follies

new stories

Ann Beattie

Scribner

New York   London   Toronto   Sydney

SCRIBNER
1230 Avenue of the Americas
New York, NY 10020

SCRIBNER and design are trademarks of
Macmillan Library Reference USA, Inc., used under license
by Simon & Schuster, the publisher of this work.

For information about special discounts for bulk purchases,
please contact Simon & Schuster Special Sales:
1-800-456-6798 or business@simonandschuster.com

Designed by Kyoko Watanabe
Text set in Aldine

Manufactured in the United States of America

1   3   5   7   9   10   8   6   4   2

Library of Congress Cataloging-in-Publication Data
Beattie, Ann.
Follies : new stories / Ann Beattie.
p. cm.
Contents: Fléchette follies—Find and replace—Duchais—
Tending something—Apology for a journey not taken—
Mostre—The garden game—The rabbit hole as likely explanation—
Just going out—That last odd day in L.A.
I. Title.
PS3552.E177F65 2005
913'.54—dc22   2004065087

ISBN 0-7432-6961-6

Some of the stories in this collection have appeared elsewhere,
in slightly different form: "Mostre" in *DoubleTake,* "The Garden Game" in
Ploughshares, and "Find and Replace," "The Rabbit Hole as Likely Explanation,"
and "That Last Odd Day in L.A." in *The New Yorker.*

For the photographic information in "Just Going Out," the author is
indebted to "Mining the Relics of Journeys Past" by Christa Worthington in
The New York Times of November 22, 1998.

For Frank Turaj

Contents

Fléchette Follies

WHEN the accident occurred, George Wissone was returning from an errand. Among the things he'd bought was a plastic container of paper clips that flew open when he slammed on the brake. Paper clips fell from his hair as he opened the door to see what damage he'd done to the car he'd rear-ended. He winced and avoided looking at the front fender of his own rental car. Most of all, he wished no one to be hurt. He was surprised to see blood between his thumb and first finger, though he had felt the key's serrated edge as he'd pulled it clumsily from the ignition. Unlike him to do things clumsily, but there would be plenty of time to introspect later. The woman did, indeed, seem to be hurt.

Being hit from behind at a red light was the last thing she needed, so she had dropped her head to her hands, which tightly clutched the top of the wheel. She was late for work, and the day before her son had called from England to say that he would not be coming home for Christmas. So much for her excuse not to work both Christmas Eve and Christmas Day at the nursing home. She finally met his eyes, but only for a second, after deciding he was not really injured. She was a round-faced woman with broad shoulders and a nervous-seeming overbite. Cars were swerving around them. Soon—when he got to know Charlottesville (to the extent that he got to know any place)—he would curse the unmannerly drivers of rush hour like everyone else.

He should not have taken a double dose of Contac and then operated "heavy machinery"—such as a Geo Metro could be dignified as representing "heavy machinery." She sat there, jaw set, not opening the door to step out. He looked back at his car and saw that he had left the door ajar. It was in danger of being side-swiped by irritated motorists, one of whom had the nerve to hit the horn as he—make that she—blared past.

"Wouldn't you know it," the woman muttered. "Are you *hurt*?"

"I'm awfully sorry," he said. "I wasn't thinking."

"Beer for lunch?" she said. "Did you think about domestic, or no: you'd go for imported, right?"

"What?"

The next car that swerved toward them was a police car. He saw a German shepherd in the back. A dog he'd never liked, along with Dobermans. Of course, he didn't like pit bulls, either. He had been driving west. The sun, which gave no heat, burned his eyes. He tried to wince it away, fixing his gaze on the police car's blue light as it pulled in behind his car. Did German shepherds have blue eyes? As a boy he'd had a mutt that was part shepherd: a dog with one blue-flecked eye, the other brown.

He had not had beer at lunch. He had not had a drink of any sort for more than four years. Another car with a dog inside passed. The dog eyed the scene, moving in the backseat.

"My *job*." The woman had finally left her car to talk to the policeman. Apparently she had the habit of loudly articulating the last words of sentences. "Doesn't he have a business card, so we can talk about this later?" she said, as if he couldn't answer for himself. "He plowed into me when I was stopped for the light." She was holding her business card between two fingers, as if it were usually clipped there. The cop reached out and took it. She said, "I think this man has been drinking."

"That hand okay?" the cop said, looking at the smear of blood on his jacket pocket. He had said something to the woman, first, but George hadn't heard it. Even she might not have understood, the wind had come up so strong. In a big tree, someone had hung wind chimes. Metal tinkled like toy swords.

"People overreact to blood," the woman said. "Blood, and tears. If it's a new mother, she overreacts to shit."

The cop turned his full attention to the woman, taking one step forward with a quizzical expression.

The cop was holding both of their licenses. He seemed to take George's word for the fact that he was driving a rental car, that the registration was in the glove compartment. George supposed you could tell a car was a rental from the license, though it had been so long since he'd rented a car, he wasn't sure about that. In any case, the cop obviously had no intention of seeing whether he could walk a straight line. "I don't want to make more of this than necessary," the cop said to the woman. "No need to waste time we don't got."

He watched silently as the cop returned the woman's registration and license. Her insurance company would talk to his insurance company. Surely he had an insurance company, though that would be a bit of trivia he'd never know. There were many things it was pleasant not to have to think about. On the other hand, it would have been nice to have some input about what rental car had been reserved for him.

The cop unwrapped some gum and folded it over, placing it in his mouth. He looked at both of them. It was obvious he knew neither would like a stick.

The driver of the other car was Nancy Gregerson—Gregerson having been her married name. Her maiden name, not resumed after the divorce, was Shifflett. The town was full of Shiffletts, so why add to their ranks? She had been divorced for twenty years, and her last name no longer reminded her of Edward Gregerson. A couple of Beatles songs did, and the way the corners of her son's mouth tightened sometimes brought his face to mind, but his last name? Not at all.

She had driven away saying, *"Late to work,"* and she realized she was being obnoxious, but couldn't help herself. She put in a full shift at Dolly Madison House without taking a break (Jenny, the nurses' aide, was six months pregnant; she let her have the time).

By the time an hour had passed, she felt slightly chagrined that she'd been so unkind to the man who'd hit her. Her instincts about who'd been drinking and who hadn't weren't always right; she tended to overestimate how many people were alcohol dependent. They made the staff watch so many films about drunks and smokers—how could she think otherwise? One recent film had been a very unfunny cartoon, and an equally humorless visiting cardiologist had pointed a laser pen at a drunken elephant on the screen as if he were making rounds with his interns and an elephant just happened to be sprawled in the bed, like any other patient.

She punched out, sorry that her son wouldn't be home for Christmas. He was an unhappy young man who expected too much from his ability to draw recognizable figures. He had been painting in London for almost two years. For a while he had lived with two other would-be painters, but as often happened in his life, they decamped and went elsewhere. One had moved to a room in someone's house. The other moved in with his girlfriend. Was that it? In any case, Nicky was there, stuck with the rent. When he'd flown in to Dulles the year before, he'd stayed only three days, and he'd spent the entire time brooding about his former girlfriend, who'd moved to Lexington. Should he visit her? Should he not? Sitting in Nancy's favorite chair, his big feet in his Doc Martens dirtying her little needlepoint footstool as he mentally plucked the anxiety daisy.

Though she alternated among several routes home, this evening she decided to take the same road on which she'd been involved in the accident earlier. There was a spritz of ice in the wind: enough to scrabble at the glass for a second before it melted. The road curved, and she realized she'd been following a van too closely. Icy road, tailgating . . . she might plow into somebody herself, and wouldn't that be ironic. An SUV sat at the curb, and just past it a tree, lit by a floodlight above it. She turned in to a driveway and walked back to where she'd been. She saw something glinting in the street, but since she'd inspected her own car carefully, she didn't much care what had broken on his. She remembered it as a crummy little car, and thought that was about right: that was what he'd be driving. She bent to see what sparkled on the asphalt, and saw paper clips scattered there. She picked up one but left the others; they would not be a clue for her insurance company. In fact, they seemed so ordinary that she felt even sorrier that she had been so unkind to him. She'd come to believe that everywhere in the world, a little something was out of place, all the time. Like one of the old ladies on floor three: you'd find a glove pulled onto one of their feet, their shoe somewhere across the room. The poinsettia's red leaves on the floor, as if a cat had attacked a cardinal. At lunch, you might see a lipstick tube dropped on their plate, shiny among the vegetables, relinquished, at last, from their fist, or even a snapshot, disguised in the folds of a skirt, pulled out and placed on the food like a trump card.

She stopped at a convenience store for Taster's Choice and milk. A young man in front of her reminded her of her son: slouched into his own body, big black motorcycle boots, ugly tattoo of some bird that couldn't become extinct soon enough etched on his forearm. He looked through her as he pocketed his change and walked past. He was someone's son—one who either would or would not be going home for Christmas.

In May, she traded in her car for one that got better mileage. Her hair had grown longer over the winter, the crown flecked with white now that she'd stopped coloring it. After much thought, she had decided, at age fifty-six, to go part-time at work. Having spent so many years there, she'd abandoned the idea of one's truly being able to prepare for one's old age. At least, she would never save enough. Even those with money could buy scant protection in this world.

On the first day off of her new four-day week, she parked and walked into a coffee shop in Barrack's Road shopping center. No one was in line. She ordered coffee and a muffin that was sinfully overpriced, but what, exactly, would she be saving money for? To send to her son to help pay his rent? She took the muffin, still as a nesting bird on its little plate, to a nearby table and returned to pay and to get her coffee. As she was returning to the table, a man rose and brushed past, touching her shoulder. Fortunately, there was a lid on his cup. "I'm sorry," he said. It was the man who'd hit her car. He'd apologized immediately, so the words were part of the stumble. He sat heavily, opened a newspaper, and began to read, all without making eye contact with her, flicking the page to keep it open.

"You're quite clumsy, aren't you?" she said.

He looked up. This time he saw her.

"I'm the woman who realized you'd been drinking," she said.

"What?" he said.

"The accident."

"Oh!" he said.

"I just traded the car in. I wasn't forthcoming about its having been involved in that little accident."

He was flustered, a page of the newspaper slipping into his lap. He clamped it between his knees.

"I wasn't having a good day before you hit me," she said. "I could have been more civil."

"I *am* sorry," he said again.

"There were paper clips on the road," she said.

"Were there? I'd been to an office supply store. Well—at least it wasn't shrapnel."

The comment stopped her. She waited for him to continue, but he didn't. She decided to tell him what had happened later with the paper clip.

"I picked one up, actually. I went back after work. I used it to make a little shiv and stabbed a balloon I'd tied to my chair at home. So there you go: my little souvenir came in handy."

He was having trouble following what she was talking about,

but he decided that she spoke in a hectic way; he'd wait to see if she gave more information or—better yet—if she'd stop talking and let him read his newspaper. He did not like women who were self-satisfied about being flaky.

He nodded and turned back to his paper. He flicked the top of the page, but she knew he was only pretending to read. She took a sip of her cooling coffee and wondered why milk didn't do much to cut the taste of such bitter brew.

"Was it your birthday?" he said suddenly. "Is that why you had a balloon?"

"No. Someone else's. I work with old people. One of the ladies was given a Mylar balloon by her son, and she thought it was a dinosaur egg. A silver dinosaur egg on a string, and naturally it was going to hatch and the thing was going to devour her. I work with people who have dementia."

"Difficult job," he said.

"You learn not to judge them. Just to do whatever it takes to solve the problem." She thought about getting up and leaving, but did not. He met her eyes and, for the first time, seemed to look into them. As quickly as their eyes locked, he refocused his gaze to some midpoint that was not her face. She said, "Something drew me back there when I'd finished work, and there was a tree lit up. No reason for it that I could see. A big, ordinary tree no one would have any reason to look at, and I had the strangest feeling that maybe it was an omen."

"I don't understand," he said.

"I'm not superstitious. I don't care what your astrological sign is," she said. "You can believe me or not: working with the elderly really sharpens your intuition. A lot of the time I know when something bad is about to happen before they do. Just sometimes, of course."

"Excuse me, is that the sports section?" a young man in a University of Virginia cap said.

"I'm done with it," he said, handing up the paper.

"A student. Not an omen of death," she whispered, as the boy walked away.

"Right," he said.

"I've never thought a thunderstorm signified anything," she said. "I'll walk under a ladder." She was talking to herself, but she felt like talking. She said, "Sometimes, though, I rely on information. For example: old people's bones break, and *then* they fall. It isn't that the fall caused the break. So when one of them becomes more fragile, suddenly, I often can tell what's coming."

"So . . . you stabbed your balloon and saved us from the next invasion of dinosaurs," he said.

She smiled. "Maybe popping the balloon was me popping my bubble. I'd talked to my son in London the day before. He was asleep when I called. Or nodding out, but if you can't look at a person, you don't know what the truth might be. With drug users, I mean. Anyway: he said he'd call back and he didn't. He disappeared."

"Disappeared?" He got up and pulled out a chair at her table and sat down. He said, "What age is he?"

"He's twenty-eight. We're not doing all that well at finding out who the other is."

"You and your son?"

"No," she said. "You and me. Or maybe I've been bothering you when you'd like a little peace and quiet."

"No—I just don't know what to say. He disappeared . . ."

"My ex-husband hired a private investigator. So far, nothing."
He frowned.

"He had a roommate whose girlfriend wrote me. She hinted that drugs were involved. That always complicates everything, doesn't it?"

He nodded.

She said, "I don't expect you to solve my problems. I don't know why I told you. Information like that is a burden for other people. You're not a drug counselor, by any chance?"

He said, "I don't talk about my job."

"CIA," she said, matter-of-factly.

He looked at the college student, leaving the coffee shop, holding the hand of a pretty girl. He said, "You could satisfy my curiosity by telling me why you did stab a balloon."

"Misplaced anxiety, I suppose," she said. "I knew there was something unusual about you the day you hit me. It makes sense that you'd be CIA."

"I'm not," he said. "I'm just not at liberty to explain. The simple version is that I take care of people, too. Sometimes medical personnel, as it happens."

"Doctors Without Borders," she said.

"You like to guess, don't you?" He pushed his empty coffee cup to the side. "No, nothing like that," he said. When he said he didn't talk about his job, more often than not, people made the same guess she had. He and the people he worked with had a nickname for those yahoos. They called them "the Rotary Club."

A few days later, waiting for coffee to go, it came to her that he must have been flirting: pretending to be so concerned that her son had disappeared. Something seemed strange about the way they'd gotten into their long, oblique conversation. She began to think that he'd maneuvered her into guessing about what he did. CIA, not CIA . . . it all seemed suspicious, once she had some distance.

But this much was certain: George Wissone did not belong to the Ivy Book Discussion Group that met the first Monday of every third month. He did not shop frequently, if at all, at Foods of All Nations (nicknamed Foods of Inflation). Increasingly, people moved to Charlottesville to retire to what they thought of as a pleasant Southern town, then didn't know what to do there. You'd see them looking puzzled, examining expensive cans of lingonberries and octagonal tins of imported teas at Foods of All Nations, wondering what other people did, why the town was so popular. Their allergies would kill them. The plane service was terrible. People didn't expect it to snow in the winter, but it snowed and snowed. The summers were so hot and humid you had to live in air-conditioning. Still, they came and drank the local wines, got excited by spotting celebrities who came into town from their so-called farms, saw foreign films at Vinegar Hill that gave them the feeling they were somewhere else—an illusion prolonged by eating at the adjacent restaurant, with its hillside garden filled with hops dangling from trellises, and sunflowers and lavender, so like a garden in France. There were stores that sold hand-shaped imported cheeses wrapped in grape leaves, oils in handblown bottles as expensive as if you were buying great perfume, satin baby booties hardly wider than a woman's thumb. Grown women still walked around in pastel-colored flats; there were the Muffies and Buffies and Fluffies (their dogs). There were the Southern boys on their lunch hour, with tasseled loafers and starched pale blue button-downs. There were fewer of them than there had been when Nancy first arrived from the county, but they were still there, keeping an eye out for antique wicker porch furniture and old Oriental rugs, going to the same watch repair shop their granddaddy had gone to, watching the Kentucky Derby on their televisions the size of boxcars and drinking mint juleps out of silver cups, the fresh mint growing along the flagstone walkways as steadily as fog rolled into San Francisco. She thought, sometimes, how amusing it would be to be one of those women; instead of the old TV program *Queen for a Day*, which really existed to let people weep tears of compassion as they maintained the class-divisive status quo, she could become "Southern Belle for a Day"—all the better if she could appear slightly pigeon-toed and carry a "cute" purse: something with a little brocade magnolia, or a silk-screened horse. She would have errands: buying bottled mixes for drinks; finding a broad-based lightbulb for the torchiere. Heirloom tomato seeds in packets beautiful enough to frame. Choosing among rosebushes named for the daughters of American presidents who "filled in" for their mothers, because they'd inevitably died so young.

By summer Nicky was still missing, and the letters from the roommate's fiancée had become increasingly bizarre, so much so that she'd begun sending them unopened to the investigator. There was not one shred of evidence that the girl had any idea where Nicky was. She was sure to be some confused, drug-addled liar whose paranoia was just another crowd-captivating embellishment, like chains on her wrist or a stud through her eyebrow.

Katie Shroeder, the activities director for the third floor, had asked Nancy to go on her lunch hour to get crepe paper and other things to be used for Fourth of July ceiling decorations. Perversely, Nancy had thought about buying a bag of plastic dinosaurs from a rack near the checkout counter to flip out Mrs. Bell. She used the facility's MasterCard to pay, got in her car, and, turning onto Route 29, saw a man in a convertible who resembled the man who'd hit her during the winter, though he was younger and more handsome in profile. In June, she had informed her ex-husband that she would no longer contribute to the cost of the investigator and put a down payment on a house in a development in Ivy. Interest rates were at an all-time low. She didn't mind the commute. The town got noisier and more expensive every day. She liked the butterflies that fluttered near the ground, and the robins and mourning doves that came to her feeders, and the way the setting sun was reflected in the pond she shared with a few neighbors that needed its water lilies thinned. It had begun to reflect little, as if it were unsilvered glass. Most days she sat by the water in the morning and again in the evening and hoped that her son was not dead. Every so often, the private investigator—whose tone was testy, so her ex-husband must have told him she no longer contributed anything—would call with what she thought was a startlingly minor question. Nicky's favorite color? Why bother to pay for the services of an idiot?

She awoke one night from a disturbing dream in which her head had fallen forward like a rag doll's and would not right itself, so that she could see only the distorted shadows of things around her (butterfly wings shadowed into airplanes). She had gotten out of bed and rubbed the back of her neck, rubbed her palms against her eyelids, puffy from sleep. She was lucky not to have gotten whiplash, she thought—which was the first time she connected her sleeplessness with the accident. She had believed for a long time, when he was in his teens, that Nicky had allergies, that that was why his eyes were often red and swollen. She, a nurse, had believed that, and wondered at the ineffectiveness of Seldane. She had been shocked when a doctor told her she'd been noticing, instead, her son's reaction to heroin. She and her ex-husband had paid for him to go into rehab, he'd spent a month there before being discharged, then he'd relapsed and been sent to a private hospital. When he got out, she had found a job for him, working in town as a photographer's assistant. Her ex-husband and his wife had rented a suite at the Hampton Inn and attended family therapy in the month between Nicky's release and his employment (she had another nurse at Dolly Madison to thank for putting them in touch with her brother, who needed an assistant). Once Nicky was settled, his father and stepmother had returned to their condo in Aspen, and Nicky had met Claudine, who loved him until she threw him over for a good-ole-boy lawyer with a prominent practice in Lexington. That was when he'd started hanging out with the old crowd again. She was never sure exactly when that started, because he'd moved out of the house the moment his relationship with Claudine began and continued to live in her apartment, sleeping with the dirty laundry and subsisting on Gatorade and Snickers, for some time after she departed. If he'd had the money to pay the rent, he might have stayed indefinitely. He had pretended for months after it ended that the relationship was still going on. He apparently thought his mother was so stupid, she'd worry less and therefore bother him less with such dismaying ideas as dinner at a restaurant. She could remember him raging: "You don't think this will last. You don't think it will last because it's a law of the universe that everything has to end badly. You think everything's a big farce, because Dad had an affair and the woman had a baby we still don't know was his. Who says that kid was Dad's? Huh? You just know it, though, don't you? It doesn't matter how you know, it doesn't matter that the woman won't have a paternity test. You still think you have to be so noble and send it money. You *like* having to sacrifice. It makes you superior to everybody. You'll never have another relationship as long as you live, and you don't want me to, either—especially with some French girl. Why do you act like she's a snob, when she isn't? She brought you *flowers*. She's going to be your daughter-in-law. That'll be soon enough to dislike her." The hula hoop of emotions spun, beginning become end, end become beginning, tilting precariously before slipping toward the ground when he at last became exhausted. Round and round: accusations, mockery, mockery, accusations. He had reverted to speed as the flip side of heroin.

Mothers everywhere, she thought. Mothers in their schlumpy bathrobes, playing back the nastiness of their children. Was anyone on the mothers' side? The drug counselor at the second rehab facility Nicky ended up in outside of Richmond had expressed surprise—quite judgmental surprise—that she claimed she could repeat verbatim Nicky's outburst regarding her thoughts on his fiancée. He was also surprised to learn that she had made no reply.

"When he became excited, what did you say to Nicholas?" the psychologist had asked her.

"What does that have to do with anything?" she had said.

"It might be productive to consider what his thoughts might have been when you were not responding after he expressed himself."

"*His* thoughts? He's never had the slightest problem expressing himself."

He started again: "You've heard the term *passive-aggressive*?"

"You're as much of a bully as he is!"

"Name-calling is completely counterproductive," he had said, with the lugubrious gentleness she had seen when doctors were examining people who might, or might not, be in a coma.

Mercifully, other details of that conversation had faded. She had talked to a psychologist she'd gotten to know over the years when next he visited Dolly Madison House, and he had applauded her for not caving in. She had examined her own heart and decided that she really had been avoiding an incendiary exchange with her son that would have gotten neither of them anywhere. She was not passive-aggressive just because she had not been sucked in. Claudine *was* just some French girl, but she had thanked her sincerely for the flowers, and she had hoped—for a long time before she met that particular girl—that some relationship would work out for Nicky.

On a Sunday in July, she was standing behind her car as a teenager from a nursery lowered a spirea bush into her trunk, the bush in its burlap-wrapped ball looking enormous when separated from the others. "I like these," he had said. "My sister had them in her bouquet when she got married. We were going to open our own flower shop, but she moved to Vancouver."

"Does she like it there?"

"I guess so. Sometimes."

Was he waiting for a tip? That was probably why he was so chatty. He had talked to her all the time he'd wheelbarrowed the bush to the car. She unzipped her handbag. He watched the zipper move as intently as a lost driver seeing the route he must take pointed out on a map. "Your asking if she liked Vancouver," he said. "She said I ought to come out. We ought to open up a place out there."

"Then I guess she likes it," she said. She folded two dollar bills and extended her hand. He reached out with a big smile. "I delivered flowers to Dolly Madison at Easter," he said. "I've seen you before."

"Well, say hello next time," she said.

"Oh, I always say hello once I've been introduced."

"Good," she said. "Well—thank you."

She started to walk around to the driver's side. Finally he said, "Mrs. Bell. You know old Mrs. Bell? She used to be our neighbor."

"Yes," she said. She was practiced in not discussing the residents, whose privacy always needed to be respected, even when they were not *compos mentis*.

"She's in there, right?"

"Yes," she said, in a tone meant to end the conversation. "She's doing well."

"Well, the ambulance guys came because I called them. I came home from school and she'd fallen on her front walk. You'd think in a neighborhood like where my parents live, somebody would have heard her."

She nodded.

"The ambulance guys—they say they find people who've been down for days. Inside, outside. Sometimes it's been days since they passed, but it doesn't really matter, because their spirits already escaped."

"Is that what you believe?"

"The spirit ascends," he said. "Accompanied by the music of nature. The call of the birds; the rustle of the leaves."

"Thanks for your help," she said dismissively. She went to her car door, opened it, and got in. He followed her and leaned toward the window. It was hot in the car, but she had no intention of rolling down the window. She put on the air-conditioning and looked straight ahead, waiting for him to take his hands off her car.

"You're a nurse," he said. "I didn't think saying something like how people depart the world would upset you."

She put the car in gear. There was something wrong with him. She'd been too slow on the uptake.

"Come back if you want more bushes!" he called.

Irritated that the nursery would have someone like that working there, she went home and popped the trunk open but did not remove the bush right away. She went inside and poured herself a Coke, listened to the two messages on her answering machine. One was somebody who'd reached the wrong number and didn't realize it; the other was from Sally, asking if she could babysit that night. She did not want to babysit and decided not to answer the message until much later, when Sally would have made some other arrangement. She had gone to the nursery wanting to get a butterfly bush, but they were all out, and the spirea—which she feared attracted bees—looked so beautiful, so much like a fountain of white confetti, that she'd decided impulsively to buy it. She took a vitamin pill with the Coke, then decided to walk to the pond. She liked it down there, though she'd started to worry about the kudzu, which was creeping up a nearby telephone pole, and she was dismayed to see that someone had thrown the top of a birdbath on the grass . . . no: it was a hubcap. Litter everywhere. The pond had been discovered; none of the neighbors would have left McDonald's bags or cans of soda near the rim. She picked them up and walked back toward the house with the trash. It was still too hot to sit outside and enjoy the day, and in any case, she should deal with the bush.

"Can I help you with that, Nancy?" her neighbor, Henry Leterson, called. He was driving by in his blue truck and had seen the bush—larger than it had looked at the nursery—cascading from the trunk.

"That would be awfully nice," she said.

He stopped and came down the hillside. "Pretty day," he said.

There had been a drought. It had been so bad the summer before that people who did not voluntarily ration water were in danger of having devices installed on their pipes. There had been so much building in recent years, and the year before it had rained so little, that there was simply not enough water. This year, though, things were better. You could buy a bush and plant it and water it.

"Have yourself some lunch down by the pond?" he said, lifting the bush.

"No. It's trash somebody left there," she said.

He frowned and nodded. The bush sat on the ground between them. He said, "Where do you think you might like it?"

He was a tall, muscular man. She'd always thought he looked like the bird in the *Peanuts* cartoon. His hair was thinning, pale blond, messy. His wife had been operated on a few months before for breast cancer.

"I'd like it over there." She pointed. "Under the side window. I'll run ahead and find the place."

"Okay," he said, and moved up the hillside almost as quickly as she did.

She patted her foot on the ground, and he put the bush there. "I can move it a little, if need be," he said.

She backed up and looked. She imagined seeing it through her bedroom window. She asked him to move it a couple of feet farther away from the house.

"Okay? That looks nice. I'll come back with my shovel, soon as it gets a little shadier."

"Oh, I can plant it," she said. "Thank you very much for bringing it up here. It's quite a bit bigger than I thought when I bought it."

"No problem," he said. "Well. You take care."

"You, too," she said. She realized that it would be possible to speak in nothing but clichés and pleasantries with the man forever. He was nice, but she felt sure that no matter how long they talked, they would never say anything meaningful. She stopped herself from asking, as so many people must all day, "How's your wife?"

"All right, then," he said, walking away. Did he feel her eyes on his back? She stared after him, thinking how often men appeared to her to be children grown tall and older. Which reminded her of her son. She walked to the shed—the previous owners had left the ugly thing behind—and dropped the litter in a trash can she kept outside. She took out the shovel, but her neighbor had been right: better to plant the bush when it was cooler. She leaned the shovel up against the shed. A wasp dangled past, seeming to come from nowhere. Again she wondered if the bush she'd selected attracted bees.

Inside the house, she looked guiltily at the "1" flashing on her answering machine. She opened a drawer and took out a letter she'd gotten earlier in the week from the girl in London and decided to open it. As soon as she started reading, she realized she'd made a mistake. The entire note was nonsense, and upsetting nonsense at that. It was a notecard with a badly drawn thatched cottage on the front. Inside, she read:

Dear Mrs. Gregerson,

I am afraid I might not have put enough postage on the last note. When I wrote before, I asked if you could send $ so some of Nick's friends could look for him. I am going to be honest and, say that he has been dating an American girl who has her own agenda over here and, that the two of them went to Leeds to get drugs to sell to a guy in Piccadilly Circus. We've figured out that he must not have come back from this trip, though the girlfriend who hates us is in their flat and won't give us information. We think he may be staying in Leeds because when somebody asked her (girlfriend) in a bar where he was and, sort of insisted on finding out, she let on that he was still in Leeds on "business." She told us to leave her alone because she'd call the police if we threatened her again and, Tony found out she sleeps with the police. It has been very hard to track him down because we are lacking in funds. I would go to persuade him to get out of this bad Leeds element and, also offer him a place to stay if he doesn't want to stay with the American anymore. Tony has an uncle we could stay with only we don't

*have the $ for a train which isn't much. We need to have Nick
back before he's sucked into something and, also we don't trust his
girlfriend not to be insisting he stay there until a certain kind of
drug arrives. We are going to go get him and get him away from
this bad element and, I want to do this before my forecoming
wedding. Please help us and we will help you because the most
important thing is helping Nick express himself through his art.
Thank you for your consideration. Even two hundred pounds not
dollars would be a lot of help. Nick is a v. good friend to us and,
we can talk to him better in person.*

Yours truly,
Marigold Howe

How had he fallen in with such an accomplished, compas-
sionate lady? From the time he was a child, he had selected friends
she could see had bad character: secretive, sly little boys who got
him into trouble when he wasn't getting them into trouble. She
remembered the game of Judge. This meant that Nicky dumped
water out of a big old cement birdbath she'd only begun filling
with water to keep him out of it, and sat in it to act as a judge in
horrible trials the boys invented. His friend Tommy (the only
murky child of the lovely Samuelsons) had sat in a lawn chair and
argued in favor of sparing an allegedly stupid turtle's life. At least,
that was the way she'd heard it, when she came out and saw the
turtle with a cinder block through its shell, the blood like cherry
Jell-O on the grass.

When he was eight, Nicky killed a cat. He'd "lassoed" a friend's
gecko in its terrarium and said he had strangled it accidentally
when he was trying to get the rope off. He took good aim with a
slingshot. Boys will be boys, so many people had said to her.
And—remember—he had kept a bird with a broken wing in a box
and nursed it back to health. He and his friend had let it go on the
Fourth of July, centering themselves, and the bird, in a ceremonial
circle of spitting sparklers. Nicky's father had been visiting that

day, bringing with him his wife, Bernadine, and her terrier that wore a little red, white, and blue vest. Nancy had expected, all day, that the dog would end up dead, but it had not. It had only caused a certain amount of confusion by running away from everyone and hiding one place or another in the house, leaving little turds whose smell attracted her attention later that night, just about the time she realized the dog must have been responsible for uncovering many of her tulip bulbs outside the kitchen window, though she couldn't be sure, since squirrels had dug them up in the past.

Meditation she thought of as a joke, though she realized that because it was an option for free time at work (newly instituted), she was biased against it. Other uses for free time (not to be confused with "break") included doing the sun salutation in a small room that had once been a large storage closet. There was also tea brewing. The nurses' stress was to be alleviated by tea brewing. She could give thanks that at least the dour cardiologist had not reappeared. The last slide show they had been required to watch had been on the subject of bedsores, and the number of repulsive close-ups—surely the cameraman had an obsession with the zoom lens—had given her a headache. Sitting there in the roar of the projector, she had felt like flotsam in space, sucked faster than the speed of light to disappear into some gaping—in this case festering—void.

When he was fourteen, Nicky and a friend had stolen the friend's father's car and crashed it into a tree less than a mile from the house, somehow managing to pin a neighbor's cat between the front fender and a willow. It was the cat she'd heard about over and over—not from the owner, who accepted its death as a bizarre accident, but from the friend's mother, who disagreed with her husband and felt the purpose of the ride had not been the driving, but driving with intent to kill. They had "stalked" the cat, the woman maintained. Vaguely, Nancy could remember reading textbooks, in nursing school, whose authors felt obliged to mention the merits of a vegetarian diet. This, before there was as much research and agreement among doctors as there was now. She could remember her own self-righteous Friday Fish Night (not for religious reasons: for the protein and low fat) and also her own Vegetarian Tuesdays: chopping broccoli and mixing it with polenta into little balls she cooked in canned spaghetti sauce. Her son grew up to eat Whoppers, and her husband—at least, the last she knew—ate "blackened" meat he cooked on a grill that cost more than they had paid for their first car. Edward and Bernadine had nervously made do with her hibachi, during the month they'd been in town years before, cooking skewers of beef and onions and handing the little sticks forward as if they were volatile tools of destruction.

At sixteen Nicky had not killed a fellow classmate, though he had fought with such energy that it had taken several courageous students and two teachers to pin Nicky to the floor. The other boy had no serious injuries: bruises, a cut knee. Nicky had broken his ankle—apparently after the fight had been broken up, kicking the tire of a parked car.

How much of it had been her fault? Had Nicky been more upset than it appeared that she and his father had divorced? He had never been a child who confided in anyone, even as a baby. If he awoke frightened in the night, there was no bad dream he could (or would) tell either of them about. From kindergarten, he had been attracted to troublemakers, though when he was home he had worked on various projects silently in his room and for a while had read so many books that she had to encourage him to go out and do something. In his teens, he had gone out with his easel and painted landscapes, though he never wanted her to look at them and he made her promise she would not discuss his interest in painting with his friends. Well: he had found things to do, and apparently those things had nothing to do with painting placid streams and towering trees. What he was most interested in now had to do with his inner landscape, which he was determined to turn dark and problematic with drugs. The Magical Mystery Tour had, like some powerful force of nature, itself, come and taken him away.

She got out a map and put on her reading glasses and looked for Leeds. Finding the dot on the map told her nothing. She went into her bedroom and sat on the bed, looking with satisfaction at the new bush planted in the lawn. It did not seem an omen of anything. It seemed only an improvement of her view. Its loveliness, though, also made her a little sad. Or its simplicity. Maybe its dainty branches blowing in the breeze saddened her. She remembered the boy saying that his sister had selected it for her bridal bouquet. She, herself, had carried white roses and baby's breath. She and her husband had been married in a garden by a justice of the peace. She had been two months pregnant. In the third month, she miscarried and Edward Gregerson had stunned her by suggesting they get the marriage annulled. They should continue to live together, he said—but whether they should be married could be rethought. She had stopped loving him instantly. They had not annulled the marriage (though she wouldn't have stopped him), and for a while they had gone on as if he'd never suggested it. He had clearly been waiting for her response, her agreement with his oh-so-logical plan, but she had not been able to say anything. She had gone into some sort of fugue state, in which she pretended to be able to do things she had done before, thereby doing them. She cooked. She had sex with her husband. She kept an appointment to take a typing test, got the results, and began a job as a secretary. After a month or so on the job, on the way home from work, she stopped and impulsively bought white roses and baby's breath. "Pretty," the young salesgirl had intoned, arranging and rearranging them. The roses had been very expensive. She had bought more than she carried in her bouquet. She had instructed the girl about how she wanted the stems cut and could still remember the girl's disappointment that such long stems were being clipped so short. The florist's paper had been patterned with pink polka dots. She remembered, because she had cried so hard, back in the car, that she had understood the Impressionists in a new way, as the dots blurred into a pink wash. She had looked at the prettiness of the bouquet and then she had begun to snap off the heads, one by one. When they were decapitated, she had broken up the baby's breath as if it were parsley she were sprinkling on a casserole. She had reached over—the whole mess was on the floor, in front of the passenger seat—and ground some into the floor until skin peeled off the ball of her thumb. She had picked up some of the roses and taken them apart petal by petal, sprinkling them back on the pile, and then she had used the heel of her shoe to mash them further into the carpeting. Then she had driven home and left them there, where her husband had seen them in the morning when he went out to run an errand. So: he, too, could choose to be silent. He did not say anything, and the crushed flowers had been removed from the car when she sat in the seat next to him later in the day. She never slept with him again, though—as she suspected—she was already pregnant.

For his part, George Wissone thought no more about her. That day he had surprised himself by coming close to lecturing her on the deficiencies of the CIA. But why should he care? You wouldn't believe the fuckups. Sad sacks who needed extrication that the bigwigs left swinging in the breeze, people you wouldn't want to get to know. Ask no questions, other than operational necessities. Try not to involve anybody, or let anybody know you'd been there. In, out, nobody gets hurt. Minimalist ops. No brands, no trophies, no Larry, no George. The Invisible Man.

He really did go on what might be thought of as medical missions, usually along with a doctor: off to the rescue of rich Americans who got themselves in trouble. He and O'Malley were just limo drivers, so to speak. O'Malley drove the car and he extricated Joe Blow. What do-gooder first thought of taking a bunch of kids on the same plane, he had no idea, but children began to be part of the haul. It started during the Carter administration. The kids were usually orphans, or kids whose adoptions had gotten fucked up for one reason or another, and there were nuns in the United States waiting to catch them when they arrived in the States. They would parcel them out to church-affiliated adoption agencies or into the arms of prospective parents. The 2002 trip to Sierra Leone had been textbook perfect. As well as some big-bucks American businessman who'd developed septicemia, they'd brought out four kids: three boys and a girl. The night before, O'Malley had gotten in a fight with a Harvard-educated Beng tribe leader on the subject of Michael Jackson's fitness as a parent, and had broken his right hand throwing a wild punch, though he piloted the plane back one-handed and they sang doo-wop songs to the kids half the way to Logan. Hadn't it been Logan that time? Rich O'Malley was Irish Catholic, married to his childhood sweetheart at age eighteen, unfortunately unable to conceive after a course of chemo for Hodgkin's at nineteen. His wife worked in Bethesda, Maryland, as a first-grade teacher; he flew planes out of Reagan ("National Airport" to Democrats) on his humanitarian rescue missions— why not call them that? They saved people who needed saving, after all.

Lawrence Krebs, aka George Wissone, had been recruited right out of St. Christopher Summer Camp of Haller Isle, Maine. Last two years of high school skipped, free college, a passport that gave his age as two years older than he was; one hundred thousand dollars in an offshore bank account; a letter of thanks from the president of the United States that consisted mostly of an uppercase warning not to frame it and hang it in public view. That was it: they came after Eagle Scouts. They loved kids whose parents were tragically dead. Let others debate flying saucers and life on other planets; Larry got to parachute out of planes nobody realized had been dreamed up. If everybody was so dumb that they could be diverted into thoughts of life elsewhere, as opposed to how truly bizarre things were in the USA—well: that was the plan. He had met Reagan and George H. W., but Dubya wanted no personal contact. Which was fine with him. He sensed he wouldn't like the guy. He had a bias against certain other ex-alcoholics. Reagan was not yet senile. George H. W. was a very focused man, out there steering his cigarette boat. Maybe after all this time he should hang the letter of long ago. Let Paula stop to read it on her way to his bathroom. Or put it on the refrigerator with one of those vegetable magnets people give other people when they're in on the joke. His offshore bank account had grown substantial. Martha's nosedive and Wal-Mart's organizational problems? Another year or two, he'd be retired to a house in Mustique.

Still: this changing-identity stuff was slightly embarrassing, the where-do-I-live-today nonsense, a lifetime without being able to befriend much of anybody except a pilot who knew exactly what he did and who was also obsessed with God's will (which apparently included both cancer and cancer treatments) and—to his own mystification—a pretty trust-fund Bard dropout who never asked qu-qu-questions, who preferred cosmetic surgery to jewelry, who, touchingly, liked his old tan terry-cloth robe better than her own Frette . . . at least he could claim he had something resembling human contact with two people.

The day after he'd moved to Charlottesville, new license wedged in a wallet (a present from Paula) made of the skin from some Gila monster du jour, 2/2 WBF condo rented in his assumed name and furnished by Ethan Allen before he arrived, he'd set out to find a place for lunch and to pick up some supplies for his home office. Some techie would come and hook up the computer, install the program, admire the desk chair. His was a life in which he was rarely questioned. He had no idea who the setup guys were, but they came in a black van, wherever he lived, and set to work immediately. His phone, though, had to be installed by non-telephone-company people, who came in an assortment of vehicles, including motorcycles (San Francisco) and a Volvo pulling a horse carrier (Atlanta). He didn't question them, they didn't bat an eye about him, or whatever they were hooking up. The first night in any place, he would call in—he had to do this at 11 p.m., a time he had chosen long ago as convenient—and when he said hello, he would immediately be hung up on. The phone would ring seconds later and the same voice he'd heard through the years would say, "Welcome to your new pad," and call him by whatever name he would now be using.

His first day on Vinegar Hill, he had called in at 11 p.m., then looked through the phone book to see where he might buy office supplies. One of the chain places was in town; he decided to go there in the morning, then stop at Red Lobster for lunch, in that his life otherwise had little continuity. Recently, Paula had represented continuity, too, he supposed, though she'd dropped hints that she was thinking of a more settled life: Paula with her enhanced cheekbones and her collagen pout, the wine she drank deepening her cheeks to a rosy glow. She often called him "hon" because she couldn't accept the name change. He loved it when it came out "h-h-hon."

He called Rich O'Malley on his cell phone. They could only chat on an unsecured line, but he didn't want more than that. Just to hear a familiar voice—though this time, O'Malley was only a couple of hours or so away. Rich picked up the conversation where they'd left off, telling him that SAD was a very real thing, and that even OfficeMax now sold lights he could sit under. Rich often confused himself with him. In a way, it was flattering. Rich, himself, stayed in the same location when he wasn't flying and ate daily at a restaurant called O'Donnell's. A worrier, Rich didn't know what he was going to do when they closed the place. There was a diner he had his eye on, that was old-time authentic (Rich's term of greatest approval), but of course that would be a step down from his favorite seafood restaurant. They hung up by saying "Spry jive," which was a variation of "high five," though the joke had become so convoluted over time that he couldn't remember how it had started: they just both signed off that way.

He had decided, at the last minute, after putting a Puppies of America half-price calendar in his shopping basket, to toss in some other items he could not imagine using. These included a large package of pencils (*pencils!*), a little stand with a clip at the top to hold a picture (he decided to leave it as it was, with Britney Spears's coarse face, smiling), a package of scissors with different-colored handles (who could possibly care?), and a sheet of bronze circles that contained the individual letters of the name George. He also threw in a large container of paper clips, already filled, with an annoying magnetized hole that both trapped the clips and made them difficult to get at, and a gallon of Poland Spring. Standing in line, he picked up a couple of things that were on a display rack near the cashier: a "theme book" with a spiral binding and a desk lamp with a clock in its base. Impulsively, he also picked up several panoramic picture frames that were shrink-wrapped together, and a pen covered in velvet. He almost put that back, ashamed of himself for squandering money, but the pen felt sensual, and Paula would like it. If he was buying paper clips, when he had not clipped together two pieces of paper in perhaps ten years, why not a pen? He slid his newly FedExed American Express Platinum card in the machine at the counter and—with an almost heartfelt laugh—answered the cashier's question by saying that no, he did not want to be added to the mailing list. When she asked his zip code, he hesitated, trying to remember.

In the last town he had bought a sound system: speakers everywhere in the faux Tudor 2/3 w/Jacuzzi. There had been perfect sound to listen to Lucinda Williams, and the setup had come with its own security system, so that if anyone tried to detach any of the speakers without hitting a code, he could . . . what? Spring out of bed and tackle the intruder? He had bought that in Columbus, Ohio. He never thought he would sink that low, after almost four years in Los Angeles, but he had. From there he'd gotten a semi-reprieve to Atlanta, for what turned out to be not even six months. Now they had a run on obscure Southern places, with their self-satisfied small-town urbanites and their eager little regional air-ports: Roanoke; Charlottesville. If this were a James Bond movie, he'd get to see who was cast in the role of the man who assigned him to those places. He had begun to think that they must be mad at him for some reason, though he'd had a run of ten consecutive successful missions, though before that . . . but who could blame him for having a guy die of AIDS in a hospital corridor, mid-rescue? Who even knew the guy had it? From Roanoke, he'd gotten a retired diplomat with an Ecstasy problem out of Haiti (though he'd had to shoot a medi-dart into the guy like he was a tiger), along with nine kids. From Atlanta, he'd gotten a counterespionage guy from North Korea, where he'd been roughed up big-time, whose prosthetic right arm the U.S. government had in the works before anybody even set eyes on him. The guy had screamed the whole way back in the plane, at one point going for the doctor's throat, scaring the one little girl he'd snatched into years of guar-anteed nightmares.

He was trying to put it out of his mind that Paula had called to say she wouldn't be coming to Virginia. She thought it was time both of them started to date other people. He'd noticed that visits to see her friend Princess Stephanie of Monaco always had a neg-ative effect on her. Afterward, Paula spoke as if she'd just learned the meaning of life from some quiz in *Glamour*.

"My *job*," he could remember the woman saying, and he had thought: Oh, tell me about it. Tell me about your all-important job in which there is no chance that you will ever be exposed to smallpox, or that anybody you work with might want your ear or your tongue as a souvenir. Tell me about the comfortable chair you sit in and the temperature-controlled room in which you work, and tell me about your personal sorrows. What would those be? Divorced? Difficult kid? Middle-aged romance gone bust?

That was the only one he hadn't found out about: the last one. He had tried not to acknowledge her at the coffee shop. He'd tried his best to pretend he didn't know who she was, hoping, at the very least, that that would bother her, and she'd retaliate by ignoring him. But no such luck. It was as if they still stood in the street, and there was still something she wanted. How happy she must have been to run into him months later at Greenberry's. It gave her another chance to make him apologize—because it was obvious she was one of those women who wanted an apology that would unfold like an accordion. He'd never heard from the insurance people, but since he'd never paid rent or any other bill, he hadn't expected to.

Nancy Gregerson was Paula's opposite: too talkative, wry, when she had no reason to feel superior. He had been surprised at how old she must have been, though; he'd come to think that only Paula looked younger, year after year. He'd forgotten that other people might just have good genes, or that not being fat, like most Americans, could make a person seem younger. He'd been unhappy to see her, and that had made him itch to put his cards on the table, in a perverse way. He had almost been able to taste the words *Sierra Leone* when she was making her silly assumptions about who he was and what he did. In the buzz of the coffee shop, he had heard their plane setting down, the caffeine he'd ingested giving him a rush that was similar to the way he'd felt running from planes in darkness. People and their questions and their assumptions. He'd never understood asking direct questions, because all you could find out from a reply was one individual answer.

But she had, finally, surprised him. Some time after they encountered each other for the second time, she had called—he supposed she must have kept the ripped-off corner of a piece of paper with his quickly scribbled phone number he'd given her after the accident, because he was not listed in the directory—and just as he was winning at computer solitaire, trying not to think about how many more days or weeks or months he'd have to wait in this pointless town before he was finally called away, which would mean, at least, that when he returned he would be sent to a new town, he'd picked up the phone, seen her name on caller ID, and frowned. He pushed the button and took the call exactly because he'd been trained not to act spontaneously, and ignoring his programming kept him on his toes; without that reflex, he would long ago have been dead.

He had thought she might be calling with some pretext for seeing him again, but instead she was calling to see if he could help her find her son.

They had coffee in the living room of her house in Ivy. When he walked in, the smell of mold contracted his sinuses as if a clothespin had been pushed down on the bridge of his nose. It took him back to summer camp, and the moldy mattress. The dog who befriended him—his dog, as he thought of it at the time—whose ruff had the same sharp, sour smell.

He had been correct in assuming she would be more nervous in person than on the phone. There he stood, on a cheap imitation Baluch runner, Nancy Gregerson nervously inviting him in and standing too close, like a skittish animal, so that entering became awkward.

He had almost no idea how other people lived, so he hadn't tried to envision where he'd be going, though the lack of anything hanging on the walls seemed odd. Hardly an art connoisseur, he put up posters, at least, when he moved into a new place. *Starry Night*; a Warhol soup can in the bathroom. It was unfortunate that people tended to save their more amusing art for the refrigerator or bathroom, because they spent so much time in both places that they naturally became blind to the house's best jokes. He saw no picture of the dearly beloved missing son. There might be one on the night table, but he was one hundred percent sure he would not be going into her bedroom.

"I don't believe in fate," she said. "This doesn't have anything to do with some vague feeling that our accident had a purpose."

Our accident, he registered. "No," he said.

"Sit down," she said. She gestured toward what looked like a comfortable chair. He assumed it was her seat, but took it anyway. She offered him something to drink. He asked for coffee. The walls of the living room were beige. A less wincingly colorful rug than the one in the entranceway filled the space between the sofa and the love seat. She had not put out a bowl of nuts, which interested him. She was not moving toward the kitchen to get the coffee, either.

"I still have it in my head that you're in the CIA," she said.

"Okay, I'm a spook," he said. "Does that make you more comfortable?"

"No," she said. "I guess it doesn't. Doesn't matter, I mean. One way or the other. You don't want hot coffee in this weather, do you?"

"Don't you have air-conditioning?"

"Central air, but the generator needs to be repaired."

"Lived here long?" he asked. He did not know how to make small talk. He seemed to alternate between complete silence and screaming instructions into someone's ear. He realized that gave him an odd demeanor when he tried to exchange pleasantries. His voice sounded mocking.

"I moved in in June," she said. "I didn't know the generator was going to stop entirely when you said you'd come over. I can open the windows. That would be better, wouldn't it?"

"Allow me," he said, rising and opening a window, which required all his strength. She would never have gotten it open. There was no breeze. He opened another window, through which he could see bees hovering around flowers. He looked into the kitchen. He wanted something to hold in his hand, was the truth; he was a little nervous because he still didn't feel certain there was no subtext to his visit.

"How much should I make?" she called. "Are you a big coffee drinker?"

"Two cups," he said.

She disappeared into the kitchen. Outside the window, he saw a bird fly into a tree. In the distance, he heard what he thought must be wind chimes. Paula liked wind chimes, but he didn't like anything that made noise, including doorbells. Better that someone knock on the door than ring a bell. When he moved somewhere new, he always disconnected the doorbell, which was one of many examples Paula returned to, again and again, as evidence that he was "crazy." He had spoken to her in New York earlier in the evening. He had assumed that Nancy Gregerson might have had second thoughts, but instead the ringing phone had been Paula, whom he hadn't spoken to in quite a while. She told him she was never coming back. She also told him—silly girl—that she had decided to have liposuction on her jiggly thighs. Her legs were one of her best features; she absolutely did not need anything done to her legs, but he had listened silently so as not to risk angering her. Before they hung up, she had said again that their relationship was over, which gave him hope. If she'd only said it once, he would have been more inclined to believe her.

Nancy Gregerson came back into the room empty-handed, though he could hear the coffee machine gurgling in the kitchen. He said, "If you got your son back, what would that mean?"

She cocked her head. "I don't understand," she said. "If I had Nicky back, I'd know he wasn't dead."

He nodded. It was a good-enough answer. He had suspected—feared—that she'd answer by saying something sentimental and unrealistic: that they'd have a rapprochement, that she'd wean him of drugs—something like that.

"Do you have children?" she said.

He shook his head no.

"A wife?" she said. She added, sounding a little bemused, "Or can't you answer a question like that, either?"

He said, "I have a girlfriend."

She moved toward the kitchen, but stopped and turned. "And you were in Vietnam, weren't you?"

"As a matter of fact," he said. "I suppose you were protesting. Right?"

"March on Washington," she said. "You've got to admit: it did accomplish something."

He had no intention of discussing politics with her. He did not have time for politics. Also, he didn't want her to think that he was going to tell her things about himself. Paula, in fact, did not even know when his birthday was. It secretly pleased him, every year, when they did something inconsequential on his birthday. This year, however, he had not seen her on his birthday at all. Or even known where she was.

"You're right that I might be able to help you," he said. "Why don't we leave it at that?"

"That's fine with me," she said. "But I want to ask you: How, exactly, might you help?"

"You called *me*," he said.

"I know, but . . ." She walked away, into the kitchen. He thought about going to help her, but he didn't want her to like him. It was easier when people didn't have much feeling for one another. He went to the chair and sat down. Now there was a slight breeze, and he waited.

"The thing is, I don't have much money," she said, handing him a mug of coffee.

"I don't imagine you'd have called me if you didn't have the money for a plane ticket," he said.

She sat in a chair covered in unpleasant yellow fabric. "But *why* would you help me?" she said.

"Let's forget the *help* word and think of this as a project," he said. "Men like to think of things as projects."

She nodded. They would drink their coffee and he would ask her some questions. He would ask her for paper and a pen and write down what he needed to remember. He thought, too late, of the "theme book" it had amused him to buy.

"How long has he been in London?" he asked.

"How long, or when did he disappear?"

"How long," he said.

She thought. She said, "A year and seven months."

He said, "Could you write down his full name and the last address and phone number you have, and his girlfriend's name and number?"

"I'm not sure there is a girlfriend."

"I thought you said on the phone that someone wrote you."

"That was his roommate's girlfriend. I have some of her letters. I used to send them to the man my ex-husband hired, but there was no point in that. I just read one of them. She's . . . if I talked like my son, I'd say, 'She's fucked up.'" She got up and went to a table, opened a drawer, and took out a package of letters held together with a rubber band. When she handed them to him, he saw that the one on top had not been opened. She handed him another letter, opened, that wasn't part of the package. "I'm worried the private investigator will be mad we're meddling," she said.

"I don't think we should waste time consulting Miss Manners."

"No. I suppose not."

"I'll buy my ticket and take reimbursement in cash."

"What if you don't find him?"

"Did you think there'd be a refund?"

"I've never been involved in anything like this before," she said. "Was that a stupid question?"

"If I don't find him," he said, "you'll have a videotape of the people who were closest to him when he disappeared. With that, you can pretty much write your own story."

She crossed her arms over her chest. She said, "That doesn't sound like something I'd like to see."

He pulled the notecard out of the opened envelope and read it. "You weren't stupid enough to send money, were you?" he said when he'd finished.

"No."

"Would you tell me if you had?"

"Yes."

"Write down the names of any close friends he has, and give me any other information, like where he had a bank account, where he was working. Do you know?"

She frowned. "I guess so," she said. "In some ways, it seems so long ago. His friends . . . he had friends I didn't know. Most of them, I didn't know. There was a woman who moved to Lexington—"

"Write it down, please," he said.

She got a notepad and bent forward earnestly, writing like a student taking a test. He drank the rest of his coffee. When she finished, she said, "What will I pay you besides the plane ticket?"

"The truth is," he said, shifting in the chair, "I'm having trouble coming up with a figure because I don't really go looking for people's sons."

"You do . . . medical things," she said. "Are you some sort of doctor?"

"Don't worry," he said, not answering her question. "This comes along at a good time, when I need a change. Do you like living in Charlottesville? I can't say that I see the charm."

"I lived here with my ex-husband, and we had Nicky, and then I went to the university and got a degree in nursing and got my job. I've never moved."

"I move a lot," he said. For him, the comment was almost astonishingly confessional.

She nodded. She seemed to understand that he didn't like questions. He could see the difficulty, of course: she was afraid he'd ask for more money than she had. Yet he didn't want to risk her liking him by saying that he wouldn't charge anything. He thought it would be fun to go to London. See a play, eat some Indian food. He had a hunch that it wasn't going to be difficult to find her son. He already knew the man to call to get things started. He'd have to call the agency to make sure he didn't have to be sitting at home for the next few days, however. They had told him, almost as if his question must be facetious, that they could easily spare him for what they called "a vacation" from Monday to Friday. He made little effort to imagine how they thought, or what they thought. He sometimes wondered if he'd met anyone he talked to on the phone and hadn't known it. The same person he talked to—if it was even the same person—might be the person who had installed his telephone, he supposed. It was pretty clear that when they spoke, it was filtered through a voice changer. In a way, they had become a bizarre form of his missing parents. He had never realized that until that minute, and it was so obvious: their disembodied voices were like the voices he heard, sometimes, in his head, except that he had to invent his parents' voices, while the agency he worked for invented false voices with which to speak. Nancy Gregerson had said nothing all the time he'd sat there, thinking. He said, "Was it a mistake to tell you this isn't what I do, looking for people's kids and bringing them back to suburbia? Because it doesn't inspire confidence?"

"No, I do feel confident," she said tentatively. "I do think you'll try your best."

"It means absolutely nothing to *try,*" he said, and when she leaned forward in her seat, he realized, with a little pang in his chest that surprised him, that of course she'd expected there would be some homily to complete the sentence.

On the flight across the pond he found himself remembering Operation Eagle Pull, which was the name of a mission you didn't talk about except by another code name, even though the name of the mission had once been printed accidentally in *The New York Times*. But that particular Vietnam mission wasn't to be referred to that way, any more than you were allowed to say "Rumpelstiltzkin." Any urge to say it, and an automatic bleep went off in your brain and the term vanished as quickly as if you'd said the *F* word on television. Maybe Madonna had gone on *Letterman* and been talking about Operation Eagle Pull; maybe she hadn't been particularly profane that night, at all.

Bleep rhymed with *sheep*. Which you were supposed to count to go to sleep. He closed his eyes and saw in the red darkness of his eyelids the lights sweeping the ground, felt his eyes tear up the way they did when rope ladders were dropped that might not bear enough weight. Eyes closed, he saw O'Malley's expression, too: eyes bright with determination.

From a tray held aloft, the steward offered poisonously strong liqueurs the color of velvet: fern green, doll's eye blue. He could feel their sting, register their warmth trickling into his stomach. The steward had assumed he was making a decision, he had looked so intently at the unnatural colors in the bottles. In the seat next to him, a gray-haired lady in a perfectly fitted suit snored, after having ingested a pill. He took the pill case out of his shirt pocket and wondered if taking an aspirin might ward off the headache he sensed coming on. He swallowed two. In the pill case were also three Viagra. Cute Paula, leaving them here and there like pocket change. Liposuction, indeed. He wondered if she would weaken, or if their relationship might really be over. In any case, she couldn't reach him now. When he'd told them he was going, he'd lied only in saying that he was being paid big bucks to bring back a friend's wayward son. Two lies, really: she wasn't his friend, and he hadn't discussed money with her. All they'd said was, "Call home, E.T." Maybe if the agency went out of business, the people he spoke to could become stand-up comics. They did not approve of the amount of time he and Paula spent together. She was on a nut list for writing her congressman so often about the pesticides used on fruit, and her car—they didn't like it one bit that it was a BMW—had been booted several times because of unpaid parking tickets. They could be nasty in Atlanta. As it had been explained to him, Paula wasn't their sort—and, by implication, shouldn't be his—because she wasn't a respectful person. The congressman had written back, but Paula had kept up her campaign. She was not respectful, he should realize, though they did admit that certain deductions taken on her 1999 taxes did seem to be something her overzealous accountant was responsible for. Their relationship was not the sort of thing that got anyone disinvolved. The word for fired was *disinvolved*. No: you'd have to do something a lot more unexpected than keep company with a Libertarian ex-hippie on Zoloft, with a love of Botox and the countryside outside San Francisco, to be told to turn in your trench coat.

It would be great if they issued trench coats. Really: they could camp it up, instead of doing everything possible to make sure no one ever had reason to laugh—their own witticisms on the telephone excepted. Talk to them on the phone in anything but a muted monotone and they'd have someone tail you for a week. He liked being on a plane, where it was difficult even to think that someone who knew him whom he didn't know could be. He took an Ambien, opening the little pill case for its last possibility, and drifted off, thinking of Paula. Paula, who could be known, to some extent, by what she was not. Not a wife, or a mother, or a good aunt (according to her). When she bought toys she ended up keeping them for herself. She bought booties for a friend's baby and decided to keep them to store her rings in. Paula got very involved in fashion magazines, though she was allergic to the fragrance sheets and ended up scratching her nose as she flipped. Paula with the teeny permanent "hairs" added to the sparse centers of her eyebrows. The false eyelashes razored apart, applied with glue for special occasions. She'd get up in the middle of the night and puree things and put them on her face: avocado; peaches mixed with milk. There would be a laugh track if there was a Paula sitcom, but he thought she'd be better as her own reality show. How would he figure in? Maybe he could have a monologue in front of the camera and ruin his career by talking about Operation Eagle Pull.

"May I offer a warm washcloth?" someone in the half-dream said.

He opened his eyes. The steward stood in the aisle, dangling a washcloth held by tongs in front of his face. No wonder he'd been thinking of the perfumed ads in Paula's magazine . . . but that was hours ago, apparently. According to his watch, there was only another hour left in flight. The lady next to him was looking into a compact and powdering her nose. He wondered, nervously, whether he might have spoken when he was dreaming.

Apparently not. The woman waved away the towel—as did he—though he took a mint she silently offered him from a little tin. The plane dipped, and the captain spoke, his voice too quiet to be heard. He heard "seat belts" and "altitude." A woman was standing outside the restroom door. The steward gestured for her to sit down, but then the door opened, and she ducked inside. The plane bounced a little before straightening out. The woman leaned toward him and whispered, "Kate Jackson is on this plane."

"Who's that?" he asked.

"Men," she said. "She was on *Charlie's Angels*."

"I know who Farrah Fawcett is," he said.

"I don't doubt that every man alive knows her. Do you know, I was watching you take a pill without water and I thought: *Men do not like to take pills with water,* and they do not like Band-Aids. A man's finger can be bleeding profusely, and he'll refuse to bandage it. Just so you don't think I'm a sexist, though, women are equally peculiar. They'll sniffle, rather than blow their nose in public."

He was glad he had not stayed awake to listen to this woman's chatter. A nun from coach came into the cabin and went into the restroom. Why did nuns so often have red cheeks? He saw the steward look at her and decide to let her use the first-class bathroom. As a teenager, Paula had lived for a winter with her mother at the American Academy in Rome, when her mother had a music scholarship. She was full of stories about the nuns in Trastevere: nuns she insisted gave tourists the wrong directions, because they did not care where people ended up, if it was not going to be inside a church. Or out of sheer malicious resentment.

"Coffee, cognac, or both?" a stewardess said, smiling like a toothpaste ad. "Coffee, cognac, or both?" she said, coming toward them.

"One day at a time," the gray-haired lady said.

He looked at her, wondering if she might just be making a personal confession.

"Because of the way you looked at the liqueur bottles," she said. "I'm in recovery, myself. Going on nine years."

"Good for you," he said, confirming nothing.

"I just wanted you to know that I knew. Now: What are you most looking forward to in London?"

It was on the tip of his tongue to say "Finding some drug-addicted loser." He thought she could handle the answer. Instead, he said, "I'm going to look for a friend's son who's been out of touch with her a little too long."

She poked his shoulder. "You're supposed to ask me what I'm going to do in London, now," she said. "That's a tendency we have. To answer, but not to extend ourselves with a question."

"Okay," he said. "Tell."

"I'll be visiting my son's family. He married the nicest Welsh girl, and they have twin daughters. We're going to the galleries. The British Museum. The Tate."

The stewardess, mesmerized by her own words, droned on and on as she passed up the aisle, as if people didn't already know what they were being offered.

As she walked by, he noticed that she was wearing a necklace similar to one he'd bought Paula: she had been happy with her intertwined rose-gold-and-silver Valentine's Day necklace, but she'd guessed, correctly, that the saleslady had suggested he buy it, which meant he didn't really get the same credit for buying it as if he'd selected it himself. The woman next to him put her bookmark in *Northanger Abbey*: an oversize bronze paper clip, which reminded him that he'd once bought paper clips just to spend the agency's money on something ridiculous. And then

Nancy Gregerson had gone back to the scene—she'd told him about it at the coffee shop—and found some on the street and picked one up, which she'd used later to puncture a balloon. That weird story she'd told him about dinosaurs . . . His mind was racing, which happened sometimes when he awakened suddenly. Again he thought of Eagle Pull. This many years later, he could remember details of the information he'd been given about land mines in the area. When stepped on, the device shot a meter into the air before sending out its fléchettes, or shrapnel fragments. Then there would be a chain reaction. It did need to be noted, however, that much in life depended upon point of view. To an ant, the spray of shrapnel would be the dream fireworks of a lifetime; a human would, of course, view the Fléchette Follies extravaganza much differently.

He supposed one reason he was doing what he was doing was because he had survivor's guilt. He was lucky he'd never had posttraumatic stress disorder, and only used Ambien infrequently to sleep. He was lucky the alcohol had numbed the memories when it had, and also lucky he'd been able to get away from liquor after not too bad a struggle when it turned against him.

"What is your position on the Elgin Marbles?" she said.

"What are they?" he said, glad to have his thoughts interrupted.

"Art. Taken from the Parthenon," she said. The plane dipped again, and she grabbed the armrest. "They're in the British Museum, but it looks like they're going to have to return them."

"People don't want them to go back, I take it."

"See?" she said, poking his arm again. "You're a better conversationalist than you knew. Your point is exactly right. The same way New Yorkers didn't want to lose *Guernica*. Look them up in a guidebook. It will make you want to see for yourself."

"I'm not big on guidebooks."

"Most people wouldn't think of taking a vacation without reading one!"

"I like to feel like I'm discovering something," he said, thinking aloud. "Almost everything's written about somewhere, but if you don't do the research, you can think you're the first one to see something." What was he saying? His life was one in which he was provided with information, went out, and found what he'd been directed to find. He knew how the things he encountered worked, how they detonated, how chain reactions began, how far shrapnel would fly. What a lie he was telling, just to see what it would feel like.

It felt frightening, he concluded. He would rather know everything about the marbles, so he could look at them and see what he was expected to see, understand what he was expected to know. He most certainly would read about them before seeing them.

"I'll bet there are plenty of guidebooks that haven't been written," she said. "As soon as the climate changes, or fashions change, people set off for different places." She closed her eyes. She said, "People didn't know about hell until Dante wrote about it."

The joke about the Lazy Day Bagpipe Band was that no one played bagpipes, being too lazy to do so. The band consisted of a senior citizen named Day Lawrence, and his twin niece and nephew, Timmy and Loni, who Nancy guessed must be in their early thirties. They had played at Dolly Madison before, Timmy hitting a tambourine and Loni strumming a guitar. Day Lawrence's former fiancée had been briefly at Dolly Madison, after a stroke, before leaving to move closer to her daughter. Nancy remembered her as a very nice lady who, afflicted as she was, seemed as embarrassed by Day's antics as with her own efforts to stand without toppling. He sang a capella songs to her that were popular during World War Two, punctuating some of the lyrics by becoming airborne and clicking his heels in the air. Mrs. Ethridge, the head nurse, was legendary for rarely smiling and even more rarely breaking stride, but she had stood in the corridor and listened to "Let Me Call You

Sweetheart" in its entirety, not only smiling, but laughing, when the heel click came. There had been talk of a flirtation between Day and Mrs. Ethridge (her name was Elizabetta, but no one called her that) that extended beyond the fiancée's relocation; someone had seen them at the frozen custard stand—though it might have been coincidence that they were both there at the same time. Surely they must gossip about her, too, Nancy thought. They must, even if only to say that there was nothing to say.

They were short-staffed, so Robins, from the kitchen, had stayed overtime to help push wheelchairs to the performance. Several times Nancy had dropped him at the bus stop, so maybe that was the gossip. She thanked him sincerely as he rolled Mrs. Bell toward the Pool Room. It was Nicky who told her that a famous New York restaurant had an area called the Pool Room, and much was determined by whether you ate in that room or another. How Nicky got his information she would never know, though he did have a snob's ability to keep track of what was happening elsewhere, what party he was missing. The Pool Room at Dolly Madison House was a room at the back of the north wing, where French doors opened onto a kidney-shaped fish pool in which a few fish swam amid many water lilies. A large sculpture of a leaping dolphin had been donated by someone and placed in the middle, which she thought ruined the ambiance. It was a place the nurses went to have a cigarette on break, or where some visitors wheeled their friends or loved ones to have some privacy.

Accounted for: Mrs. Bell, Mrs. Albaharis, Miss Heller, Mrs. Beaumont, Mr. Freeley, Mrs. Jones and her day nurse, Mrs. Lanahan and her nephew, who was a professor at the university. Several more wheelchairs were being pushed past the nurses' station. The light went on in Mrs. Dowler's room, and Nancy stood to respond, because Mrs. Dowler was a screamer. Jenny, wheeling Mrs. McCall past, looked at the light above the door and rolled her eyes. It was a rule that if your hands were on a wheelchair, only in an emergency could you stop pushing the person to aid someone. Mrs. Dowler had somehow gotten herself out of bed, though, Jenny and Nancy saw at the same time. Mrs. McCall asked, "Why aren't we going anywhere?" as Jenny and Nancy rushed forward to catch Mrs. Dowler before she fell. No such luck: she crumpled at Jenny's feet. "Why aren't we moving?" Mrs. McCall said. "Why aren't we moving?" "Just a minute, Mrs. McCall," Jenny called. "Why aren't we moving?" the old lady said. "Just one minute," Jenny said, all the time looking frantically at Nancy, who was trying to figure out if Mrs. Dowler was hurt. Mrs. Dowler screamed, but rarely spoke. At night, sometimes, when she was dreaming, you might hear a few words, or even a sentence, but mostly she screamed, and it might be a bad sign that she was at this moment silent. "Why aren't we moving?" Mrs. McCall hollered. She attracted another nurse's attention, who began pushing her and speaking to her reassuringly, without knowing what was happening in Mrs. Dowler's room. "Blink if anything hurts," Nancy said, forcing herself to sound matter-of-fact. "How did you get up, Mrs. Dowler?" Jenny said. Seeing Jenny's face close to hers, Mrs. Dowler began to scream. Her favorite assertion, which she sometimes alternated with screams that sounded horrified and indignant, rather like an animal who was sprung upon by another, was: "I've been shanghaied." She screamed it loudly several times, then rolled onto her side and began to cry. "All right, we're going to get you up," Nancy said. "Here we go," Jenny said, chiming in. "I've been shanghaied!" the old lady screamed. At this point, Katie Shroeder ran into the room, hands clasped nervously. "Oh my goodness, is there anything . . ." "Here we go, now," Nancy said, bearing most of Mrs. Dowler's weight. "Take me to the bank," someone said loudly, as she was wheeled past. "Tell us if you're in any pain, Mrs. Dowler," Nancy said. The old lady was upright, Katie supporting one shoulder and Nancy with a hand firmly around her waist. The old lady had gone stone-faced. "Does Mrs. Dowler understand how she had an accident?" Katie said to Nancy. "I was on my way to punch out," Sally muttered, rolling the wheelchair up behind her. "I've been shanghaied!" Mrs. Dowler screamed. "She's all right," Nancy said. *"Of course she is!"* Katie said. "Were you getting ready for our *musical performance,* Mrs. Dowler?" "I'm getting out of here," Jenny said. The voices of the Lazy Day Bagpipe Band could be heard, not yet in harmony, above a strummed guitar that seemed badly out of tune. "Help me, I've been shanghaied!" Mrs. Dowler screamed. "Everything is *fine,*" Katie said. Katie had the nervous habit of quickly licking her bottom lip, so red lipstick was often on her teeth. Nancy pointed to her own lips, to let Katie know. Katie looked in the mirror, and began to run her finger over her front teeth. "In the good old summertime, in the good old summertime," the voices sang. "Strolling down the avenue . . ." "Who knows what an avenue is?" Nancy heard, shouted above the music. It was the director, who often blurted out things so unexpectedly that Nancy wondered if he liked to complicate things, or whether it was nervousness. "Take me to the bank!" someone hollered. The music began again: "In the good old summertime . . ." "I've been shanghaied!" Mrs. Dowler screamed, unfastening the bag Velcroed to the arm of her wheelchair. "Mrs. Dowler, you are *fine!*" Katie said, taking the wheelchair and rolling it into the corridor, tongue moving like a metronome over her bottom lip. Nancy lingered to look at a greeting card on the old lady's bulletin board. The front was a photograph of a very yellow butterfly flecked with blue. Inside, she read the message: "How does a butterfly fly? / How does a butterfly soar? / How many clouds move 'cross the sky / How many, how many more?" It was signed, in shaky handwriting, "Sister."

On her way back to the nurses' station, she overheard someone in one of the rooms helping someone else make a telephone call. "No, I'm not going to do it for you, you just put your finger on the number when I say it. No, you can't put your finger there, that won't work. Pick up your finger and put it on the seven, but just . . . Let's try again. You aren't trying. You don't have to dial the area code. I've told you that. This is a local call. Just dial seven. *Seven.* All right. Now, no, pick your finger up, you know how to push a button. They don't *make* rotary phones anymore, I've told you that."

"I've been shanghaied!" Mrs. Dowler hollered. "I need half a glass of water."

There was spilled something—coffee?—in the hallway. Since she was right by the broom closet, Nancy opened the door and took out the mop. She cleaned up the spill, then flopped the mop into the sink. "Somebody help me," came Mrs. Tanley's tiny voice. Nancy sighed and rinsed the mop and dropped it in the bucket before responding.

"Yes, Mrs. Tanley?" she said. She was too tired to admonish her for calling out instead of ringing.

"Honey, look out that window at my bird feeder," the woman said. "What do you see?"

"You'll have to give me more of a clue about what I'm looking for," Nancy said.

"On the bird feeder. Do you see that dead bird hanging from the bird feeder?"

"No," Nancy said.

"You don't see it?"

"Mrs. Tanley, didn't you want to hear the music?" Nancy asked. Mrs. Tanley was peeking over the top of her afghan, bunched under her chin. The song had changed to "Ghost Riders in the Sky" and the tambourine was shaking wildly. Through the window, Nancy could see that the sky outside was very blue. There were a few clouds, but only a few. Three, that she could see. That was the answer, in response to the question in the greeting card, its nonsensical verse masquerading as a koan.

George Wissone's dossier on Paula, obtained by inserting a telephone card and calling her sister Jan: *Actually, she has been seeing someone else. She actually decided to get out of your orbit for a little while* and see what it felt like. Well—more to be alone than to be with someone else, actually. I don't want to be in the middle. I've always liked you. I've actually wished she wouldn't tell me so many personal things, like medicine she orders over the Internet and stuff like that, but what do you do, tell your sister not to confide in you? Actually it might not be a bad idea, meeting someone new. You know, they say true love will stand the test—not that I'd be eager to subject my own husband to temptation, but actually, I don't think he'd go anywhere if I can't even get him to the movies unless it's Julia Roberts. You marry somebody and they're so lively and then hardly any time goes by and it's like they get a cold one day, like they're run down and they get a virus and they aren't themselves, and weeks pass and before you know it, years have gone by and you're still waiting for the virus thing to pass. Fred wouldn't give me a gift for my birthday unless the kids insisted. I mean, we do have too much stuff. That's not something Paula's encumbered with, is it? She's got her laptop and those jackets from France she can wear forever, they're so classic, and she has zero interest in trinkets and jewelry and things like that. I suppose she does think a lot about how she looks, but at this age, who doesn't? She's got those beautiful almond eyes. I used to be so jealous, with my beady little eyes. My skin is my best attribute, I think. That, and the little waist. Everyone in the family has that, except that our older sister looks so much like an hourglass because of her breasts and hips. Paula and I were always happy we didn't get our mother's hips because a big butt usually comes along with them, right? And that crazy husband and the four children. I mean, I've got two and I certainly didn't plan the first one, but those things happen and even though they're a lot of work, you've got to love 'em. You never met Christie, did you? Christine, as she's always correcting me now. If they didn't drive through here to see his mother, I don't think I'd see as much of her as I do. I love her, but we don't have much in common, actually. So what should I do if Paula calls? I promised I wouldn't talk about her, and here I've gone on and on—but hey, she must know I like you. She introduced you, after all! And you know. You know how much you move. She used to like that. Well, actually, I think she liked getting out of Manhattan. I mean, she loved the city but for a while all that travel served its purpose, and now after 9/11 everything's such a mess, who could possi-

bly want to put themselves through it? She bought a new car. I don't see the harm in mentioning that. She's got some notion of driving somewhere. I never actually realized she hadn't owned a car since college, except for that leased car that was always getting towed. Look, if you want my personal opinion, she's just a teeny, tiny bit of a bitch, and she's decided to test your affection. She hasn't made this man sound particularly important, except that our mother is jumping up and down, because, hey, doesn't it figure that she thinks it's the best thing in the world if a woman has a doctor for a husband? Paula is a very loyal person. She went through her wild days and pulled out of it really well, but lately it seems like she just wants a fling or something. I know she loved wherever it was you two were in San Francisco, outside of San Francisco, and then you had to move . . . it is mysterious, all this moving, though it's none of my business. It might have been a good idea to go to Manhattan with her just for a while, if you could have. If she hadn't had such wanderlust, she would have finished college. It wasn't her grades that caused any problem. Even if she wasn't there when the Towers went down, it has to have done psychic damage because it was her special place, along with tens of thousands of others, right? When she lived in the Village after her sophomore year, she was very impressionable. The dry cleaner knew you back then. The people at "your" coffee shop. That's the nice thing about New York: you can feel special there just because of a little nod and a wave. I never thought Paula wanted children. Actually, I feel like she dislikes her nieces and her nephew. It shouldn't be held against the kids that they have no manners. That's Christie's fault. Well, anyway. Paula's a conservative girl, at heart, and it might just be that all the travel, to say nothing of how mysterious you could be, sort of got to her, and then along came this doctor guy. In no way can I imagine Paula with someone else. She'll miss the travel and the dislocation. You might have a problem if she'd left in order to be with this man, but hey: it's just . . . he had an idea, she decided to go along. She might have felt a little—how should I say this? Pissing in the wind of her own fate, I guess would be the way I'd put it. Paula is a very unique person. I was going to say special, but that has so many PC connotations, you might have thought I was saying she was retarded! We both know Paula is fun-loving and devoted . . . don't you think she's devoted? But she never quite figured out what she wanted to do after she left Bard. She started that novel. Then she took that course at Columbia with that jerk who discouraged her. I mean, what would he have suggested? Not even trying to write? Maybe he had a lot of stuff rejected himself, is what I think now. She got so hurt. She changed then. But San Francisco came along, and she really liked it. She loved the opera. Or am I thinking of the ballet? I shouldn't talk about her so much. I'll tell you the truth: I don't know where she is right now, but people need breathing room every now and then. It's a shame you couldn't have lived in the Valley, because I never knew her to be happier. It could all happen again. Even as a child, she'd get disagreeable. She had tantrums, but we weren't allowed to use that word because you had to pretend the person wasn't having a tantrum, or you'd be disciplined yourself. You could actually think of it as a growth move: Paula about to find out how good she had it, being lonesome without you, all that. Think of it as a little trip. A little exploration. You could do the same. Though God knows, men don't have to be told that. They always know it in their bones. Actually, she'll be lucky if she comes back and you're not attached to somebody else. From what I understand, you had a very good relationship. She wished you'd talk to her more, but I told her: Dream on. He's a man.

He took a deep breath, exhaled, and pushed open the unmarked door with three peepholes at varying heights—presided over by no one, that night—that opened into Forever. Max sat in the back booth—the one George Harrison favored, before he died—longer-haired than when he'd last seen him, coughing in the fumes of his own cigarette smoke. His wrist was in a cast. A blonde was with him who immediately excused herself before any introduction.

"Max. Did I do something wrong?" he said.

"Give a girl one glass of white wine, she has to take a whiz immediately," Max said. "She'll come back all smiles, bladder empty, dying to know your name so she can begin to forget it."

"You're in a good mood."

"I'm in pain, I hate pain pills, and I've always called a spade a spade, even if what I was talking about was a white woman pissing," he said. "Never mind what happened to my wrist."

"Max, our lives don't matter," he said solemnly. He was echoing Max, checking to see if he remembered. He did, and it got a smile.

"I'll have an orange juice," George said to the server.

"Vodka for me, another white wine for my lady friend in the loo," Max said. "This man is the only alcoholic among us."

The waitress went off, expressionless. Over her flat breasts she wore a white bustier, and black slacks tucked into black boots with a fringe of little bells. She had curly red hair and freckles. She was probably 34A, and nineteen years old. O'Malley would have eyed her seriously, then pronounced her not the equal of his wife. He had never once seen anyone he thought equaled his wife. That included a brief chat with Cindy Crawford, who had believed that both of them were writers for *Variety*.

"That's the truth about white wine," Max said. "If you order them a vodka—and believe me, that's like asking them to drink their own blood, it's so hard to persuade them—they drink it and sit for hours. But one white wine and they race for the loo."

"Other than info on your girlfriend's bladder, what have you got for me?"

The waitress put down the vodka, white wine, and glass of juice. "Cheers," she said, walking away fast.

"I'd ask for nuts, but I'm tired of leaving big tips," Max said. "Sometimes I think, If they don't bring the nuts, the hell with them. I don't want nuts anyway. Something better, but not nuts. I get tired of living in London. Rotten weather. Nobody bathes."

"And you didn't care for the monarchy, the last time I inquired."

"Right. One of them dies, Elton John comes out of hiding and plays the piano."

"She was the only one who would have gotten an Elton serenade," George said.

"*Sir* Elton," Max said, correcting himself. "And did you know he *chose* to live in Atlanta? That'll tell you how pointless this place is."

He thought briefly about defending Atlanta, but the truth was, it was something of a blur. Really, he missed Los Angeles. The blonde came back to the table and sat down, sniffing and smiling. "Never mind introductions. Let's pretend we're all old friends and we're just picking up where we left off," she said. "That would make me feel less lonely."

"She always has nice ideas," Max said. "Doesn't that strike you as a nice idea?"

"It would be a fake name, anyway," she said. "Like you're Max. Right. I saw a driver's license that said something else, and then a credit card that was different from that. Aren't you supposed to have these things coordinated, like sweater sets? Anyway, I don't want to pretend. I don't want to feel weird and lonely just because I'm out on a date."

"He's the Dormouse," Max said, pointing to George. "Jet-lagged Dormouse."

"There's stuff being developed for jet lag that's supposed to be on the market soon," she said. "Real stuff doctors would prescribe."

"That would be good," George said.

"ZZZZZZZZZZZZ. 'That would be good,'" Max said.

"I look that tired?"

"He's mean, isn't he?" the blonde said. "My real name is Cary. I'm from Oklahoma."

Mick Jagger was singing "Angie." He lived around the corner from Max. They'd gone to the movies together a couple of times, and Mick had given him a tape of an Irma Franklin song Max had been trying to find for years.

"Your candle burned out long before . . . ." Max sang, fingering the tabletop like a piano in perfect imitation of Sir Elton.

"I never know what you're doing," Cary said. "I'd really like it if you wouldn't start singing, and tell me what you're really thinking."

"Princess Diana's death," Max said flatly.

"Oh," she said, dropping her eyes. "Sometimes, for no reason, I start to think about her, and I get so sad."

Everyone was silent.

"So, Max, before I fall asleep, as you're going to accuse me of doing: What information have you got?"

"Everything. I don't usually ask, but who is this Nicholas person?"

"As far as I know, he's some druggie not worth finding, but his mother—a woman I hit in a minor fender bender—asked me to locate him. I agreed as a kind of dare to myself: to do something easy, just once." He had also thought that it would be instructive to find someone who was sincerely missed by someone who wanted him back.

"You hit a woman?" Cary said.

"I was in a car accident with the guy's mother," he said. "I don't hit women."

"Don't believe him," Max said. "He'd say anything to get you in bed."

Cary screwed up her face. She said, "Do you think you're funny?"

"Let's all have a drink," Max said, drinking his down. "Now," he said. "Here's what I have, and it took a precious ten minutes out of my day, George Wissone." Max let the name reverberate for a second. In Los Angeles, Max had known him as Arthur Hyde— though even then, Max had been Max. Max lit a cigarette and fanned the smoke into George's face. He said, "I have his address, a key to his apartment—excuse me: flat—and the name and cell number of his dealer. I have his phone bill from the previous month, before service was cut off, and a picture of him with a girl outside the Piccadilly Circus stop whose name I didn't get, I'm sorry to report."

"Excellent," he said. "It sounds like I've got about fifteen minutes of work left."

"Explain what you said before," Cary said. "Max never will. You're bringing this guy back for somebody?"

"Cary. We never overhear anything, so we have no questions to ask," Max said.

"What does it matter what I know? Who would I tell? This is about some druggie who's being shipped home. Right?"

"Maybe you need to powder your nose," Max said.

"Ha ha," she said. "If I did have powder, you'd be surprised, wouldn't you?"

"Powder for *outside the nose*," Max said. He handed George an envelope. "Everything I know, you now have," he said. "We'll settle later."

"You shouldn't drink when you're taking codeine," she said.

"Next she'll be offering me oxygen," Max said. He had turned his chair toward George. He said, "Share with me some impression of Nick's mother. I need some visuals on the lady who brought you all the way to London."

Either Max's drink had been very strong, or he was pretty far gone by the time he'd arrived. How obnoxious he must have been, those times he put people on the spot. He wondered how often he had acted that way with Paula, and whether that might not be something she resented. He wondered what kind of doctor she'd taken up with. How much her sister's compulsive talk reflected anything she knew, beyond a love of telling stories.

"Whiskey per tutti!" Max called to the waitress, in a convincingly heavy Italian accent.

"More, luv?" the waitress said.

"Hon, I wouldn't order more," Cary said. "Those pain pills—"

Max looked at her. "A woman of caution?" he said. "You?"

The waitress took the discussion to mean that she should come back. She turned toward another table and put down some beers. Max called, "One whiskey for me, nothing for my friends."

George slipped the envelope Max had put on the table into his pocket. "Thanks," he said. "I'll let you know how things turn out."

"It turns out that Cary is sulking," Max said. "I observe this, though drunk out of my mind. Insensible. I want to go on record, though: I'm not stupid. Before I fell into this terrible state, I picked up on certain vibes between Cary and you, and you and Cary. If you two want to leave me here, I'll drink my drink in peace."

"Maaaaaax," Cary said. "I hate it when people say crazy things like that." She got up and walked stiffly toward the bathroom. George watched her go.

"You couldn't seriously think that," he said.

"Why not? I heard Paula broke up with you."

"You always did have your sources," he said. The waitress returned and put a drink in front of Max, said, "Okay, luv," and left quickly. "But I'm not sure Paula's staying gone, and I'm not interested in your girlfriend. Maybe you ought to be glad she's looking out for you tonight, instead of trying to get rid of her."

"There's really nothing going on?"

He shook his head no.

"If I get paranoid, everything's lost," Max said.

"You're not paranoid. You just had a bad couple of seconds."

"No footsie under the table?"

He shook his head again. "Let me write you a check," he said.

"Gratis," Max said. "Though I would be interested in hearing how it turns out. I envy you being able to have a quick turnaround and go back to the States. I wish I could."

"Passport still no good?"

"No good," Max said. The waitress started to put a beer bottle on the table but realized her mistake and dipped toward the table on the left. Two young men with punk haircuts bobbed toward each other across the table like toy ducks with magnets in their bills.

"Scum," Max said, following George's glance. He turned back to George. He said, "Count backwards from sixty for me. Go as slow as you want, but count out loud so I'll think we're making progress with Cary coming back to the table. What's that look for? If you're so sure she didn't go out the window, give me the count, so I don't jump out of my skin."

"Sixty," he said. "Fifty-nine, fifty-eight, fifty-seven, et cetera. After that, fifty-six, going backwards to . . . number fifty-five, and before that comes fifty-four—we're doing fine here—that was fifty-four, fifty-three, fifty-two. There she is."

Max looked up. He had been concentrating, eyes closed, tapping his thumb on the table. Cary, hair neatly combed, approached the table, still walking stiffly. She had a tentative smile on her face.

"Love you, honey," Max said. "For a minute, I just went a little out of focus."

She waved her hand to indicate that it was nothing. Her lips were bright pink, which George didn't think they'd been before. Rattled, though, she took a sip of orange juice before she realized it was his.

"That's okay," he said, encouraging her to keep it.

"I'm awfully sorry. I wasn't thinking," she said. Which had an odd echo. In fact, he had said those exact words to Nancy Gregerson after the accident. As for Max's question earlier: he found Nancy Gregerson absolutely ordinary-looking. This was also true of her eyes—and people often had expressive eyes, even if they weren't special in any other way—but her eyes were absolutely ordinary, like a drab, military-issue shirt. Well, he thought: there were ways out of having to wear those shirts, time had proven. But what could a woman do about her eyes? He'd spent enough time with Paula to know the answer: accentuate your best features, and play down the others. Yet she really had no "best" feature. He had come to London to see if he could still be a responsive human being who'd do a person a favor when he wasn't motivated by money, or sex, or—in this case—danger. He was trying to do something he thought a more normal person, with a more normal life, would do. Something kind, and also a little unexpected: the way a person might decide to let someone with fewer packages step in front of them in line. It did feel strange to do a favor. It was nowhere near as thrilling as acting covertly, assessing all the variables, calling on his training, using his instincts when the training failed him. In fact, he felt almost as numb as he'd expected to feel, and self-conscious, too. When he was working, self-consciousness was not an emotion he'd ever experienced.

The next morning he walked out of the B and B off Bond Street, having eaten two poached eggs on toast, strawberry compote, and something called a "gala" muffin. At the innkeeper's insistence, he pocketed a piece of fruit (a banana).

He had lied outlandishly at breakfast to an Australian couple sitting across from him, who insisted on dragging him into conversation. He had told them he was a retired IRS agent, married, with a son who'd dived the Great Barrier Reef. The last seemed a particularly nice detail. The man had informed him that recently, more and more blind fish were turning up at the reef; there was speculation that chemicals in the water had led to their mutation, so that now many were born without eyes. Diving and looking at the head of a "blindie" (as the man called them) was a very strange thing. You might think a fish was inherently beautiful, but when you found yourself looking at two thumb-size (he held up his thumbs) indentations and nothing but a big snout, you . . . and then the man's wife had interrupted and insisted he be quiet.

A lone German at the end of the table had clearly not understood a word. The innkeeper told them he was a visiting scholar from Munich, though she had no idea what his area of specialization was. That would have to wait for the arrival of the bilingual Irish cleaning girl. Meanwhile, she pantomimed to the German that he, too, should not leave the table without fruit. She went so far as to tap an apple to her lips. The second time she tapped, the German blushed and shook his head.

Outside, there was a ray of sunshine that quickly faded. George zipped his jacket, wishing he'd brought a scarf, and walked to the corner, where he was surprised to see a Starbucks. Where McDonald's goes, can Starbucks be far behind? He'd used the cash machine at Heathrow, so he took out pounds to buy a ticket for the underground. He went through a turnstile and walked past posters advertising plays and liquor, clothes and movies. Richard Burton's daughter looked matronly, but then, she was appearing in a Chekhov play.

He had memorized the address he was going to, but he had no idea what he would say to Nicholas if he found him. He thought he might be out of cash—even relieved to know he was missed by Mama. At the same time, though, he knew that wasn't realistic. London had a way of making ne'er-do-wells into real losers, and when drugs were involved, you could be sure that the concept of home resided in whatever pill or powder was ingested or shot. Love, hate, God, Christmas, beauty, power, where you were starting from, where you were going. Where you already were didn't matter at all, because being drugless was the most temporary state imaginable.

Getting off two stops later, he passed a woman in an orange and silver sari and nearly tripped when the mother of a small child yanked the boy across his path. He zigzagged a second time to avoid colliding with a Doberman on a leash that had stopped to stare at him. *Never could stand those dogs.* Someone was selling scarves from a black nylon bag, and he stopped and looked—the man selling them didn't speak, probably because he knew no English—and then pointed to a fake Burberry plaid, which amused him to buy. He looked at the man's five raised fingers, put up four of his own, and the deal was complete, the scarf pulled around his neck. Max had drawn him a map from the underground exit to Upper Middlesex Street. At the corner he turned and walked toward the end of the block, where there was a building with windows open on the second floor. Nicholas, though, lived in the basement, according to Max's drawing. A side entrance was marked with an *X*. Once he stood in front of the building he felt a little tingle in his fingers, a little frisson, which was a word he'd learned from Paula. The feeling he'd most certainly had long before he met her. He went down several broken concrete steps littered with cans, bottles, and rotting newspapers, past a Dumpster piled high with broken furniture. A window beside the door was covered with a dark curtain. He paused outside the door and listened for any sound. Though he had the key, he knocked and stepped to the side: an old habit. In his peripheral vision he saw a cat jump from a broken chair into the Dumpster. There were more chairs on their sides, broken and scorched. He knocked again.

"Come in," a woman's voice said.

He didn't have a gun. He wouldn't have gotten it past security, though he supposed he could have had Max give him one. But why would he need a gun? He turned the handle. In front of him, in the entranceway, hung a wrinkled dark curtain that smelled intensely of cigarette smoke. He decided that if the person did not speak again, he would move to the side, with the outer door open, and wait.

"Hi," said the woman who pulled back the curtain.

"I'm looking for Nicholas Gregerson," he said.

"It's me," the woman said. "Do I look that different with a ponytail?"

It was Cary, from the night before. Confused, he said nothing.

"Get it?" she said.

"No," he said.

"I'm the girlfriend. Nick's girlfriend. Max, or whoever he is, paid for my company last night. Some people really go in for practical jokes, but I guess I knew that already, growing up with three brothers."

"And what exactly does this joke consist of?" he said, following her into the dim apartment.

She spread her arms. She said, "This, I guess."

There was a mattress on the floor with an almost threadbare Oriental rug thrown across half of it. The apartment was so dim, it was hard to see. She saw him squinting and turned on a floor lamp. The only other window he could see was high up, at the back of the room. No Nicholas Gregerson. No Max—unless he was about to jump out of a closet. If so, he might explain the joke a little better.

She sat on a corner of the mattress and gestured to the other possible places to sit: one of two director's chairs that faced a big television placed crookedly on top of cement blocks. There was a lava lamp on top, though it was not plugged in. Also, a photograph of somebody.

"Tea?" she said. She bent forward to scratch her ankle.

"Nick lives here?" he said. "And how do you happen to know Max?"

"Don't, really. He came around the same way you did. Said somebody from the States was going to be looking for Nick. Then he asked if I'd consider helping him pull a prank. For the money he offered, I thought I would, though you don't seem as amused as he thought you'd be."

"I'm still trying to figure this out," he said.

"I thought you'd understand it better than I do," she said. She took off her sock and scratched her ankle harder. She put the sock back on. "I microwave the tea," she said. "I'm not English. So what I mean is, no problem."

"Max hired you," he said slowly.

"Yeah. You know, to me it was more or less a business deal. I mean, what am I saying? It was completely business."

"So what's the deal?" he said. "I hire you, and we call him to meet us for drinks?"

"I'm not doing it," she said, as though he'd made a serious proposition. "I think this is going to get way kinky. And if Nicky finds out about it, he'll kill me. I'm lucky you came when Max said you would, because if this was tomorrow, he'd be here."

"Where is he now?" he said.

"Sung Ho Lo," she said.

"And what is that?"

"Jeez, I'd expect you to take out a little notebook or something. I mean, look, put my mind at ease and tell me whether you're going to tell him you stopped by."

"I don't know why I'd have to mention anything," he said.

"Good. What about tea?"

"I don't want tea."

She shrugged. She said, "I don't, either. In answer to your question, it's a Chinese restaurant. He's a waiter there three nights a week, but Tuesdays he goes in as a dishwasher." She got up. "You're not going to do anything bad to him, are you?" she said.

"No."

"It's what Max told me? His mother wants him to go home?"

He nodded.

"Okay," she said, "because we've been having some problems and everything, but if he got kidnapped . . . I mean, he'd go back if he wanted to. You know?"

"I'm not going to kidnap him."

She went into the kitchen and got a little can of juice out of the refrigerator. She did not offer him juice. She opened the can and stood leaning against the wall, sipping. "Did you think I was a hooker or his girlfriend?" she said.

He assumed she was asking about Max. He said, "Girlfriend."

"From Oklahoma," she said. "I had to have one lie, myself. It wasn't much of one, though. I just thought, *I wonder if he'll ask why I don't have an accent?* I'm really from Wisconsin."

He nodded.

"I told Nick I was at my mother's last night."

"She's here, not in Wisconsin," he said.

"Oh, yeah, she married an English guy and she's a legal resident."

He nodded.

"I have to go to work," she said. "I guess I can assume—"

"I might walk over to the restaurant," he said. "What did you say the name was?"

"Hey, if you'd written it on your little spy tablet, you'd remember!" she said. "Kidding. It's Sung Ho Lo. Just one street over. Everybody knows it."

"Don't be late for work," he said, standing.

"No. So. Good-bye. Maybe I'll never see you again, right?"

"Right," he said.

"So. This is the end, except that you're going to talk to Nick and not kidnap him."

"That's right."

"Okay," she said. "It didn't turn out to be much of a joke, did it?"

"I don't think so," he said.

"Okay. Well. You've been awfully nice. I'm glad it wasn't the other way around. That it wasn't you I went to that place with. That didn't come out right. What I meant was, if I'd gone out with you, it would be Max who was sitting here today, right? And he sort of gives me the creeps, to be honest."

"He's definitely getting creepy."

When he left, she stepped out of her shoes and socks and didn't see him to the door. He pushed aside the curtain and went out, just in time to see a huge rat drop into the Dumpster.

Paula was trying to do origami. The instructions were badly translated from the Japanese, in print so small the lines looked like dead gnats. *Take two fold,* she read. *Other fold point one and four.* She put down the square of paper because it was getting damp and puckered by her fingertips. She looked ahead in the directions. Some sentences made sense, others made very little. It was not likely she would have her yellow giraffe any time soon, but she prided herself on patience. Lately, she'd gotten little cuticle scissors and begun patiently doing her own nails, going to Spa of the Seven

Senses only for an occasional pedicure. Since moving to her fiancé's house she'd gained five pounds, making her the only person in history to gain weight, rather than lose, in health-obsessed California. At the same time she was trying to figure out how to fold the pretty pieces of paper, she was mixing cookie batter. Stirring was a good distraction from trying to understand how to fold. The wedding would be a week from Saturday. She had still not bought a dress, though she had Peter Fox satin heels with sparkly little flowers that were so exquisite, no dress could compete with the footwear.

After a year of therapy she had realized how much George was like her aloof, undependable father, and that her self-esteem was severely lacking, which was something that George counted on, she'd come to think. Her career had been derailed when she met him, then ruined. She was a big girl, and also to blame, but he had made it impossible for her to work, he moved so many times. Once she had thought she would learn how to do something she could do anywhere, like quilt, but she had no talent for quilting, and stained-glass-making required . . . well, it required a studio and tools. She had given the one small coaster she made to her sister and given up. Her sister thought she should write, but she had no talent for writing. The course at Columbia had proven that.

They had moved every time he got a call from "the Starship *Enterprise*." Condescendingly, he did not even tell her who phoned him, who determined their lives. "Conjecture," her therapist had said, raising one hand, as if to stop something—which might have been the doctor's own urge to speculate, she supposed. "Conjecture, Paula: Think CIA."

Well, *duh,* as the kids said. But the therapy had helped. She had reestablished something of a relationship with her mother, though it was too late to try to talk to her dead father. Her mother, Flyineye@aol.com, sometimes wrote two or three cheery messages a day, eager to prove—Paula supposed—that their earlier, rancorous exchanges about Paula's not working (not "putting your brain to use") and not marrying (not "making a commitment that will sustain you through good times and bad") were at an end. Paula didn't care for e-mail, though every letter she'd attempted to write to George—at the behest of the therapist, for "closure"—seemed so overwritten that she'd begun to think one sentence on the computer would suffice to say she was okay, she wished him the best, and if he had any doubt, their relationship was over. How many commas would that sentence need? She was about to marry a radiologist named Kendall Llewellyn, whom she'd met at a meeting in Washington, D.C., arranged by the American Enterprise Institute. She had gone to the meeting with a friend, stopping to see an old school chum on her way to Charlottesville, Virginia, to swallow her pride and rendezvous with George, when she met the doctor (her friend's plan, it seemed) and stayed in town an extra day to have lunch with him. He had been at NIH, but was about to move back to California, where he had a research grant at UCLA. It wasn't San Francisco, but it was close. It also seemed that he was so fond of her, he was willing to consider going into private practice there, once his research fellowship ended. She could not quite believe she'd met someone when she wasn't looking—though the therapist maintained that in the back of her mind, she had been looking, and that this was evidence that she had good instincts about self-preservation. Paula thought that refusing to have the big wedding he'd envisioned was also a step in the right direction—she hated formal gatherings, and hated to be the center of attention—and was grateful that Kenny agreed to marry at City Hall. It was a shame so few people would get to see the Peter Foxes, but she would know she had them on. She would be wearing the old gold locket she had gotten from her grandmother, along with a borrowed Lady Elgin watch she had admired on a female doctor's wrist, who'd insisted she have it for her wedding, and as for something blue she thought she might tuck a photograph of George in her brassiere, because on her wedding day, she did not doubt that—at long last—she would be able to say with certainty how he would feel.

She turned the piece of paper, smoothing a wrong fold, then rather quickly shaping the giraffe's long, fragile neck, which completed its shape. It didn't stand up, though. There was no way to balance it. The directions didn't say anything about the figures standing upright, she supposed. She decided to do one more, and to let her menagerie lie prone on the tabletop, as if winds from Chernobyl had done them in.

Two more completed: a leopard (easy) and a horse (moderately difficult). She was trying *not* to finish the cookie dough, because she still thought fresh fruit might be just as nice. Though whoever heard of having someone for tea and *fresh fruit*? The tea had been Kenny's daughter's idea. She had asked her to lunch, when Kenny said his daughter wanted to meet her, but his daughter had suggested tea instead. The animals looked colorful and sad. She remembered, vaguely, some poem by Yeats about animals that she had loved in her college days, but she couldn't remember how it went. A poem of regret, as she recalled. All she could remember, as she searched her mind, was the beginning of a poem by Robert Frost: "Some say the world will end in fire, / Some say in ice."

She got up and cracked an egg into the cookie dough, then lowered the blade and set the mixer on "medium." The noise reminded her of George's and her blender period: protein powder, bananas, and white grape juice, with a squeeze of liquid vitamins and a few ice cubes, pureed for breakfast. There had also been their cinnamon toast period (the cinnamon sugar kept in a shaker intended for Parmesan cheese), and the yogurt with lecithin granules. She'd never liked that gloppy stuff, and the lecithin reminded her of the hideous pinworms she'd contracted over and over as a child. These days, she drank fresh-squeezed grapefruit juice (as sweet as orange juice), and, more mornings than not, ate a sinfully buttery almond croissant from the bakery at the shopping center. The juice was very California, but the bit of La Belle France was beyond delicious. You could believe you were in Paris, rather than the Hollywood Hills.

Kenny's house had six bedrooms and seven and a half baths. The back windows overlooked a small plot of land on which the neighbor's Appaloosa stood. The neighbor was divorced, and the horse sometimes came and spent the weekend. It was as affectionate as a dog. She would look out the window and see the neighbor picking up droppings and wonder if he might not be happier if he got himself a dog. He could get a very big dog, like a Great Dane, and think of it as a horse.

The Christmas before he died, Paula's father had sent her sister Christie a tape of *The Godfather* with a note saying that he remembered her fascination with horses, and also the many dinners he had sat through, entirely devoted to his girls' enthusiasms. Jan's interest had been ballet, but to Paula's knowledge, she had not been given the tape of a dance performance. Her own interest had been . . . well, that wasn't so easy to say. She had loved her Barbie dolls, but she had also been a tomboy who liked softball, though for a while she played checkers, then chess, every night. Her sister Jan had played checkers with her; her father had played chess though he often wandered off and shut himself in the bathroom, or went to bed and left her sitting there. She could remember one time, after she'd made a particularly clever move, her father rising and exiting the room, when she'd felt sure in the knowledge she should not wait for him to come back. She'd grabbed up Hawaiian Barbie and used the doll as a broom, sweeping the ivory pieces to the floor and running from the room, herself. Both she and Jan had been sent to see someone about their anger. Christie had not, and Christie had taunted them with: "Crazy, crazy, crazy." See who was crazy now, with four brats driving her nuts and a husband who could barely support them. Jan had married well, leaving aside the fact that her husband was too much of a homebody. And she, herself, would be marrying a man who expressed his political opinions, who had religious beliefs (he had been raised going to church), who knew where he would be living for the next two years, and who was so responsive to her that he seemed quite willing . . . but there was no point in thinking of San Francisco. She should look out the window and continue to try to like the Hollywood Hills, where Gore Vidal and his companion were said to be in residence (this was rare), and where there were roses tended by a Mexican gardener who came twice a week, though he loved the flowers so much he often stopped by on Sunday. It was a strange feeling, to be near so many famous people. Christie envied her that, she knew. It was Christie who had given her a subscription to *Vanity Fair*. Come to think of it, she had not changed the subscription. *Note to self: change address.*

She swirled a spatula around the side of the bowl and put the bowl on the counter, licking the beaters. She licked them well, then put them in the sink. In about half an hour, Talia would arrive. She must put the cookies in the oven, so the timing would be perfect. She hurried to drop rounded tablespoonfuls on the cookie sheet.

She thought, for the first time: a cookie sheet. What man had one of those? It had been shipped, along with many other kitchen items, and everything had been put away in drawers by the moving men, while she and Kenny stayed at the Hotel Bel Air. He must have lived with someone, though in telling her about the last five or six years of his life he had omitted mention of any serious relationship and said only that he had been lonely, and that he thought he'd never find the woman who was right for him. Still: a cookie sheet . . . she should try to find out whom he'd dated before her. Kenny had more or less prepared her for Talia's excessive loyalty to her mother (who had never remarried), explaining that his daughter was "eccentric" and dropping other hints that the meeting might not be all that pleasurable. She supposed she was happy the girl was coming for something less time-consuming than lunch, though she would have preferred to have Kenny there. At dinner, you would have thought. Talia lived with two roommates in

Topanga Canyon and worked as a legal secretary. Paula had an image of her as reclusive and unattractive, though that was probably a guarantee that she'd be stunning and slim. How could she be so worried about five pounds? She was ashamed of herself for being so silly. At the same time, she set herself a limit: three cookies. That way, it would look like she was enjoying them, though she wouldn't eat too many. When Talia left, she would take them immediately to the neighbor (did horses eat cookies?), saving only a few for Kenny.

The doorbell played the first four notes from *The High and the Mighty*. He'd had to tell her what it was.

She opened the door and put a smile on her face before she saw Talia. Which was just as well, because Talia's mouth curved wryly, though she did formally extend her hand. A man stood at her side. "Mr. Corcoran," Talia said. "And I'm me, of course."

"Talia, come in," she said, freezing the smile. "And Mr. Corcoran."

"Mr. Corcoran is one of the partners at the law firm where I work."

"Something is baking!" Mr. Corcoran said appreciatively, sniffing the air.

"Come in and sit down," she said, heading toward the living room. Talia was tall and pretty, though her poker face and protruding bottom lip made her seem only strange. She was pouting. That was the way she'd describe Talia later on the phone, when she called her therapist back in New York: pouting. Mr. Corcoran was as nice as Talia was distant. She asked if she should brew some tea, or whether they would like green tea she'd bought at the market, which was cold. "Whatever is easiest, I like both," he said. Talia said, "Is there any Irish tea?" as Paula went into the kitchen.

"I'm afraid there's only a box of Earl Grey and the tea I bought—"

"Earl Grey," Talia said. Paula almost added: *please.*

"I used to know someone on this road. We had some pool parties at his house, but that was years ago," Mr. Corcoran said. "I see you have a lovely pool out there. That's something I miss, living in a high-rise. Beautiful, beautiful view at night, but no pool. There is one, but it's overrun with children, so I never go."

"You should go and tell the mothers to control them. Or the au pairs. Forgive me, what was I thinking: *au pairs*."

Unsure whom Talia was mocking, Paula picked up the plate of cookies, then put it down, deciding to carry it in with the drinks, on a tray. She took an inlaid tray from a rack under the counter, put water on to boil, and poured two glasses of green tea. She picked up a little bowl of sugar packets and put it on the tray. She put napkins patterned with tiny green frogs on the tray. For the hell of it, she put the pink swan in among the cookies. She looked at the other little animals she'd assembled. She had already begun to feel like lying on her side, herself. She rearranged the swan so it was perkily upright. She carried the tray into the living room.

"What do you think of this furniture?" Talia said. "Do you think furniture like this is part of male menopause?" She was ignoring Paula and asking her employer his opinion. Paula said quickly, "I like it. It's comfortable."

"It certainly is," Mr. Corcoran said. "Isn't that pretty? You made those, obviously."

"Yes, the swan, too. I'm creative, don't you think? I had to be, to read the directions, which were translated into English by someone who didn't speak the language."

"Tell me about it!" Talia exclaimed. "They call the office, and if you don't speak Spanish, forget it." She shifted in the chair. She said, "Are you planning to work in Los Angeles, or will you be making origami?"

"Talia!" Mr. Corcoran said.

"It was a question," Talia said.

"She's her own person! Blunt and to the point!" Mr. Corcoran said. "Well, I've never had a better secretary in fifteen years, and as long as she doesn't find fault with me, it's to my advantage to look the other way."

It was the first time it really registered that Talia had brought a *lawyer* with her. She could no longer pretend to herself that this was a meet-the-bride tea party. The kettle whistled, and she got up immediately, trying to think—which she thought she might do better out of the malevolent girl's presence.

She opened drawer after drawer, looking for a tea ball. She had seen one, but could not remember where. The tea was loose; she had only thought she'd bought tea bags. She opened another drawer, and wondered at the moving men: there were several rolled pairs of socks, and a few corkscrews lay to one side. Jeweled fruit filled the rest of the drawer. This was another hint, she was certain: a cookie sheet; *jeweled fruit*. She found a strainer and put loose tea in it, poured boiling water through, and decided she was glad that the tea looked weak. She went back to the living room, knowing that Kenny must have recently bought new furniture. That he must have been living with another woman. That Talia was angry with her. Few mysteries remained, though what Mr. Corcoran was there for, she could not have guessed.

"Mr. Corcoran has drawn up some papers pertaining to my share of my father's estate, which my father thought you should consider," Talia said. "If you grant the fairness of my inheriting something, you shouldn't have any problem. Of course we'll leave them with you to consider at your leisure."

"I would have waited another few minutes," Mr. Corcoran said, more to himself than to anyone else. He quickly took a cookie.

"If you think I'm going to ask if you'd like milk, I'm not," Paula said. She thought it was a fair way to speak to a woman who spoke to her like a dog she needed to scold: *Let's show you this rolled-up newspaper and let you think about it at your leisure, before I smack you.* "Do you have any interest in what sort of person I am? Or do you have so much disdain for your father, you think he must have picked just *anybody*?"

"You're one of several women he's 'picked' lately, as you put it. And the first one made off with a truckload of my grandmother's Victorian furniture and a considerable amount of his money," Talia said.

"Please, please, ladies, please," Mr. Corcoran said. "This can all be handled much differently. Talia, you don't realize what your tone of voice sounds like."

But Talia had grabbed up her little quilted Chanel bag and was on her way out the door.

"You'll never believe it now," Mr. Corcoran said, "but she has many nice qualities, she really does. Her father's involvement with the Argentinean woman . . . ."

She looked at him, glad that at least the awful daughter had left before tears sprang to her eyes.

"I feel like shit," Mr. Corcoran said. "We talked about this. She wasn't going to bring it up this way. I can see that you're a lovely person. Do you think I could go out to the car and talk to her, and maybe we could get to know each other before this subject is discussed? These are wonderful cookies. I can see you went to great trouble. My daughter made an origami bird in summer camp last year. We're all decent people here, there's no reason she should have spoken to you that way."

But Paula wasn't listening. Like Paula's father, Talia had exited because that was what was most convenient, abandoning the other person to helpless frustration. Like her sister Jan, the lawyer had logorrhea. You never got away from your family, she supposed. George had been like her father, and now it seemed Kenny was more like him than she'd realized: secretive, smooth, a coward.

Of course she was crying. The surprise was that for a few seconds, it looked like Mr. Corcoran might join her.

In the restaurant, the lighting was dim. When he knocked on the door, someone opened it a crack and hollered over his shoulder in

Chinese. "Sung Ho Lo not open," the man said, turning back to him. He had a towel thrown over one shoulder. In the room, George could see a bucket and a mop. Another man came through a swinging door and said, "Sung Ho Lo opens twelve o'clock. Thank you."

"I'm looking for Nicholas Gregerson," he said.

The two men spoke to each other in rapid-fire Chinese. There was a pineapple-y smell: probably the water in the bucket, rather than food, he thought.

"Thank you come back," the second man said, moving forward as if to butt him in the chest. The first man grabbed the towel and walked away.

"Nicholas Gregerson?" he said again, nodding his head in the direction of the kitchen.

"Twelve o'clock. Gregerson twelve o'clock."

"He will be here at twelve o'clock?" George asked.

"Gregerson twelve o'clock," the man said, moving so close that George did, finally, take a step back. This was the point at which—if he happened to be stupid—he would give the man the business card he didn't have (that would be a good one: What information could possibly be printed on his business card?) and he simply astonished when he returned and Nicholas had fled.

He took his leave without saying good-bye, trying not to be irritated that the door closed so loudly behind him. The pineapple odor was still in his nose, and he patted his pocket, wishing a tissue might appear. He wiped his thumb quickly against both nostrils and walked to the street, sniffing, looking left, then stepping down. The cab that ran over him was driven by a twenty-year-old Bengali who—had he been born a few generations earlier—would have been a priest in his country. Instead, he was driving a minicab in London, transporting a massively pregnant woman to a doctor's appointment. On impact, the woman vomited, hitting the Bengali's neck. Then the woman was screaming, pedestrians were screaming, and two men from a car behind him were racing toward the minicab, with George Wissone, dead on impact, trapped beneath it.

Cary found out about the accident later in the afternoon, when Nicholas—who had gone to the restaurant late, having sat at Starbucks much too long with a friend he'd run into, who had very kindly bought him a grande latte with cinnamon, and two biscotti to dunk—called to say that some man had been hit, that blood was being cleaned up in front of the restaurant, and that if business remained slow, he might be home early. How did she know, even before he repeated what information the Chinese had given about the body, that the person who'd died was the man who'd left the apartment not long before? But she did know. And she remained convinced that it was no accident, that George Wissone's weird friend had something to do with it, and that her world was about to cave in, because she would somehow be dragged into the mess. Then, and ever after, she did not tell anyone that she had met the dead man. She lived in fear that Max would show up at her door— so much so that she picked a fight with Nicholas and left London that evening for quite a while.

For her part, Nancy Gregerson had no idea whom to call. She could imagine that finding someone might be a lot more difficult than it appeared, though she didn't think the situation would be complicated because Nicky had done anything drastic, like having plastic surgery. Having no evidence to the contrary, she continued to assume he was in London, unless some woman was involved, and then if the woman left, she could imagine him following her, whether he was wanted or not. What he'd said so long ago was true: she could only assume his relationships would end; she never considered them equal relationships, and it wasn't likely the right sort of person would be attracted to Nicky in the shape he was in. She waited another couple of weeks for word from George Wissone, blaming herself for not asking approximately when she might expect to hear from him, and then did something she vowed she'd never do: she wrote the girl in London who had sent the letters asking for money. Her note said: "My son's trouble with drugs has led me to be suspicious of what he says and does, and also to be skeptical of what his friends say and do. I'm sorry if this does you a disservice. If you can give me any substantial information about where Nicky is, I will fly to London and we can discuss remuneration then." She crossed out *remuneration* and wrote *payment*. She did not rewrite the note, which she had written on lined paper she'd torn out of a tablet. She put six stamps on the envelope because she didn't have time to go to the post office to get it weighed. They were understaffed at work: another pregnancy, with the aide having to take off work months early because of toxemia, and Bonita Villasenor's angioplasty. Jenny had quit the month before. Her mother had offered to pay for her to go to nursing school full-time if she left her husband, and Jenny had decided to do it. For some time Jenny hadn't been particularly friendly toward her, but Nancy still missed seeing her in the hallways, and almost anyone besides Osama bin Laden would have been appreciated for pitching in, there was so much work. Any notion that her son might help take care of her in her old age was ridiculous, she knew, but planning for a future she could not anticipate also made less and less sense. The lives of others, Nancy thought. You could spend so much time thinking about them, it subsumed your own life. Not that distractions weren't welcome. As it was, she often paced restlessly during the night, wondering where Nicky was, increasingly skeptical about whether she had been wise to put her trust in George Wissone.

The more certain she became that the situation in London must be complicated, the more she dreaded that eventually he would return with a videotape, but no Nicky. Perhaps by the time she paid off her credit card bill, he would be back. What amount of money would he ask for if he somehow had Nicky with him? More often, though, she feared that George Wissone had simply absconded. What proof did she have that he'd ever gone to London? Still, she couldn't believe that he'd left town, just like that, simply because she'd reimbursed him for an airline ticket. He didn't seem to need money. He dressed well—though she did remember the crappy little car he'd driven. But people were unpredictable about the cars they bought: people who couldn't afford Mercedes went into debt to buy them; rich people bought Jeeps. She had not thought about the time she'd gone back to the scene of the accident recently, but suddenly the one big tree with the bright light aimed at it came to mind, and she remembered what a creepy feeling the spotlight on something ordinary— something toward which she wasn't sure her attention should be directed—had given her; except for the verticality of the light, it had reminded her of the much talked about light at the end of the tunnel so many people reported seeing in near-death experiences. She had turned her back and gone on her way, though once seated in the car she had wondered if the light might portend something. For her, or for him? She'd had premonitions of other things that materialized, though maybe everyone had. She'd known that the neighbor's cat—the long-ago neighbor's cat—was going to die, and that Nicky was going to be involved. She had noticed the way he looked at it, though she never could account for why Nicky would like a creature or hate it. Images of the crushed turtle no longer came back to her—except momentarily, when she didn't stop herself from thinking about troubling, gloomy subjects. She had imagined the death of her husband's wife's dog, and that hadn't happened, had it? Though, on the other hand, she had seen something in Mrs. Sanderson's eye, and the woman had died soon thereafter. The eyes were known to register bad health. Good doctors always looked into a patient's eyes.

The light went on above the desk, indicating a patient was calling. Usually, between getting them in bed for the night and the beginning of bad dreams, there was a longer lull. It had been a busy night.

"Yes?" she said, entering the room. It was Mrs. Bell, whose covers were on the floor. "Your covers," she said, answering her own question.

"Don't go," Mrs. Bell said, raising a shaky hand. "You haven't told me when we'll leave."

"It's midnight, and you're in your bed. You don't have to go anywhere, Mrs. Bell."

"I have to go to my son's," she said. Her hand moved restlessly across the newly replaced covers. Nancy stepped forward and grasped Mrs. Bell's hand. "Your son and his family are in Richmond," she said. "You're in your bed, and it's almost midnight."

"Richmond?" the old lady said. It was always a calculated risk: give a detail, and it might soothe; give a detail, and it might perplex them further.

"You know," she said, trying to distract her, "I met a boy who used to be your neighbor, not too long ago. Do you remember a blond boy who works at a plant nursery?" *Plant nursery,* not *baby nursery.* Words were endlessly misleading.

"I fell and he called the ambulance," she said.

"Is that right? Well, he said he'd delivered flowers here."

"He's an angel," Mrs. Bell said.

He hadn't seemed very nice to her, but that was not something she'd mention. "Well, he was very nice to carry my bush to my car," she said.

"His sister was so bright. She won a spelling contest for all the state. She's no longer with us, though, bless her heart."

A mistake: any nighttime conversation could elicit unhappy memories.

"Oh," she said, trying to speak as if that settled the matter, and was not a question.

"Yes. She died on Afton Mountain, in a car none of them were supposed to be in. The car fell all the way down, and it was the headlights pointed at the sky that made them find them."

"How awful," she said. "I'm sorry to have brought up—"

"Her father never worked another day. He bought groceries, after that. His wife made him. Sitting in his chair, never again working another day. Her son had to be everything to her. He was his mother's own angel boy."

"At least she has her son," Nancy said, unthinkingly. As soon as she'd spoken, she bit her lip, but the old lady didn't seem disturbed.

"Richmond," Mrs. Bell said. "Of course they're in Richmond. What time did you say it was?"

"Ten after twelve," Nancy said, looking at the clock.

"In the afternoon?"

"No. At night."

"Richmond," the woman repeated, and Nancy let go of her hand.

No response came to the letter she wrote the girl in London, sitting at the nurses' station later that night, and no word from George Wissone, though in another week's time a letter arrived, postmarked Washington, D.C., from someone named Rich O'Malley. He said he was trying to track down a friend whom he thought she knew, George Wissone. He gave her his telephone number and asked her to call him collect; he had tried her number many times and not reached her. So: George had told someone about her, and about the trip. She wondered if Rich O'Malley might also be a spook, because she had understood when George sat in her living room and joked that he was a spook that he *was*. Because of his age, he had probably retired.

She had planned, when she went part-time, to buy new clothes, but time had passed and she hadn't done that. At work she wore pants and a matching top, with rubber-soled clogs and a pair of socks or, more often, trouser hose that stopped at the knee. Her only jewelry was the Bulova her ex-husband had left behind when he moved. The younger nurses saved their money to buy gold bracelets and gold earrings. She cared nothing about jewelry. She did not attend any political fund-raisers, or go to lunch at places where people wore subtle, expensive earrings. She certainly did not ever attend formal occasions, though a grateful patient's son had asked her to join him and his wife when they were invited for drinks at Ash Lawn. She had been invited, a few times, for one occasion or another at someone's house: a croquet party—that was the South!—or a Christmas party, though she always declined. It was an easy time of year to pretend you had something else to do. This past Christmas, instead of a Christmas tree, she had gone to a greenhouse—*not* part of the nursery where the strange boy worked—and bought a large white azalea, which she'd decorated with twinkling lights and a few red felt miniature cardinals she'd bought at the fabric store. She had cooked herself a filet mignon and had it with baked artichoke hearts with Parmesan cheese and a half bottle of red wine that did not come from the area. She'd worn her jeans and a comfortable, oversize blouse with unfashionable shoulder pads she kept meaning to cut out. She'd listened to Christmas carols on the radio, then put on Norah Jones—a gift from the director of Dolly Madison, along with a check for one hundred dollars—and sat in her chair, warm and comfortable, wondering how people took on so many obligations. She and her then-husband had bought their tree the week before Christmas, decorated it two or three days before the twenty-fifth, unwrapped gifts on Christmas Eve, then driven to his cousin's for Christmas Day breakfast, then home to receive visitors in the afternoon, followed by an evening recital of music by the sons of her neighbors, at their house, along with homemade eggnog—then back to their own house to make Christmas night resolutions, which did not cause as much guilt as broken New Year's Eve promises. Once or twice she had enjoyed the routine. Three times, even. And then the neighbors' children became awkward teenagers with acne and unpleasant tenor voices, and the resolutions she and Edward made had an edge to them: *I'll give up desserts, but you should think about that, too.* When Nicky got older, they couldn't have a tree in the house because of his allergies. Well, of course she'd assumed his eyes were red, all those years later, because of some other

allergic reaction. They stopped going to the cousin's in Winter-
green. People still came by in the afternoon, but a little apologetically, because they thought she and Edward might be napping,
they were both so sleep deprived. Nicky never went to bed before
ten o'clock, and he never slept through the night. Nicky was a
problem in kindergarten: he bit, he threw things. She was always
getting calls. He had trouble reading. He had to repeat second
grade. He would scream bloody murder if either of them tried to
help him bathe, and sometimes months would pass when his hair
was unwashed, and he dug at his scalp but refused to shampoo his
head. He begged for a dog, and when neither of them would
relent, cut up his toy animals with pinking shears and threw them
on their bedroom floor. She called the pediatrician, crying and
fingering the once-beloved, decapitated Snoopy in her pocket. He
saw her that day and set up an appointment with a psychologist.
Nicky went. And then, perhaps even the same week, he had a
seizure. Their world seemed to stop. Tests, more tests. Then a
reprieve: years in which there was no second seizure, though the
medicine he took made him put on weight. With his rounder face,
he looked more like her. After three years—the last year with no
medicine at all (and there had been no more horrible incidents)—
she had been telling her husband the doctor's cautiously worded
but still reassuring good news (a much better drug had been
developed, if and when Nicky might need it) when he had stood
up from his chair and said, "I need to tell you something." Just
like that, she had heard about his long affair with a woman who
had become pregnant. He answered her questions: it was not a
woman she had ever met; the woman lived in the county; he was
not in love with her, but he was nevertheless asking for a divorce.
"You wouldn't even blink if I had a seizure," he said. *What?* It was
as if it was neatly woven together in his mind: his unfaithfulness,
the woman, the pregnancy, her failure to drive him home after
he'd had a root canal; her failure—a nurse's failure!—to ask the
result of his colonoscopy, during which they had removed polyps.

It might have been funny, except that he frightened her. For the first time, she noticed the redness of his face, which was the same prickly purple blush Nicky had gotten when he became adamant that he would not bathe or wash his hair. She wished she could remember how her ex-husband had segued from his mistress's pregnancy to the discovery of polyps. In her wildest dreams, she could not imagine the transitional sentence, so perhaps there had not been one. Perhaps he had just begun yelling any grievance he could think of . . . but what had been wrong with Nicky, years later, when she and he and his father and his father's wife were all in family therapy, to maintain that never once had his father raised his voice? She asked him whether he didn't remember that night: the night of the tossed-over lamp, his father clomping out in a rage, and he said he did remember the incident, though he had been chilled by his parents' silence. It was the small click of the door that meant the family would not be together again that he remembered. The way, in the middle of it all, she had answered the phone and said, "Hello?" According to Nicky, there had been only the softest sounds: a whisper, a click. He thought he might have become so hypersensitive to sound not because he was used to living amid shouting and crying, but because everything that happened happened as gently as something ephemeral, drifting to a stop. And he had turned his own round, blank face to her to see if she would disagree. "My son lies in a very calm tone of voice," she had said to the therapist. "He wants to provoke the other person into such frustration, she raises her voice." The man had looked from her to her ex-husband, who did not verify or deny what had been said, and then he had searched Nicky's face, to no avail. Next he looked at Bernadine, who looked stricken, but said nothing. She, herself, had determined that she would sit there silently, since she had spoken the truth. For the remaining ten minutes of the session, no one had said a thing, as if whoever was the most silent would be the one absolved.

Could Nicky have done something similarly maddening to

provoke George Wissone? He would certainly lie when it suited his purposes. She hadn't thought what might happen if Nicky presented a different version of things—if he convinced George that he was put upon, unfairly characterized, a young man trying to detach from his crazy mother. Maybe George had gone all the way there and come back—that was it: he might have come back!—and just hadn't known how to tell her that she should butt out, things were fine. How likely was that? Not very. What would be the scenario? Nicky would show the man his paintings, explain that his mother was a smothering woman who wanted him back in Virginia because she was lonely, and couldn't let go, and she thought he was her property . . . he was not being supported by her; he was fine, on his own in London, working. . . . That was, of course, absolutely impossible. More likely, he would be stoned and arrogant and devious. George would try to talk to him, but fail. What evidence did she have that he knew how to talk to someone like Nicky? George, the nonspook spook. Knowing how to maneuver in Vietnam when you were young would give you little preparation for functioning in London when you were old. She had been crazy to contact him. The cost of the plane ticket was nothing, but a failed mission overseas could actually work against her. The next time, Nicky would be more savvy; he'd elude the next person. *What* next person? Another ineffectual private investigator like the one her husband had hired? Maybe the two men had collided over there, smacked each other with their foreheads as if they were two actors in an English farce.

She dialed the phone and missed a beat, surprised when Rich O'Malley's wife answered. "Hello?" Linda said. She almost hung up. In part because she was still recovering from her own shock that she had dialed the number. "Is Mr. O'Malley at home?" she said.

"Yes. May I say who's calling?"

"Nancy Gregerson."

"Oh, good!" the woman said. "My husband was hoping you'd call."

"Well, he . . . wrote me," Nancy said.

"Oh, we've been so concerned. Honey, it's Nancy on the phone. Nancy Gregerson."

"Hello?" It was a man's voice.

"I almost didn't call," she said, though what she might have said was that she wished she had not. The second the phone was answered, she'd felt a knot in her stomach. She was more reluctant about this phone call than she had been about asking George Wissone to help her. *Calm down,* she told herself. Of course the man has friends. Though whoever was on the phone wasn't the problem; the problem was that she felt even more sure that George must have failed in his mission, if these people also felt he had been out of touch too long.

"Tell me about your son. It's your son he went after, right?" the man was saying. She could hear the woman whispering.

"I don't know who I'm speaking to," she said. "Who are you, and why did you want me to call?"

"I'm his best friend. He's dropped off the face of the earth. We need to know how to get in touch with him."

"I don't know," she said. There seemed little harm in stating the truth.

"When did you last hear from him?"

"He's never called."

"He hasn't?"

"I can't help you," she said. "I should hang up."

There was a long pause.

"I appreciate your not doing that," he said. "How long did he tell you he was going to be gone?"

Again, she said, "I don't know you."

"Would it help to meet me? *Us?*" he said. "He's my best friend. He called and said he was on his way to London to find your son."

"Maybe he hasn't called because he doesn't have anything to report," she said.

"He calls us all the time," he said.

She let this register. She wondered if Nicky was capable of hurting someone and knew that he was.

"I would like to hear from him, myself," she said.

"Where in London was he going?"

"If I'd had an address, I could have gone there myself."

Again, she heard the woman whispering. Her stomach felt sick. She didn't answer. "I don't want to get in any deeper," she said. "It might have been a mistake to talk to George. I'm thinking now that it might have been."

"What does that mean?"

"It means that you've got every right to look for your friend, but I can't have anything more to do with this."

"Why would he go in the first place?" the man said. "I never knew him to do anything like this."

"I don't like to hang up on people, but I'm not going to help you, and I'm not giving information to a stranger," she said. It was easier when she pretended that this man was the one causing trouble, and all she had to do was get rid of him. Still, she could not bring herself to put down the phone. After a long pause, the man said, "If there's a problem, did it even occur to you that you might bear some of the responsibility? In that you suggested this to George. In that you asked him to do you a favor."

"Don't lecture me," she said. "This was a business proposition he agreed to take on." She took a deep breath and said, "I'm upset there's no word on my son."

She could hear him putting his hand over the phone, whispering.

"We've got a problem here. We've definitely got a problem," he said, though she could tell that he was speaking to his wife, not to her. Afraid she would cry, she said nothing. She was thinking: Nicky might be hurt; Nicky might have hurt George. How like a seesaw negative thoughts were: one would weigh you down with its certainty, the other become airborne, then the airborne worry would wobble and become heavy with its own possibility, then thud to the ground.

Nicky had always been afraid of seesaws, but had screamed excitedly for her to push him in the swing until it went dangerously high, out of her control, and her hands could no longer control it.

Paula tipped 25 percent. Her hair had never looked better. It felt silky, too, in spite of the chemicals that had been painted on to make it various shades of blonde. She was now highlighted and lowlighted, the darker tones an ash blonde that matched her roots. Her nails had been painted "I'm Not Really a Waitress" red. She had returned her engagement ring but arranged a consolation prize: she'd had a stone taken from one of her rings—a turquoise—and had it set in gold, with two diamond baguettes at either side. She missed her therapist in New York and hadn't wanted to stay in California. George was the man for her, and ultimately, what had happened had been for the best. She thought, secretly, that her own (sort-of) disappearance had been more of a factor in George's going away than it would be modest to let on. His friend Rich O'Malley had been delighted to hear from her; she was going to Rich and his wife's, and they were going to brainstorm and find him. She had met them only once, at a Fourth of July party when Rich's wife had passed out sparklers and everyone had had a little too much to drink, but both had seemed nice, and they were certainly being helpful now. She made light of her broken engagement to the people who knew about it, omitting mention of it entirely with Rich and Linda, saying only vague things about how the California way of life wasn't for her. It certainly wasn't. Imagine a man that age, that accomplished, that horrible, that he'd send his daughter to do his dirty work for him.

She was relieved that her tenant had agreed to vacate the New York apartment early, in exchange for not paying that month's rent. The lease would have been up in two months, anyway, and then Paula would have to have dealt with finding another tenant, long-distance. Her sister had volunteered to help, but really: she went out of control about everything; she would have interviewed so many people, and then been so confused, she would never have reached a decision. Just imagining the phone call was exhausting.

In New York, she had stopped long enough to be there when a cleaning service came in, and then she had made an appointment uptown and gotten her hair done, her nails, and had a massage and a seaweed wrap . . . it was as if she already knew the date and place of her reunion with George.

She took the Metroliner. She could have taken the faster train, but the Metroliner was fast enough. She was reading the new biography of Benjamin Franklin and liking it. He reminded her, in odd ways, of George. George's name wasn't George, but Larry didn't seem to suit him, and of course she'd gotten used to calling him George, so . . . God: she was beginning to dither like her sister, though at least she did it silently. At Union Station, she would be picked up by Rich's wife, who had errands downtown that day. Then they would drive to someplace called . . . she consulted her BlackBerry: *Bethesda,* and then the three of them would put their heads together and figure out how to find George.

She fell asleep on the train and must have slept until the stop in Philadelphia. She sat up straight and put on her earphones and listened to a CD of old radio comedies. She listened as Rochester informed Jack Benny that he had made a mistake, and had showered using a peeled potato instead of soap. It kept her awake, and Ben Franklin, however interesting, put her to sleep. She looked around the car and noticed that almost everyone wore ugly shoes. Hers were Jimmy Choo. She studied them, the pretty laces that tied around her ankles, and decided they were worth every penny.

She pretended that George would be waiting inside the station. She knew she gave too much time to thinking about appearances, but if you presented yourself well, you felt good about yourself. That had been one of her therapist's points, and she'd decided it was correct, though it was silly to think that if she looked even better, George would be at her side. He was the one who called her neurotic when she talked about cellulite. He was the one who loved to kiss her toes. The woman in Charlottesville had to be involved with him. That was obvious. Rich had tried to see the woman, but she had resisted. They were going to have to see her, whether she wanted to meet them or not. How unhelpful to change her phone number. Rich had gotten the unlisted number with no trouble, though he was waiting to talk to her before he made a second call. He had hinted that the call might be taken more seriously if she placed it herself. It would be just like a man to say something to displease the woman; he had hinted that she'd "gone off" on him and didn't know why. Probably because he'd been too aggressive, that was why. You had to establish contact first. Men thought you established contact by saying hello.

One of her fondest memories of George was being in the bath with him. Slipping in and sitting behind him and embracing his broad back as if they were kids, sleigh-riding. Or as if they were on a motorcycle—which they'd been, when they lived outside San Francisco. The therapist had called to her attention the fact that she associated that locale strongly with the person. But come on: she knew a landscape was a landscape, and a person was a person. Admittedly, she'd had her fantasy about getting him to move back there with her. But she'd love him, anyway. How could you be this age and not be 100 percent certain that you loved someone? she wondered. How could you be certain that you loved your *shoes* and not be completely sure . . . but she never thought he'd been sure, either. He kept distance between them. In the bath, once, he had said the strangest thing. He had started talking about lynx. He had seen one, in a petting zoo, and an old woman had come along and gone into the cage with a dish, and she had said to George: You never, ever turn your back on them. If you can't remember that, you deserve to be jumped from behind. She'd run one hand down the side of the cage in a clawing motion, watching the lynx all the while. "Imagine those claws in your back," she had said. It had been a rather sad affair, the petting zoo: a lot of goats wandering around; birds that looked glutinous, it was so hot; rabbits with signs on their cages saying they were available for adoption.

What she knew about her former fiancé's former girlfriend was that she made jeweled fruit. She did not remember why the awful daughter had been talking about that, but somehow the jeweled fruit business had been brought into the discussion. It was a blessing when certain details disappeared off your radar screen. It was embarrassing to have been engaged to a man who loved (she assumed) a woman who made jeweled fruit.

"L-l-l-linda," she said, smiling, coming through the doors of the train station. Linda was where she said she'd be, standing there in Keds, hair pulled back in a headband. When Paula was prettier than another woman—which was often the case—she'd learned to rush the woman, to get her arms around her and seem to like her before the woman had time to become jealous. "So glad to see you again, Paula," Linda said. "Your trip was okay?"

Small talk. She let Linda buy her an iced tea at a little coffee counter before they continued to the parking lot. She was carrying everything she thought she'd need for a few days in one of George's old nylon duffel bags. Like a psychic going to look for someone, she thought: she'd washed in his favorite soap (verbena); she'd dropped one of his pens in her purse; she'd even taken one of his suitcases, which, like others through the years, had migrated to her New York apartment and stayed there. Having some of his things around might somehow lure him back.

Linda drove well, flipping on the directional signal and changing lanes as quickly as a short-order cook flipping burgers. She said, "Did Rich tell you about the wedding we're having at the house over the weekend? I'm so excited. I knew about their relationship when it was still a secret."

"This weekend?"

"Umm. He didn't tell you? That is just like him. I was setting things up with the caterer today." Linda's hand dropped, and the car flew into the inside lane. "Trucks." Linda sighed.

"Whose wedding is it?" Paula said.

"Sister Mary Matthew and Steve Shannon. I mean . . . listen to me! Mary and Steve. She left her order, and he never took his vows. Can you believe that he's eleven years younger than she is, but he's thrilled out of his mind? She was one of the nuns who received the children."

"What?" Paula said.

"The children," Linda said.

Paula shook her head.

"Well, forgive me for trespassing on one of their many important secrets—I will never know why it pleases men so much to keep women in the dark—but when George and Rich fly, they usually bring kids back with them. It's been going on for years. They get the kids out, and the nuns have Catholic families to adopt them."

Paula had no idea what she was talking about, but was too embarrassed to say so. She hoped Linda would continue. This was certainly very informative.

"Mary decided she wanted children of her own. What a big decision that must have been, to be forty years old and realize after twenty years in a convent that you wanted to be married and have kids! Not the nuns I knew back in school, I'll tell you that! They never rethought anything. It was no joke that they thought boys could look at your patent leather shoes and see up your skirt. They were so sex-starved, it made them demented."

The signal blinked; they went into the next lane to pass an old Cadillac convertible barely going the speed limit. Two gray-haired ladies were driving, all smiles. "I take it you weren't raised Catholic," Linda said.

"No."

"Lucky you," Linda said. "It never *occurred* to me that he wouldn't say anything about the wedding. There are going to be people setting up a tent, and everything. Anyway: enough of that. Tell me about you."

Paula froze. She never dared say she wanted to be a writer, but that was what she'd thought about, leaving California: getting back together with George; having a career that would be flexible, that would allow her to travel with him. She envisioned a novel based on her own life: a woman who's the companion of a mysterious man . . . well, the part about herself wouldn't be too hard, but the rest of the plot . . . how was she going to give a sense of who George was? Now she felt sure that if she kept quiet, Linda would explain a lot more about him than she'd figured out through the years. She said, "Oh, I've got two really beautiful sisters and I'm sort of the one in the middle. I'm just beginning to take myself seriously. Years ago, in school, I wanted to write, and I think right now the most important things to me are getting back with George and starting to do that. Write," she said. It sounded just as lame as she thought it would.

Linda looked at her. "Great," she said. "It's not so important when you get it together, it's just important that you do. I really admire Mary."

"Isn't it kind of a f-f-funny time for me to be coming?" Paula said.

"Oh, the second Rich heard from you, you *had* to come," Linda said. "He's hyperventilating about George. Wedding or no wedding, he wants to be back in touch *now*."

"Do you think he went to Mustique?" Paula said.

"Why there?" Linda said. So: Linda didn't know everything. She knew at least one thing Linda didn't know.

"Because he's got land there. He was going to go there when he retired."

"Do me a favor," Linda said. "Wait until after the wedding to ask Rich that question. Otherwise, he'll get a plane and put you on it and you'll be gone tonight."

"Okay," Paula said. "I actually do think we should get that Nancy woman to talk to us. I mean, why would he just cut off contact with everybody, even if he was going away?" She feared the answer: because he was done with them. All of them. She had waited too long to join up.

"I know," Linda said. "This is going to sound really disrespectful, but I'll say it anyway. My husband is a real creature of habit. He's really unhappy because his favorite restaurant closed so some building could be built on the land, and he ate there every day. He had names he'd made up for the fish in the fish tank. He even called the rum buns they served 'my rummies.' He tipped so much, they loved him. Knew his order so he didn't have to say anything—which is surprisingly important to some people. And then, no more does the restaurant close—I mean, they asked him if he wanted some of the fish. The fish swimming in the tank, I mean. Anyway, no more does it close than he loses contact with George. I mean, this wouldn't put most people in a tailspin, but if you knew how much Rich depends on routine, you'd see how it would."

Linda turned left, into a housing development with a waterfall to one side, above which rose a sign: BEECHWOOD VILLAGE. Underneath it, someone had spray-painted on the rocks: SUCKS SHIT. "We weren't able to have children because of treatments Rich had for an illness, long ago. We should adopt, you'd think. But I've never felt like doing that. If it's God's will that we can't have children, maybe we should honor that. Not that it wouldn't be a great idea and all that, but I just don't really . . . the thing is, I've sort of said to Sister Mary Matthew that we'd do it, one day, but I really think it's enough that Rich gets the children out. There are families waiting for them. I mean, lists of families. It's just not something Rich and I ever talked seriously about doing, even though Mary sort of thinks it is. You know what I mean?"

"You mean she assumes it's going to happen, and it isn't," Paula said.

"Exactly!" Linda said. She pulled into the driveway of a big house and touched a button on her visor. The garage door began to rise. "I mean, we let her think it, because she couldn't imagine *not* thinking it. You know what I mean?"

She knew, and had known since childhood: she meant that the course of least possible pain was to let somebody retain his view of how things were, even though you knew otherwise.

Father Ambrose raised a champagne flute. "In the thirteenth century," he began, "Saint Francis was blessed and privileged to live in times of compelling significance. Today, in times whose complexities we may dread, and in an age that may lack so many qualities we identify with Christian charity"—he drank most of his champagne—"with Christian charity," he repeated. "But, like Francis, there are always those individuals who stand apart and distinguish themselves from others not through any feeling of superiority, but because they understand that they have been called. The message received may be humble. It need not be the case, as it was with Francis, who saw around him the disorder of the state and the paucity of honorable examples and felt compelled to take a stand. One's being selected can come not as an epiphany, but begin as an enigmatic question, a thing confusing rather than enlightening." A man stepped forward and poured more champagne into the empty glass. "Thank you," Father Ambrose said. "As a longtime friend of the groom, I am here today to say that one must act according to one's conscience, which may mean . . ."

Paula wandered off. The next morning, the wedding couple would be gone and the three of them would finally set out for Charlottesville, the town where George had last lived, where he had met a woman who somehow persuaded him—she must have persuaded him, though Paula described him repeatedly to her shrink as intractable—to move outside his usual parameters. And what exactly were they? she thought, bringing herself up short. So much analyzing, when she had only limited information to go on. She supposed that if she thought like some of the people at the wedding, she would have to say that she had committed the sin of Pride. What a surprise to find out that he and Rich went to the aid of ailing honchos in places they shouldn't be, the U.S. government—and even American Express, if she could believe what Linda had later told her—entering into bribes and blackmail with foreign governments, and if that wasn't problematic enough, they got to be heroes by hauling back children, like remora, along with the sharks. What had she, with her brilliant novelistic imagination, thought he was doing? She had thought he was killing people, was the answer. She had not wanted to ask because she had been so sure. For years, she had assumed he was an assassin, and she had been relieved but also let down, as if his life were downright ordinary, when she began to piece the puzzle together from what Linda described and what bare-bones details Rich O'Malley assumed she knew.

Father Ambrose was reading from something called *Canticle of the Sun*. He was a little tipsy, which added to the strangeness of the day. She shuddered to think that she had almost married the wrong man. If only she could see George again, she might think seriously about proposing to him. What she'd thought all those years she didn't ask questions was that he was an assassin, and she had always assumed that because of his ability, he would be all right; now, even though she'd had it verified that he'd been involved in dangerous activity, she felt less sure that he was safe. There was her inimitable reasoning, as her shrink liked to call it: if he could kill people, he wouldn't be killed. If he was just some glorified body snatcher, somebody might be able to kill him.

She walked around inside the house, where it was darker and cooler, and the young bartender followed her with his eyes. What did he make of these people with their flushed faces and their purses stashed here and there, as if they were squirrels, burying nuts? Her own purse was upstairs, in the bedroom where she'd slept the last two nights, bizarrely papered in gingerbread wallpaper, with a mobile of gingerbread boys and girls suspended from the ceiling, as if the room awaited children. She had pulled the door closed when she went down to meet the bride and groom, so she was surprised to see it open when she walked upstairs to comb her hair. A teenage girl was sitting on the side of the bed, reading a magazine. She had stepped out of her high heels, and one foot was tucked under her, the other planted on the woven rug on the floor. The girl looked surprised. No—just unhappy to be discovered. She had been reading a thick issue of *Vanity Fair*, Paula saw; the girl put her thumb inside and closed the magazine.

"Hi. I'm Paula."

"Shalissa Ray," the girl said. Her black hair was pulled back in an elastic band. "Am I in your room?"

Paula nodded.

"I don't like weddings," the girl said. "My sister was killed the night of her wedding."

"How awful," Paula said.

"I know," the girl said. Like many teenagers wearing their best clothes, she looked uncomfortable. "I'm not going to get married. Not because my sister died, just because you can just live with somebody."

"I used to think that way," Paula said. "Then my boyfriend disappeared, and suddenly I'm missing him so much I'm thinking about getting married to him."

The girl shrugged. "How come you've got a room that looks like a kid's room?" she asked.

"Well, I'm only staying here temporarily, so it isn't really my room. I came up because the ceremony didn't make a lot of sense to me."

"Yeah. The stuff about Saint Francis taming the wolf."

"He *was* talking about Saint Francis. I'm afraid I didn't quite understand the point, so I thought I'd take a breather."

"He practiced what he was going to say last night, at my parents' house. He's my uncle," the girl said. "And his boyfriend's my stepuncle, supposedly. I don't care if people are gay. I just don't understand why weddings are such a big deal. I mean, I guess if I'd been a nun, a wedding would be a surefire way to let everybody know I was having sex and all."

"T-t-true," Paula said.

"My sister used to stutter. You didn't even ask how she died. A tire came off a truck and turned their car over, and he lived, but she didn't. Anyway: she learned how not to stutter by using puppets. She'd put on these little finger puppets, and they'd say everything she was saying, but it came out perfect. She didn't do it in public, but she did it at home, so really all she had to learn was how to think her fingers were talking."

"Never heard of that," Paula said.

"Nobody's ever heard of it," the girl said.

"Want to go back down together?" Paula said, combing her hair.

"I guess so," the girl said. "Especially if my uncle's done with his speech. I never understand what he's talking about. He's obsessed with Saint Francis, though. He's got a blind bird named Francis, which makes sense, with Saint Francis having so much trouble with his eyes and hiding in that dark cave and all."

"I went to Assisi once," Paula said. "With the person I was telling you about. We went to a monastery because I wanted to see the garden."

"What was it like?"

"The person who showed us around was very nice. He spoke Italian very slowly and gestured, so I could pretty much understand him. There was a cat there that they took care of. Everywhere else, the cats were starving. Pretty scary cats, actually. The guy who showed us around was there because the brothers had helped him to give up drugs. He wasn't one of them. He was more or less just there to live a clean life."

"That's a lot more interesting than that myth about Saint Francis and the wolf," Shalissa said. "One really lucky cat shut up inside a monastery, being taken care of—that's something you can understand if you believe in good luck and bad luck." She looked at Paula, to make sure that it went without saying that her sister was still part of the conversation; her sister who'd had *bad luck*.

"What's the luckiest thing that ever happened to you?" Paula said, dropping her brush in her purse.

"Being rescued from Vietnam. But long after the war," she added. "You might say I was lucky not to be born yet, during the war."

"You were rescued? Your sister, too?"

"Yep. We went to Massachusetts, but I don't remember it. It was really cold. I think that's something I do remember, not just something I was told. But nobody knew we were sisters, and we weren't reunited for a whole year. Then I went to live in Louisiana with Nora. They gave her an American name. I don't know what, exactly, the point of my name is supposed to be. Anyway, they found out we were sisters, and then Sister flew with me to New Orleans."

"My boyfriend might have been the one who got you," Paula said.

"Really? Did he fly with Rich?"

"Y-y-yes," Paula said.

"That would be way cool if I was meeting the girlfriend of one of the guys who saved me," she said. "Worms were eating my intestine. I had to have surgery once I got here. I don't remember anything about it, but Sister Mary Matthew kept me all that year, while my sister was gone."

"You must be very fond of her."

"She wasn't all that nice. If my sister was alive, you could ask her. She was four years older than me. There was even a letter from Sister Mary Matthew to the people who adopted both of us, saying that they could give us back if we didn't get healthier. I mean, what's so nice about that?"

"Wow," Paula said. "You're right. That's not very reassuring."

"I think maybe I was fated to meet you," Shalissa said. "Since I don't much like Sister, somebody nice showed up that I could like instead."

"My new friend," Paula said, putting her hand lightly on top of the girl's shoulder.

"So what's your boyfriend's name?" Shalissa said.

"I've always called him George, but his real name is Larry."

"Then why do you call him George? *I know!* It's his middle name."

"No, he—he has aliases."

"What's that?"

"An alias? It means you have an assumed name. A made-up name."

"A pen name."

"Well, yes. But I think you only call it a pen name if the person has written something."

"Hey, he should write about his adventures. Uncle Ambrose told me a couple of things when he was drinking, and I know they risk their lives to get kids and all."

Maybe he should, Paula thought. Maybe she could advise him. Help edit whatever he wrote. Wouldn't that be nice? Just the two of them by the fireplace, as she held a pen in her hand and learned about his adventures. Well, that was obviously not going to happen. If they got together again, he would be just as secretive— perhaps even angry that she'd found out all she had. She flashed on an image of herself in the kitchen in California, taking the cookie sheet out of the oven. She had tried to be nice, to be liked by her fiancé's daughter. That was what happened when you tried too hard: you usually got fucked. In a way, she was like George. *Larry*. She sometimes imagined scenes in which what she wanted came true, but she always made them so sticky-sweet (like the damned cookies), she always sensed the hidden cliché, she inflated everything until it became ludicrous, in order to dismiss the possibility of happiness, because she didn't believe in it. She had picked a man who didn't believe in it, either. His way of coping was to run away, while she sat still long enough to play out the fantasy, subverting it until its sugary unreality made her run, too. She thought again of California, with a shudder. And even in Sonoma . . . she had stayed there, but she was the one who'd bought the motorcycle to ride farther and farther from home. So far out into the country, and the sunshine, and the moonlight, and the breeze, that she really lost him back then, long ago. Even though she'd returned every time, it was during that time that she'd lost him.

"I'll tell you what," the girl whispered. "Let's say what we really think about people. I'll go first. Mary's fat, and her husband has nasty, narrow eyes. Now you say."

Paula looked around. Speeches were over, and an orchestra was playing. She finally located her host and hostess and said, "Those people are unhappy, and neither one will admit it. He's looking at women out of the corner of his eye, and she's scared she's not pretty enough to keep him."

"She's *not* pretty, is she?"

Paula shook her head no.

"It's all about how a person looks. It's a lie that it isn't. Some people are never going to have what they want because they're not attractive enough."

Paula looked down and saw that the girl had walked downstairs barefoot. Her feet were a child's: soft skin on her heels; toenails badly polished—no doubt, she'd done them herself. Paula felt the sudden urge to hug her tight, to reassure her that she would be a beauty, but that right now—like a puppy—her paws were too big, and she had too much energy so that certain people who'd forgotten their own youth—or never really lived it—would want to punish her.

In fact, she did say those things. She started by mentioning Shalissa's sister, though. She said, "Was your sister beautiful? I'll bet she was. And you worry you won't be that pretty, or you worry she might have been punished for being beautiful, right? But none of it is true. People are in the wrong place at the wrong time sometimes, that's why bad things happen to them. You're going to be every bit as pretty as she was, and your feet will stop growing and you'll learn how to make your hands look pretty by wearing rings and putting perfume on your wrist, and even if you don't get married, there'll be someone who loves you."

"How could you know that?" the girl said. "There's no way you could know."

"I know it the same way I know those were the things you *would have* asked."

The girl looked at her. Hesitant, she almost drew back, but didn't. The bartender from inside the house circulated through the tent, with a tray of salmon arranged on little rounds of melba toast to look like roses.

"Don't be fooled," she whispered, high on her own certainty about what Shalissa thought and wanted and liked. Hands cupped around the girl's ear, she leaned closer and whispered so softly she risked her missing what she had to say, "Don't fall for it. It's fish."

So, just like that, after having come from New York to Bethesda, Maryland, Paula didn't continue to Virginia. She got up early and left a note thanking them for wanting to help. She thanked them for inviting her to the wedding, which she still thought it was extremely strange not to have mentioned. That thank-you was insincere: the only good thing about the wedding had been Shalissa, and she felt more than a little sorry that she would probably never see her again. Sure, they'd exchanged e-mail addresses, but friendship depended on gestures, and smiles, and whispered words, and how could you do that with e-mail? If she called, and got the girl's parents, it might have been fine once, but beyond that, they would have wondered about her. She also thought—gratefully, not egotistically—that the girl had served her purpose. It had been in talking to her that she reconnected with her own hopes and fears at that age that still made her insecure. More than that, she had learned something from trying to console the girl. She had learned that her relationship with George—if it was ever to get back on track, which she seriously doubted—would require a lot of renegotiating, because *she* had ended it in Sonoma and only retained the necessary delusion that it continued. But that wasn't something she wrote in the note. They wouldn't have known what she was talking about. What did they know about her relationship with George, and what could she have told them? Their own relationship seemed to be coming apart, and adoption was the least of their worries. If he spent so much time grieving for an out-of-business restaurant, then it was displacement, pure and simple. He was grieving something else.

She snuck out of the kitchen and turned on her cell phone. There must be a Yellow Cab. There was a Yellow Cab everywhere in the world. Or she'd walk a little, take the metro back to Union Station. It was a beautiful day, and quite frankly, she was glad that Sister Mary Matthew was on her honeymoon and that she wasn't. It would have been a disastrous mistake to marry her fiancé, and it would be equally disastrous, she thought, to propose to George. She had just been there for his convenience, and she was proud of herself for not following him to Charlottesville, and equally proud that she'd come to her senses and not gone there with Rich and Nancy. What was their plan? To waylay some woman on her way out of her house? To gang up on her and demand that she explain her relationship to the Mystery Man, who was obviously less of a mystery to Rich and Linda than he'd been to her all those years? She had some mild curiosity about what the woman looked like, and how much of a factor that had been in his taking off for London. Though she didn't feel sure he'd really gone to London. She thought he might be in Mustique, and pictured him there, alone, hands plunged in his pockets, in Bermuda shorts and a T-shirt, surveying his land with a builder at his side. If there was a woman, as well as the builder, she didn't want to know about it. She had a strong suspicion that that was where he was, and she should leave him there. Let him return to her, if that was what he wanted. She had returned, but not returned to him, one too many times.

The bartender had given her his phone number, but she was not going to call him. He was too young. The Demi Moore thing was faintly embarrassing. The Cher thing.

She found the entrance to the metro and went down the stairs, following the crowd. It was probably too soon to get sentimental about the good times they'd had. She felt sweaty and wished she could have taken a shower, or a bath, but she hadn't wanted to risk awakening Rich and Linda. Thinking about how refreshing water would have been, she remembered, again, hugging George's back in the bathtub, and how it had provoked the story about the lynx in the petting zoo. Had it ever really happened? If so, what had taken him to a petting zoo? And what had the woman really been saying, as she clawed the cage like an animal, herself, giving the advice George would of course want to hear: that he should watch his back.

Let him watch it in Mustique. Let him lie in the sand, where nothing more dangerous than pesky sand fleas would attack his back. He could watch his back, and from now on, she'd watch hers.

All the way to New York, though, she kept thinking about him. If she'd known he was in Virginia, or that the woman could have pointed her toward him, would she have gone? She envisioned a woman much more attractive than Nancy Gregerson, pointing a finger toward a sunlit island paradise, and then she imagined that finger twisting into the finger of someone else: the woman in the animal's cage. Finally, she looked at her hand and remembered the girl's advice about puppets and thought that really, as advice went, it was rather interesting. She wiggled a finger, but had nothing to say, either aloud or simply where most of her dialogue happened—in her head.

For days she wouldn't speak, as it turned out. Confusion and guilt began to seep in about why, exactly, she'd run out on George's friends, why she hadn't at least let things play out. She would become increasingly doubtful about whether he'd made it to Mustique, and be surprised, also, that Rich didn't call, and neither did Linda. Were they ever going to get in touch, or would she just be someone who'd passed through their lives on her way somewhere; or from somewhere, in a nursery that wasn't a nursery, and then ran out before they could help her look up her boyfriend? Boyfriend. He wasn't her boyfriend. He was an elusive man who made up stories that had a moral not so easy to decipher—nothing as easy as Saint Francis taming his wolf. What did it mean that all those days she passed in silence she could *see* the lynx up in a tree, looking down, and the woman, looking up, telling George that she knew how to outsmart it?

The memorial service for Mrs. Bell had been attended by angels—people who dressed as angels and announced themselves to be angels—and among the mourners had been the blond boy Nancy had come to suspect was retarded—*correction: mentally challenged*—at the nursery where she'd once bought a bush and ever after avoided. He'd approached her, wearing his flowing white robes with high-set shoulders and wings folded down as if he were a sleeping bird, and explained that he and the other angels were making an appearance as "guardians of the spirit." Mrs. Bell was still alive in what he called "every real sense" ("Riding on the back of *Tyrannosaurus rex*?" she'd wanted to ask), as was his sister (Ah: Vancouver was synonymous with heaven). She understood there was something wrong with him, though he stood amid four other adults with shortly cropped hair and pale faces she did not want to inspect closer for evidence of powder, their costumes lushly multilayered.

While that didn't make her think they were sane, at least she saw that he was not alone in his delusion. The minister was either a very cool customer, or the angels had made other appearances at memorial services. One thing they did do was sing very nicely. The boy's tenor was joined by the stronger tenor voice of an older man, who—because he moved in with no space between their shoulders, and because he had the same sharp nose and thin lips—she assumed must be his father. The singing transported her back to her former neighbor's children, whom she'd lost touch with . . . those stepladder little boys who had sung, well, so angelically every Christmas, the sheet music in their hands, their mother accompanying them on the piano, their father piping out inexact little notes from a flute and looking self-conscious. Well—whatever people needed to get them through the night, she supposed: the afterlife of Mrs. Bell; the reappearance of a girl who had died on Afton Mountain, alive again in British Columbia. By such reasoning, her son could be dancing with the Tin Man down the Yellow Brick Road, and maybe he was: those druggie friends had such odd nicknames for one another. Some scraggly speed freak would be Toto. The private investigator her husband hired had come up empty-handed, and her own brilliant idea had resulted in nothing but a lot of money lost in plane fare. Instead of a white shirt, perhaps the private investigator should have worn angel wings, and then he could just have announced where Nicky was. The man had come to Virginia and searched Nicky's computer, which he'd given to a friend when he left town, since—like the majority of things the boy owned—it was perpetually broken, and in searching the hard drive had found messages back and forth from Toto and Tin Man and Judy Garland (if you suffered enough in life, were you awarded the distinction of being, simply, yourself?). What he found turned out to be nothing but drivel: code names for drugs that were so obvious, she could figure them out without being told; bleak jokes about the uselessness of normal people; plans to meet at boring places in the county deemed lively because they would grace them with their presence, and also because Sam Shepard was known to show up at the bar. Wade Butler, Private Investigator (he had handed her a business card on which was embossed the face of Sherlock Holmes), had hinted that he'd like to stay in her guest room, but she hadn't picked up on the suggestion. She gave him a few phone numbers that she copied out of the phone book and a cup of coffee, and she also did him the courtesy of pretending he was a serious person, even though his questions continued to be pathetic: Nicky's sports interests in high school (none); the name of the by now long-married girlfriend who'd gone to Lexington (she'd called Information). And pets—that was a good one! She did not say that he'd killed a turtle, while others might have tried to adopt it. She did not mention the neighbor's cat. She lied and said that he had been very fond of Bernadine's dog. If he'd asked a second time, she would have told him that blue was Nicky's favorite color. Perhaps he didn't remember that crucial question he'd asked so long ago.

At the end of the service, which, to Nancy's surprise, Jenny had attended with her older daughter (who rushed to Nancy's side for a hug), the two women exchanged raised eyebrows about the angels. Mrs. Bell's son from Richmond was there. Mrs. Bell's doctor attended: a young man who had surprised them all by actually visiting his patient at the facility, instead of having her transported to his office. He seemed friendly with the son, and the two men stood chatting, ignoring the angels who milled about, telling anyone who would listen that death was just a journey.

In a memo that had circulated back in December, it had been suggested that each nurse consider attending at least two memorial services a year, unless she was particularly fond of the deceased and wished to go more often. No: it hadn't been a memo. It had been a brochure, with hypothetical questions written in italic type: *What number of memorial services is it proper to attend?* Perhaps they could revise the brochure to include: *What questions is it proper to ask an angel?* She had gone to more than her share of memorial services. Because she was one of the older members of the staff, she supposed she had some notion of setting an example.

The day before, she had gotten a much-delayed response to the letter she had written the girl in London: *Why pretend you're interested in his well being? If there's no money to send me on a train out to Leeds forget it. I can get there myself and, don't think I won't. What did you think I'd show you for proof? That I'd cut off his ear or something? I told you he wasn't in London. I heard something happened where he worked that he didn't want to be part of. Mrs. Gregerson keep your money.*

That afternoon, after stopping at her favorite grocery store to get some cookies she liked (a reward for being such a conscientious person), she returned to Ivy and knew the minute she saw the car in her driveway that it would be the man who had called long distance, who wanted to know where his missing friend was. She felt discouraged more than alarmed. When she saw a woman sitting on the grass outside the car with him, she felt relieved. They would be like two children she could appease, sharing her cookies with them, and then she would send them on their way because they would understand that she knew nothing.

"Please. We won't take much of your time," the man said.

"When you realize how little I know, you'll want to be on your way," she answered.

Even in person, the woman whispered. "You could have introduced us," she said.

"Nancy Gregerson," Nancy said, coming closer to extend her hand. The man was already standing. He gave his wife his free hand, and shook Nancy's hand firmly with the other. "Rich and Linda O'Malley," he said.

She took out her key and opened the door. She said, with exaggerated patience, "Your friend and I met by chance. He hit my car when I was stopped at a light." This fact still irritated her; she could feel herself clenching her jaw. "We met another time, and we started talking. I paid him"—she thought how strange it was that the subject had never come up between her and George, but didn't want to falter. If she could make the story simple enough, they would go away. Her paying him was part of the story; the plane ticket had cost money, after all—"to go to London, because I thought—and you can bear me out on this—that he'd been involved in things like this before."

"What do you mean?" Rich said. She had sensed from the moment she saw him—no different from the way she could sense the unpleasant contents of certain unopened letters—that their encounter wouldn't be over as quickly as she'd hoped. She walked into the kitchen and put her package down. One of them closed the front door, as she knew would happen. They were all going to be polite, and understand one another, and then they would go away, no more enlightened than all the other people who wanted answers to things that had no answers. Oh, certainly: you could declare yourself an angel and make an assertion, but the audience would have to be desperate, or downright silly, to believe anything that was said.

She'd put the cookies on a plate. She brought with her a bottle of seltzer and some plastic cups. She felt under no obligation to be inordinately hospitable. In fact, she left the cups stacked: if he or his wife wanted a drink, they could disturb the pile. She did not address the man's question, which he'd hollered while she was in the kitchen.

The woman sensed her distance and tried to bridge it. "We've been so close to George, all this time. We're terrified to think that something might have happened to him, because it's not like him to be out of contact."

"I'll say," her husband said. He was going to be something of a problem, but she reminded herself that she was a nurse. She was used to worse problems.

"I miss my son," Nancy said. "I'm so disappointed that the trip hasn't resulted in anything yet. If it ever might. I'm as perplexed as you about why he hasn't contacted me, or you. I don't know what else to say."

"Did you have an affair with him?" the woman asked.

She hadn't counted on a question like that. She decided to indicate her disdain—people and their dumb assumptions about human behavior—by simply staring at the woman until she realized how ridiculous her question had been. It did not take the woman three seconds to drop her eyes.

"I hope you don't think you can stay and question me indefinitely," she said. She should not have spoken her worst fear; her voice went too high, and revealed her nervousness.

"Did you call the police?" the woman said.

"How much did you pay him?" Rich O'Malley asked. It was the first time she seriously considered that she might have a big problem on her hands. That the man might assume something crazy, such as that she had something to do with George's disappearance. The police . . . she really hoped the police would not have to be involved.

"That isn't a factor," she said.

"He didn't really need money," Rich said. "He couldn't have done this for the kind of money you'd pay him, I don't *think*, so I guess what my wife was getting at was that he might have done it for love."

"He hit my car at a red light," she said. "I saw him two other times. At a coffee place where we ran into each other, and here, when I called him and he came to discuss the trip."

"You told him what you wanted," Rich said, "and he came over."

"You can understand that we're confused," the woman said.

"Oh, and I'm not?"

"Rich, she's made it clear she doesn't know where he is," Linda said.

"She gets him over to her house by telling him some kid he's never met is missing, he comes, he goes to London, he takes her money, he never returns, she never calls the cops. Why do I think something doesn't make sense?"

"What do you think this is? One of those party games where everyone gets to guess who killed the victim? Is that what you're thinking—that I'm involved in something like that? Maybe he stopped at your house on the way to London, and *you* killed him for all the money I gave him, and you're here to try to pin it on me because the cops already contacted you. You being his best friends and all. Do you see how dangerous paranoia can be, Mr. O'Malley? Now leave. Please."

Linda had put her hand over her heart. She was biting her bottom lip. She said only her husband's name, tentatively.

"Do you know Paula?" he said, frowning. "Did she not come here because you'd already met?"

She didn't know who Paula was, but she'd decided the time had come to insist that they leave. It was her house, and she had done nothing wrong. But that thought only empowered her for a few seconds. Yet again, fallout from her son's actions had ended up as rubble in her own life. If it took calling the police to get these people to leave, so be it. Some of the police might remember her: the distraught lady whose son was always causing problems. The woman whose husband had left her. The nurse who hadn't realized her no-good son took drugs. What had she failed to understand this time?

Paula. Of course there was always a Paula. She had probably gotten involved with a man who wanted to get away from his wife. People disappeared more than was reported, changed their identity. There were books about those people; there was the witness protection program. With or without reason, secrecy was part of those people's lives.

A plane flew over, angling darkness across the living room floor. Rich looked up, and she understood from the flash in his eye that it brought George to mind—though *spry jive* would have been nonsense words, had he said them aloud. Linda's eyes went not to the ceiling, but to her husband. I know that habit, Nancy thought; when a marriage ends, the body retains its habits: that swivel of the head toward the other person, the assumption that someone is with you in the moment and will reply, wordlessly, to any unasked question. What she saw on a day-to-day basis had convinced her that nobody and nothing lasts forever. The big questions had been precluded, so if any of them returned now, they'd be safe: no longer would any responses be expected. She supposed that—had she been better at self-deception—she might experience the wind as the caress of an angel that had just passed over: a modern angel that, paradoxically, also embodied darkness. An angel that, like people on Earth, made a bold announcement of itself, then disappeared.

Find and Replace

TRUE story: my father died in a hospice on Christmas Day, while a clown dressed in big black boots and a beard was down the hall doing his clown-as-Santa act for the amusement of a man my father had befriended, who was dying of ALS. I wasn't there; I was in Paris to report on how traveling art was being uncrated—a job I got through my cousin Jasper, who works for a New York City ad agency more enchanted with consultants than Julia Child is with chickens. For years, Jasper's sending work my way has allowed me to keep going while I write the Great American I Won't Say Its Name.

I'm superstitious. For example, I thought that even though my father was doing well, the minute I left the country he would die. Which he did.

On a globally warmed July day, I flew into Fort Myers and picked up a rental car and set off for my mother's to observe (her terminology) the occasion of my father's death, six months after the event. It was actually seven months later, but because I was in Toronto checking out sites for an HBO movie, and there was no way I could make it on June 25, my mother thought the most respectful thing to do would be to wait until the same day, one month later. I don't ask my mother a lot of questions; when I can, I simply try to keep the peace by doing what she asks. As mothers go, she's not demanding. Most requests are simple and have to do with her notions of propriety, which often center on the writing of notes. I have friends who are so worried about their parents that they see them every weekend, I have friends who phone home every day, friends who cut their parents' lawn because no one can be found to do it. With my mother, it's more a question of: Will I please send Mrs. Fawnes a condolence card because of her dog's death, or, Will I be so kind as to call a florist near me in New York and ask for an arrangement to be delivered on the birthday of a friend of my mother's, because ordering flowers when a person isn't familiar with the florist can be a disastrous experience. I don't buy flowers, even from Korean markets, but I asked around, and apparently the bouquet that arrived at the friend's door was a great success.

My mother has a million friends. She keeps the greeting-card industry in business. She would probably send greetings on Groundhog Day, if the cards existed. Also, no one ever seems to disappear from her life (with the notable exception of my father). She still exchanges notes with a maid who cleaned her room at the Swift House Inn fifteen years ago—and my parents were only there for the weekend.

I know I should be grateful that she is such a friendly person. Many of my friends bemoan the fact that their parents get into altercations with everybody, or that they won't socialize at all.

So: I flew from New York to Fort Myers, took the shuttle to the rental-car place, got in the car and was gratified that the air-conditioning started to blow the second I turned on the ignition, and leaned back, closed my eyes, and counted backward, in French, from thirty, in order to unwind before I began to drive. I then put on loud music, adjusted the bass, and set off, feeling around on the steering wheel to see if there was cruise control, because if I got one more ticket my insurance was going to be canceled. Or maybe I could get my mother to write a nice note pleading my case.

Anyway, all the preliminaries to my story are nothing but that: the almost inevitable five minutes of hard rain midway through the trip; the beautiful bridge; the damned trucks expelling herculean farts. I drove to Venice, singing along with Mick Jagger about beasts of burden. When I got to my mother's street, which is, it seems, the only quarter-mile-long stretch of America watched directly by God, through the eyes of a Florida policeman in a radar-equipped car, I set the cruise control for twenty and coasted to her driveway.

Hot as it was, my mother was outside, sitting in a lawn chair flanked by pots of red geraniums. Seeing my mother always puts me into a state of confusion. Whenever I first see her, I become disoriented.

"Ann!" she said. "Oh, are you exhausted? Was the flight terrible?"

It's the subtext that depresses me: the assumption that to arrive anywhere you have to pass through hell. In fact, you do. I had been on a USAir flight, seated in the last seat in the last row, and every time suitcases thudded into the baggage compartment my spine reverberated painfully. My traveling companions had been an obese woman with a squirming baby and her teenage son, whose ears she squeezed when he wouldn't settle down, producing shrieks and enough flailing to topple my cup of apple juice. I just sat there silently, and I could feel that I was being too quiet and bringing everyone down.

My mother's face was still quite pink. Shortly before my father's death, after she had a little skin cancer removed from above her lip, she went to the dermatologist for microdermabrasion. She was wearing the requisite hat with a wide brim and Ari Onassis sunglasses. She had on her uniform: shorts covered with a flap, so that it looked as if she were wearing a skirt, and a T-shirt embellished with sequins. Today's featured a lion with glittering black ears and, for all I knew, a correctly colored nose. Its eyes, which you might think would be sequins, were painted on. Blue.

"Love you," I said, hugging her. I had learned not to answer her questions. "Were you sitting out here in the sun waiting for me?"

She had learned, as well, not to answer mine. "We can have lemonade," she said. "Paul Newman. And that man's marinara sauce—I never cook it myself anymore."

The surprise came almost immediately, just after she pressed a pile of papers into my hands: thank-you notes from friends she wanted me to read; a letter she didn't understand regarding a magazine subscription that was about to expire; an ad she'd gotten about a vacuum cleaner she wanted my advice about buying; two tickets to a Broadway play she'd bought ten years before that she and my father had never used (what was being asked of me?); and—most interesting, at the bottom of the pile—a letter from Drake Dreodadus, her neighbor, asking her to move in with him. "Go for the vacuum instead," I said, trying to laugh it off.

"I've already made my response," she said. "And you may be very surprised to know what I said."

Drake Dreodadus had spoken at my father's memorial service. Before that, I had met him only once, when he was going over my parents' lawn with a metal detector. But no: as my mother reminded me, I'd had a conversation with him in the drugstore, one time when she and I stopped in to buy medicine for my father. He was a pharmacist.

"The only surprising thing would be if you'd responded in the affirmative," I said.

"'Responded in the affirmative!' Listen to *you*."

"Mom," I said, "tell me this is not something you'd give a second of thought to."

"Several *days* of thought," she said. "I decided that it would be a good idea, because we're very compatible."

"Mom," I said, "you're joking, right?"

"You'll like him when you get to know him," she said.

"Wait a minute," I said. "This is someone you hardly know— or am I being naive?"

"Oh, Ann, at my age you don't necessarily want to know someone extremely well. You want to be compatible, but you can't let yourself get all involved in the dramas that have already played out—all those accounts of everyone's youth. You just want to be— you want to come to the point where you're compatible."

I was sitting in my father's chair. The doilies on the armrests that slid around and drove him crazy were gone. I looked at the darker fabric, where they had been. Give me a sign, Dad, I was thinking, looking at the shiny fabric as if it were a crystal ball. I was clutching my glass, which was sweating. "Mom—you can't be serious," I said.

She winked.

"Mom—"

"I'm going to live in his house, which is on the street perpendicular to Palm Avenue. You know, one of the big houses they built at first, before the zoning people got after them and they put up these little cookie-cutter numbers."

"You're moving in with him?" I said, incredulous. "But you've got to keep this house. You are keeping it, aren't you? If it doesn't work out."

"Your father thought he was a fine man," she said. "They used to be in a Wednesday-night poker game, I guess you know. If your father had lived, Drake was going to teach him how to e-mail."

"With a, with—you don't have a computer," I said stupidly.

"Oh, Ann, I wonder about you sometimes. As if your father and I couldn't have driven to Circuit City, bought a computer—and he could have e-mailed you! He was excited about it."

"Well, I don't—" I seemed unable to finish any thought. I started again. "This could be a big mistake," I said. "He only lives one block away. Is it really necessary to move in with him?"

"Was it necessary for you to live with Richard Klingham in Vermont?"

I had no idea what to say. I had been staring at her. I dropped my eyes a bit and saw the blue eyes of the lion. I dropped them to the floor. New rug. When had she bought a new rug? Before or after she made her plans?

"When did he ask you about this?" I said.

"About a week ago," she said.

"He did this by mail? He just wrote you a note?"

"If we'd had a computer, he could have e-mailed!" she said.

"Mom, are you being entirely serious about this?" I said. "What, exactly—"

"What, *exactly,* what *one single thing,* what *absolutely* compelling reason did you have for living with Richard Klingham?"

"Why do you keep saying his last name?" I said.

"Most of the old ladies I know, their daughters would be delighted if their mothers remembered a boyfriend's first name, let alone a last name," she said. "Senile old biddies. Really. I get sick of them myself. I see why it drives the children crazy. But I don't want to get off on that. I want to tell you that we're going to live in his house for a while, but are thinking seriously of moving to Tucson. He's very close to his son, who's a builder there. They speak *every single day* on the phone, *and* they e-mail," she said. She was never reproachful; I decided that she was just being emphatic.

Just a short time before, I had relaxed, counting *trois, deux, un.* Singing with Mick Jagger. Inching slowly toward my mother's house.

"But this shouldn't intrude on a day meant to respect the memory of your father," she said, almost whispering. "I want you to know, though, and I really mean it: I feel that your father would be pleased that I'm compatible with Drake. I feel it deep in my heart." She thumped the lion's face. "He would give this his blessing, if he could," she said.

"Is he around?" I said.

"Listen to you, disrespecting the memory of your father by joking about his not being among us!" she said. "That is in the poorest taste, Ann."

I said, "I meant Drake."

"Oh," she said. "I see. Yes. Yes, he is. But right now he's at a matinee. We thought that you and I should talk about this privately."

"I assume he'll be joining us for dinner tonight?"

"Actually, he's meeting some old friends in Sarasota. A dinner that was set up before he knew you were coming. You know, it's a wonderful testament to a person when they retain old friends. Drake has an active social life with old friends."

"Well, it's just perfect for him, then. He can have his social life, and you and he can be compatible."

"You've got a sarcastic streak—you always had it," my mother said. "You might ask yourself why you've had fallings-out with so many friends."

"So this is an occasion to criticize me? I understand, by the way, that you were also criticizing me when you implied that you didn't understand my relationship with Richard—or perhaps the reason I ended it? The reason I ended it was because he and an eighteen-year-old student of his became Scientologists and asked me if I wanted to come in the van with them to Santa Monica. He dropped his cat off at the animal shelter before they set out, so I guess I wasn't the only one to get shafted."

"Oh!" she said. "I didn't know!"

"You didn't know because I never told you."

"Oh, was it *horrible* for you? Did you have any *idea*?"

She was right, of course: I had left too many friends behind. I told myself it was because I traveled so much, because my life was so chaotic. But, really, maybe I should have sent a few more cards myself. Also, maybe I should have picked up on Richard's philandering. Everybody else in town knew.

"I thought we could have some Paul Newman's and then maybe when we had dessert we could light those little devotional lights and have a moment's silence, remembering your father."

"Fine," I said.

"We'll need to go to the drugstore to get candles," she said. "They burned out the night Drake and I had champagne and toasted our future." She stood. She put on her hat. "I can drive," she said.

I straggled behind her like a little kid in a cartoon. I could imagine myself kicking dirt. Some man she hardly knew. It was the last thing I'd expected. "So give me the scenario," I said. "He wrote you a note and you wrote back, and then he came for champagne?"

"Oh, all right, so it hasn't been a great romance," my mother said. "But a person gets tired of all the highs and lows. You get to the point where you need things to be a little easier. In fact, I didn't write him a note. I thought about it for three days, then I just knocked on his door."

The candles were cinnamon-scented and made my throat feel constricted. She lit them at the beginning of the meal, and by the end she seemed to have forgotten about talking about my father. She mentioned a book she'd been reading about Arizona. She offered to show me some pictures, but they, too, were forgotten. We watched a movie on TV about a dying ballerina. As she died, she imagined herself doing a pas de deux with an obviously gay actor. We ate M&M's, which my mother has always maintained are not really candy, and went to bed early. I slept on the foldout sofa. She made me wear one of her nightgowns, saying that Drake might knock on the door in the morning. I traveled light: toothbrush, but nothing to sleep in. Drake did not knock the next morning, but he did put a note under the door saying that he had car problems and would be at the repair shop. My mother seemed very sad. "Maybe you'd want to write him a teeny little note before you go?" she said.

"What could I possibly say?"

"Well, you think up dialogue for characters, don't you? What would you imagine yourself saying?" She put her hands to her lips. "Never mind," she said. "If you do write, I'd appreciate it if you'd at least give me a sense of what you said."

"Mom," I said, "please give him my best wishes. I don't want to write him a note."

She said, "He's DrDrake@aol.com, if you want to e-mail."

I nodded. Best just to nod. I thought that I might have reached the point she'd talked about, where you have an overwhelming desire for things to be simple.

We hugged, and I kissed her well-moisturized cheek. She came out to the front lawn to wave as I pulled away.

On the way back to the airport, there was a sudden, brief shower that forced me to the shoulder of the road, during which time I thought that there were obvious advantages in having a priest to call on. I felt that my mother needed someone halfway between a lawyer and a psychiatrist, and that a priest would be perfect. I conjured up a poker-faced Robert De Niro in clerical garb as Cyndi Lauper sang about girls who just wanted to have fun.

But I wasn't getting away as fast as I hoped. Back at the car-rental lot, my credit card was declined. "It might be my handheld," the young man said to me, to cover either my embarrassment or his. "Do you have another card, or would you please try inside?"

I didn't know why there was trouble with the card. It was AmEx, which I always pay immediately, not wanting to forfeit Membership Rewards points by paying late. I was slightly worried. Only one woman was in front of me in line, and after two people behind the counter got out of their huddle, both turned to me. I chose the young man.

"There was some problem processing my credit card outside," I said.

The man took the card and swiped it. "No problem now," he said. "It is my pleasure to inform you that today we can offer you an upgrade to a Ford Mustang for only an additional seven dollars a day."

"I'm returning a car," I said. "The machine outside wouldn't process my card."

"Thank you for bringing that to my attention," the young man said. He was wearing a badge that said "Trainee" above his name.

His name, written smaller, was Jim Brown. He had a kind face and a bad haircut. "Your charges stay on American Express, then?"

An older man walked over to him. "What's up?" he said.

"The lady's card was declined, but I ran it through and it was fine," he said.

The older man looked at me. It was cooler inside, but still, I felt as if I were melting. "She's returning, not renting?" the man said, as if I weren't there.

"Yes, sir," Jim Brown said.

This was getting tedious. I reached for the receipt.

"What was that about the Mustang?" the man said.

"I mistakenly thought—"

"I mentioned to him how much I like Mustangs," I said.

Jim Brown frowned.

"In fact, how tempted I am to rent one right now."

Both the older man and Jim Brown looked at me suspiciously.

"Ma'am, you're returning your Mazda, right?" Jim Brown said, examining the receipt.

"I am, but now I think I'd like to rent a Mustang."

"Write up a Mustang, nine dollars extra," the older man said.

"I quoted her seven," Jim Brown said.

"Let me see." The man punched a few keys on the keyboard. "Seven," he said, and walked away.

Jim Brown and I both watched him go. Jim Brown leaned a little forward, and said in a low voice, "Were you trying to help me out?"

"No, not at all. Just thought having a Mustang for a day might be fun. Maybe a convertible."

"The special only applies to the regular Mustang," he said.

"It's only money," I said.

He hit a key, looked at the monitor.

"One day, returning tomorrow?" he said.

"Right," I said. "Do I have a choice about the color?"

He had a crooked front tooth. That and the bad haircut were distracting. He had lovely eyes, and his hair was a nice color, like a fawn's, but the tooth and the jagged bangs got your attention instead of his attributes.

"There's a red and two white," he said. "You don't have a job you've got to get back to?"

I said, "I'll take the red."

He looked at me.

"I'm freelance," I said.

He smiled. "Impulsive, too," he said.

I nodded. "The perks of being self-employed."

"At what?" he said. "Not that it's any of my business."

"Jim, any help needed?" the older man said, coming up behind him.

In response, Jim looked down and began to hit keys. It increased his schoolboyish quality: he bit his bottom lip, concentrating. The printer began to print out.

"I used to get in trouble for being impulsive," he said. "Then I got diagnosed with ADD. My grandmother said, 'See, I told you he couldn't help it.' That was what she kept saying to my mom: 'Couldn't help it.'" He nodded vigorously. His bangs flopped on his forehead. Outside, they would have stuck to his skin, but inside it was air-conditioned.

His mentioning ADD reminded me of the ALS patient—the man I'd never met. I had a clearer image of a big-footed, bulbous-nosed clown. If I breathed deeply, I could still detect the taste of cinnamon in my throat. I declined every option of coverage, initialing beside every X. He looked at my scribbled initials. "What kind of writing?" he said. "Mysteries?"

"No. Stuff that really happens."

"Don't people get mad?" he said.

The older man was looming over the woman at the far end of the counter. They were trying not to be too obvious about watching us. Their heads were close together as they whispered.

"People don't recognize themselves. And, in case they might, you just program the computer to replace one name with another. So, in the final version, every time the word *Mom* comes up it's replaced with *Aunt Begonia* or something."

He creased the papers, putting them in a folder. "A-eight," he said. "Out the door, right, all the way down against the fence."

"Thanks," I said. "And thanks for the good suggestion."

"No problem," he said. He seemed to be waiting for something. At the exit, I looked over my shoulder; sure enough, he was looking at me. So was the older man, and so was the woman he'd been talking to. I ignored them. "You wouldn't program your computer to replace *Mustang convertible* with one of those creepy Geo Metros, would you?"

"No, ma'am," he said, smiling. "I don't know how to do that."

"Easy to learn," I said. I gave him my best smile and walked out to the parking lot, where the heat rising from the asphalt made me feel like my feet were sliding over a well-oiled griddle. The key was in the car. It didn't look like the old Mustang at all. The red was very bright and a little unpleasant, at least on such a hot day. The top was already down. I turned the key and saw that the car had less than five hundred miles on it. The seat was comfortable enough. I adjusted the mirror, pulled on my seat belt, and drove to the exit, with no desire to turn on the radio. "That's a beauty," the man in the kiosk said, inspecting the folder and handing it back.

"Just got it on impulse," I said.

"That's the best way," he said. He gave a half salute as I drove off.

And then it hit me: the grim reality that I had to talk sense to her, I had to do whatever it took, including insulting her great good friend Drake, so he wouldn't clean her out financially, devastate her emotionally, take advantage, dominate her—who knew what he had in mind? He'd avoided me on purpose—he didn't want to hear what I'd say. What did he think? That her busy daughter would conveniently disappear on schedule, or that she might be such a liberal that their plans sounded intriguing? Or maybe he thought she was a pushover, like her mother. Who knew what men like that thought.

The cop who pulled me over for speeding turned on the siren when I didn't come screeching to a halt. He was frowning deeply, I saw in the rearview mirror, as he approached the car.

"My mother's dying," I said.

"License and registration," he said, looking at me with those reflective sunglasses cops love so much. I could see a little tiny me, like a smudge on the lens. I had been speeding, overcome with worry. After all, it was a terrible situation. The easiest way to express it had been to say that my mother was dying. Replace *lost her mind* with *dying*.

"Mustang convertible," the cop said. "Funny car to rent if your mother's dying."

"I used to have a Mustang," I said, choking back tears. I was telling the truth, too. When I moved from Vermont, I'd left it behind in a friend's barn, and over the winter the roof had fallen in. There was extensive damage, though the frame had rusted out anyway. "My father bought it for me in 1968, as a bribe to stay in college."

The cop worked his lips until he came up with an entirely different expression. I saw myself reflected, wavering slightly. The cop touched his sunglasses. He snorted. "Okay," he said, stepping back. "I'm going to give you a warning and let you go, urging you to respect your life and the life of others by *driving at the posted speed.*"

"Thank you," I said sincerely.

He touched the sunglasses again. Handed me the warning. How lucky I was. How very, very lucky.

It was not until he returned to his car and sped away that I looked at the piece of paper. He had not checked any of the boxes. Instead, he had written his phone number. Well, I thought, if I kill Drake, the number might come in handy.

I also played a little game of my own: replace *Richard Klingham* with *Jim Brown*.

He was probably twenty-five, maybe thirty years younger than me. Which would be as reprehensible, almost, as Richard's picking up the teenager.

Back over the bridge, taking the first Venice exit, driving past the always closed House of Orchids, dismayed at the ever-lengthening strip mall.

My mother, again in the lawn chair, reading the newspaper, but now not bothering to look up as cars passed. I could remember her face vividly from years before, when my father and I had turned in to our driveway in Washington in an aqua Mustang convertible. She had been so shocked. Just shocked. She must have been thinking of the expense. Maybe also of the danger.

My mother seemed less timid now. Obviously, she, too, could be quite impulsive. I was just about to tap the horn when my mother stood and took a minute to steady herself before heading toward the house. Why was she bent over, walking so slowly? Had she been pretending to be spry earlier, or had I just not noticed? Then the door opened, and a man—it was Drake, that was who it was—stood on the threshold, extending a hand and waiting, not going down the steps, just waiting. He stood ramrod straight, but, even driving slowly, I got only a glimpse of him: this man who was not my father, with his big hand extended, and my mother lifting her hand like a lady ascending an elegant, carpeted staircase, instead of three concrete steps.

There was nothing I could say. It had all been decided. There was not a word I could say that would stop either one of them.

I turned left just before the street dead-ended, not wanting to risk passing by a second time. I realized that there was someone waiting to hear from me: possibly two people—the kid *and* the cop—if not three (my mother, who was probably hoping for an apology for my dire warnings about Drake). I could have made a phone call, had the evening go another way entirely, but everyone will understand why I decided otherwise.

You can't help understanding. First, because it is the truth, and second, because everyone knows the way things change. They always do, even in a very short time. Back in Fort Myers, the transaction was all business: another shift was at work at the rental agency, and there was only the perfunctory question as I opened the door and got out about whether everything was all right with the car.

Duchais

V AN Allan Wrightsman appeared at Professor Duchais's office just as the older man was taking off his coat. It was cashmere, he realized, when he reached out to help, softer than the blanket on his own bed. The professor was much gossiped about: he was said to have a farmhouse in France; he'd dated (and written a screenplay with) a famous actress who'd later become a nun. He taught literature one day a week, one semester a year. Even leaving aside fantasies of his enviable life, his teaching schedule was enough to ensure the man was talked about behind his back.

Van Allan had gone to Professor Duchais's office to volunteer to replace his roommate, Tim Foxx, as the professor's assistant. Tim had worked for Duchais briefly before being hospitalized with mono. The way Van Allan saw it, temporarily taking his roommate's job would be more interesting than working at the library.

"He's feeling better?" Duchais squinted over his half-glasses. His eyes seemed uncomfortable in the air; they narrowed and sank below the level of the frames. "Or should I take your silence to mean I'm mistaken?"

"No, sir. Actually, he might not get out of the hospital for a while. Professor Duchais, if there might be a possibility of stepping in to help while Tim recuperates, I'd be most willing."

"Would you?" The man put down a pile of messily stacked papers. Out of his backpack he took a bottle of Tums, a book, and yet another pile of papers, so disorganized they fanned out like an enormous deck of cards. "How would you file these?" Duchais said, holding out the clump of paper.

Van Allan reached for it. The problem was, nothing was titled.

He flipped to the end of one stapled manuscript. He checked another. No name of the author appeared. "File by first line?" he asked, trying not to sound tentative.

"No! Who remembers beginnings? File according to subject, I think is best. Did Tim tell you he worked at my house, instead of in this neon-lit monstrosity of an office? You work for the same money as your friend." The last remark seemed not to be a question.

"I would, sir. I don't know exactly what Tim was making."

"Eight dollars an hour."

"Eight it is, then," he said. Glancing again at a manuscript page (was it Duchais's own work?), he worried that his frown betrayed the fact that he was not at all sure he could ascertain the subjects, even with repeated readings.

That night, late, Van Allan's phone rang.

"On the way here, could you stop by Brown's and pick up my dry cleaning?" Professor Duchais said. "There should be several items. If there's only a blue robe, tell them there's more. Have them call me if they need the ticket numbers. By then I might have found them."

"Yes, sir. Is this the cleaner's on Preston Avenue?"

"It is. And if you have time, run into the market and get me a bunch of bananas. Coffee of any kind, bananas, any sort of orange juice."

"Yes, sir. A half gallon of orange juice?"

"A can of concentrate."

"Okay," Van Allan said. "What time would be good to bring them by?"

"Three o'clock," Duchais said. "The only time there is. We'll pretend that F. Scott Fitzgerald was talking p.m. instead of a.m."

Van Allan needed clarification, but he was worried that if the man thought he was slow-witted, he wouldn't hire him. He said,

"Sir, Tim did tell me you were off 250 just before Montgomery's, but what do I do after I turn?"

"Ask Tim to describe it."

"He's pretty sick. They thought he'd be better in the hospital when he got bronchitis on top of the mono."

"The lamentable fragility of the human body," Duchais said. "Sadly, even for the young."

"So—three o'clock. And when I turn off 250—"

"Less than a quarter of a mile on the right. Stay on Kensington. You'll see balloons tied to the mailbox. If you have time, call before you set out and pick up a few books for me if they've come through interlibrary loan."

"I can do that."

"When you talk to Tim, tell him how sorry I am. As for the dry cleaning, I could reimburse you or call the store with my credit card number."

"It would be appreciated if you called, sir."

"Just call me Duchais. Drop the Professor part, too, if you don't feel too uncomfortable. Even if you do, it's the way to make me feel more comfortable."

"Will do, Duchais."

"I don't hear your TV in the background. Mute the gunfire when you picked up?"

"No, sir. I mean, no. We don't have cable right now because somebody threw a football into our dish."

"Called another student tonight and thought I'd interrupted a beheading," Duchais said.

Van Allan, himself, hated violent television shows, but Tim had never missed either *24* or *The Sopranos*. On Saturdays, he retaliated by listening to the Car Guys on the radio. The laughter often drove Tim out of the apartment.

"They killed him in jail, didn't they?"

"Sir?"

"Jeffrey Dahmer. Didn't an inmate murder him?"

"I believe that is what happened. Yes," Van Allan said, figuring he had missed something.

"Happened when I was in Cahors. The account was rather garbled. The way the French saw it, refrigeration itself was at fault. Newspaper printed the dimensions of the refrigerator. I'll call the cleaner's in the a.m.," the professor said, and hung up.

It was raining when Van Allan turned by the mailbox from which floated one collapsing Mylar balloon. There were also two bronze chrysanthemums flanking the mailbox, which was itself a flying goose atop a cedar pole. Numerous other small errands had been requested in an early-morning phone call: Van Allan was to stop at the stationery shop for the *International Herald,* pick up Duchais's mail at the department, and bring in mail from the mailbox out front, as well, if Duchais hadn't yet lowered the goose's wing. Duchais set upon him the minute he walked in: in the future, the broom propped against the side of the vestibule could be used to sweep out any autumn leaves. If the thermostat was still set at sixty—which Duchais often didn't notice, dressed, as he almost always was, in cashmere sweaters—it was to be put at sixty-six: the housekeeper's optimal temperature. She would turn it down when she left.

In his arms, Van Allan carried the transparent dry-cleaning bags, blue robe on top. Duchais took them from him and held them, in their slightly damp crinkly plastic, against his chest.

"My mother will be coming for drinks at four," Duchais said. "We like to have a glass of wine in the study, with the ficus tree moved aside so we can enjoy a clear view of the backyard. The tree isn't hard to move, because it's on a rolling stand. Please put her blue robe on the sofa, so she can slip into it."

"Do you want me to serve the drinks?" Van Allan asked.

"Yes. I'll take down special glasses. You might open some nuts, or see if there's cheese in the refrigerator. One of the things I hate to do is go foraging through the refrigerator, looking for cheese. Nuts and cheese should not appear on the same plate."

"Okay," Van Allan said, trying to keep his voice level.

"The driver should be invited to join us. He sometimes declines, and if he does, it means he'd prefer a bath, which you should draw. Take him red wine, but no food."

Van Allan nodded.

"The driver's religious beliefs are not my own, but I've found it's better not to engage him on the subject. Some days these things seem to mean more to him than others. You should do as you think best."

"Your mother's robe," he said, figuring out to whom the clothes belonged, reaching out to take them from Duchais's hand. "I just put it on the sofa?"

"That's right."

"I remove it from the bag?"

"You operate, at all times, using common sense."

Van Allan nodded.

"My mother and I, on rare occasions, have differences of opinion. If that happens, common sense requires that you not get involved."

"I wouldn't," Van Allan said.

"What sort of relationship do you have with your own mother, if I may ask?" Duchais said. He was adjusting the venetian blinds.

"Oh, we talk on the phone and everything. She sends me cookies and everything. It's, you know . . . it's fine. She and my dad are divorced."

"My mother has no idea who my father was."

"Sir?"

"Duchais," Duchais said emphatically. "She didn't tell me about the confusion until I was grown. Amazing the things one might never be filled in on. My mother is quite the lady."

Van Allan looked down. The tip of a leaf protruded from the sole of his shoe.

"You'll want to be getting the study ready. There's a rheostat by the door. I'll leave the lighting up to you. Hors d'oeuvres should be put on the coffee table. As should the drinks, when you bring them."

"Okay, Duchais," he said. He gave a little wave he regretted, for its obvious halfheartedness. He did not know what a rheostat was, but hoped he could figure it out. He went into the study, turned on and adjusted the lights downward, noticed dust on the coffee table and wiped it away with the side of his hand. He looked at the ficus tree, centered in the window. He tried to push the stand, but it wouldn't budge. Where a third wheel should have been, balancing it, there was a brick. With great effort, he picked up the pot and set it on the floor. He pushed the stand several feet to the right, replaced the brick, and—again, barely managing— slowly bumped the heavy pot to the lip of the stand. Concentrating fiercely, he lifted it onto its platform. He picked up the dry-cleaning bag from where he'd draped it on the back of the sofa and slid the blue robe off a hanger. He draped the other things, still on hangers encased in plastic, across the back of a chair. Outside the window, migrating birds fanned across the sky.

"Another thing," Duchais said, and Van Allan jumped, so certain had he been that the professor had gone away. "Nice lighting," Duchais said. "What I wanted to say was that the linen cocktail napkins are in the top drawer of the Hoosier cabinet in the kitchen. I've taken the cut-glass wineglasses from the top shelf, but it's always best to rinse them beforehand."

"Absolutely."

"It's very nice your mother sends you cookies," Duchais said. "Does she make them herself?"

"She tends to buy them at the farmers' market in the summer. She tends not to send them in the winter."

Duchais nodded. "If the driver doesn't want to join us, and doesn't want a bath, he prowls the house, which is perfectly fine. I guess that's everything."

"Okay," Van Allan said. "I'll go wash those glasses."

"They should be used even if my mother might prefer a drink you wouldn't ordinarily think of serving in a wineglass, such as a scotch and soda. Don't worry: you're doing a fine job," Duchais said. "The driver is a longtime employee of my mother's. He is, of course, entitled to his religious beliefs."

Kryptonite, the German shepherd, had gone unmentioned. Once past his initial shock at the dog's immensity, Van Allan realized it was docile, even if it did carry a deflated Mylar balloon in its teeth. The driver, whose name was either Kenny or Benny Smith—he did not look like the sort of person you would ask for clarification—was so tall and broad-shouldered that he obviously needed no such dog to walk at his side. Duchais's mother also was not what he expected. She held Kenny/Benny's elbow and teetered in high heels that still put her not much over five feet. She wore a red dress, a fur cape, and a hat trimmed with fur. "Here we go again," she said, instead of hello.

"Very nice to meet you. I'm Van Allan Wrightsman. Please come in," he said.

There was a moment of confusion as the dog, whose leash had been dropped, ran into the house and the driver picked up Mrs. Duchais, who seemed as light as a leaf, and carried her in. Van Allan felt like a child, scurrying after them, not sure what to do. The driver seemed to know exactly where he was headed, though, and Kryptonite converged at the door to the study at the same moment, having already circled the house. Mrs. Duchais was deposited on the couch. She took off her hat with trembling hands, and the driver removed her fur cape and placed it next to her on the sofa.

"If you'd care to put on your robe—" Van Allan began.

"Wouldn't fit me," the driver said. When he saw the expression on Van Allan's face, he smiled, revealing several spectacularly gold-filled teeth. Mrs. Duchais settled herself farther back on the sofa.

"What can I get you to drink?" Van Allan said, wondering why his employer was not making an appearance.

"Whiskey sour, no orange or cherry," the driver said. "Not in one of those heavy antique glasses, either. I like a simple juice glass."

"Merlot," Mrs. Duchais said. "Not in one of those heavy antique glasses, either. Just out of the bottle is fine."

"Ma'am?"

"That was a joke," she said. "Kenny, are you going to help me into my caftan, or am I going to sit here freezing?"

"I've done enough for the present," Kenny said. "I think this is just the man to put that thing on you, while I mix my own drink."

Mrs. Duchais turned toward Van Allan. The dog followed Kenny when he left the room. "I'm rich," she said. "And you must be another of my son's underpaid helpers. A student, I suppose."

"Yes, ma'am."

"Grew up in the South, with the 'yes, ma'am' stuff," she said. He nodded.

"I have a cousin in Atlanta, but I consider the South unfit for habitation. Kudzu and salty ham. Unfortunately, I'm all alone in the world and my son chooses to teach at a Southern university. All of Kenny's relatives are in Richmond."

He nodded.

"Well, I hope I don't have to hint again that I'd like to put on the caftan, which I hope has been to the cleaner's."

"I just picked it up," he said. "The bag is over there." He pointed. She squinted, but did not turn her head. In the kitchen, cabinet doors opened and closed. Mrs. Duchais leaned forward, extending an arm. He quickly pulled the robe from the back of the sofa, gathered up some material, and eased her arm into the arm-hole. The material wadded up behind her back. He eased it around as best he could, and held the opening for the other arm where he thought she could easily reach it. She said, "My grandfather's money was from Armour Meat, in Cuba."

In the distance, Kenny's words were now clear, with long pauses between every word: "Where is the sweet vermouth?" As if in answer, the dog began to whine. The light had begun to dim, and Van Allan wondered if he should turn up the lights. Before he could move, she said, "Do you have any idea where my son is? He makes it a point not to greet me. As you can see, Kenny and I have it worked out perfectly, but my son thinks we come in peculiarly, and he won't come to the door."

"Should I call him?" Van Allan said.

"Oh, he'd love that. Just like Rochester and Mr. Benny. Don't you do it. Have more gumption than that," she said.

He had no idea what she was talking about. From the kitchen, he heard Kenny say—so clearly, he assumed Duchais must be with him—"Nothing wrong with a martini for a change." The dog walked into the study and sat by the sofa, panting, then thumping down with a great sigh.

When Van Allan heard footsteps, he expected to see Kenny. Instead, Duchais stood in the doorway, wearing a green tank shirt and neon blue swimming trunks patterned with fish. A towel was slung over one shoulder. He let his appearance register before he strode barefoot into the room. "Mother," he said. The dog beat its tail, but did not rise.

"What *ever* are you doing?" she said.

"Mother, we're on vacation today. I'm going to let you have the heat as high as you want, and I'm going to stretch out here on the sand, hoping there are no fleas." He dropped the towel on the rug and lowered himself, settling onto his side. He recited:

> *"For dogs have fleas upon their backs*
> *Upon their backs to bite 'em;*
> *The fleas themselves have lesser fleas,*
> *And so ad infinitum."*

He coughed. "Jonathan Swift," he said. "Van, could you get me a glass of wine? I assume you've asked what my mother is having."

"This is *stupid,*" Mrs. Duchais said. "I don't know what point you think you're making."

Van Allan did not know where to look. He looked at the dog, who had dropped its snout between its paws and closed its eyes. When Kenny emerged with his drink and began to laugh loudly, the dog did nothing more than blink.

"May the good Lord bless and keep me," Kenny said. "Whatever is happening here, may the good Lord abide with me."

When there was no response, Kenny sat in an uncomfortable-looking chair with a straight back and, shaking his head, began to sip his drink.

"Put on some clothes!" Mrs. Duchais said. "You embarrass yourself, Harry."

"This is Barbados, and I am at the Sandy Lane, basking in the sun," Duchais said quietly. "In a minute I'm going to put out this cigarette"—he looked at his first and second finger, no cigarette clasped between them—"and have a delicious rum punch, which my new friend Van will procure."

"Get up," Mrs. Duchais said. She kicked a shoe in her son's direction. "Harry, this is not an appropriate way for a man to greet his mother."

"I'll get that drink," Van Allan said.

"I'm glad I settled on a martini," Kenny said, behind closed eyes. "It's a drink I can sip slowly."

In the doorway, Van Allan looked over his shoulder. It was the moment when everyone might have begun to laugh, if that moment was going to come. There was silence. He no longer gave any thought to getting more light in the room. "Okay," he said under his breath, as he went into the hallway.

In the kitchen, there was a perplexing array of glasses, which he thought might have been taken down and rejected by Kenny. He looked at a tall beer glass and at a tiny glass on an inch-high stem.

He picked up the corkscrew to open the bottle of red wine—it was, he saw with relief, Merlot—that was prominently centered on the kitchen island and eyed the glasses until he found the ones he thought Duchais had been referring to: stemmed, cut-crystal wine goblets, clearly superior to the others. He filled two of them slightly more than half full, then poured an inch of wine into the beer glass, drank it down quickly, wiped his mouth, and carried the two glasses to the study.

Remote control in hand, Duchais was skipping through music. Something vaguely Hawaiian began to play: an instrumental, with lush, muted tones. Both of Mrs. Duchais's shoes were on the towel, one near her son's hip, the other near his shoulder. Her face was frozen. She reached for the glass of wine without speaking. Outside, it had turned darker. In the chair, Kenny had slid a little forward and seemed to be sleeping.

"Oh, ah kooka wooka la, oh, wooka wooka la-la," Duchais sang. He reached up and said, "Thank you," as Van Allan handed him the glass. "Oh, the shores of bee-yoo-te-ful Bar-ba-dos, ooooooh, Waikiki or Montego Bay, Jamaica, oh la laaaaaaaaa."

Van Allan went back to the kitchen, poured another inch of wine, looked at it, puzzled, for some time, then tossed it down. Silence in the study. What he did finally hear, above the soaring music, seemed to be crying, which he decided not to investigate. He debated with himself when, if ever, he should return to the study to offer more wine. He could not decide what to do. He opened the kitchen door quietly and walked outside, breathing the cold air. He did not begin to run until he was almost to his car.

"Honest to God, the guy was a real stiff," Tim said. "What you're telling me does not compute in any way."

"Did you meet the mother?"

Tim was hooked up to an IV. Not only did he have mono and bronchitis, he now had jaundice. The whites of his eyes were yellow. Even with pain medicine, it was difficult for Tim to talk. He shook his head no. He was bug-eyed from hearing Van Allan's account of the day, which made his eyes more frightening.

"Okay, I'm gonna let you get some rest, buddy," Van Allan said.

"Guy's nuts," Tim said.

Liquid dripped slowly through the IV.

"You get well," Van Allan said.

Tim nodded. "Nuts," he repeated hoarsely.

"Van?" Duchais said. "Am I calling too late? I left a couple of messages on the machine, but I thought you might be avoiding me."

"No, sir," he lied. "Sorry I said 'sir,'" he said.

"When you're older, you'll realize relationships take all sorts of weird twists and turns. If things don't get worked out between parents and children, things can get very odd, indeed. It's one of the reasons I never wanted to have children."

"Listen, the thing is, there's a job in Special Collections I might take. More regular work and all. I was going to call you."

"I'll double the money," Duchais said. "What would they pay you at the library? Eight bucks an hour? I'll pay you sixteen. Then if you're not happy with the job, you can quit. I should have told you before I pulled that little prank on my mother, but it wasn't planned. It just happened."

"Okay, well, the thing is, I might be happier working in the library and not having a lot of errands, is the thing. I don't think—"

"My mother doesn't come every day," Duchais said. He added quietly: "Far from it."

"Okay, I know, but I'm really not sure about this, you know? I didn't—" He hoped Duchais would break in, but he didn't. He said, "I didn't know whether I should come back and pour more wine, or what. I thought you'd understand. I just went out the back door."

"We heard the car drive away."

"I'm really sorry. I didn't know what to do."

"It's behind us," Duchais said. "Come next Wednesday, and if the job's not for you, it's not for you. All I'm requesting is some books from the library, and that you stop for the *Herald*. You can skip the paper, if it's too out of the way."

There was a pause.

"Okay," Van Allan said, picking up a pen. "What are the books?"

Corinne, Tim's girlfriend from freshman year, who had transferred to Columbia, was back in town to see her brother. She was staying at the apartment, slightly flustered to be there without Van Allan's previous knowledge when he returned from school. Corinne had no idea Tim had been hospitalized after he'd mailed her the key, and no idea, either, that in the confusion he'd forgotten to mention her arrival. She couldn't stay with her brother because the landlord was already trying to evict him for having "transients" in the studio apartment.

What happened the day after she arrived was pretty bizarre, Van Allan thought though perhaps not so bizarre if you got caught up in Duchais's orbit.

Duchais appeared at the apartment with a peace offering: a box of chocolates from a store that had apparently chosen between manufacturing chocolates or manufacturing gold and decided that chocolates would be more profitable. Van Allan was out running, but Corinne opened the door, and there stood Professor Duchais, who asked if Van Allan was home. She told him where he was, he identified himself as someone Van Allan was doing some work for, and she invited him in. They started talking, and soon Duchais had told her the story of what he continued to call the "prank" he'd pulled on his mother, laughing apologetically about how flipped out Van Allan had been. As a funny story, it was funny. Afterward, Van Allan couldn't make Corinne understand how upsetting it had been. At any rate, he arrived home winded and sweaty, to find Duchais and Corinne drinking his seltzer, eating chocolates. They were having a very merry time. It was Tuesday night, and perhaps because he hadn't yet picked up the books with their unpronounceable German titles at the library, perhaps because he was sweaty and out of sorts, he did not smile when he saw Duchais.

"I never knew my father," Duchais said, turning serious. "It's the source of a lot of anger. In no way did I mean to implicate you, Van. I hope Corinne, here, can convince you I'm an okay guy."

There was a smear of chocolate at the corner of Corinne's smile.

"Apology accepted. But what are you doing here?" he asked.

"I came to apologize."

"Okay, well, apology accepted. I've got to jump in the shower and get some work done now."

"Are you coming tomorrow?" the professor asked.

"Yeah, I already told you that. I'll see you tomorrow."

Duchais stood, holding out his hand. He looked somber. Corinne had wiped the smile off her face. "So, okay," Van Allan said, shaking the man's hand. "Tomorrow at three."

"You'll come?" Duchais asked, turning toward Corinne.

"She's here to visit her brother."

"Perhaps all three of you could come. I could fix lunch. I'm sorry I overstepped my bounds."

"It just sounds *funny*," Corinne said. She brushed her hair behind her ears. She looked questioningly at Van.

"Okay, look, I'm really feeling on the spot. I said I'd be out on Wednesday, with the books and the newspaper. I'd just as soon leave it that way, if you don't mind."

"With me staying here," Corinne said.

"Yes," he said. "You here. Me at my job."

There was an awkward silence. Finally, Duchais spoke. "Well, if you change your mind, please bring along your delightful friend," he said, beaming at Corinne. His shoulders were slumped as he walked out of the apartment.

Corinne looked at Van, open-mouthed. "Did I *do* something?" she said. "What?"

"You don't get it that that guy's creepy?" he said. "A box of chocolates? Was he going to bring roses, too? I'm his sweetheart or something? I went to be his fucking research assistant, and he recruited me for a day to be his houseboy, and he did this very flipped-out thing that *wasn't funny*."

Corinne raised both hands to hip level and splayed her fingers. "You are *so* overreacting," she said.

"I am? I am? I'm trying to cover for my roommate, I'm putting up his ex-girlfriend, I get home and some flipped-out professor is here yucking it up—"

"You are being, like, impossible," Corinne said. She whirled and went into the bedroom. It had already been established the night before that he would sleep on the foldout couch.

He didn't go on Wednesday. He called and left a message on the machine saying that he quit. He went to visit Tim, but Tim had been taken for an X-ray and didn't return during the hour in which Van Allan sat in his hospital room, thinking things over. Finally he wrote a note, saying he'd be back that evening if not before. He thought better of worrying Tim with any specifics of what he still thought of as Duchais's odd visit; he just underlined the part of the note saying he'd return.

He stopped for a burger at Anthony's and looked at the freebie newspaper to see if a movie he'd been waiting to see had opened. It hadn't, and he was disappointed. Corinne had left the apartment without saying good-bye, apparently tiptoeing past the couch without his having awakened. She had never been his favorite of Tim's many girlfriends. It was something he couldn't put his finger on. That she felt entitled to things, he supposed. She hadn't protested that she'd take the sofa when he volunteered. But maybe he was a petty person. Maybe he didn't have an adequate sense of humor. Somebody else might have delighted in the weirdness of Professor Duchais's afternoon. Ed, for example. Ed, who always told such good stories, and who could mimic anyone and anything, including a trash can. He flipped through the paper, eyed a tall blonde girl he recognized as one of the women's basketball players, who clomped past in her Doc Martens. He had just bitten into his overcooked hamburger when the thought occurred to him that Corinne might have gone to Duchais's. In fact, he thought, forcing himself to swallow, that must be exactly what she'd done.

He wiped his fingers and asked for the check. "Something the matter?" the waitress asked. Across the restaurant, the basketball player bit her nails and studied the menu. *Why would she go there?* he asked himself, but he was sure she had, driving in the rental car she'd picked up at Dulles. He had never seen the car, but he imagined it to be small and dark, and he also imagined that whatever was happening, it wasn't good. He told the waitress he needed to be somewhere else and left too much cash. He ran for the bus and got it, and sat in the seat with his heart pounding as it passed down Main Street. He got off two stops short of his apartment and took a shortcut through the backyard of a dead-end street, where the old people yelled if they caught you on their lawn. He ran, and made it to the far side of the parking lot of his apartment in very little time. In a few more minutes, he was in the car, headed west.

Sting was on the radio, singing about fields of barley. He made a fist and hit the dashboard, then turned the radio off.

He sped. He barely missed a squirrel in the road, almost forgetting to turn right past Montgomery's restaurant. He realized he was holding his breath, and forced himself to breathe, remembering, for some odd reason, his mother's advice, shouted to him when he was learning to swim: "Turn your face to the side and *breathe,*" skidding on gravel, coming to a stop just short of Duchais's goose, with its raised wing. Past it, in the driveway, were two cars and a truck with a gun rack. Just before his father left his mother, he had taken him hunting for the first and last time. His father had given him a lecture about the proper cleaning—not handling, cleaning—of a gun, and then he had told him that he was in love with a woman from Puerto Rico.

Duchais's driveway was strewn with leaves. The sight of vehicles was reassuring, though he had the sinking feeling that of course one of the cars was hers, and of course he was going to be walking into something he'd give almost anything to avoid. He flashed on his last image of Tim, with his yellow eyes, rasping that Duchais was nuts.

Twigs were scattered on the front steps. Inside, the house seemed to vibrate with noise. He knocked, though he might have used the doorbell. Hanging beside it was a small, weathered plaque, calligraphically lettered: *Ad Infinitum*.

A vacuum was turned off. An elderly lady opened the door.

"Is Professor Duchais here?" he said. He looked past her to where someone wandered through the house. He saw Kenny, in profile, though Kenny never looked to see who'd come to the door. For a second, he thought the old lady was simply going to close the door in his face. She had that deep a frown. She had powerful arms, and she could easily have slammed the door shut before he could make his way in. Suddenly, the German shepherd moved quickly around the vacuum, no doubt fearing it would turn itself on, and stood by the open door. The dog's muzzle was whiter than he remembered. Its dull eyes met his.

"Kenny!" he called into the house.

At this, the woman simply stepped aside, as did Kryptonite, who took several paces back. "Corinne?" he called. He looked at the cleaning woman again. He said, "Where is Professor Duchais?"

When the woman pointed to her lips, and then to the side, he understood that she could not speak.

"Corinne?" he called past her. "Kenny? Duchais?"

He found Duchais in the study, playing solitaire. He looked up from the card table set under a broken limb of the ficus tree, which was propped against the window ledge at a precarious angle. Clumps of soil were scattered across the floor. On the table was an empty bottle of wine and one of the crystal wineglasses, also empty. It cast a prism of jagged colors across the rug where, dead center, sat the brick. "You said you weren't coming," Duchais said. He had on a yellow cashmere sweater and sagging sweatpants. He was wearing slippers. His mother sat on the sofa, head fallen forward, shoes placed neatly beside her dangling feet. She really did look like a broken doll. Except for Duchais's having spoken, he might have thought he was in a dream. No one acknowledged his presence, including the dog, who thumped down and closed its eyes.

"Is Corinne here?" he said, suddenly feeling very foolish.

"Corinne?" Duchais said, as if he'd asked about a rare species of bird he might have recognized, had he known its name.

"Corinne. From my apartment. Last night. You invited us to lunch."

"Yes," Duchais said, putting down a card. "But you called and said you quit."

"I know that," he said stupidly. He looked around. Mrs. Duchais's head had fallen so far forward, it looked as if her neck had been broken. He said, so loudly his voice cracked, "Are you all right, Mrs. Duchais?"

"We would have had such a nice lunch," Duchais said. "Walnut chicken salad."

Van Allan walked forward and touched the woman's shoulder. She twitched, and he felt simultaneously relieved and repulsed. He could smell alcohol on her breath. Worse: it was vomit, splashed thickly on the front of her dress. He looked at Duchais.

"What are you, the morality police?" Duchais said. "She's been a drunk all her life."

"Is Corinne here?" he said. He still had the queasy feeling she was somewhere in the house, though he was slowly realizing that one vehicle must belong to the driver, one to the maid, and one to Duchais.

The dog flicked open its eyes, then closed them. Oblivious to anyone's presence, Kenny drifted past with a glass in his hand. He was wearing the old lady's blue robe, or caftan, or whatever the thing was called. When the vacuum started again, Kenny snapped out of his stupor and threw the glass. The cleaning woman jumped back, her heavy arm raised over her face. "Oh, my God, why hast thou forsaken me?" Kenny said, pushing past the woman, disappearing around a corner.

"He has a bit taken, but he's certainly entitled to his religious beliefs," Duchais said, moving one card, then another around with his fingertips, as if following the pointer of a Ouija board.

It was another day in the life of Professor Duchais, who drank, and whose mother drank, and whose mother's driver drank. It was very cold in the house. Slowly, Van Allan went from room to room, to satisfy himself that Corinne was nowhere inside. Only the housekeeper was sober, and when he'd arrived at the door, of course she had assumed that he was just another potential drunk.

He found Kenny in a room with the curtains drawn, and Mary Tyler Moore on the TV, without sound. He was slumped in a chair with his cheek turned against the chair's back. On the TV sat a framed photograph, spotlit underneath the one keen light in the room, of a young man standing next to a nun, shoulder to shoulder, smiling, their eyes narrowed against the flash. Beside the TV on a bath towel was a dish piled high with dry dog food. Next to that sat a bowl from which rose the odor of alcohol, an inch or so glistening in the bottom.

"Corinne?" he said, moving from room to room, whispering her name as if the sound itself could lead him to something—though eventually, exhausted and certain she was not there, he continued to think her name, but not speak it. As a boy, he had played a game—would you call it a game?—with himself, after his father left, pretending that he might encounter, if not his father, his father's ghost. Sometimes, late at night, he got silently out of bed and prowled the house with his finger pointing the way like a gun, and sometimes in the draft kicked up by his heels, he thought he did feel his father's presence, though everything he'd heard about ghosts led him to believe that they vanished in front of you.

She was not in the house, and he felt simultaneously relieved and sad—sad because not only had he not found Corinne, but she had not been with Duchais, either. He walked to the front door, down the leaf-strewn steps, across the driveway, and back to his car. It was late October; daylight savings time had ended, and it was cold and it seemed arbitrarily dark, which suddenly angered him. He jabbed his key in the ignition and started the car, pulling on the headlights, registering the dull click of his seat belt. He could not have predicted that years later, when he was a lawyer in Boston, he would return to Virginia for a twentieth class reunion and find himself accompanying his wife on a garden tour, which ended directly across the street from the house where he had wandered as a young man, a place where he had gone to prove to himself that he was the sort of person who could face difficult things, though instead he had felt like a helpless child in a chilly house, who was nevertheless intent upon saving someone named Corinne, whom he did not even really like.

There he stood, years later, squinting at the house as the group moved on. He was remembering what a particular person Duchais had been, with his fine sweaters and his special wines and his specific glasses and his old-fashioned oak kitchen cabinet, whatever the thing had been called. . . . It was a paradox: how vaguely Duchais had lived in a world of specific things. "The Do-chess house," he heard the blonde, bright-eyed Southern lady say, as she led people in the opposite direction. *She doesn't even know how to pronounce the name,* he thought, as the woman dismissed the dilapidated house with a wave of the hand. He could remember that time in his life when he had not known the words for so many things—being in the kitchen, having what would not turn out to be the last sneaked drink of his life, the confusing word *rheostat* taking form as a little pinprick in his brain, provoking a huge desire in him to run from all his inadequacies, including what, prophetically, turned out to be a not very good sense of humor.

The front door was shuttered, and the shutters were missing slats. There was no sign of the mailbox, but on the lawn the boxwoods had grown higher, oddly discordant because they did not seem to have been planted with any intention of forming a hedge. There was no telling what had become of Duchais and the others. Tim Foxx had recovered from his sickness but died in a freak accident, helping a motorist who'd broken down on the Verrazano Bridge. Van Allan dreamed, sometimes, not of Tim, but of Tim's eyes, which he'd more than once felt the presence of, those times he stared too long at certain leaves, in autumn.

"Are you coming?" his wife called back to him.

He followed behind.

Tending Something

CURLED on the sofa in her apartment, Mandy wrote down names, though it seemed silly, because she meant to include the whole gang. Oh, sure, some of the people at the surprise party she was planning for Kathy's birthday would not be all that happy to see certain other people, though she wasn't inviting anyone—that was it; that was why she was making the list—she would not invite anyone who couldn't at least act civil. It made her feel slightly embarrassed and self-conscious to be thinking about people acting properly, but she supposed that was her Southern heritage, and besides: the world could do with a little more civility.

In their early twenties, her crowd's who's-sleeping-with-whom? game had been preoccupying: one-night stands, affairs, betrayals confessed over vodkas on ice. All those years of pushing ice cubes out of trays. No apartment ever seemed to have a refrigerator with an ice maker. She remembered Trey, hitting a mass of 7-Eleven ice, having to go to the emergency room after breaking his thumb. Mandy had gone to the hospital with him and his twin sister, Tina, who—as they waited in the corridor—wondered aloud if they should call Alicia, because he'd been sleeping with her. At that time, Alicia had been low on the totem pole of women the other women liked, but now that she worked at *Vogue,* it was clear that when Alicia wasn't liked, it was jealousy. Mandy jotted Genine's name onto her list. She'd decided against getting take-out from the Mexican place on Thirty-sixth, and decided instead to order a sheet cake from the supermarket. Cake and champagne would be enough, since all people really wanted to do was talk. Carter and Jake should be invited. Colin Jaye, from Oak Park, who—after he'd ranted about cults and followers of gurus—Alicia had nicknamed "Sri So Sensible."

A year ago at this time, Mandy had wondered if she might be in love with Trey's good friend Jake Nemeyer, though the joke had been on her: he'd thrown an out-of-the-closet party, and afterward, Mandy had gone alone to the last showing of the night to see *You Can Count On Me,* which moved her to tears. Though she could see that she acted like the sister in the movie—dependable; loyal; someone who could be relied on to fix things—she identified with the wayward brother. When she got out of the theater she found it had been snowing. Late at night, snow: everything blurry; the air freezing. The cabdriver had said, "Unless somebody died, you shouldn't be crying. What are you? Thirty? Did somebody die?" He had even guessed her age as older than she was. She had him take her uptown to the building where she worked. She told the night watchman she'd forgotten something in her office. He looked at her and let her in and didn't call out when she walked past the after-hours book without signing in. She'd guessed correctly that he wouldn't come looking for her if she didn't emerge. She curled up on the fake leopard-skin rug spread over the wall-to-wall carpeting on her boss's floor, her damp coat a good enough blanket that she eventually fell asleep. When the sky brightened, she went to the bathroom and washed her face, using a dot of liquid soap to clean her teeth. Back in the office, she saw that she had written on a memo pad: "Unless somebody died, you shouldn't be crying." She didn't remember writing it, but in any case, the cabbie had been right. She thought of her grandfather, and his months of suffering before he died. She went to the window and looked into the snow in the general direction of where, on a different day, the sun would rise. She returned to the bathroom for hot water to fill her mug and emptied a packet of instant cocoa she took out of her boss's desk drawer into it. She should have known, because of the way Jake always avoided kissing her on the lips. Her lips were chapped, so she put on lip balm, then brushed her hair. There were most certainly worse mistakes than the one she'd almost made. She went to her own desk and drank the tepid cocoa and resolved to buy the shoes with the impractical high heels. She did, slogging through the snow on her lunch hour to get them. Back in the office she dropped the box in the trash, and also the piece of paper, which she crumpled as she tore it from the memo pad.

The last details of Kathy's party: buy birthday plates and napkins; get more wineglasses; make sure the florist on Lexington will have pink roses at the end of the week. At that same flower shop, Jake had once bought Mandy roses during a storm. As they exited, hail balls began to fall, and Jake had said, "With every half dozen roses, you get a bonus of diamonds."

An e-mail from Alicia said that her trip to Paris had been extended: no chance of getting back for the party. Then Markson called to say he'd run into Kathy at Blue Boy and that she'd mentioned going to her boss's house in Connecticut after work on Friday to meet the woman's new grandson. Wouldn't you know? Now Mandy would have to call Kathy's boss and tell her about the party and get her to disinvite her to Connecticut. Other changes included: Trey and Tina Greene fighting about which artists should be in their gallery and deciding not to interact so often socially (she urged them to make an exception for the party); Reva Calistanova calling to ask if Mandy would like her old denim jacket, since she'd decided to change her look, and Mandy spontaneously inviting her to the party. An e-mail to Elizabeth had turned up the name of the guy Kathy spent so much time talking to at the watercooler, but also the information that he was living with someone. Just forget it, was her inclination. Still, the party grew: Markson would be bringing his cousin. Colin Jaye accepted with a handwritten note on off-white paper so thick and beautiful that Mandy saved it to use as a bookmark. She didn't have an actual head count—that sort of thing was the preoccupation of an older generation—but she was glad she'd opted for the larger cake. She would pick up the twenty-seven roses the morning of the party. She borrowed her neighbor Mr. Parini's crystal vase to hold the flowers.

It snowed, but late in the afternoon the sun came out. Rivers of slush overflowed clogged gutters and the skylight above her stove began to leak, but since she used the microwave and never heated anything on the burners, it didn't much matter. It was what living in New York was about: accepting and improvising.

Things worked out with Jane, Kathy's boss: she not only said she could figure out a way to rescind the invitation, but hinted she'd like to be invited to the party. She'd visited Kathy every day the previous spring, when she'd been hospitalized with a burst appendix. Kathy had come out of Sinai loving the former "bitch on wheels." So of course Mandy invited her, and her husband, to the party—though Jane said that her husband had to go to Connecticut on Friday night, so he'd pick her up the next morning at the train. Just as well—other people's husbands were like blind dates: the guy could be a bore; an egomaniac.

The napkins were dark blue with *Happy Birthday* written in silver. They were by far the prettiest napkins. Kathy was not a Garfield sort of girl.

It had been Markson's idea to invite Clerey Dey, Kathy's writing professor from NYU. He RSVPed by e-mail, but phoned the morning of the party to ask if people were bringing gifts. Of course! Was he trying to get out of that? But then she thought: he's older; maybe his friends don't exchange presents. "It could just be something small," she said, and he said, "Oh, fine, that's what I thought."

Mandy had bought two Miles Davis CDs to play at the party, to be mixed in with Alicia's Japanese hip-hop and Kathy's beloved Eva Cassidy. So: the roses; the music; the Freixenet; the six Waterford wineglasses her grandmother had willed her, the six new ones from Pottery Barn. Then there was the Ambien: somebody would be sure to steal a pill or two, so she hid the bottle. She put statice— brightly colored and cheap—in a mug on the back of the bathroom sink. She planned to light all three of her vanilla-scented candles. When her father had visited New York at Christmas, he'd brought chocolates from her favorite store and the imported candles from France she'd loved as a teenager (pleased to tell her vanilla was the newest scent), installed a dimmer switch so she could fine-tune the lighting. She tried it low, then a bit brighter. She decided that she was obsessing: she could adjust the lights when people arrived.

Mr. Parini, from whom she'd borrowed the vase, had given it to her with some marbles encased in netting at the bottom. Mandy extracted the sack and looked at it, cupped in her hand. She herself had a metal holder with spikes. She supposed that wasn't the sort of thing one wanted to risk lowering into crystal. The marbles in netting were neither light nor heavy, which reminded her of the way her pet hamster had felt, cradled in her hand as it was dying. There she went: traveling back in time and getting morose. Is this marbles encased in plastic, or a living thing? she asked herself. She filled the vase with water.

Clerey and his fiancée, Monique (never before mentioned), were the first to arrive. Mandy didn't really know what to say to them. Clerey wore a tweed jacket and looked like the academic he was. His fiancée didn't seem to understand English very well, though she might just have been a person who frowned. She was older than he: fifty? Still, she had such elegance: suede boots of an indescribable color; her hair just so, with little wisps escaping to soften its perfection. Carter and Jake came next. To Mandy's surprise, Carter was fluent in French; after introducing himself, he began to converse animatedly with Monique, though Mandy had no idea what he might be saying. Jake exclaimed over the flowers, and she thought: I should have known. Then she winced, embarrassed by her own stereotyping. Her *father* liked flowers. Her father had grown gladiolas in his garden in Virginia. Markson and his cousin came next. Markson had on his jacket lined in purple and a corduroy shirt and jeans: his winter uniform. Unlike the others—or at least as far as she knew—Markson was a Sunday churchgoer. Trey and Tina seemed fine. Paula—she'd forgotten inviting Paula!—looked right through Trey. They were still on the outs because he'd criticized her for having too much to drink at an opening at the gallery. She carried a beautifully wrapped box in telltale blue for Kathy.

When McLafferty came in, dusting the shoulders of his long black coat as if snow clung to it, he gravitated to Trey's side. Trey, seeing Mandy's finger raised to her lips, whispered his hello. Genine came next. "Does this dress look terrible?" Genine said, throwing her jacket on the bed. It was one of her thrift shop finds: a wool knit with pleated skirt. The way it fell below the knee detracted from her pretty legs, but who would tell a friend that? Behind Mandy stood Reva, her curly red hair held back with a headband. She was wearing jeans and a soft white sweater and carrying a box that she said contained a globe that glowed in the dark. "Is this pretty, or is it really not Kathy's thing?" Genine said, showing Reva and Mandy the present she'd brought in an unwrapped jewelry box. It was a sweater guard, studded with fake pearls and bright stones. Kathy would never wear it in a million years. "Perfect," Reva said.

Everyone seemed excited and ready to party. It was a miracle they'd all been free on the same night, and that no one had canceled for some neurotic reason. She'd gone back and forth about inviting Trey and Tina, because they weren't really comfortable when they couldn't be the center of attention, but now that they were here, she knew she'd made the right decision. She'd known Tina since they'd gone to camp together, the year they were fifteen. That early, Tina had resolved to live in New York City, which she'd made seem exotic and slightly frightening—though she supposed exotic things were exciting exactly because they contained an element of danger.

Kathy's boss was overweight and soft-spoken. As she came

through the doorway she almost collided with Jake, who'd opened a bottle of Freixenet and was sipping from a glass filled to the brim. Mandy went to the door and opened it for Markson's cousin, entering a second time, holding a hastily bought birthday present: pineapple tops protruded from a brown bag. The last to arrive were Elizabeth, her nose Rudolph-bright, and Colin Jaye, whose attention was riveted by Elizabeth, though he seemed to be talking to himself about Tolstoy.

"My fuckin' boss," McLafferty said. "I knew he'd do this. I took the afternoon off, saying I had to go to a funeral, and the prick took off in the corporate plane and left a message on my machine to get myself to Colorado first thing in the morning."

Markson fiddled with his gift: something in tissue paper, stuffed in a bag.

"Marky, you've looked wonderful ever since you dumped me," Genine said, rummaging in her coat pocket. With the same intonation, she said, "Damn it, I lost another scarf."

6:53–4–5. Mandy had a sudden idea that Kathy's professor might be good at hushing people. She went up to Clercy and asked if he'd try to quiet them. Markson, sensing his reluctance, began to shush people himself. Mandy did not much like Clercy. It was a mystery, what a Frenchwoman would be doing with him, but life was a mystery (thank you, Daddy). She suggested that Reva get behind the chair, meanly interrupting the little flirtation that had begun between her and Markson's cousin. She gestured to Paula to go into the kitchen, herded others into the bedroom. People giggled as the excitement built. "Where did you get such *beautiful* roses?" Tina said breathlessly. Mandy whispered the name of the shop, told her, also, the roses' name: "Miss Maureen." Tina giggled: "Named after some dominatrix."

At five past seven Kathy was not yet there, but people had fallen silent. Mandy adjusted the lights. She looked at her watch. She felt a little like Gulliver among the Lilliputians, though everyone in the apartment was the same size.

7:20, 7:25. Another round of whispering: someone's suspicion Kathy might have forgotten. 7:30. That was the point where it got to be bad manners, Mandy's father always said: when you were a full half hour late.

From the apartment next door she could hear the gay guys bickering. She liked the older man, but his partner was a pain: sure enough, complaints about the lack of excitement in their lives. The complaining and the response were completely predictable. Paula's cell phone rang, and she turned it off, embarrassed. It was 7:33.

At eight, there was clearly reason for concern. It wasn't as if no one ever got mugged in New York. Mandy's phone call had gotten only Kathy's machine. It made her think of the way cameras panned violent scenes in the movies: someone's outgoing message chattering as the camera recorded the destruction. There was a doorman at Kathy's West End apartment, at least. Although she, herself, when she first moved to the city, had roomed with a girl from Georgia who bought heroin from her doorman.

"I'm afraid we're going to have to push on," Clerey said, in something between a stage whisper and a pantomime. "I'll give Kathy a call tomorrow." Oh. That would make everything fine? Monique looked at the floor. She did not seem to be studying her pretty boots.

"You might run into her in the elevator," Mandy said.

He considered her remark. He said, "Are there stairs?"

Self-absorbed man, Mandy thought. But she said, simply, "Yes."

Ten minutes later, only a few people remained in the bedroom, and Paula was talking quietly on her cell phone. "I'm starving," Jake said. "I didn't eat lunch."

Everybody had a theory about where Kathy was, but they were only guesses.

Then the doorbell rang. Mandy froze. Elizabeth ducked behind the chair. It was as if she'd broken a spell: everyone went somewhere, vanished. McLafferty's eyes darted to the bedroom, and Mandy gestured for him to go there *now,* but instead he moved in the opposite direction.

"Mandy?" Kathy called, tapping instead of ringing a second time.

"Coming," Mandy said.

It all happened at once: Mandy opened the door and Kathy walked in with a tall man just as McLafferty, who had snatched his coat from the back of the chair and was milling around the room, tripped and knocked the vase of roses to the floor. The shattering glass made for a missed beat before the people in the bedroom rushed out, knocking shoulders, grinning widely, shouting, "Surprise!"

"*Oh my God!*" Kathy said.

"Happy birthday!" Reva said. "Happy birthday, sweetie!" Paula said, and was the first to hug her.

"Oh, no," Kathy said. "I can't believe it. Is this . . . I'm late to my own *party*?"

McLafferty, on his knees, was picking up glass.

"Everybody, this is Steven," Kathy said. "We almost got married, but we . . . it was, I mean, it was just the craziest afternoon." She looked at the handsome man who stood at her side and smiled tentatively.

"We're engaged," Steven mumbled. "We just don't have a ring."

"Oh, that's so *great,*" Reva said.

"*Jane!* Steven, *Jane* . . . Jane is my *boss.* I'm just, oh, this is so incredible."

Everyone smiled, but they weren't all that happy, Mandy supposed. Forget her lateness; she was engaged, and they weren't. But who was this Steven? Mandy suddenly got a strong whiff of alcohol and stepped back. Steven had become unsteady on his feet. Kathy was propping him up with her elbow. Out of the corner of her eye, Mandy saw McLafferty picking up glass. He, alone, had not gone to greet Kathy. She looked at him, puzzled, and saw him walking quickly toward the bathroom, his coat slung over one shoulder. She had the strange feeling that something was more wrong with him than with Kathy and Steven.

"Champagne!" the Greene twins said, rushing out of the kitchen.

Everyone remained huddled in the doorway, giving their attention to the birthday girl. Mandy took a few steps backward, smiled gratefully at Reva, approaching the spill with a sponge and a roll of paper towels, and turned toward the bathroom door.

"McLafferty?" she said. No response. She turned the doorknob. The door opened. He was sitting on the side of the tub. His hand was bleeding onto his coat. The coat lay wadded up between his feet.

"What are you doing?" she said. She pulled the guest towel off the towel bar and clamped it against his skin. Then, just as quickly, she lightened the pressure. "Is there glass inside?" she said.

"I got fired," he said. "That was bullshit about taking the plane tomorrow. I got caught manipulating prices. If I'm lucky, it ends with getting axed." He nudged his jacket with the toe of his shoe, exposing the Bilzerian label. "I broke your vase and now I'm ruining my fuck-you cashmere coat," he said. "I still owe eight hundred bucks on it."

She felt slightly sick. They were all just starting their careers. Everyone got promoted. Nobody she knew had ever been fired.

"Maybe I can use the Twinkie defense," he said. "The meds my shrink was giving me made me feel sort of foggy and invincible at the same time, like everything was a big joke, and since I was down the rabbit hole anyway . . ."

Instead of finishing his sentence, he stood and kissed her.

When everyone was gone—when they'd all gone, including Markson's tipsy cousin . . . after Carter came back to see if his wallet had fallen on the bedroom floor (it had)—Mandy turned off the music, drank the dregs of champagne that remained in one bottle, and thumbed a frosting rosebud back into shape before putting the cake in the refrigerator.

McLafferty was leaning against the kitchen door. "My father used to go ballistic if we forgot to cover food," he said. "He claimed it wasn't about stuff drying out—he just couldn't tolerate what he called 'haste.'"

"Am I being criticized?" she said.

"Jesus, no. Don't mistake me for him. He's just been on my mind, is all."

To test this assertion, she opened the refrigerator door and smeared her finger through more icing, licked it, then closed the door. She said, "In our house, it was my mother's job to make sure we never ran out of anything. He'd look at an empty toilet paper roll like it was the skeleton of something he'd loved. Carry it out and show it to her."

"How old were you when your mother died?" he said.

"Fifteen," she said automatically. It was not quite true; she had been fourteen and a half. That summer, when she turned fifteen, she had been sent to summer camp against her wishes, and only Tina's friendship had gotten her through. Back home, her grandfather had moved in and would be living with them, to help out. She would soon find out that he was not as vigilant as her mother about replacing supplies.

"I guess that was pretty awful," he said. "It would have to be. You're an only child, right?"

"You think that made it worse?" she said.

"Well, yeah. I mean, I don't know about you, but I was always happy my older brother was there to suck up all the attention. I mean, I wouldn't have wanted my father watching me any closer than he was."

"What does your brother do?" she said.

"He does the whole nine yards. CEO of a nonprofit in Seattle. Wife. Baby."

"What's the baby's name?"

"Its name? It's funny you ask, because they haven't named him. His wife wants an Asian name. He wants him to be called William, for my father."

All the time they'd talked, she had been thinking that what happened next would probably determine whether or not her life would change. But what was McLafferty doing, endlessly discussing their families?

"You don't intend to say anything about the kiss?" she said.

"I felt the urge to kiss you."

"Oh. Like you were a politician and I was somebody's baby?" He snorted.

"Or you were Mr. Magoo and I was a fishbowl?"

He looked at her.

She took a deep breath, tried again. "I guess if I was the shrink on *The Sopranos* I'd ask, 'How did that make you feel?'" she said.

He said, "If I was Tony Soprano, I would have kissed you last season."

Once out of the bathroom, he went to the coatrack and took down her coat, pulled on his own crumpled coat, and said, "Walk?"

She pulled his scarf from the pocket, draped it around her neck without asking, and preceded him to the door. In the corridor, she thought about whirling around and forcing him to kiss her again, but she questioned why she'd do that. They took the elevator, which smelled like Tide and popcorn. They went through the lobby, and he held the door for her. They walked to the end of the block. She saw, he probably also saw, two rats diving into a trash can.

"If I'm lucky, I'll have another job by the time my old man gets back from Germany," he said.

They walked in silence. A cab slowed, but sped up when neither of them broke stride.

"Another effect of the wonder drug is that I can't get it up," he said. "I would guess you might already have heard that from Genine."

McLafferty and Genine? She hadn't had a clue. She said, "I wouldn't overreact. It's not *The Sun Also Rises,* you know. All you have to do is get the doctor to switch your meds."

He looked at her. "Listen," he said. "It'll probably sound like I'm making this up now, but I'd thought about calling you a couple of times to see if you wanted to do something, but I don't seem to have done that."

She had never been as happy to see anything as she was to see the lobby of the Algonquin, on Forty-fourth, when he suggested a drink and they stepped in out of the wind.

"Hurry up," a bald man in a tuxedo said urgently, as they entered. "Come on, you'll miss it!"

They were not whomever he thought they were, but McLafferty put his arm around her and gave her shoulder a squeeze. "What are they going to do, throw us out when they realize their mistake?" he said, steering her forward. The White Rabbit, who happened to be a human being wearing a tux, went rushing off, hand raised in the air, calling back, "You're late."

At the entrance to a room off the lobby, the man had come screeching to a halt. Mandy looked at him full in the face, giving him every opportunity to realize his mistake, but she could tell that he hardly saw her. They could say, later, that they'd just been following orders, she supposed. She could give the excuse that her father always said was the lamest excuse in the world. They moved forward quickly; she and McLafferty seated themselves at the table the man gestured to. Here was a party-giver who instilled his guests with anxiety; here was someone too determined, too . . . desperate. It was the worst thing you could be, she'd always thought, because desperation made you transparent.

There were a few people sitting at other tables, where little candles flickered, but the room was almost empty. She'd noticed, with pleasure, that as hurried as they were, McLafferty had remembered to pull out her chair.

A pianist in a particularly elegant tuxedo smiled briefly in their direction. He sat just outside the spotlight illuminating the singer, who was seated and ready to begin: a woman in a shimmery blue-green gown, one leg crossed over the other. She wore shoes a million times more beautiful than the ones Mandy had splurged on. The slim, gold-tipped heels must have been four inches high and accentuated her delicate ankles. Because her head was bowed, it was difficult to see the woman's face, but when she did look up, Mandy was startled to see such an open, benevolent visage. Her voice was a clear soprano, and when eventually she reached the high notes, her eyes narrowed and her lips quivered like a choirboy's. A pale green gossamer scarf was thrown loosely over one shoulder and moved in a breeze blowing from some invisible source. Only when the woman touched a hair clip did Mandy notice the slight tremor of her hand. Occasionally, one pointed toe moved against the beat. "Two for the Road," the piano player said quietly to the singer, though she didn't seem to be taking requests. She only pointed one elegant finger and wagged it playfully, as sure as a high-wire performer taking the first step on invisible wire.

The man who'd gestured to them so desperately sat alone, a pile of coats on the chair next to him. There were two empty champagne glasses on the little tabletop, where the candle had either blown out or been snuffed. The table was cluttered with an empty plate and an ashtray and a vase holding an orchid, as well as a lady's fur hat and the man's gray lamb's-wool hat with earflaps. When Mandy felt McLafferty's fingers on her shoulder, she'd been so preoccupied taking inventory that she jumped, but he only meant to help. They had come in so quickly that neither of them had removed their coats. After she struggled out of hers, he kept his own coat on, clasping his hands on the tabletop and giving the singer his full attention. When she concluded, there was a polite ripple of applause. The woman nodded without looking at anyone, then had a moment of silence to compose herself before beginning another song. Mandy felt a little as if she were spying, because the setting and the low lights were so intimate.

McLafferty had turned so she could see him in profile. She saw a little pulse beating below his jaw and kept her eyes on it as the singer began the next song. At some point, Mandy leaned just slightly forward and realized that he was looking not at the singer, but at the bald man. "Cassandra Stevens," the man said, timing his words so they came only half a second after the singer's long-held last note vanished, his voice filled with adoration.

Then everything changed. It was as abrupt as a knock on a door. Mandy was jostled as a young man in a herringbone jacket sideswiped her chair, rushing toward the singer in her puddle of light. His energy was alarming; he swooped down on the singer, motionless on her stool, then lifted her, the fabric of her dress rustling, and handed her to the man who'd first rushed them into the room—the man in the tuxedo, who sprang up with outstretched arms. Instead of staring, though, people in the room averted their eyes, or pretended to look elsewhere. Then they were gone, the sequins of the singer's dress like the green flash said to appear on rare occasions in the tropics, as the sun sinks below the horizon line.

McLafferty was grabbing Mandy's thigh so hard she winced. He was staring at the after-image, his bandaged hand pressed against his mouth. She had to fight the urge to say: *Let's go, let's sleep in my bed, I don't expect anything, not even a kiss.* Instead, she heard herself say, "Don't you think this would be a good time to leave, before he discovers his mistake?"

He looked puzzled, the way he'd looked when he knocked over the vase, as if he, himself, could not imagine what he was doing, or how something had happened so quickly. "It wasn't a mistake," he said. "He wanted an audience for the performance."

"Would it be rude to leave?" she persisted.

It made her nervous, he looked at her with such incomprehension.

"I'll get a cab," she said quickly. "You stay."

He stood immediately. "What do you think I am?" he said.

The piano player, who'd taken no notice of them, suddenly crushed out his cigarette and turned in their direction. A thin stream of smoke wafted from the ashtray. "Next set, she's going to sing 'Two for the Road,'" he said.

McLafferty sank back into his seat. He looked at Mandy, but no words came. She heard an echo of something, though. In the silence, she remembered her father's voice at Christmastime, asking, "Why would you want to live in a place like this? Why don't you come back to Virginia? There are cities in Virginia. Richmond is a city." That was what he'd said the day he installed the dimmer switch, as her grandfather lay dying.

In the apartment, she left the mess as it was, though she carried the roses, which someone had gathered up and put in water in the blender, into the bedroom. She set them on the night table. It was disappointing that they had no smell at all. She undressed, pulled on her nightshirt, and checked her answering machine. There was one message, and as she hit "play" she wondered if it might be McLafferty, saying that he was on his way, or, even if he was not, that he loved her.

"I can't get to sleep unless I confess," Kathy said. "But first of all, let me say that that was the best party ever, and I really, really thank you. I ran into Clerey in the stairwell. My fiancé, or whatever he is, always has to take the *stairs*. We stood there face-to-face, and he blurted it out. Like I would ever have guessed he was there for a party for me! I would *never* have guessed. But anyway, it doesn't matter: it was the nicest thing anyone's ever done for me. It couldn't have been any better, even if it had been a surprise. Really, Mandy. I'll never forget it."

She pressed "delete" and got into bed and looked out the window at the lamppost, flickering because of a short in the wire.

What were you supposed to do if you couldn't sleep? Count sheep, of course. It went without saying that they must be silent sheep, though tonight's seemed to be someone's pets that came with pretty collars dangling bells. They jingled in a minor key, making the same sort of sound she might have heard if she'd stayed at the hotel, listening to the piano. She turned on her side and slid one arm under the pillow in her favorite position for sleep. The sheets, newly laundered, smelled like new-mown hay. The simple smell of them transported her to Virginia, where she could see herself standing in a vast green field where no sheep stood, though her grandfather, with his eyes cast down, must certainly have been tending something.

Apology for a Journey Not Taken: How to Write a Story

WHAT can I possibly say? I should have been there, and I was not.

I can explain what happened, but perhaps the story should evolve.

In my imagination, I was there. Not that that did anyone the slightest bit of good, but still, in my imagination, I was there.

I was preoccupied with being there. *Obsessed* is an overused word, so let's say preoccupied. It has a nice, old-fashioned sound: some old lady, sewing, listening to a radio drama, so riveted to the story being told, she drops her needle.

The Shadow knows.

(Even as a throwaway allusion, it's surely obscure, having vanished from most people's consciousness.)

Though you can never underestimate the appeal of something old, newly packaged. Perhaps a painting on the CD cover by Cy Twombly would make some people curious about the Shadow.

Back to the beginning. I intended to come, up until the last minute, but then I became a coward. I worried that I might, sleepless, the night before. To avoid making my worry materialize, I had a cup of chamomile tea, which I drank from a cup, instead of a heavy mug that would preoccupy me with its size and weight, rather than with what was inside, and attempted to get a good night's sleep. You know how things can be when you drink out of a mug, though: getting lost in thought, seeing, again, the mug from the airport in Denver, with snowcapped mountains rising toward the lip, only the handle obscuring the view.

I am aware that I've taken some very nice vacations, and that that money could be used in other ways—such as sending it home.

No point at all in digressing about what "home" means, these days. It says a lot that I usually carry a heavy leather suitcase with no wheels, and that I place this suitcase horizontally on two small birchwood stools bought in Vermont many years ago, thus raising it off the ground to function as a coffee table.

I just don't know whether it's worth it—ordering heirloom tomato seeds.

Other worries include: Is there really a difference between regular and premium gas?

I understand such questions to be diversionary tactics. And I'm mad at myself, and I'm just not going to take it anymore. No, I am going to be straightforward about this and explain my absence, as best I can.

I was drugged on the train. I got caught in the rain. I drank contaminated tea. I really had to pee. I overslept. I drank too much. I got chicken pox.

I was mugged. Verbally abused. Censured by the Tribunal.

GREETINGS FROM SUNNY FLORIDA.

WISH YOU WERE HERE.

OU SONT LES NEIGES D'ANTAN?

I began to watch a taped episode of *24*.

Kiefer Sutherland reminding me of Donald Sutherland, I watched a tape of *Klute*.

I looked at old tabloids, explaining the breakup of Kiefer Sutherland and Julia Roberts.

I investigated, on Google, the possibility of going to Anguilla.

I called an old chum. I got very glum. I ate a plum.

Realizing that Howard Dean had blown it, I went to bed.

Hearing "Walk On By" on the radio, I became nostalgic.

Finally atoning for forgetting the birthday of my sister two years in a row, I bought her a chenille throw, a cute stuffed monkey that chattered when a button in its navel was pushed, a carton of oranges, a bottle of champagne, and enrolled her in the Flower of the Month club.

Realizing I could not mail the bottle of champagne, I drank it.

Subsequently, I ate one orange and enjoyed several imaginary conversations with the monkey.

I called UPS, while there was still something to call about.

Is one supposed to say "waxed nostalgic"? And if so, why?

To explain more thoroughly: I awoke with a migraine, took an Excedrin especially formulated for maximum pain relief, got frustrated and drank a little champagne, turned on the tube and saw Kiefer, screaming. What is wrong with our society? I wondered. Why am I watching this violent show, with this man screaming orders at a volume one might use when asking for an oil change? What was Howard Dean thinking of, being exuberant—that he was already on *Saturday Night Live*?

The death of Belushi. My astonishing mistake, earlier in the week, of referring to Jim Carrey, overdosing in a bungalow at the Chateau Marmont.

Which is legendary for having a swimming pool that is hard to find.

Where someone recently exited, and drove into a wall, dying.

I should have come. I could have come. I could have come along and listened to the lullaby of Broadway. The hip hooray, etc.

Setting out presents difficulties. As an adult, not having to wear boots in the rain. Then your feet get wet.

I wonder how many people do not take a journey because their feet might get wet.

Because they get cold feet, so to speak.

Some travel with their own linen.

Many take their pets, or stay home if this can't be arranged.

But let me explain more thoroughly: Meaning to set out early, I wrapped my sister's late birthday presents in a box and called to have the box picked up. On the box, I saw a black bug. I reflexively hit it with the toe of my shoe, blurring the address. I went into the house to get a Magic Marker. The Magic Marker leaked, obscuring both addresses. Cursing, I threw it into the bushes. Inside, I attempted to wash Magic Marker leakage from my hands. No go, until I scrubbed gently with Comet. Then I found a piece of cardboard, found a regular pen that did not leak, wrote the address on the cardboard, and affixed it to the box with tape. I then decided to use more tape, in case rain might fall on the address, yet again obscuring it. This done, I put the box back on the front step. For no reason at all, it fell off. It was slightly dented. I put it where the sidewalk meets the step and left it there. It began to rain, and no amount of tape would be dependable as a water repellent, so I took the box back inside and sat with it. It was like sitting with a wounded friend. Of course, I did not talk to the box, but still, I felt a sort of unspoken exchange going on, in which I expressed sympathy for the box's plight. I waited for UPS, as one would wait for a friend to go through security at the airport, or as one would wait with an elderly person at the bus stop. I felt that having done it some harm, I should atone by protecting it. Therefore, I turned on the TV. Therefore, I had thoughts of Donald Sutherland, which reminded me of my youth. My youth reminded me that I was no longer youthful. I was glad I had drunk the champagne, which I equated with youthful enthusiasm.

I was also enthusiastic about setting out on my trip, wearing shoes, but thinking that perhaps I should carry an umbrella. Which kind? Sturdy and large-ish, or less sturdy, but more compact? I considered the merits of each, deciding on sturdy and large-ish. I went outside to make sure it opened, it being bad luck to open an umbrella in one's house, and saw that the UPS truck was rounding the corner. Then, the driver slammed on the brakes, and a squirrel dashed into the underbrush, including my stalks of asparagus, which thrive in sandy soil. The truck did not stop. It hit a utility pole. Open umbrella tossed onto the lawn, I ran toward the driver to offer assistance. The umbrella blew away, no matter, but in my mind's eye I saw the Morton's salt container, which I believed to be decorated with an umbrella—though not one tossed on the lawn.

The driver was fine. That bloody squirrel, he said, explaining further that if he had known it was a squirrel rather than a cat, which he had assumed it to be, he would not have braked. Well, that wasn't the problem, he said. The problem was his job. And the job wouldn't have been a problem to him if not for his wife. His wife's attitude toward the job. Which was negative. He had married a woman with high aspirations, he said. She played the dulcimer and he played the guitar, and she aspired to be a famous musical duo. He offered to sell me a CD of their songs, which included "Irish Melody."

We spoke of Ireland, and of the Cliffs of Moher, where the updraft was so strong that one time when a movie was being filmed there, a dummy dressed as a woman was repeatedly tossed from the cliff, only to sail back up again.

Might this be untrue? Since he had visited the cliffs, he thought not, though in saying such a thing, which certainly might be analogous to an urban legend, I realized there might be cause for doubt.

He gave chase to my umbrella, finding it slightly entangled with the neighbor's rosa rugosa. In disentangling a spoke, he pricked his finger, which put us both in mind of a particular fairy tale. Remembering it, we each filled in parts the other had forgotten. We were quite the duo ourselves, we laughed. Of course, I was pleasantly disposed to him for returning my umbrella, and frankly, I had worried for him and the out-of-control truck much more than I worried for the slightly dented box that he had come to pick up.

I attempted to purchase his CD, only to find that there was a hole in my pants pocket, and my wallet was nowhere to be found. Hoping against hope, I looked at the surface of my dresser, in the bathroom, and through every room, concentrating on the floor.

Finally, I saw that I must call the floor refinisher. As coincidence would have it, the driver's brother was in the business. I took down his brother's number. When putting the pen back in the mug in which I keep twenty or so identical pens, I found my

wallet, which was wedged between a bookend and the wall—
a place where surely I could overlook it forever. Happy to have my
wallet, I removed a twenty-dollar bill, hoping the CD would not
cost more. The bill was fragile—one that should be exchanged as
quickly as possible for a better, stronger twenty-dollar bill, we
both agreed. He gave me seven dollars' change and asked to watch
my expression as I listened to the first song, which he said was his
favorite. This required me to tell him that while I did not have a
CD player, my best friend had a CD player in his car, so when we
next went out together, I would hear the CD that way.

He said, "Some loser! Your umbrella blows away, this box here
is fucked up, I hope at least you can watch television."

No, I said, I couldn't, because I was about to set out on a
journey.

GREETINGS FROM SUNNY FLORIDA, I said, having a
little in-joke with myself, though he took it to mean that I would
be going to Florida. In the event, he had a cousin who could give
me a discount ticket to Disney World. I had to explain that this was
not my destination, however. I said more than I should about my
difficulty in setting out. There were pills for that, he said. His wife
took them. Otherwise, she'd never go to the grocery store. The
pills allowed her to go repeatedly to the grocery store.

I was getting some idea of his life: a man married to a woman
he had some problems with, who liked cats and who enjoyed
making music. Making music in the literal sense, I mean. I had no
indication about whether he and his wife liked to "make music,"
so to speak.

In checking the salt container for the umbrella image, a plastic
jar of honey fell on my head, causing the immediate return of my
headache. I went into the bathroom, where I had been only a little time before, for aspirin. This time, my wallet was clearly on the
floor, because after paying the UPS man, I put the wallet in my
pocket without thinking and went into the bathroom, and when I
bent over to open the drawer in which the aspirin was kept, the

wallet (apparently) slipped to the floor. Noiselessly, because there was a blue shag bath rug where I stood.

Though I did not remember saying good-bye to the UPS man, I exited the bathroom, wallet in hand, aspirin ingested, to find that he was gone, his truck was gone, and the box remained. Why did the box remain? Because he had forgotten that it was his job to pick up the box? Because I had somehow given offense? Well, it turned out that he was only moving the truck. He came back in and we had further discussion of the fairy tale, as I heated water for tea, which could be drunk with honey. If he had to be on his way, I could give it to him in a Styrofoam cup. But it seemed that he was in no hurry to be on his way, which somewhat inconvenienced me, in that I knew I should be making preparations for being on my way.

I had never visited Disney World, and I gave a moment's thought to stopping there either on the way to, or on the return from, my planned trip. The discount coupon was an incentive. He did not want any tea, it seemed, whether regular or herbal. He informed me that he was allergic to ragweed, and that chamomile was in the ragweed family, therefore he could not drink chamomile. He *could,* but he did not.

I began to realize that if I was to get going, I would have to hint to him that he should leave the house. However, he had gone into the living room and sat with his feet on the footstool. At least, I thought it was the footstool, until I entered the room and saw that he had put his feet up on the box. He had turned on the TV with the remote control and sat there, channel surfing. Finally, I said that it was nice to have met him, and that I would enjoy listening to his CD, but that at present I must continue my preparations to set out. This elicited a longer story about his cousin, including mention of the fact that his cousin had sued Disney World after slipping on a wad of cotton candy discarded not in a trash basket, but on the ground. The cousin had been dressed as a pirate at the time, and the sword, though made of rubber, had nonetheless pierced his thigh. In fact, if I needed a lawyer for any reason in Florida, he knew one to recommend.

But let me be honest and say that the man who had come to live in my house did not stop me from setting out on my trip. I felt that I should go to the drugstore and buy more aspirin, so that I would have some packed, if needed, as I traveled.

Once there, I was greeted by an old friend who inquired about my health. The friend's health was not good. I was of course aware that my friend suffered from near deafness, and therefore had a perspective on why he spoke so loudly, but felt very embarrassed as he loudly expounded upon his problems. An old lady sitting in a chair, waiting for her prescription, sighed loudly many times and frowned at my friend, but he did not lower his voice and, in fact, went into greater and greater detail about his possible hemorrhoid surgery. As we parted, I saw her deliberately stick out her foot and trip him.

As a responsible citizen, and perhaps having just considered the issue of lawyers, I felt obliged to tell the manager what had happened, since my friend was unconscious. The only thing I could do was wait with him until the ambulance came and took him away, and once that happened I went quickly home, shaken. I had forgotten, entirely, about the necessity of acquiring aspirin. Disappointed in myself, I returned to the drugstore, where a man was mopping up blood. This reminded me of what might have happened had the UPS man run over the squirrel. I very much disliked patches of blood in the street—especially those with feathers or fur protruding. The thought made me retch, which suggested to me that I was feeling queasy, and therefore indisposed to travel.

Though I intended to come, instead I returned home and walked past the UPS man, who was channel surfing, and went upstairs and stretched out on my bed. If, twice, I could forget to buy aspirin when I had set out expressly to obtain them, was it in my power to take a journey?

No one would be chronicling my journey, of course, so there was, say, no Boswell to disappoint.

The man who had been mopping blood appeared at my door, and was admitted by the UPS man. It seems he was the nephew of my next-door neighbor, who recognized me and who took note of the fact that I seemed very upset. Upon returning to his aunt and uncle's house, he decided to stop by to make sure I was taking the accident in stride.

The UPS man invited him in to watch television, so both of them were there, engrossed in a horror movie, when the phone rang. Was I going on a journey, or was I not going on a journey? a friend inquired. The reason for the inquiry being: Could he use my house while I was away, because his wife had kicked him out. I explained that he might find my house rather crowded, even if I did set out on my journey, which I was rethinking. That is, I was thinking that perhaps all that had happened was in some way a message to me that I should immediately set out.

I thought of calling a cab, but hesitated. It might be better, after all, to drive. As I considered taking a cab to the airport, versus driving, I saw the UPS man and the man from the drugstore back out of the driveway in my car.

I considered calling the police, but have always had my doubts about calling the police. I suspect this aversion is somewhat generational.

I took a suitcase out of my closet, then a duffel bag, then a different suitcase. One, being a Vuitton, had probably actually appreciated in value. It would be a shame to check it as baggage, however, so the duffel bag made more sense. However, it would not hold an adequate amount of clothes, I decided. That is, unless I shortened my journey, which might make sense, since what was keeping me from setting out was probably an unwillingness to be away from my house for so many days.

I consulted the calendar and realized that I had not canceled my dentist appointment, and thought that it might be best to keep the appointment, so I could set out after the mystery of the tooth sensitive to pressure was solved.

In putting the suitcases away, I tripped over the duffel bag. An image of my friend, bleeding on the drugstore floor, came back to me, and forced me to sit on my bed, cradling my head, waiting for the dizzy feeling to subside.

As things sometimes come to one when least expected, I conjured up an image of the dental hygienist, whose name I thought was Sally. This, in turn, reminded me that she had once asked to borrow twenty dollars, which I had not, to the best of my recollection, been repaid.

I consulted my ledger, but found tiny holes in the paper, probably caused by silverfish. An article in the newspaper had convinced me, previously, not to have the exterminator come to the house anymore, but I was irritated that they had returned so quickly.

Because I was unable to read the notation I had made about the money borrowed, I wrote a note to myself re the hygienist, assuming her to be an honest girl, who would confess, if necessary, that she had not yet returned the money. I then put the note in my wallet, pushing it into the slot where I kept the credit card I always used when paying the dentist.

It was then that I noticed that the credit card had expired. Had I been sent a new credit card and it had not arrived? Was someone, at this very moment, forging my name? Or had it not been sent for some reason? I consulted a credit card bill and took note of the 800 number to call if there was a problem.

When reached, I spoke of my impending journey and it was decided that, having not received my new card for reasons unknown to the company, they would FedEx a new card to me the next day. I informed them that regular mail would be fine, in that I would have to wait for my dentist appointment to be completed before I set out, anyway.

The next phone call was to tell me that my friend was dead.

With a funeral pending, I did not see how I could get away until after the dental appointment, after the new card arrived, and after the funeral. Still, I made a firm decision to drive, if the car was ever returned to me. I gave fleeting thought, once more, to calling the police, and decided that my mistrust of them was indeed generational, but not to be overcome this particular night.

Yuri, the neighbor's dog, ran across several lawns to greet me, as I searched the empty streets, hoping to see my car returning. He had in his mouth a newly killed bird, which repulsed me and caused me to make a startled movement, mistaking it, at first, for a stick or something Yuri wished me to throw for him, but upon touching it I realized that it was, indeed, a dead bird. "Drop," I said authoritatively, and Yuri did, tail wagging.

I realized I must bury the bird and went into the garage to get a trowel. It was then that I noticed that my gardening bag was missing. Had I failed to put it back in the garage, or had someone made off with it?

I did not have long to wonder, because what happened next required my full attention. Yuri's owner, a teenage girl, came for him, waving a rolled-up newspaper in the air. Upon seeing her, Yuri ran off, which distressed her. Both she and I set off to chase down Yuri, who eluded us and disappeared under a hedge. The girl began to cry, dropping the paper. In picking it up before comforting her, I noticed the date on the paper and realized that it was my birthday.

What a good birthday present I could give myself, to set off on a journey. Though I had previously convinced myself that there were impediments, I decided, instead, to simply leave. Calling a cab would surely be best, since I had no car. I put my arm around Cissie and told her it was not her fault, really, that the dog had run away, though I was lying and knew that I, too, would probably run away if someone came after me with a rolled-up newspaper.

I invited Cissie into the house, so that we could call her parents and explain that Yuri was missing. Her line was busy, however, so

I gave her a can of ginger ale and opened a Perrier for myself, but after the first sip I had to quickly set the bottle down, in that Cissie was taking rapid, deep breaths and her pupils were dilated. Allergy to ginger! I knew what it must be. I had an epi pen that the doctor had given me, in case I was stung by another bee, so that I would not go into shock. To give the girl a shot or not? I did not hesitate long, as her eyes were bugging out of her head. Immediately upon injecting her, she began to recover, though in her recovery she seemed even more distraught about her conduct toward Yuri, who, it seemed, had killed another bird earlier in the week. Her real worry was that her parents were going to force her to give up Yuri, in that they were bird lovers. I promised to bury the bird and not tell her parents, and that is exactly what I was doing when my car reappeared in the distance, driven by the UPS man. The man from the drugstore exited, carrying a six-pack of beer, as did the UPS man. They seemed somewhat surprised to see a red-eyed girl in my kitchen, but upon hearing her story, all agreed that I was doing the right thing, and that the bird must be given a funeral and that, this one time, her parents should not be notified. To this end, we all went searching for the bag missing from the garage so enough implements for burial could be found, and who should find it but Cissie: it had slipped off the table and landed near a spare tire, which, I noted with consternation, had gone flat.

In burying the bird, we bonded. I was asked what, exactly, I did: meaning, what job did I hold? That of writer, I answered. This engendered a discussion in which all three present revealed that they also planned to be writers, because each had a story to tell. Cissie, in fact, was required to write a story for school, and she thought that she might write about the funeral of the bird, though she hesitated to do so in that her parents might subsequently ask to read her composition. Similarly, the UPS man had already written an entire book in his head, about a musician who delivers packages and the amusing things that happen to him. The man from the drugstore, to whom English was a second language, was waiting for the arrival of his brother, from Buffalo, who would help him with his story concerning his innermost thoughts when mopping and vacuuming, after which the brother's wife would type it.

Upon hearing that I was about to set out on a journey, all urged me to incorporate the upcoming trip in my writing, however it turned out. It was a good idea, but it was not, in itself, enough incentive to take the journey. In thinking about my obligations to myself and others, I decided that it would be best to remain at home for an indeterminate period of time, during which, of course, I could write.

However, the daily roar of the television distracted me, and I continued to see the pros and cons among my choice of suitcases. I considered seriously the advice that I should flip a coin, but in picking up a coin from my dresser top, I clumsily knocked over a bottle of aftershave, which I feared would ruin the wood. I ran into the bathroom for a towel, and in so doing stubbed my toe, forcing me to hobble, which would make walking on a journey difficult.

After a day, Yuri returned to my house and barked loudly on the front lawn. I hobbled out to greet him, relieved that he had reappeared after whatever journey he had been on, and gathered him up in my arms to take into the house, in order to call Cissie.

Cissie had the flu, unfortunately, though her older sister came to get the dog, and in so doing, she met the man from the drug-store. They hit it off and decided to take a walk together, so I went into the living room to keep the UPS man company.

I should have come. I understand that people think I have an exciting life, and those who do not think that seem to believe that I am a recluse. I have entertained the possibility that both things are true simultaneously, though it seems equally possible that neither is true.

Had I come, I had decided to leave the Vuitton at home, but had still not decided between the other suitcase and the duffel bag.

I intended to phone and explain, but the power went out and I could not use the telephone. Though telephone service resumed, by the next morning the man from the drugstore and Cissie's sister asked to borrow my car to go to Las Vegas and get married. Though the UPS man offered to drive me to the airport, it was understood by both of us that this was not an approved use for his vehicle.

The caulk in the bathtub was inadequate, and the kitchen ceiling flooded as I was bathing.

I wanted to come, but I was forced to remain home for the plumber, the plasterer, and then for the painter.

Winter is, of course, a very good time for travel, in spite of possible inclement weather.

I intend to come, but summer may be best.

Though my life is temporarily unsettled, in that two people are living with me, and my car will not be available to me for a significant amount of time, it may all be for the best; while the funeral of the bird was accomplished rather easily, the funeral of my friend was a much more complicated affair, and emotionally exhausting.

It is best to set out when one has had a good night's rest.

One likes to tie up loose ends, such as the twenty dollars still owed me by the dental hygienist. Someone else's dental emergency required me to delay my appointment for three days, and as my visit to the dentist is still pending, I must, at this time, delay my departure.

Mostre

S HE hadn't done very well in Rome, not knowing the language. The buses were hard to figure out, and even when she did get the right bus, she stood all the way to her destination. She avoided the 64 entirely, because of pickpockets. More often she walked, and held her breath as the motorcycles and motor scooters whizzing by missed touching her legs by only a fraction of an inch. On a late-night walk, she stood looking at the Trevi Fountain, thinking like Evel Knievel, imagining what it would be like if a motorcycle jumped the whole thing. Forget Anita Ekberg: Romans—if any natives at all stood looking at the fountain—would appreciate much more the unexpected sight of a beautiful, silvery machine flying overhead. It would make a wonderful children's book: some gutsy little bastard on his *motorino* flying over the fountain's grand massive statues, shaking the men's fig leaves, setting the nymphs' nipples aquiver.

The Gypsies wouldn't like it, though, because then everyone's camera would be clicking, not snug in a pants pocket, where nimble fingers could delicately extract it. The guidebooks were full of warnings: so many that she thought it must be the paranoiac's ideal to write for them. Sort of like offering inmates the opportunity to build ships in bottles, encouraging fantasies of escape as they worked on the tiny masts and sails until the vessel was complete, and then the state could sell their dreams for profit.

Her brother, Larry, was in jail. Though he had told her in detail what he had done, it was so complicated that she could barely grasp the concept. As best she could understand, Larry's company had applied to the FDA for a patent for something that he had bribed a researcher from another company to supply him with information about. But Larry had gone too far—as when had he not?—and threatened the researcher when he realized the information was incomplete. The researcher went to the FDA, the FDA investigated Larry's company, and the company made Larry the scapegoat and saw to it that he alone was indicted. Larry maintained that he had been set up: the lawyer he had been working with quit their firm and resurfaced six months later in Silicon Valley, working for the researcher's brother's company. Larry's lawyer intended to use that new information in his appeal.

About one thing, though, she was perfectly clear: she had custody of her thirteen-year-old nephew, Chandler. This is what her brother had wanted: that she become the legal guardian of his son and, as soon as that was accomplished, that she leave Chandler and go to Europe to see the place her brother had always most wanted to see. Of course she agreed to the first request, which she had assumed would happen. After all, who else did the boy have? Private detectives had never turned up his mother. His grandmother on his mother's side lived in West Virginia and had four young boys of her own from her third marriage and made it clear she wanted nothing to do with Chandler. Their own parents—Larry's and hers—had died prematurely a year apart, their mother from pneumonia, their father from a heart attack.

Well, she thought, everyone travels with baggage. The bags you pack and check and lug to the hotel and unpack are the obvious ones, and then there are all the others: the little silk pouch in which you've tied your delicate dreams; the steamer trunk of worries (never big enough to contain them); the lovely little Hermès suitcase that contains elegant ideas; the last-minute duffel bag for the leftover things not yet dealt with, that will probably never be dealt with; confusions that bury themselves amid your socks and underwear and the paperbacks you know aren't great literature, but who doesn't enjoy a good mystery?

What was mysterious to her was why she'd come. It would have been too awkward to write a letter to Chandler at his boarding school in Connecticut—for which she was somehow going to have to come up with the next year's tuition. . . . The fact that she'd been too cowardly to tell him on the phone, afraid he'd see it as another abandonment. . . . But here she was now, buying a postcard of the Trevi Fountain, composing in her mind a message to Chandler about how much she was enjoying herself, which even she did not believe. She felt sorry for herself—an emotion she did not like to indulge, if only because admitting it usually cast things in stone, so that the complainer would be left frozen in a tableau of unhappiness that would grow enormous, like the lying Pinocchio's nose.

A bird landed on the head of one of the figures of the fountain (Abundance, she would later learn). She put the postcard in her money belt—she dared not carry a purse—and knew she would write nothing on it. Later, back at her hotel, she looked up the fountain in her guidebook. She read:

> The custom in Imperial times of building a monument where the new water arrived in Rome was copied by the later Popes, and some of Rome's fanciest fountains were the result. These were called Mostre (Shows), and were also a monument for whichever Pope built them.

The next day, she looked at her checklist of places to see and left it deliberately on the night table. She had seen a banner flying from one of the galleries, announcing a show of photographs by Lartigue. She thought France might be the perfect antidote to Rome. Better yet, France in the 1920s. She bought a ticket by holding up one finger for the cashier and handing her the correct number of lira. She was given a little red disk that she had trouble separating from its sticky backing. But apparently she was not supposed to do that: she gave the disk to a second woman who worked there. The second woman returned the peeled-off disk unsmilingly, and she took it and placed it on her collar. She gathered, from what the woman said, that the show she had come to see was on the second floor, which was called, perversely, the first floor: the *piano nobile.*

She saw a beautiful enlarged photograph of three women at the racetrack, viewed from behind in their confectionery hats, the vertical lines of their stylish skirts echoing the railing before which they stood. But the skirts reminded her of prison uniforms—no, they didn't look like that any longer: Larry wore a pastel-blue jumpsuit that made him look like a rumpled Easter bunny; still she was reminded that Larry was there and she was here, and that seeing Lartigue was cheating because it wouldn't have been Larry's notion of seeing Rome. But she couldn't stop: it was like a seduction, that long-gone world, those beautiful women, the countryside, the stylish cars, the ridiculous airplanes, and a woman in a long skirt, her face a happy blur, caught in midair as she was jumping down the stairs.

"I hope she timed that right," a man said. She turned to see another American, alone, who seemed to have come from nowhere. He was wearing a long raincoat, unbuttoned, the belt almost trailing the floor.

"Because if she didn't, I'm sure he wasn't able to photograph anymore that day," the man said. He smiled—more a smile to himself than to her—and moved past her to look at the photographs on the other wall. To avoid him, she decided to stay where she was, which required looking longer at the photograph.

It was a photograph that couldn't help but make you smile. You could feel the woman's happiness. Her skirt was like a blurry whorl of cotton candy, and her jump was so high, it did not look as if she could possibly have known where she'd land.

Out of the corner of her eye she watched the man, who moved slowly, examining each photograph. He did not stop concentrating when one of three teenagers in the room became giggly. He tuned them out; she tuned them out as best she could. Better laughing voices than the insistent buzz of motorcycles, she thought. The relentlessness of the sound had given her afternoon headaches every day she'd been in Rome.

Hardly anyone was at the show: a couple (German?); the teenagers talking to each other, trying to hush their silly friend, only occasionally noticing a photograph; the man; and an elderly woman who walked with a cane and did not closely consider any of the photographs.

The man left the gallery and she began to look at photographs he had already examined. How Lartigue must have loved those women, with their lips painted in shapes no unadorned human face has ever possessed, attired in their fabulously ludicrous, feathery, gauzy hats, their expressions of absolute self-possession. She stood in front of one bizarre beauty—a face transformed from inherently beautiful into artificial beauty, but still—and lost herself, contemplating the woman's alabaster skin. The face was not quite in profile, but not looking into the lens, either. As she squinted to see any imperfection, another face came into focus behind the first face—her own, of course, mirrored back from the deeply saturated black tones of the background.

Ah, my little moment of comeuppance, she thought: I realize that if what I'm seeing is a little too glamorous, it still deserves more contemplation than the plain, rather sullen, unangular face that lurks behind. She lowered her eyes and moved away. There was much more of the show to see, and she saw it all, and then she went around one more time, avoiding the photograph in front of which she had already lingered.

The man was nowhere, and she was glad. She would report a chaste trip to her brother, who would have to settle for hearing about the sights she described, without the vicarious thrill of hearing about a traveler who connects with an unexpected person, caught up in an unexpected romantic encounter that must of course be an end in itself.

Larry was handsome. He had married twice. He had been in the army. She knew about several of his affairs. He'd had all that, so she had no regrets about not providing him with more. Besides, if the appeal worked—if Larry's excellent, expensive lawyer prevailed— he might even get out of jail. And if she was really lucky, that would happen before she had to figure out a way to pay her underachieving nephew Chandler's tuition.

It started to rain, so she cut short the rest of her plans— meaning: whatever occurred to her that had not been on Larry's damned list of things she must do—and went back to the hotel. The Asian man behind the desk finally recognized her, after four days, and took down her key without her having to say her room number. She hated her Italian pronunciation. She sounded like what she was: someone who had taken a couple of semesters of French in college twenty-five years ago. She went up to her little room and dropped her coat on the bed. The motorcycles in the street were loud. The hotel was not in a quiet location. Her room was only on the second floor (the *real* second floor), and she was jolted awake an hour later, next to her coat, by a crash outside the hotel. She got up and went to the window: almost at the corner, someone had been knocked off his motorcycle. A small blue car had come to a stop. A crowd had already gathered, including the Asian man from the desk and several children as well as men and women with briefcases and cell phones and grocery bags, all of them attracted and repelled by the scene, so that first a woman would rush forward, then recoil; a man would peer over people's shoulders, then turn away and speak into his cell phone. A woman with red hair, who might have been with the motorcyclist, seemed particularly distraught. There were sirens. Police raced onto the street, but by then the motorcyclist was standing, and the Asian man was helping him. Two children seemed to be playing tag but then ran away, and it was only then that she realized that they were Gypsy children. The woman with red hair pointed and screamed, and one of the policemen gave chase, the Asian man following behind. She could do nothing, had no idea how the accident had happened, and the motorcyclist seemed to be all right, so she turned away from the window and picked up her coat and put it over her shoulders. She was about to go into the bathroom when she glanced one last time out the window and saw the man from the museum, recognizable because of the gray raincoat that fell to his ankles. He was one of the men who had been holding a briefcase. Now that he had stopped peering at the no-longer-fallen cyclist, she was sure it was him. She left the room immediately, the keys in her coat pocket, the door left unlocked. She took the stairs instead of the elevator. By the time she got to the man's side, she had come to: This wasn't some dream, or some movie, so what was she to say? Though just by seeing her, the coincidence—the near impossibility of their meeting again in a city of two and a half million people—would say it all, she supposed.

She was out of breath. And since she hadn't thought of what to say, she stood there feeling foolish—which was only an intensification of the way she'd felt ever since arriving in Rome.

The man turned in her direction and did a double-take. "The woman in the air," he said.

She nodded.

"And the boy is okay," he said, looking at the motorcyclist, who had hobbled away and was leaning against the policeman's van. "He's okay," he repeated, as if it were required of him to narrate events for her. But then he paused, as if unable to finish the story. "Everyone has landed on his feet," he said, giving it one last try.

"I wasn't in any danger," she said. It was the first time she had spoken to him. "It was only the woman in the photograph. And she was so obviously"—she faltered—"*joyful,* that there was never any real danger for her, I imagine." She thought, but did not say, that she had never been a woman who'd leapt for joy, but a woman in the shadows, a woman who saw herself when she least expected it—saw herself against a deeply saturated black background, a background as empty as Rome was chaotic, that revealed her to be unexceptional, startled, plain.

Her brother had wanted to know why she had never married. That was why.

"This is incredible, I still can't believe it," the man said. "We must have coffee." He looked back at the policeman's van, a little confused but also riveted, as if the blue vehicle itself symbolized his past. "I mean," he said falteringly, "now that everything has worked out."

Fontana di Trevi

I have not been to Italy and neither has my dad, but when I go it is my idea to see the Trevi Fountain. The fountain is located in downtown Rome. About Rome, Robert J. Hutchinson has written in his book *When in Rome,* subtitled *A Journal of Life in Vatican City* (Doubleday, 1998), that "I forgive Rome all its petty sins, because it has one redeeming quality that it shares with a few other large European cities and which strikes Americans with particular force: it's tremendously safe." Sometimes in the downtowns of some cities safety can be a problem and interrupt the pleasure of the traveler. I feel that in Rome it is a necessary thing to see the Trevi Fountain, known to the Italians as Fontana di Trevi.

It can easily be explained what the fountain is. First of all, the fountain is very big and is very much like looking at beautiful scenery in a Broadway play. The building behind it was left with a blank wall so that the fountain could be there. People come from all over the world to see it, and some say it is one of the most romantic spots in the world. It is lit at night. One of the best things about the fountain besides its size is that there are many statues of people and also bigger-than-life sea horses. In my books I have many pictures of sea horses alive in the ocean.

The mixture of sea horses and people is very interesting.

The people are called Abundance and Good Health. In the middle is the Ocean. Very much work had to go into carving the things that you see at the Trevi Fountain. It was done for the Pope, but we still enjoy it today.

In summary, when I go to Rome, Italy, I will go first to see the Trevi Fountain. It is said to be beautiful at night when the lights are on and the lights can even make it look like things are really moving. It is safe to see the Trevi Fountain, and almost every tourist goes there.

The man used the cash machine around the corner from the Trevi Fountain. Rome was turning out to be more expensive than he had expected, even with the dollar strong against the lira. Also, there had been the store with the broken machine that had prevented him from using his credit card to buy Marissa's cashmere sweater. What was he going to do? Walk away, when she'd finally found the perfect style, the perfect color? His wife liked the colors that were popular in Italy that fall: the burnt oranges, the dark purples. Aubergine, his wife always called the color. She painted her nails aubergine. He and Marissa liked pale colors: pale peach, that shade of pink that is almost not pink at all. Unlike his wife, Marissa chewed her fingernails. That and her quick step—she could be in a hurry even when she didn't know what she was doing—made her very different from his wife. The strange thing was, she looked like Paula. They had the same long, auburn hair. Even their expressions were sometimes the same: both women often looked at him quizzically, when he thought he had just been saying something inane. He would find it necessary to explain that what he'd said was just a cliché or that he had meant a remark ironically.

His wife was a lawyer and could only manage to get away from her job for the first week he was in Rome. He would be in Rome for two more months—three months total. Marissa, the youngest daughter of a French businessman, had Daddy's blessing about traveling while she was young and unattached. Perhaps because she was the youngest, her father didn't want her to grow up. The week before, she had turned twenty-eight, though she looked five years younger. In Rome, as opposed to France, people sometimes looked at him a few seconds too long as he and she walked down the street. He had met her in Paris, when she acted as a translator at a business meeting. He had been surprised, astonished, when she'd flirted with him. Her father supplemented her income and didn't ask questions. She had flown to Rome to see him at her own expense. She had suggested the restaurant in Trastevere where they had met on the first night. It wasn't far from the apartment his company was renting for him, on the hill above Trastevere, near Ireland's Embassy to the Holy See.

October in Rome was sometimes rainy but often lovely: warm; blue skies. As was Marissa: warm; blue eyes.

They had had the stupidest fight that morning. He had put two small plastic bags in each of his raincoat pockets because he would be stopping to buy milk and other small things on the way back to the apartment. She had looked up from the sofa—insouciant: he had asked himself why she wasn't getting up, as usual, to kiss him good-bye. Why didn't he have a nicer sack, she wanted to know? The plastic bags would do fine, he told her: it was what they gave you when you made a purchase, after all. She accused him of being cheap. He turned, frowned at her. Was that a serious comment? Was she really saying that it wasn't *stylish* to carry things— things for both of them—in simple plastic bags? Did she, perhaps, think the problem might really be that she cared a little bit too much about appearances?

She got up, walked up the curving iron staircase to the bedroom loft, and went into the bathroom—about the size of his sink at home—and slammed the door.

"Bravo!" he said, and applauded. Imagine calling him cheap, when the night before he had bought her a 400,000-lire cashmere sweater.

There was no response. Did that mean that she still intended to meet him at the Palazzo di Esposizione to see the Lartigue exhibit? Would she be embarrassed to meet a man wearing a mere 725,000-lire raincoat? More than 350 dollars for a raincoat; he couldn't believe he'd spent that. And it wasn't exactly the sort of raincoat one could wear easily in Cincinnati. Then again, his plan—his and his wife's plan—was to relocate to New York by the spring of the following year. His wife's cousin was selling his brownstone in Brooklyn. His wife would be going there to look at it while he was on this trip.

Amazing that Marissa had gotten mad at him about two plastic bags. Just amazing.

He stopped for an espresso. Real Italian coffee was something he was going to miss back in the States. He would miss the late-night walks on the cobblestone; the way the moon looked through the sycamore trees; the people who lingered on the Spanish Steps, all in their own worlds, eating their gelato, looking at their maps, eating their chocolates, looking at their maps.

He would like to feel that he would miss Marissa most of all, but he hated her pointless outbursts. He hated her pouting. Though she did have very pretty lips with which to pout . . .

He paid for the espresso and left. He saw, in a store window, a sweater remarkably similar to the turtleneck he had bought Marissa, for 260,000 lire. He went inside and peered at it, draped over a satin pillow like some luxurious cat. A saleswoman asked if she could help him. "No, *grazie*," he said, but she could tell that he was looking at the sweater. She gestured to the shelf behind her and extracted the exact same sweater from a neat pile. He felt it with his thumb. If it had purred, he wouldn't have been surprised. He asked if they accepted credit cards—he could manage that in Italian—and nodded when the saleswoman said they did. He gave her his American Express card. "*Grazie*," she said. She walked to the back of the store and processed the card and wrapped the sweater in tissue paper. He took a plastic bag out of his pocket. She was scandalized: no, no, she would put it in a bag. She put it in a lustrous green bag with the name of the store lettered in gold and closed it with the store's seal. The sweater was an indescribable color somewhere between orange and peach. He would give it to his wife.

Outside, he opened the bag, took the sweater out of its little bundle of tissue paper, and threw the bag in the trash. He placed the sweater in one of his plastic bags and slid it into the deep satin-lined pocket of his raincoat. He smiled, somehow feeling much better.

He called Marissa to make sure that she would meet him at the museum. She had been delighted to hear about the Lartigue show. Her grandfather had once had an affair with one of Lartigue's models in Corsica, and she knew detail after detail about his photographs.

Marissa was due back at her job, teaching an intensive course in German for businessmen, in two days. There was not time for them to fight. He decided to show her the sweater and, if she liked it, give it to her. About Lartigue, he knew almost nothing. A famous photograph of a man standing on some jetty by the sea, the water splashing high.

Three hours later, he climbed the steep steps to the museum and paid the cashier. A woman in a dowdy blue uniform stepped forward and took the little red badge he'd been handed, peeled off the backing, and handed the badge back to him. He took it with his thumb, was reminded of his thumb's having recently touched cashmere, was reminded of the very nice sweater in his pocket, hoped that Marissa would meet him at the entrance to the exhibition as they'd arranged.

The horizontal stripes of yellow on the walls were a shock: exactly the color of his kitchen in Cincinnati. It was a bright, insistent primary color—very odd, he thought, as a background against which to display photographs.

There were only a few people at the exhibition: a tall blonde in platform boots who seemed to have come to strut up and down the long corridors. He did not look closely at her as she passed by, because he knew she wanted him to notice her. Why should he stare—just because she'd dressed so that men would? He admired his wife's understated style. He admired Marissa's mixing and matching and layering and tossing some grand scarf over everything. He had the distinct feeling that he was not going to rendezvous with Marissa at the exhibition. Preoccupied, he had passed halfway down a line of photographs. He turned and retraced his steps to examine the smiling face of Picasso. There were four photographs of Picasso looking intense and, sometimes, happy. A couple passed by, pointing to the photographs and saying something he didn't understand, in German. If Marissa had been there, she could have translated. "How do you know I am telling you the truth?" she liked to tease him, after she'd reported on some overheard conversation. "How do you know I am not just having fun with you?"

He decided that she was not coming. Could she really have been so upset that he'd made a faux pas by carrying two balled-up plastic bags? How could she stand him up when they had only two more days together?

Maybe it was her way of detaching. Maybe the parting was going to be painful, and if she pretended that she had abandoned him, rather than vice versa, she could make things easier on herself.

But surely she'd be at the apartment at the end of the day, wouldn't she?

He found the photograph he knew: the man looking sideways, the white burst of water in the background. Another, of three women at the racetrack, was also familiar, but it had been greatly enlarged and was a little disconcerting because the figures looked so real in the room. Real figures, intent upon watching something that had nothing to do with him, or with anyone else.

It was so quiet in the gallery that a woman examining a photograph heard the rustle of plastic in his pocket and gave him a look as he passed by. He had been fingering the bag nervously, as if it were pocket change. "Don't jiggle your damned change!" his wife always said to him. It set her nerves on edge.

Three teenagers were moving through the room, welded to one another's sides. One wore glasses and too much makeup but was, he decided, the prettiest of the three. Another was giggly and chatty. The third girl stepped away to actually look at a photograph or two.

Again he saw the woman—American? English?—examining a photograph of a woman with a painted mouth, the same dark lipstick one of the teenage girls was wearing.

He looked at photograph after photograph: people in cars, portraits, ladies in their fabulous dresses. And then he came upon the American (he'd decided) once more, standing and staring at an image he had seen before but had not realized was by Lartigue: a woman in a billowing skirt, jumping at an impossible angle above the stairs she was descending. He felt stricken. He felt as if he, too, had jumped but that his landing was not going to be easy. That he was going to make a fool of himself, crumple to the ground, end an ecstatic leap with dreary clumsiness.

He realized from the way the woman stood that she sensed his presence. He said something inane—he didn't know what: it just came out of his mouth—and then moved on, lest she think he had been studying her instead of the photograph.

He thought of the photograph as he was descending the stairs outside the museum. Halfway down, a beggar with one leg sat on a dirty blanket. She turned toward him and raised her cup as he passed. He felt light-headed: no lunch, no Marissa, no response from the woman to whom he had made the remark, as if all the world disdained him. He did not know whether he'd been right and she'd been an American. She could at least have smiled, if she didn't deign to speak. And Marissa could at least have been honest about her feelings instead of orchestrating that ludicrous moment in which she tried to make him look foolish.

Well, he wasn't buying it. He wasn't foolish. He plunged his hand into the pocket that held the sweater. If not for a last second of sanity, he would have handed the sweater to the beggar. As he hesitated, the beggar bent forward and he saw that she was holding a McDonald's cup. It was so grotesque he almost laughed. Instead he gave her all the change from his pocket and continued down the stairs.

There were motorcycles, buses, scooters, trucks, and vans, all honking, spewing exhaust, riding bumper to bumper, everyone trusting that everyone else would stay in motion, because if one vehicle stopped, it would mean disaster for them all. He waited for the light, crossed the street, and walked away from the noise, down a cobblestone street that finally, blessedly, became quiet. In a doorway, he took the sweater from his pocket and pulled a bit of cashmere from one end of the neatly wrapped parcel, touching it to his lips and his nose, then using the soft wool to absorb the tears in his eyes.

Fontana di Trevi (Revised Version)

The beautiful Fontana di Trevi in Rome, Italy, may have gotten its name from two Italian words "tre" and "via" ("three" and "road"), which means that three roads met where the fountain was built. It was built for Pope Clement XII, but it is more famous because in a movie by director Federico Fellini, the actress Anita Ekberg cavorted in the Trevi Fountain. Because of its beauty, too many tourists to count visit the Trevi Fountain each year.

I intend to be one of those tourists when I am older. Right now, all I can do is imagine what the Trevi Fountain is like from reading about it. (All guidebooks about Rome give information about the majestic Trevi Fountain.)

The Trevi Fountain is an enormous fountain that is brightly

lit at night so that tourists can better enjoy it. I imagine that the lights shimmer in the water and that when you look at it, it seems like the sea horses are really jumping. In my personal experience, when I have been to Sea World with my dad you sometimes can't tell when something is really moving due to the rushing water. Adding shimmering lights to this situation would further present things as really being in motion. The carved statues which must have taken a long time to create are very big, and although they do not seem to be in motion they are beautifully carved and they stand above the action in the fountain.

It is said (in guidebooks, etc.) that if you want to return to Rome, all you have to do is throw a coin in the Trevi Fountain and your dream will come true. I will be sure to take some coins there, because once I see the Trevi Fountain, I am sure I will want to return many times.

What I imagine happening is that I will probably go to the Trevi Fountain in the middle of the night, when it is lit brightly but there are not so many tourists, so I can be alone with my thoughts. I look forward to the excitement of seeing something so famous and I will be sure to take pictures for my friends. I feel that pictures you take yourself have more personal meaning than postcards you buy of famous places. If I am alone in Rome, I will ask someone in the crowd to take my picture. I imagine that people who go there are happy and excited and in a good mood on their vacations, so someone will be glad to take the picture to provide me with a keepsake of my trip to Rome. Even though it might be a while before I get there, the Trevi Fountain will be waiting for me since it has been there as a welcoming place for young and old, friends and lovers, since 1762.

The Garden Game

MY aunt Leticia could be counted on to explain the family mysteries. She'd forget I didn't know something and drop it into conversation, or use the occasion of having a fever—or being ill in any way—to let down her defenses and tell me things I hadn't been told. Sometimes the words flew out of her mouth like frogs jumping onto the road after a rainstorm.

She was never the heroine of the stories. Neither was Beaumont, her husband. Infrequently, a dog was the hero. She had two dogs: one a collie; the last one a mutt from the pound who could not be cured of sniffing under women's skirts, who died after being struck by a go-cart. A little monster who was visiting *his* aunt and uncle hit it. The young man buried it twice, once in the field across from Leticia and Beaumont's house, and again the next day, after Leticia rethought the final resting place.

I liked the first dog, Tyke, better, though of course I felt sorrier for the dog who'd been run over. Tyke had lived to be thirteen, which I think is ninety-one in human years: exactly the age Leticia was when she died.

I used to visit my aunt and uncle for two weeks during the summer. I was driven there by my parents, who were divorced though they got together to do things with me on significant days, such as my birthday, and once or twice I remember trick-or-treating with them on Halloween. They attended all graduations and more musical performances than necessary. They no doubt gave thanks that I never played sports.

I always loved to work in a garden, though. Now I grow herbs, along with some Better Boy tomatoes I've staked in a washtub I leave on the front stoop so the deer won't eat them. Around the lantern at the end of the walkway are sweet peas, in with the morning glories, and so far no animals have sniffed them out.

Going to visit my aunt and uncle was one of my favorite things. My mother did not approve of my father's family, but she knew how much the Maine vacation meant to me. I started thinking about it at Christmas, which helped get me through winter in Cleveland. Leticia and Beaumont were nothing like their names: she wasn't prim and proper at all—in fact, she guffawed instead of laughing—and although you might assume Beaumont was a Southerner, he was from a tiny mining village in Michigan. He was six feet tall, and his scowl was deeply etched below and above his eyes. He was self-conscious when he laughed along with his wife. Did I think Beaumont was always a lot of fun? Well, he most surely wasn't, but that was due to the terrible death grip alcohol got on him after he was fired from his factory job, Leticia told me when she was in the hospital recovering from pneumonia.

This was the routine: my pajamas were kept from year to year and placed on the bed as if I'd just slipped out of them that morning, replaced only if I outgrew them (Leticia queried my mother before my arrival). I was sent a catalog of flower seeds in March, from which I could pick a dozen different kinds to be planted in the garden that spring. Uncle B. would write a letter in which he enclosed "gas money" to pass on to my parents, who always protested but ended up saying, "Well, we don't want to put her in the middle, so just this once, we'll take it." My father did all the driving from Cleveland to Maine. We stayed at a Howard Johnson's, where we ordered fried clam dinners and had mint ice cream for dessert. My mother and I slept in one bed, my father in the other. The second day, we were there. I wonder, now, what the ride back must have been like. In those days I did not think much about anyone except myself. I remember times when it felt like my life was unraveling like the ball of string it was, and me the little surprise inside, freed, after some necessary untangling, to the place where I belonged.

I never knew Leticia fought breast cancer.

I didn't know that B. sold his Mustang convertible because his best friend died when a convertible rolled over, which made B. decide it was time for a sensible car.

I knew, the year I was thirteen, that my father had left my mother for another woman, who subsequently decided she didn't want him, but that was top secret, and I never asked for details, even from Leticia, who told me the bare facts amid sneezes from a fit of hay fever, saying it was time I understood things. My first morning in the garden was always golden, whether or not the sun shone. Leticia rarely followed us to the rectangular patch of plowed soil, just down the slope from the peonies that multiplied every year. Herbs had been planted along one edge before I arrived, but somehow herbs never seemed to be magic to begin with. I would step carefully over the lush oregano, kept from spreading everywhere by a channel of mint planted between bricks. Then, amid the smell of lemony mint, I would begin to move the dried grass off the little yellow tendrils of chives, being careful to avoid any bugs that might be crawling near my fingers as I uncovered the garden in preparation for the planting of bug-repellent marigolds and nasturtiums.

That first year, I uncovered a plethora of wiggly worms and numerous bottle caps, along with some not-quite-decomposed trash that had blown in and been trapped between soil and dry grass. Beaumont saw my excitement when I found the unexpected, of course. My eyes lit up when I was surprised. That must have been what gave him the idea: to deliberately scatter things in the garden at the end of the season, and to let them weather over the winter—durable things such as marbles and coins and miniature plastic animals. Eventually, larger things began to appear: an old green glass bottle, a ceramic perfume container, quite a bit of money, and even a rusted tin that contained a little silver squirrel pin. In the future, some mother-of-pearl buttons, fine when soaked clean, as well as something called a NEV-R-Rust-Cake-

Serv (not rusted), and a plastic finger puppet like the Munch figure with its mouth open, a very rusty but still workable Slinky, a paperweight with a perfect autumn leaf suspended inside, a cowrie shell, a purple Frisbee uncracked by winter weather. He had to have tossed them in after I left, because the crust of dry grass weighted down here and there by bricks showed no signs of having been disturbed.

I wish I had asked him what gave him the idea: whether, the first year, the coins might simply have fallen from his pocket; whether he himself had no idea about the partially decomposed letter written by no one either of us knew that had somehow lodged, half faded, underneath the grass cuttings. The bottle caps were clearly junk. I suspect I didn't ask because the discovery began as our secret—so mysterious and private that after the first year, we didn't even speak of it. There must have been only my puzzled frown, my moment of suspicion during which I looked at him and asked a silent question. Or maybe I questioned him many times. Maybe he denied it. It seems he may have denied it— honestly, at first, but later disingenuously when treasure after treasure littered the garden. That might have been when it occurred to me that adults could lie and mean no harm by it; that lying was a game, and sometimes it was not wrong to be complicit. I went there at least ten times, but somehow, the last few summers, I lost interest in the garden. "Don't make her do it if it's a chore," Leticia said to Beaumont.

Everything was a chore except thinking about Paul Kellogg, the cutest boy in school, and the way we'd danced together, once in the high school gym, once when nobody saw us, circling around a Dumpster at the shopping center. I spent the summer on the phone with my girlfriends. I was petulant and didn't want to take the ride to Brown's ice cream because the only flavor I liked was chocolate, and chocolate might give me acne. For three years I refused to go near the garden, complaining of blackflies and dirt under my fingernails.

I didn't know Leticia's cancer recurred, and that she beat it a second time. I didn't know how much the photograph on the wall above the phone of B. smiling in the driver's seat of his once-new Mustang meant to him. I heard, but somehow did not hear, that my father had numerous girlfriends (not one of whom I ever met). I did not know that my mother had been engaged before she married my father, and didn't really want to know, I guess, which is why I disappeared from the room as Leticia went to get more Kleenex.

What is childhood, except things intruding that you aren't prepared for: facts, like unexpected guests, suddenly standing right in front of you. I tried to ignore my parents' past, as well as the details of Leticia and B.'s present (how worried she was when he got together with former colleagues, though he always, resolutely, only had coffee).

The year I went to college, my mother married the high school geography teacher. I liked him—everybody did—though I never knew she'd secretly dated him, then broke it off, only to resume the relationship after I graduated. My father remarried, divorced, then married his third wife, buying a van and driving her from town to town as she toured with her band.

The summer they married, they asked if I wanted to go on tour with them, and I almost said yes. Maine was no longer a possibility: the house had been sold to someone who put up a string of town houses on Leticia and Beaumont's four acres. I like to think the garden is thriving, but I doubt it. If people were smart enough, they saved the peonies, which never mind being transplanted. Whether or not they intended to save the oregano, it's as hearty as anthrax and probably just seeped off to grow somewhere else.

I try not to think about the garden treasures that might have been plowed under forever. It was so wrong of me, so self-centered and wrong, to simply end my secret collusion with Beaumont. I've come to think it was misplaced anger on my part: that I did it simply because he was a man, and for a long time I no longer wanted to trust men. I don't mean that I came to mistrust them: I mean that in order to be myself, I arbitrarily stopped trusting men and instead put my trust in women. I decided that women were more often straight shooters: after all, my mother had filled me in on more than I wanted to know about her romance with Mr. Cattrelli; Leticia had given me her diary and asked me not to read it until she died, and I had done as she said, finding out only afterward the extent of B.'s drinking and her own premonition of dying prematurely.

If he'd upped the ante from bottle caps to mother-of-pearl buttons, what else might have frozen, unfound, in the garden I never again explored? The herbs took over, and B. stopped packing on grass to dry atop the soil. He turned his attention to pruning the lilacs for maximum flowering. There is no sign, in the diary, that Leticia knew anything about our garden game. I think the first year I told her my suspicions, but as I recall, she was as adept as any adult is when asked the Santa question.

I'm thinking of the garden because I'm in B.'s room, which is modern and characterless and has absolutely nothing in common with the garden—and little in common with the house in Maine—except that the picture of his Mustang sits on the night table, and the wall-to-wall carpeting is ironically reminiscent of the dried grass cuttings. No one wants a relative to be in such a place, but what else could happen? He needed someone to give him the fifteen medicines he takes every day; he needed to start eating meals again; he never could figure out the portable oxygen tank. It got so he couldn't understand that he had to turn off a ringing alarm. So my mother and father—reunited again—explored the possibilities, and Beaumont became a resident of an assisted-living facility with the ludicrous name of some British manor house. You would expect mutton to be served, to be eaten with real silver. Ridiculous! But so is the name of the town houses that now stand on my aunt and uncle's former property: Gentry Gardens.

I went back years ago when the land was being plowed and the foundation was being laid, but didn't get out of the car. I saw it with as much tunnel vision as possible, then drove quickly away in case the neighbors recognized the out-of-state car and stoned it, having figured out who'd sold the property to the developer.

Now B. has taken a turn for the worse and has been hospitalized. He has sent me from the hospital to Highland Manor, room 301, to look for his father's penknife, so he can open his mail. This is absurd because the only mail consists of useless advertisements ("We pave your driveway in 1 hr.!"), and what are the odds, anyway, that B. is capable of telling me where to find anything? He's in a time warp and thinks he's his father's son, and that the knife is, predictably, in his top bureau drawer, and furthermore, that having the knife will empower him and, once again, make him the man he was meant to be.

I'm on the verge of tears because of the pointlessness of my search—embarrassed because I found this silly errand preferable to sitting in B.'s hospital room. I nodded and patted his hand. I let him believe there was a real chance I could find it. And if a miracle occurs, I might find it still—down on all fours, looking through the clutter dumped on the carpet: the knife a needle in a haystack magnetized to my iron hand—my hard fist hammering the floor in frustration.

The garden is surely gone, though years from now someone planting a bulb or scattering seeds might unearth a screaming figure, as corroded as a carpenter's nail, and remember for a moment—like an aged man recalling the thrill that came from the quick click of a knife—that there has always been so much more than the present.

The Rabbit Hole as
Likely Explanation

MY mother does not remember being invited to my first wedding. This comes up in conversation when I pick her up from the lab, where blood has been drawn to see how she's doing on her medication. She's sitting in an orange plastic chair, giving the man next to her advice I'm not sure he asked for about how to fill out forms on a clipboard. Apparently, before I arrived, she told him that she had not been invited to either of my weddings.

"I don't know why you sent me to have my blood drawn," she says.

"The doctor asked me to make an appointment. I did not send you."

"Well, you were late. I sat there waiting and waiting."

"You showed up an hour before your appointment, Ma. That's why you were there so long. I arrived fifteen minutes after the nurse called me." It's my authoritative but cajoling voice. One tone negates the other and nothing much gets communicated.

"You sound like Perry Mason," she says.

"Ma, there's a person trying to get around you."

"Well, I'm very sorry if I'm holding anyone up. They can just honk and get into the other lane."

A woman hurries around my mother in the hospital corridor, narrowly missing an oncoming wheelchair brigade: four chairs, taking up most of the hallway.

"She drives a sports car, that one," my mother says. "You can always tell. But look at the size of her. How does she fit in the car?"

I decide to ignore her. She has on dangling hoop earrings, and there's a scratch on her forehead and a Band-Aid on her cheekbone. Her face looks a little like an obstacle course. "Who is going to get our car for us?" she asks.

"Who do you think? Sit in the lobby, and I'll turn in to the driveway."

"A car makes you think about the future all the time, doesn't it?" she says. "You have to do all that imagining: how you'll get out of the garage and into your lane and how you'll deal with all the traffic, and then one time, remember, just as you got to the driveway a man and a woman stood smack in the center, arguing, and they wouldn't move so you could pull in."

"My life is a delight," I say.

"I don't think your new job agrees with you. You're such a beautiful seamstress—a real, old-fashioned talent—and what do you do but work on computers and leave that lovely house in the country and drive into this . . . this crap five days a week."

"Thank you, Ma, for expressing even more eloquently than I—"

"Did you finish those swordfish costumes?"

"Starfish. I was tired, and I watched TV last night. Now, if you sit in that chair over there you'll see me pull in. It's windy. I don't want you standing outside."

"You always have some reason why I can't be outside. You're afraid of the bees, aren't you? After that bee stung your toe when you were raking, you got desperate about yellow jackets—that's what they're called. You shouldn't have had on sandals when you were raking. Wear your hiking boots when you rake leaves, if you can't find another husband to do it for you."

"Please stop lecturing me and—"

"Get your car! What's the worst that can happen? I have to stand up for a few minutes? It's not like I'm one of those guards outside Buckingham Palace who has to look straight ahead until he loses consciousness."

"Okay. You can stand here and I'll pull in."

"What car do you have?"

"The same car I always have."

"If I don't come out, come in for me."

"Well, of course, Ma. But why wouldn't you come out?"

"SUVs can block your view. They drive right up, like they own the curb. They've got those tinted windows like Liz Taylor might be inside, or a gangster. That lovely man from Brunei—why did I say that? I must have been thinking of the Sultan of Brunei. Anyway, that man I was talking to said that in New York City he was getting out of a cab at a hotel at the same exact moment that Elizabeth Taylor got out of a limousine. He said she just kept handing little dogs out the door to everybody. The doorman. The bellhop. Her hairdresser had one under each arm. But they weren't hers— they were his own dogs! He didn't have a free hand to help Elizabeth Taylor. So that desperate man—"

"Ma, we've got to get going."

"I'll come with you."

"You hate elevators. The last time we tried that, you wouldn't walk—"

"Well, the stairs didn't kill me, did they?"

"I wasn't parked five flights up. Look, just stand by the window and—"

"I know what's happening. You're telling me over and over!"

I raise my hands and drop them. "See you soon," I say.

"Is it the green car? The black car that I always think is green?"

"Yes, Ma. My only car."

"Well, you don't have to say it like that. I hope you never know what it's like to have small confusions about things. I understand that your car is black. It's when it's in strong sun that it looks a little green."

"Back in five," I say, and enter the revolving door. A man ahead of me, with both arms in casts, pushes on the glass with his forehead. We're out in a few seconds. Then he turns and looks at me, his face crimson.

"I didn't know if I pushed, whether it might make the door go too fast," I say.

"I figured there was an explanation," he says dully, and walks away.

The fat woman who passed us in the hallway is waiting on the sidewalk for the light to change, chatting on her cell phone. When the light blinks green, she moves forward with her head turned to the side, as if the phone clamped to her ear were leading her. She has on an ill-fitting blazer and one of those long skirts that everybody wears, with sensible shoes and a teeny purse dangling over her shoulder. "Right behind you," my mother says distinctly, catching up with me halfway to the opposite curb.

"Ma, there's an elevator."

"You do enough things for your mother! It's desperate of you to do this on your lunch hour. Does picking me up mean you won't get any food? Now that you can see I'm fine, you could send me home in a cab."

"No, no, it's no problem. But last night you asked me to drop you at the hairdresser. Wasn't that where you wanted to go?"

"Oh, I don't think that's today."

"Yes. The appointment is in fifteen minutes. With Eloise."

"I wouldn't want to be named for somebody who caused a commotion at the Plaza. Would you?"

"No. Ma, why don't you wait by the ticket booth, and when I drive—"

"You're full of ideas! Why won't you just let me go to the car with you?"

"In an elevator? You're going to get in an elevator? All right. Fine with me."

"It isn't one of those glass ones, is it?"

"It does have one glass wall."

"I'll be like those other women, then. The ones who've hit the glass ceiling."

"Here we are."

"It has a funny smell. I'll sit in a chair and wait for you."

"Ma, that's back across the street. You're here now. I can introduce you to the guy over there in the booth, who collects the money. Or you can just take a deep breath and ride up with me. Okay?"

A man inside the elevator, wearing a suit, holds the door open. "Thank you," I say. "Ma?"

"I like your suggestion about going to that chapel," she says. "Pick me up there."

The man continues to hold the door with his shoulder, his eyes cast down.

"Not a chapel, a booth. Right there? That's where you'll be?"

"Yes. Over there with that man."

"You see the man—" I step off the elevator and the doors close behind me.

"I did see him. He said that his son was getting married in Las Vegas. And I said, 'I never got to go to my daughter's weddings.' And he said, 'How many weddings did she have?' and of course I answered honestly. So he said, 'How did that make you feel?' and I said that a dog was at one of them."

"That was the wedding you came to. My first wedding. You don't remember putting a bow on Ebeneezer's neck? It was your idea." I take her arm and guide her toward the elevator.

"Yes, I took it off a beautiful floral display that was meant to be inside the church, but you and that man wouldn't go inside. There was no flat place to stand. If you were a woman wearing heels, there was no place to stand anywhere, and it was going to rain."

"It was a sunny day."

"I don't remember that. Did Grandma make your dress?"

"No. She offered, but I wore a dress we bought in London."

"That was just desperate. It must have broken her heart."

"Her arthritis was so bad she could hardly hold a pen, let alone a needle."

"You must have broken her heart."

"Well, Ma, this isn't getting us to the car. What's the plan?"

"The Marshall Plan."

"What?"

"The Marshall Plan. People of my generation don't scoff at that."

"Ma, maybe we'd better give standing by the booth another try. You don't even have to speak to the man. Will you do it?"

"Do you have some objection if I get on the elevator with you?"

"No, but this time if you say you're going to do it you have to do it. We can't have people holding doors open all day. People need to get where they're going."

"Listen to the things you say! They're so obvious, I don't know why you say them."

She is looking through her purse. Just below the top of her head, I can see her scalp through her hair. "Ma," I say.

"Yes, yes, coming," she says. "I thought I might have the card with that hairstylist's name."

"It's Eloise."

"Thank you, dear. Why didn't you say so before?"

I call my brother, Tim. "She's worse," I say. "If you want to visit her while she's still more or less with it, I'd suggest you book a flight."

"You don't know," he says. "The fight for tenure. How much rides on this one article."

"Tim. As your sister. I'm not talking about your problems, I'm—"

"She's been going downhill for some time. And God bless you for taking care of her! She's a wonderful woman. And I give you all the credit. You're a patient person."

"Tim. She's losing it by the day. If you care—if you care, see her now."

"Let's be honest: I don't have deep feelings, and I wasn't her favorite. That was the problem with René: Did I have any deep feelings? I mean, kudos! Kudos to you! Do you have any understanding of why Mom and Dad got together? He was a recluse, and she was such a party animal. She never understood a person turning to books for serious study, did she? Did she? Maybe I'd be the last to know."

"Tim, I suggest you visit before Christmas."

"That sounds more than a little ominous. May I say that? You call when I've just gotten home from a day I couldn't paraphrase, and you tell me—as you have so many times—that she's about to die, or lose her marbles entirely, and then you say—"

"Take care, Tim," I say, and hang up.

I drive to my mother's apartment to kill time while she gets her hair done, and go into the living room and see that the plants need watering. Two are new arrivals, plants that friends brought her when she was in the hospital, having her foot operated on: a kalanchoe and a miniature chrysanthemum. I rinse out the mug she probably had her morning coffee in and fill it under the faucet. I douse the plants, refilling the mug twice. My brother is rethinking Wordsworth at a university in Ohio, and for years I have been back in this small town in Virginia where we grew up, looking out for our mother. Kudos, as he would say.

"Okay," the doctor says. "We've known the time was coming. It will be much better if she's in an environment where her needs are met. I'm only talking about assisted living. If it will help, I'm happy to meet with her and explain that things have reached a point where she needs a more comprehensive support system."

"She'll say no."

"Regardless," he says. "You and I know that if there was a fire she wouldn't be capable of processing the necessity of getting out. Does she eat dinner? We can't say for sure that she eats, now, can we? She needs to maintain her caloric intake. We want to allow her to avail herself of resources structured so that she can best meet her own needs."

"She'll say no," I say again.

"May I suggest that you let Tim operate as a support system?"

"Forget him. He's already been denied tenure twice."

"Be that as it may, if your brother knows she's not eating—"

"Do you know she's not eating?"

"Let's say she's not eating," he says. "It's a slippery slope."

"Pretending that I have my brother as a 'support system' has no basis in reality. You want me to admit that she's thin? Okay. She's thin."

"Please grant my point, without—"

"Why? Because you're a doctor? Because you're pissed off that she misbehaved at some cashier's stand in a parking lot?"

"You told me she pulled the fire alarm," he says. "She's out of control! Face it."

"I'm not sure," I say, my voice quivering.

"I am. I've known you forever. I remember your mother making chocolate-chip cookies, my father always going to your house to see if she'd made the damned cookies. I know how difficult it is when a parent isn't able to take care of himself. My father lived in my house, and Donna took care of him in a way I can never thank her enough for, until he . . . well, until he died."

"Tim wants me to move her to a cheap nursing home in Ohio."

"Out of the question."

"Right. She hasn't come to the point where she needs to go to Ohio. On the other hand, we should put her in the slammer here."

"The slammer. We can't have a serious discussion if you pretend we're talking to each other in a comic strip."

I bring my knees to my forehead, clasp my legs, and press the kneecaps hard into my eyes.

"I understand from Dr. Milrus that you're having a difficult time," the therapist says. Her office is windowless, the chairs cheerfully mismatched. "Why don't you fill me in?"

"Well, my mother had a stroke a year ago. It did something. . . .

Not that she didn't have some confusions before, but after the stroke she thought my brother was ten years old. She still sometimes says things about him that I can't make any sense of, unless I remember that she often, really quite often, thinks he's still ten. She also believes that I'm sixty. I mean, she thinks I'm only fourteen years younger than she is! And, to her, that's proof that my father had another family. Our family was an afterthought, my father had had another family, and I'm a child of the first marriage. I'm sixty years old, whereas she herself was only seventy-four when she had the stroke and fell over on the golf course."

The therapist nods.

"In any case, my brother is forty-four—about to be forty-five—and lately it's all she'll talk about."

"Your brother's age?"

"No, the revelation. That they—you know, the other wife and children—existed. She thinks the shock made her fall down at the fourth tee."

"Were your parents happily married?"

"I've shown her my baby album and said, 'If I was some other family's child, then what is this?' And she says, 'More of your father's chicanery.' That is the exact word she uses. The thing is, I am not sixty. I'll be fifty-one next week."

"It's difficult, having someone dependent upon us, isn't it?"

"Well, yes. But that's because she causes herself so much pain by thinking that my father had a previous family."

"How do you think you can best care for your mother?"

"She pities me! She really does! She says she's met every one of them: a son and a daughter, and a woman, a wife, who looks very much like her, which seems to make her sad. Well, I guess it would make her sad. Of course it's fiction, but I've given up trying to tell her that, because in a way I think it's symbolically important. It's necessary to her that she think what she thinks, but I'm just so tired of what she thinks. Do you know what I mean?"

"Tell me about yourself," the therapist says. "You live alone?"

"Me? Well, at this point I'm divorced, after I made the mistake of not marrying my boyfriend, Vic, and married an old friend instead. Vic and I talked about getting married, but I was having a lot of trouble taking care of my mother, and I could never give him enough attention. When we broke up, Vic devoted all his time to his secretary's dog, Banderas. If Vic was grieving, he did it while he was at the dog park."

"And you work at Cosmos Computer, it says here?"

"I do. They're really very family-oriented. They understand absolutely that I have to take time off to do things for my mother. I used to work at an interior-design store, and I still sew. I've just finished some starfish costumes for a friend's third-grade class."

"Jack Milrus thinks your mother might benefit from being in assisted living."

"I know, but he doesn't know—he really doesn't know—what it's like to approach my mother about anything."

"What is the worst thing that might happen if you did approach your mother?"

"The worst thing? My mother turns any subject to the other family, and whatever I want is just caught up in the whirlwind of complexity of this thing I won't acknowledge, which is my father's previous life, and, you know, she omits my brother from any discussion because she thinks he's a ten-year-old child."

"You feel frustrated."

"Is there any other way to feel?"

"You could say to yourself, 'My mother has had a stroke and has certain confusions that I can't do anything about.'"

"You don't understand. It is absolutely necessary that I acknowledge this other family. If I don't, I've lost all credibility."

The therapist shifts in her seat. "May I make a suggestion?" she says. "This is your mother's problem, not yours. You understand something that your mother, whose brain has been affected by a stroke, cannot understand. Just as you would guide a child, who does not know how to function in the world, you are now in a position where—whatever your mother believes—you must nevertheless do what is best for her."

"You need a vacation," Jack Milrus says. "If I weren't on call this weekend, I'd suggest that you and Donna and I go up to Washington and see that show at the Corcoran where all the figures walk out of the paintings."

"I'm sorry I keep bothering you with this. I know I have to make a decision. It's just that when I went back to look at the Oaks and that woman had mashed an éclair into her face—"

"It's funny. Just look at it as funny. Kids make a mess. Old people make a mess. Some old biddy pushed her nose into a pastry."

"Right," I say, draining my gin and tonic. We are in his backyard. Inside, Donna is making her famous osso buco. "You know, I wanted to ask you something. Sometimes she says 'desperate.' She uses the word when you wouldn't expect to hear it."

"Strokes," he says.

"But is she trying to say what she feels?"

"Does it come out like a hiccup or something?" He pulls up a weed.

"No, she just says it, instead of another word."

He looks at the long taproot of the dandelion he's twisted up. "The South," he says. "These things have a horribly long growing season." He drops it in a wheelbarrow filled with limp things raked up from the yard. "I am desperate to banish dandelions," he says.

"No, she wouldn't use it like that. She'd say something like, 'Oh, it was desperate of you to ask me to dinner.'"

"It certainly was. You weren't paying any attention to me on the telephone."

"Just about ready!" Donna calls out the kitchen window. Jack raises a hand in acknowledgment. He says, "Donna's debating whether to tell you that she saw Vic and Banderas having a fight near the dog park. Vic was knocking Banderas on the snout with a baseball cap, Donna says, and Banderas had squared off and was showing teeth. Groceries all over the street."

"I'm amazed. I thought Banderas could do no wrong."

"Well, things change."

In the yard next door, the neighbor's strange son faces the street lamp and, excruciatingly slowly, begins his many evening sun salutations.

Cora, my brother's friend, calls me at midnight. I am awake, watching *Igby Goes Down* on the VCR. Susan Sarandon, as the dying mother, is a wonder. Three friends sent me the tape for my birthday. The only other time such a thing has happened was years ago, when four friends sent me *Play It as It Lays* by Joan Didion.

"Tim thinks that he and I should do our share and have Mom here for a vacation, which we could do in November, when the college has a reading break," Cora says. "I would move into Tim's condominium, if it wouldn't offend Mom."

"That's nice of you," I say. "But you know that she thinks Tim is ten years old? I'm not sure that she'd be willing to fly to Ohio to have a ten-year-old take care of her."

"What?"

"Tim hasn't told you about this? He wrote her a letter, recently, and she saved it to show me how good his penmanship was."

"Well, when she gets here she'll see that he's a grown-up."

"She might think it's a Tim impostor, or something. She'll talk to you constantly about our father's first family."

"I still have some Ativan from when a root canal had to be redone," Cora says.

"Okay, look—I'm not trying to discourage you. But I'm also not convinced that she can make the trip alone. Would Tim consider driving here to pick her up?"

"Gee. My nephew is eleven, and he's been back and forth to the West Coast several times."

"I don't think this is a case of packing snacks in her backpack and giving her a puzzle book for the plane," I say.

"Oh, I am not trying to infantilize your mother. Quite the opposite: I think that if she suspects there's doubt about whether she can do it on her own she might not rise to the occasion, but if we just . . ."

"People never finish their sentences anymore," I say.

"Oh, gosh, I can finish," Cora says. "I mean, I was saying that she'll take care of herself if we assume that she *can* take care of herself."

"Would a baby take care of itself if we assumed that it could?"

"Oh, my goodness!" Cora says. "Look what time it is! I thought it was nine o'clock! Is it after midnight?"

"Twelve-fifteen."

"My watch stopped! I'm looking at the kitchen clock and it says twelve-ten."

I have met Cora twice: once she weighed almost two hundred pounds, and the other time she'd been on Atkins and weighed a hundred and forty. *Bride's* magazine was in the car when she picked me up at the airport. During the last year, however, her dreams have not been fulfilled.

"Many apologies," Cora says.

"Listen," I say. "I was awake. No need to apologize. But I don't feel that we've settled anything."

"I'm going to have Tim call you tomorrow, and I am really sorry!"

"Cora, I didn't mean anything personal when I said that people don't finish sentences anymore. I don't finish my own."

"You take care, now!" she says, and hangs up.

"She's where?"

"Right here in my office. She was on a bench in Lee Park. Someone saw her talking to a woman who was drunk—a street person—just before the cops arrived. The woman was throwing bottles she'd gotten out of a restaurant's recycling at the statue. Your mother said she was keeping score. The woman was winning, the statue losing. The woman had blood all over her face, so eventually somebody called the cops."

"Blood all over her face?"

"She'd cut her fingers picking up glass after she threw it. It was the other woman who was bloody."

"Oh, God, my mother's okay?"

"Yes, but we need to act. I've called the Oaks. They can't do anything today, but tomorrow they can put her in a semiprivate for three nights, which they aren't allowed to do, but never mind. Believe me: once she's in there, they'll find a place."

"I'll be right there."

"Hold on," he says. "We need to have a plan. I don't want her at your place: I want her hospitalized tonight, and I want an MRI. Tomorrow morning, if there's no problem, you can take her to the Oaks."

"What's the point of scaring her to death? Why does she have to be in a hospital?"

"She's very confused. It won't be any help if you don't get to sleep tonight."

"I feel like we should—"

"You feel like you should protect your mother, but that's not really possible, is it? She was picked up in Lee Park. Fortunately, she had my business card and her beautician's card clipped to a shopping list that contains—it's right in front of me—items such as Easter eggs and arsenic."

"Arsenic? Was she going to poison herself?"

There is a moment of silence. "Let's say she was," he says, "for the sake of argument. Now, come and pick her up, and we can get things rolling."

*

Tim and Cora were getting married by a justice of the peace at approximately the same time that "Mom" was tracking bottles in Lee Park; they converge on the hospital room with Donna Milrus, who whispers apologetically that her husband is "playing doctor" and avoiding visiting hours.

Cora's wedding bouquet is in my mother's water pitcher. Tim cracks his knuckles and clears his throat repeatedly. "They got upset that I'd been sitting in the park. Can you imagine?" my mother says suddenly to the assembled company. "Do you think we're going to have many more of these desperate fall days?"

The next morning, only Tim and I are there to get her into his rental car and take her to the Oaks. Our mother sits in front, her purse on her lap, occasionally saying something irrational, which I finally figure out is the result of her reading vanity license plates aloud.

From the backseat, I look at the town like a visitor. There's much too much traffic. People's faces inside their cars surprise me: no one over the age of twenty seems to have a neutral, let alone happy, expression. Men with jutting jaws and women squinting hard pass by. I find myself wondering why more of them don't wear sunglasses, and whether that might not help. My thoughts drift: the Gucci sunglasses I lost in London; the time I dressed as a skeleton for Halloween. In childhood, I appeared on Halloween as Felix the Cat, as Jiminy Cricket (I still have the cane, which I often pull out of the closet, mistaking it for an umbrella), and as a tomato.

"You know," my mother says to my brother, "your father had an entire family before he met us. He never mentioned them, either. Wasn't that cruel? If we'd met them, we might have liked them, and vice versa. Your sister gets upset if I say that's the case, but everything you read now suggests that it's better if the families meet. You have a ten-year-old brother from that first family. You're too old to be jealous of a child, aren't you? So there's no reason why you wouldn't get along."

"Mom," he says breathlessly.

"Your sister tells me every time we see each other that she's fifty-one. She's preoccupied with age. Being around an old person can do that. I'm old, but I forget to think about myself that way. Your sister is in the backseat right now thinking about mortality, mark my words."

My brother's knuckles are white on the wheel.

"Are we going to the hairdresser?" she says suddenly. She taps the back of her neck. Her fingers move up until they encounter small curls. When Tim realizes that I'm not going to answer, he says, "Your hair looks lovely, Mom. Don't worry about it."

"Well, I always like to be punctual when I have an appointment," she says.

I think how strange it is that I was never dressed up as Cleopatra, or as a ballerina. What was wrong with me that I wanted to be a tomato?

"Ma, on Halloween, was I ever dressed as a girl?"

In the mirror, my brother's eyes dart to mine. For a second, I remember Vic's eyes as he checked my reactions in the rearview mirror, those times I had my mother sit up front so the two of them could converse more easily.

"Well," my mother says, "I think one year you thought about being a nurse, but Joanne Willoughby was going to be a nurse. I was in the grocery store, and there was Mrs. Willoughby, fingering the costume we'd thought about the night before. It was wrong of me not to be more decisive. I think that's what made you impulsive as a grown-up."

"You think I'm impulsive? I think of myself as somebody who never does anything unexpected."

"I wouldn't say that," my mother says. "Look at that man you married when you didn't even really know him. The first husband. And then you married that man you knew way back in high school. It makes me wonder if you didn't inherit some of your father's fickle tendencies."

"Let's not fight," my brother says.

"What do you think other mothers would say if I told them both my children got married without inviting me to their weddings? I think some of them would think that must say something about me. Maybe it was my inadequacy that made your father consider us second-best. Tim, men tell other men things. Did your father tell you about the other family?"

Tim tightens his grip on the wheel. He doesn't answer. Our mother pats his arm. She says, "Tim wanted to be Edgar Bergen one year. Do you remember? But your father pointed out that we'd have to buy one of those expensive Charlie McCarthy dolls, and he wasn't about to do that. Little did we know, he had a whole other family to support."

Everyone at the Oaks is referred to formally as "Mrs." You can tell when the nurses really like someone, because they refer to her by the less formal "Miz."

Miz Banks is my mother's roommate. She has a tuft of pure white hair that makes her look like an exotic bird. She is ninety-nine.

"Today is Halloween, I understand," my mother says. "Are we going to have a party?"

The nurse smiles. "Whether or not it's a special occasion, we always have a lovely midday meal," she says. "And we hope the family will join us."

"It's suppertime?" Miz Banks says.

"No, ma'am, it's only ten a.m. right now," the nurse says loudly. "But we'll come get you for the midday meal, as we always do."

"Oh, God," Tim says. "What do we do now?"

The nurse frowns. "Excuse me?" she says.

"I thought Dr. Milrus was going to be here," he says. He looks around the room, as if Jack Milrus might be hiding somewhere. Not possible, unless he's wedged himself behind the desk that is sitting at an odd angle in the corner. The nurse follows his gaze and says, "Miz Banks's nephew has feng-shuied her part of the room."

Nearest the door—in our part of the room—there is white wicker furniture. Three pink bears teeter on a mobile hung from an air vent in the ceiling. On a bulletin board is a color picture of a baby with one tooth, grinning. Our mother has settled into a yellow chair and looks quite small. She eyes everyone, and says nothing.

"Would this be a convenient time to sign some papers?" the nurse asks. It is the second time that she has mentioned this—both times to my brother, not me.

"Oh, my God," he says. "How can this be happening?" He is not doing very well.

"Let's step outside and let the ladies get to know each other," the nurse says. She takes his arm and leads him through the door. "We don't want to be negative," I hear her say.

I sit on my mother's bed. My mother looks at me blankly. It is as if she doesn't recognize me in this context. She says, finally, "Whose Greek fisherman's cap is that?"

She is pointing to the Sony Walkman that I placed on the bed, along with an overnight bag and some magazines.

"That's a machine that plays music, Ma."

"No, it isn't," she says. "It's a Greek fisherman's cap."

I pick it up and hold it out to her. I press "play," and music can be heard through the dangling earphones. We both look at it as if it were the most curious thing in the world. I adjust the volume to low and put the earphones on her head. She closes her eyes. Finally, she says, "Is this the beginning of the Halloween party?"

"I threw you off, talking about Halloween," I say. "Today's just a day in early November."

"Thanksgiving is next," she says, opening her eyes.

"I suppose it is," I say. I notice that Miz Banks's head has fallen forward.

"Is that thing over there the turkey?" my mother says, pointing.

"It's your roommate."

"I was joking," she says.

I realize that I am clenching my hands only when I unclench them. I try to smile, but I can't hold up the corners of my mouth.

My mother arranges the earphones around her neck as if they were a stethoscope. "If I'd let you be what you wanted that time, maybe I'd have my own private nurse now. Maybe I wasn't so smart, after all."

"This is just temporary," I lie.

"Well, I don't want to go to my grave thinking you blame me for things that were out of my control. It's perfectly possible that your father was a bigamist. My mother told me not to marry him."

"Gramma told you not to marry Daddy?"

"She was a smart old fox. She sniffed him out."

"But he never did what you accuse him of. He came home from the war and married you, and you had us. Maybe we confused you by growing up so fast or something. I don't want to make you mad by mentioning my age, but maybe all those years that we were a family, so long ago, were like one long Halloween: we were costumed as children, and then we outgrew the costumes and we were grown."

She looks at me. "That's an interesting way to put it," she says.

"And the other family—maybe it's like the mixup between the man dreaming he's a butterfly, or the butterfly dreaming he's a man. Maybe you were confused after your stroke, or it came to you in a dream and it seemed real, the way dreams sometimes linger. Maybe you couldn't understand how we'd all aged, so you invented us again as young people. And for some reason Tim got frozen in time. You said the other wife looked like you. Well, maybe she *was* you."

"I don't know," my mother says slowly. "I think your father was just attracted to the same type of woman."

"But nobody ever met these people. There's no marriage

license. He was married to you for almost fifty years. Don't you see that what I'm saying is a more likely explanation?"

"You really do remind me of that detective, Desperate Mason. You get an idea, and your eyes get big, just the way his do. I feel like you're about to lean into the witness stand."

Jack Milrus, a towel around his neck, stands in the doorway. "In a million years, you'll never guess why I'm late," he says. "A wheel came off a truck and knocked my car off the road, into a pond. I had to get out through the window and wade back to the highway."

A nurse comes up behind him with more towels and some dry clothes.

"Maybe it's just raining out, but it feels to him like he was in a pond," my mother says, winking at me.

"You understand!" I say.

"Everybody has his little embellishments," my mother says. "There wouldn't be any books to read to children and there would be precious few to read to adults if storytellers weren't allowed a few embellishments."

"Ma! That is absolutely true."

"Excuse me while I step into the bathroom and change my clothes."

"Humor him," my mother whispers to me behind her hand. "When he comes out, he'll think he's a doctor, but you and I will know that Jack is only hoping to go to medical school."

You think you understand the problem you're facing, only to find out there is another, totally unexpected problem.

There is much consternation and confusion among the nurses when Tim disappears and has not reappeared after nearly an hour. Jack Milrus weighs in: Tim is immature and irresponsible, he says. Quite possibly a much more severe problem than anyone suspected. My mother suggests slyly that Tim decided to fall down a rabbit hole and have an adventure. She says, "The rabbit hole's a more likely explanation," smiling smugly.

Stretched out in bed, her tennis shoes neatly arranged on the floor, my mother says, "He always ran away from difficult situations. Look at you and Jack, with those astonished expressions on your faces! Mr. Mason will find him," she adds. Then she closes her eyes.

"You see?" Jack Milrus whispers, guiding me out of the room. "She's adjusted beautifully. And it's hardly a terrible place, is it?" He answers his own question: "No, it isn't."

"What happened to the truck?" I ask.

"Driver apologized. Stood on the shoulder talking on his cell phone. Three cop cars were there in about three seconds. I got away by pointing to my MD plates."

"Did Tim tell you he just got married?"

"I heard that. During visiting hours, his wife took Donna aside to give her the happy news and to say that we weren't to slight him in any way, because he was ready, willing, and able—that was the way she said it to Donna—to assume responsibility for his mother's well-being. She also went to the hospital this morning just after you left and caused a commotion because they'd thrown away her wedding bouquet."

The phone call the next morning comes as a surprise. Like a telemarketer, Tim seems to be reading from a script: "Our relationship may be strained beyond redemption. When I went to the nurses' desk and saw that you had included personal information about me on a form you had apparently already filled out elsewhere, in collusion with your doctor friend, I realized that you were yet again condescending to me and subjecting me to humiliation. I was very hurt that you had written both of our names as 'Person to be notified in an emergency,' but then undercut that by affixing a Post-it note saying, 'Call me first. He's hard to find.'

How would you know? How would you know what my teaching schedule is when you have never expressed the slightest interest? How do you know when I leave my house in the morning and when I return at night? You've always wanted to come first. It is also my personal opinion that you okayed the throwing out of my wife's nosegay, which was on loan to Mom. So go ahead and okay everything. Have her euthanized, if that's what you want to do, and see if I care. Do you realize that you barely took an insincere second to congratulate me and my wife? If you have no respect for me, I nevertheless expect a modicum of respect for my wife."

Of course, he does not know that I'm joking when I respond, "No, thanks. I'm very happy with my AT&T service."

When he slams down the phone, I consider returning to bed and curling into a fetal position, though at the same time I realize that I cannot miss one more day of work. I walk into the bathroom, wearing Vic's old bathrobe, which I hang on the back of the door. I shower and brush my teeth. I call the Oaks, to see if my mother slept through the night. She did, and is playing bingo. I dress quickly, comb my hair, pick up my purse and keys, and open the front door. A FedEx letter leans against the railing, with Cora's name and return address on it. I take a step back, walk inside, and open it. There is a sealed envelope with my name on it. I stare at it.

The phone rings. It is Mariah Roberts, 2003 Virginia Teacher of the Year for Grade Three, calling to say that she is embarrassed but it has been pointed out to her that children dressed as starfish and sea horses, dancing in front of dangling nets, represent species that are endangered, and often "collected" or otherwise "preyed upon," and that she wants to reimburse me for materials, but she most certainly does not want me to sew starfish costumes. I look across the bedroom, to the pointy costumes piled on a chair, only the top one still awaiting its zipper. They suddenly look sad—deflated, more than slightly absurd. I can't think what to say, and am surprised to realize that I'm too choked up to speak.

"Not to worry," I finally say. "Is the whole performance canceled?" "It's being reconceived," she says. "We want sea life that is empowered." "Barracuda?" I say. "I'll run that by them," she says.

When we hang up, I continue to examine the sealed envelope. Then I pick up the phone and dial. To my surprise, Vic answers on the second ring.

"Hey, I've been thinking about you," he says. "Really. I was going to call and see how you were doing. How's your mother?"

"Fine," I say. "There's something that's been bothering me. Can I ask you a quick question?"

"Shoot."

"Donna Milrus said she saw you and Banderas having a fight."

"Yeah," he says warily.

"It's none of my business, but what caused it?"

"Jumped on the car and his claws scratched the paint."

"You said he was the best-trained dog in the world."

"I know it. He always waits for me to open the door, but that day, you tell me. He jumped up and clawed the hell out of the car. If he'd been scared by something, I might have made an allowance. But there was nobody. And then as soon as I swatted him, who gets out of her Lexus but Donna Milrus, and suddenly the grocery bag slips out of my hands and splits open . . . all this stuff rolling toward her, and she points the toe of one of those expensive shoes she wears and stops an orange."

"I can't believe that about you and Banderas. It shakes up all my assumptions."

"That's what happened," he says.

"Thanks for the information."

"Hey, wait. I really was getting ready to call you. I was going to say maybe we could get together and take your mother to the Italian place for dinner."

"That's nice," I say, "but I don't think so."

There is a moment's silence.

"Bye, Vic," I say.

"Wait," he says quickly. "You really called about the dog?"

"Uh-huh. You talked about him a lot, you know. He was a big part of our lives."

"There was and is absolutely nothing between me and my secretary, if that's what you think," he says. "She's dating a guy who works in Baltimore. I've got this dream that she'll marry him and leave the dog behind, because he's got cats."

"I hope for your sake that happens. I've got to go to work."

"How about coffee?" he says.

"Sure," I say. "We'll talk again."

"What's wrong with coffee right now?"

"Don't you have a job?"

"I thought we were going to be friends. Wasn't that your idea? Ditch me because I'm ten years younger than you, because you're such an ageist, but we can still be great friends, you can even marry some guy and we'll still be friends, but you never call, and when you do it's with some question about a dog you took a dislike to before you ever met him, because you're a jealous woman. The same way you can like somebody's kid, and not like them, I like the dog."

"You love the dog."

"Okay, so I'm a little leery about that word. Can I come over for coffee tonight, if you don't have time now?"

"Only if you agree in advance to do me a favor."

"I agree to do you a favor."

"Don't you want to know what it is?"

"No."

"It calls on one of your little-used skills."

"Sex?"

"No, not sex. Paper cutting."

"What do you want me to cut up that you can't cut up?"

"A letter from my sister-in-law."

"You don't have a sister-in-law. Wait: Your brother got married? I'm amazed. I thought he didn't much care for women."

"You think Tim is gay?"

"I didn't say that. I always thought of the guy as a misanthrope. I'm just saying I'm surprised. Why don't you rip up the letter yourself?"

"Vic, don't be obtuse. I want you to do one of those cutout things with it. I want you to take what I'm completely sure is something terrible and transform it. You know—that thing your grandmother taught you."

"Oh," he says. "You mean, like the fence and the arbor with the vine?"

"Well, I don't know. It doesn't have to be that."

"I haven't practiced in a while," he says. "Did you have something particular in mind?"

"I haven't read it," I say. "But I think I know what it says. So how about a skeleton with something driven through its heart?"

"I'm afraid my grandmother's interest was landscape."

"I bet you could do it."

"Sailboat riding on waves?"

"My idea is better."

"But out of my field of expertise."

"Tell me the truth," I say. "I can handle it. Did you buy groceries to cook that woman dinner?"

"No," he says. "Also, remember that you dumped me, and then for a finale you married some jerk so I'd be entitled to do anything I wanted. Then you call and want me to make a corpse with a stake through its heart because you don't like your new sister-in-law, either. Ask yourself: Am I so normal myself?"

Banderas nearly topples me, then immediately begins sniffing, dragging the afghan off the sofa. He rolls on a corner as if it were carrion, snorting as he rises and charges toward the bedroom.

"That's the letter?" Vic says, snatching the envelope from the center of the table. He rips it open. "Dear Sister-in-law," he reads, holding the paper above his head as I run toward him. He looks so different with his stubbly beard, and I realize with a pang that I don't recognize the shirt he's wearing. He starts again: "Dear Sister-in-law." He whirls sideways, the paper clutched tightly in his hand. "I know that Tim will be speaking to you, but I wanted to personally send you this note. I think that families have differences, but everyone's viewpoint is important. I would very much like—" He whirls again, and this time Banderas runs into the fray, rising up on his back legs as if he, too, wanted the letter.

"Let the dog eat it! Let him eat the thing if you have to read it out loud!" I say.

"—to invite you for Thanksgiving dinner, and also to offer you some of our frequent-flier miles, if that might be helpful, parenthesis, though it may be a blackout period, end paren."

Vic looks at me. "Aren't you embarrassed at your reaction to this woman? Aren't you?"

The dog leaps into the afghan and rolls again, catching a claw in the weave. Vic and I stand facing each other. I am panting, too shocked to speak.

"Please excuse Tim for disappearing when I came to the door of the Oaks. I was there to see if I could help. He said my face provoked a realization of his newfound strength." Vic sighs. He says, "Just what I was afraid of—some New Ager as crazy as your brother. 'I'm sure you understand that I was happy to know that I could be helpful to Tim in this trying time. We must all put the past behind us and celebrate our personal Thanksgiving, parenthesis, our wedding, end paren, and I am sure that everything can be put right when we get together. Fondly, your sister-in-law, Cora.'"

There are tears in my eyes. The afghan is going to need major repair. Vic has brought his best friend into my house to destroy it, and all he will do is hold the piece of paper above his head, as if he'd just won a trophy.

"I practiced this afternoon," he says finally, lowering his arm. "I can do either a train coming through the mountains or a garland of roses with a butterfly on top."

"Great," I say, sitting on the floor, fighting back tears. "The butterfly can be dreaming it's a man, or the man can be dreaming he's . . ." I change my mind about what I was going to say: "Or the man can be dreaming he's desperate."

Vic doesn't hear me; he's busy trying to get Banderas to drop a starfish costume he's capering with.

"Why do you think it would work?" I say to Vic. "We were never right for each other. I'm in my fifties. It would be my third marriage."

Carefully, he creases the letter a second, then a third time. He lifts the scissors out of their small plastic container, fumbling awkwardly with his big fingers. He frowns in concentration and begins to cut. Eventually, from the positive cuttings, I figure out that he's decided on the train motif. Cutting air away to expose a puff of steam, he says, "Let's take it slow, then. You could invite me to go with you to Thanksgiving."

Just Going Out

MY cousin Renny and I were raised in Minneapolis by my
mother's brother and, occasionally, women hired to help
around the house: boarders or (we supposed) Uncle Roy's lady
friends, our favorite female anything being Gladys the dog.
Shortly before we arrived, Roy found Gladys panting at the door
and took her in to give her a drink of water. She waited politely in
the kitchen (he always began the story at this point) as he looked
for a suitable bowl. Then he called the police, who told him to call
the Animal Rescue League and have the dog taken to the pound.
Instead, he asked around the neighborhood, ran an ad, then
checked out many books about dog ownership from the library.
Gladys became an early subject of my cousin's photographs,
wearing various headdresses Renny made. Except that she was a
mongrel and ducked her head in an embarrassed way, Renny's
photographs were much in the spirit of William Wegman's Wei-
maraners. In spite of the difficulty he must have experienced,
suddenly having a twelve-year-old girl and a fifteen-year-old boy
to raise, Roy gave a fair share of his attention to Gladys (who made
it clear, when she dragged certain things from one woman's room,
that the boarder wasn't the old maid she presented herself as
being).

I had been sent to Minneapolis to stay with my mother's
brother while she had surgery. She died as a reaction to anesthe-
sia. My grandmother was supposed to take me, but she remarried
and moved to Florida. It was Roy's idea to have me joined by my
cousin Sarah, from a broken home, though when the day came
her brother Reginald showed up instead, a *20,000 Leagues Under
the Sea* lunch box at his feet, his collection of miniature flags of

the world in the backseat. Reginald's sister had promised to start attending school again if she could stay with her mother; Renny asked to go in her place, saying he needed a father figure in his life.

Several months after we arrived, one of Roy's neighbors called, saying that her son, a film student at NYU, wanted to come over to talk to the family ("We're a family, we're a slightly unconventional family" was another of Roy's refrains). Nelson Crawford was tall, with red hair and what turned out to be a temporary tattoo salamander disappearing under the sleeve of his T-shirt. He wore a silver stud in one ear and had little, bony hands that looked almost vestigial.

We liked Nelson—we being Renny and me—though Gladys showed little interest, and Uncle Roy was wary about anyone coming in to make a film of us living our lives. Elizabeth Brown, one of the boarders who had rented my room before I arrived, advised against letting Nelson into our home. She had heard that he was an atheist, and also that he belonged to some group that went swimming naked in the middle of winter. She did not believe he was a student at NYU. He was, though. He had changed his major from religion to philosophy to film. He'd once had a cup of coffee with Robert De Niro, and he lived in his own apartment on lower Broadway. As much as possible, as he explained his project to us, he wanted to disappear into the background (it would be an understatement to say that all of us were used to people disappearing), and film us doing everyday things like the laundry, or eating dinner, but he also wanted to talk to us about our individual interests. Tape recorder running, Renny started right in about flags, while Uncle Roy hinted strongly that things sometimes tended to be a little chaotic, and he worried that whatever was captured (as he put it) might give the wrong impression. He warmed up a little, though, when Nelson said that he'd heard Roy was an artist.

Roy's hobby was making herbal wreaths. He grew most of the herbs, drying them over the summer and working in his heated garage in the winter, late at night. He spray-painted pinecones, bought little birds at the craft store in town, and sold his wreaths at a crafts fair that took place every Saturday in August, near the lake.

"What's your interest?" Nelson asked me.

"She's a big reader," Uncle Roy answered.

"Then I'll bet you're going to be a writer," Nelson said.

Being a writer became synonymous, for me, with New York City (which was synonymous with Robert De Niro) and also with my assumption that I'd know more people like Nelson, who seemed filled with self-assurance. I had never met a man who wore two scarves, twined together like a twist ice cream cone—in clashing colors, no less. I was grateful that Nelson had not jumped to a more likely possibility—one I'd heard mentioned by my mother: that I should be a librarian.

Nelson came every day for a week. He'd go home and have dinner with his parents, then return. By the third night some of the novelty had worn off; we got tired of clowning around, and stopped making remarks to the handheld camera. We tuned him out as we did homework, watched TV, or talked on the phone. When Gramma Abby called from Fort Lauderdale, she was surprised to learn that a film student was in Roy's house. She acted like I was slow-witted and didn't realize Nelson must be a boarder. Nelson filmed and recorded as I explained to her that he lived in New York, and had decided to come to our house to show people how ordinary, yet exceptional, a typical American family could be. (He had told me this, drawing invisible quotation marks in the air around *typical.*) I had begun to keep a journal, which I planned to turn into a novel when I was more mature. Renny had demonstrated how flags were used in various military exercises in Greece, marching back and forth with tennis balls held atop his shoes with rubber bands, a down vest pulled over his pajamas.

The house seemed empty, in spite of Gladys's reemergence, when Nelson went back to New York. When the phone rang, Renny and I raced for it, wanting to know if Nelson had been able to get a grant for a plane ticket back in March. We were delighted when the approval came through. "You don't want to get your hopes up," Roy said. "Remember, this won't be shown in a movie theater. It's a school project."

I sang in the school choir. Renny became interested in coins. Renny explained to Roy that we could not do our assignments without a computer. Roy bought us one to share, saying that he knew nothing about them and to please not ask him to help us. In the same way Gladys disappeared when either Nelson or the vacuum appeared, Roy passed by quickly when he saw the screen glowing.

Soon afterward, Renny and Nelson began e-mailing. Renny was RennywhenUR. Nelson was Nelfilm@nyu.edu. Nelson reported primarily on his love life: a triangle with two women who were only sort of friends (one pretended to be friendly in order to gather information, then stabbed her friend in the back). Pru was pretty, Janine plain. My mother had explained to me that *plain* was a euphemism for *ugly*. I explained that to Renny, who involved me in his e-mailing. He wrote Nelson that I was in concert choir because the only alternative had been drama club, which I'd joined, and then been selected only to play a butterfly in one production, and as the understudy for another, in which I would have been an old woman with a broom who opens a door. He told him things about Uncle Roy: that he'd given up smoking, but was biting his nails to the quick. He told him I wanted to live in New York, but he wanted to go to the desert (he hated the cold). Nelfilm e-mailed back about Pru and Janine. Pru had a good body, but was a bitch who said she wanted to have sex, then didn't show up; Janine had ham-butt thighs and was obsessed with Pru's perfection, though she sneered at Pru's having had a nose job and hinted that if Pru took the subway instead of walking, she'd gain weight instantly. Janine showed up (inevitably late), but accused Nelson of really caring only for Pru. Janine was too defensive; Pru was insecure. Both of them were ballbusters. We were amazed when it was revealed that all three of them, in their clothes, got in Nelson's bed and drank a giant margarita they sipped from the pitcher, Pru licking the rim to reapply salt, Janine poking her foot out of the covers to have Nelson apply polish, which she requested that Pru blow on.

To hear Nelson tell it, they'd get into these situations with no forethought, and just happen to have margarita mix and special salt, while Janine carried a bottle of Ming Dynasty Red wherever she went (in this case, her father's apartment. He let her stay there when he was in Denmark). They drank his liquor, watered down the bottle, smoked marijuana, said sarcastically funny things about one another's deficiencies; they switched locales not only from downtown to uptown, but as far as Stowe, Vermont, where they built a snowman they carried into their friend's ski chalet, taking the shower curtain off its hooks to protect the antique rug they had sex on, in front of the melting snowman. We also learned of a blow job in the ladies' room at Kennedy airport, as a cleaning woman worked her way up the stalls, singing in Spanish.

I think we stopped telling Nelson about our lives because we realized they were dull. We were embarrassed to ask for details of things we didn't understand. We were also embarrassed to be reading them in each other's presence. Sometimes when Renny turned on the computer and opened one of Nelson's messages, I could tell from the check mark he'd already read it. He'd leave me alone and pretend to have something to do in the other room. For a while we tried to think of nasty things to report about everyone, because if we couldn't talk about our nonexistent sexual exploits, at least we could be cruel. But it was difficult to keep imagining bad things. Our schoolwork took a lot of time, and we still had the habit of walking Gladys together, at night, and we also worried—at least, I did—that our nasty streaks might stain us. Then Renny got pneumonia. He was hospitalized for several days and nobody looked at e-mail for a week; when we did, it was obvious that Nelson had gone over the top. There were more than sixty messages waiting, many of them very long, growing more and more insistent that we respond, because we owed him that. He'd spent a lot of time enlightening us. He'd thought we were his friends. The last few turned accusatory: we were losers, unsophisticated kids who couldn't handle the truth about adult life. Even Pru sneered at us—or Nelson pretending to write as Pru. We figured that out.

We were amazed that someone who had been our friend could turn against us so viciously, just because he'd misread our silence. Renny ripped up the list he'd been keeping of words he hadn't understood. I was disgusted when Nelson said Renny was a limp dick who'd probably spend the rest of his life trying to hump Gladys, though when I look back at my diary, I realize that I had no idea that *hump* meant intercourse; I'd thought it had something to do with Renny's grabbing Gladys's haunches when her body seemed to go in two directions as she tried to hold on to a ball. Renny thought we should say something about the whole bizarre (as we now understood) exchange to Roy.

"Enough! You need rest!" Roy finally said, and we all but did a body block, fearing he might see what was on the screen. I stood by the printer in case he had any curiosity about its spewing pages. But Roy (we'd told Nelson that Roy was cannibalistic, gnawing his own flesh from the fingers up) only seemed concerned we had so much homework, and the e-mails made us think of him by contrast as blessedly levelheaded, rather than an old fogy. In one of the last messages, Pru said that if we stopped corresponding, we would experience phantom pain. She wrote at length about Viet vets who couldn't sleep at night, tortured by the pain of their scorched, amputated feet, or their aching missing arms. In a message that started out chiding, she ended up saying she could send out bad vibes to bring down cowards.

What do you imagine? That somehow, perversely, she was right? That something awful happened? Gladys hit by a car? Roy found out and called Gramma Abby and we were gone from his house like sand blown down a beach?

Those things didn't happen. After Pru's dismissal of us as "fuck-faces," the messages ended. Roy came home with a box of éclairs. Gladys, on her leash, walked at heel. Renny's cough did not turn out to be a recurrence of pneumonia. In the spring concert, I sang a capella, with the other altos, "The Pasture," adapted from a poem by Robert Frost. Roy clapped. Renny got an exciting new book about Roman coins. After another week or so, Renny said, walking home from school, "It's over." It reassured me. We still sat side by side to sign on to e-mail, but we stopped holding our breath. Every junk e-mail was a relief. Renny pressed "delete" and "delete" and "delete." He got permission to order another book about numismatics by the author of the library book on Roman coins. I rarely thought about Nelson. When I came into the room, Renny was never e-mailing. Take the rest of this story as a report from a would-be fiction writer. Like any story worth telling, it isn't easily paraphrased. But don't worry: Roy never found out; Renny married into a big Southern family the year he graduated from Duke. He still collects coins and flies an American flag from the front porch in Savannah, where, for many years, he has created artwork in his workshop. He is president of a Nations-Bank. Gladys lived to be thirteen, having eaten scrambled eggs the morning she died in her sleep, her favorite toy, the SS *Uncle Roy,* clamped under her chin.

You will realize that I have omitted mention of myself.

In August 2003 I was on my first trip to Paris, engaged to a man named Steven whom I'd met at a deli in New York, whose older sister had married a Parisian. We were staying with them in the Fifth in a sunny apartment with speckled glass vases on the deep windowsill. The vases had curling lips that looked like cresting waves, and it seemed as if confetti were mixed into the water. They were the ugliest thing I had ever seen: Murano glass, I learned. Perhaps ugly, but coveted by many, including my future brother-in-law.

The next day I would fly to New York and my fiancé would go to Chicago; he had decided to start law school and eventually join the family practice in Evanston. I would put things from our New York student housing into storage, room with a friend in midtown to save money, and fly to Chicago on the weekends, while I finished my MFA at Columbia. In the years I'd already spent there, I'd thought of Nelson a few times, but the evil spell was long broken. The episode had not been important enough to tell Steven about.

Another American couple, Charlie and Annette, had been invited to dinner at Steven's sister's apartment. Charlie was in a program in Paris as an apprentice to a museum curator; his much nicer girlfriend, Annette, was flaxen-haired and had a shy smile; she wore dangling turquoise earrings and pale lipstick and looked like a model from my mother's generation. She was up on everything: what was in the museums; the new fashions; books that were being discussed.

It came up in conversation that Annette's sister was the assistant manager of a café a few blocks from where I planned to live when I returned to the States. Her sister, she said, was the creative force behind the place: she had added magazine racks up front and changed the music. Annette's best friend worked at *Vogue* and had gotten the place mentioned. The ficus had been removed, a piece of sculpture moved in. For a while, we were caught in a whirlwind of detail: the sculptor's work had been selected for the Whitney Biennial, making Annette's sister look prescient. "You have to meet her," Annette said, writing on the back of her boyfriend's card: "Café Risqué, 134 E. 66th Street." In block letters: "PRUDENCE WINTER."

It was Pru's name; Pru, Nelson's girlfriend.

"Did she go to NYU?" I asked, already knowing the answer.

Yes! Did I know her?

"No. I just remember the name. I knew somebody who knew her."

In the Murano glass, bits of color seemed to swarm upward, like fish at feeding time.

It wasn't really surprising that so many years after I'd stared at a computer screen and realized I was dealing with a crazy person, I'd met someone who had a close connection to Nelson Crawford. Would I look up Pru when I returned to New York? I must have looked perplexed: Annette touched one of her blue, blue earrings to still it, as if it had been moving, as if pretty jewelry was responsible for diverting my attention.

On a September morning two days after I'd returned, still jet-lagged, I walked to Café Risqué and took a seat. A young waitress came up immediately. I ordered a cappuccino, hoping that Pru was working that day. When an Englishman and a stylish older woman crossed in front of my table, Pru suddenly appeared with a menu. She did not resemble her sister. She had mousy brown hair and was a small, ordinary woman dressed in de rigueur New York black. Dark-rimmed, square glasses. Bangs, which accentuated her already magnified eyes. She looked tired, on a rainy day. I smiled as she started to leave me a menu. "Pru," I said. It wasn't a question.

"Yes?" she said, turning back.

"I knew Nelson Crawford," I said.

Pru's sister, to my surprise, had told her nothing about me. What I'd said to Annette had been sketchy: only that I'd known a friend of her sister's. I'd let her assume that the friend had spoken warmly of Pru. I started to feel uneasy about what I was doing in the café. In part it must have been because I was still recovering from one of those evenings everyone has experienced—people wanting to connect; everyone's love of coincidence, as if it added magic to the world.

The day after Steven and I had flown back, separately, he'd called and said he wanted to rethink our engagement. What he really said was "I don't think we connect. You're always preoccupied. I took you to Paris to meet my sister, and all you could talk about was their taste in glassware. What am I supposed to think? That it's just a writerly approach to life? I think we need to rethink our commitment."

Pru was standing there, staring at me. Finally she picked up a blue metal chair across from me. I had the funny feeling, because of the way she gripped it, that she might raise it, lion-tamer style. In my experience, women tended to pull chairs back, rather than lift them. "You know Nelson," she said. "And why did you come here?"

"I met Annette in Paris." I added: "I'm a little jet-lagged," as if saying something truthful might allow us to start again.

"*Annette* thought I might like to meet a friend of Nelson's?"

"I guess . . . I'm not really sure his name came up."

From her reaction, I understood that I was about as welcome as the rain.

"You're here because he fucked you over," she said. "Obviously, that's why you're here."

"I don't know why I'm here. Because I met your sister, and . . . because my fiancé ended our engagement. By phone. Just the night before last."

She looked confused, but then, so was I. She fidgeted with the ends of her hair. She said again, as if prompting me, "Nelson fucked you over."

"I guess."

"You *guess*?"

"Well, I was twelve years old. In Minneapolis. He came to

make a film about my cousin and me. In Minneapolis," I heard myself repeating. "It was 1992. Would that be right?"

"Right for *what*?" she said.

I crumpled. I said, "I don't really know why I felt like I had to meet you. I happened to meet—"

"*A twelve-year-old!*" she said. "What kind of film?"

"It never got finished," I said. It was the first time I'd realized that was so.

"Oh yeah? Well, the one of me did, but it didn't exactly get distributed. My father got a lawyer. Nelson ended up plea-bargaining himself into a hospital in Connecticut. He'd tied me up and filmed me for twenty four hours, like he was Andy Warhol and I was the Empire State Building. When he got out, he wasn't allowed to contact me. A rather destructive person, I'd say. You talked to Annette about this?"

I shook my head no.

"Nineteen ninety-two?" she said. "Is that what you said? How interesting that I was still in his thoughts two years after they let him out. Those Connecticut hospitals are nothing if not liberal. Detox, and they think it's the same thing as recovery."

"Could you help me?" the woman from the kitchen said. She had a dish towel over her shoulder. One hand was covered in something sticky.

"Excuse me," Pru said. "But don't pretend to yourself he didn't fuck you over," she said over her shoulder, by way of good bye.

I stood and took my damp raincoat from the back of the chair, put it on, and smoothed it, though it retained its unpleasant shapelessness. Of course Pru's information had upset me: it confirmed that Renny and I had had the misfortune of meeting a crazy person, and the good luck to have escaped him.

Some of Nelson's words came back to me. Dirty words. Slang I'd never heard for parts of the body. Nelson had e-mailed Renny that he should try what he called "a few tricks" with me. I could remember my cousin's red face, his legs jumping nervously.

I walked a couple of blocks before I realized I hadn't paid for my cappuccino. As if to atone, I went into a Starbucks and ordered another coffee, saying the magic words to have it delivered to me in the biggest cup, with just the right combination of low-fat milk and my favorite flavoring. It was probably a bad idea to be drinking a sweet, caffeinated beverage when I was suffering from jet lag, I realized. I put my hand on my stomach and had an image of the melting snowman from years before: another Nelson legend, or lie: the snowman that would eventually be nothing more than its jaunty scarf and a carrot nose and button eyes. Though Nelson might also have invented a more original snowman, I thought, walking quickly across the street, against the light. The jet lag persisted, and by the next morning I'd convinced myself that my life was a mess. I began to think of calling Roy and telling him all about the game Nelson had played with us, even though Roy had recently been ill with complications from diabetes. I told myself that I should go to Minneapolis to visit, though I knew the real reason for that wouldn't be concern for my uncle, but to purge myself by giving him information on the chance it might make me feel better. I knew better than to do it.

A story: a woman finds herself in Savannah, Georgia, her older cousin seated at the end of an elegant, bird's-eye maple table. He is a flag-flying Republican businessman whose life seems as pleasant as it is incomprehensible: a man whom she nevertheless loves. Also at the table are his nice wife, a daughter, an au pair, and a man (Renny's friend), recently divorced, who often eats there.

Behind her back, it is whispered that the woman seems unhappy and a little on edge. If she was aware that her cousin's daughter was throwing a ball against the side of the garage, why did she jump out of her seat on a random thunk? Like the rest of the world, the woman had a difficult childhood. Her father left before she was born. She never knew him, but she was always

aware of him: his absence made him constantly present. In philosophy class at Columbia—which philosopher was it?—she
perked up when she heard that a thing can be known by what it is
not. She decided that adulthood had to do with not being a child.
She has no religious beliefs to sustain her (an area neglected by
her agnostic uncle, who raised her). Until recently, she had been
engaged to an (apparently) immature man who broke off their
engagement.

Dialogue: "Don't you be silly, honey. That Steven wasn't worthy of you. What would you want with a lawyer who was going to
sit in his daddy's lap all his life? People make jokes about lawyers.
Come on down South. We love you."

The woman tells her cousin's wife a story, beginning at a rather
unlikely place: a New York café, in the rain. She segues into pointless detail about her raincoat. She believes the material actually
absorbs water. The raincoat is a shapeless thing, and she needs to
replace it. (Does she, or does she not, realize that she is saying
she's no longer comfortable in her own skin?)

In childhood, she and her cousin Renny became involved in
an e-mail correspondence with a would-be filmmaker who was
previously hospitalized for mental problems. The man burdened
them with provocative (and, she now understands, untrue) stories
about his sexual exploits. E-mail was a good medium for such
provocation. She and Renny had also tried on various attitudes
simply because they seemed to be sent into space. Technically,
they could be retrieved, reread . . . but really, they'd tried on different identities because e-mail existed to be used that way. For a
while, they'd felt grown-up. They'd liked the thrill of scandal. A
prolonged secret had been told to them; by implication, they must
keep it.

Flip forward: Paris. The woman learns that a woman in New
York may be the clue to a puzzle that was not so much missing a
piece as missing the entire picture, so to speak.

New York. The woman meets one of the e-mailer's purported

girlfriends. Though one is rarely able to question people who appear in stories, she is able to ask questions. Did they pile into bed together and drink? No. Did he ever have sex with her in an airport? Well—who hasn't? But in this case . . . no.

So what, exactly, does this explain? Whatever the game had been, one player ended up winning, completing college with honors, marrying, moving to Savannah, having a daughter, while the other's life remained unfocused.

One night she goes downstairs and takes a sip of scotch from the bottle in the liquor cabinet and remembers this: Nelson and the girls in someone's house . . . their having watered the liquor. The specifics come back: it was a ski chalet. She pours another shot, then waters the Cutty Sark, the water from the faucet twining down thinly. She sits at the kitchen table and cries. She has on her cousin's wife's nightgown, warmer than anything she brought with her. This part of the South has been having a cold spell. The nightgown is flannel, lace-trimmed. She wipes her tears with the hem and is disgusted to see that her mascara has rubbed off on the material. She feels like she's melting into a dark smudge. She hears footsteps on the stairs. Her cousin comes downstairs for a drink of water. His face is flushed. He is surprised to see her. She can tell that he's just had sex with his wife. "You're just not present," her fiancé had said to her on the phone. Who can be totally present on the phone? She has no idea what he was talking about. When they were apart, they spoke every day. She always held his hand.

She gets Steven's number from information and calls but hangs up, though he probably has caller ID. She starts eating again. Before the trip, eating had been neglected. Soon she has trouble buttoning her jeans. She has no faith in her writing talent. She looks at herself in the mirror, straight-on, and realizes she is unphotogenic. Her eyes seem glazed, unseeing, the way Gladys's did when they teased her by holding her up to a mirror and trying to make her look at herself.

She sleeps with her cousin's friend the next night, knowing

she's just biding time, that she will leave and break his heart. (She does. That is not the story.)

Alone with Renny (now called Reginald), she brings up the subject of Pru. He listens, but from his response she understands that he has not been focusing on various details of Pru's life, but rather his own. She worries this may be because she was not a good storyteller; that she had trouble animating Pru, who, after all, did not spend her entire life in bed, bottoming out. He interrupts, and says that what Nelson did was "exploitation." He calls it, "Exploitation, pure and simple." He views the e-mails as analogous to pornography shown to an unsuspecting viewer. He points out that in their sheltered world, they'd had no idea their uncle was gay. He presents them as having been naive children who bonded as they put up a brave front about how little they meant to their parents. Bitterly, he says that his mother could have visited, but chose not to. At the same time he went to Roy's, she took up with a man. He knows little about her subsequent life: his sister left the moment she could, when she turned eighteen; his mother and her boyfriend had a dog that bit a child and had to be put down. Saying this pleases him—perhaps because it makes Gladys shine by comparison.

If Renny assumed she knew Roy was gay, she hadn't. As so often happens, someone says something in passing, assuming the other person knows. But she'd never taken the overview, or the long view (and she is supposed to be a writer?). Had Renny not spoken, Roy would have remained their slightly eccentric uncle.

Renny pours them each a vodka on the rocks with a splash of tonic. She is surprised to realize that she has a preference about what she drinks. She wishes he'd poured scotch. She notices that his hand trembles as he holds a lemon to cut it. He squeezes juice into his glass, makes a cut in the other section, and gently pushes it onto the rim of her glass so she can squeeze it herself. Right:

they were raised by a gay man, and Renny picked up some of his mannerisms.

Taking their drinks, they go to the attic. She has asked to see it many times. Renny converted the space: gleaming oak floor; massive workbench; horizontal files. A section walled off: his darkroom. She peeks in. A red light shines dimly. There is a not-unpleasant chemical smell. Outside, a loose-pelvised-Elvis clock hangs on the wall, legs doing a metronome swing. A clock is attached to the stomach: 11 p.m. They sip their drinks. It is quiet. Everyone asleep.

He gestures to a rocking chair. He sits in a wicker chair with a bulging back. He says his friend introduced him to a woman who runs a gallery in Atlanta, who wants to give him a show in the spring, though (artists always say this) he is nowhere near ready (*RennywhenUR*). They discuss what visual art can do that writing can not, and vice versa. For a moment she thinks he is going to ask how things went when she went out with his friend, but he does not. There is a Balthus poster framed and hung on the wall: a girl in profile before a mirror.

"I want to see something you've done," she says. She can hear the pout in her voice.

He tries to change the subject. He is like Steven: she seems to be on one track, he on another. He seems to want her to admire the space. It is as though she's there for an architectural tour. She walks to the window, but there is no view. She can make out the outline of a gym set in the side yard, but only because she knows it's there. The trees are pale in the night. She looks down on a willow. She likes willows. She once had a children's book about a girl with an enormous comb who combed a willow's hair. She has no idea what Renny photographs. She teases him: he's read many of her rough drafts (she never finishes anything: what else could she have shown him?), so fair is fair. Another irrelevant late-night memory: one of the witches in *Macbeth,* saying, "Fair is foul and foul is fair." What line follows? Renny is saying how embarrassed he is, because for so long he hadn't realized what artistry was involved in developing and printing your own film. He had delegated the printing to a stranger. As a young man, he'd thought photography had to do with subject matter.

"Show me something," she says. "Don't you trust me?"

"Why wouldn't I trust you?" he says.

He gets up and opens the door of an under-the-counter refrigerator. So: he keeps a bottle of vodka in the attic. He cracks little cubes out of a blue plastic tray, asking silently, by raising an eyebrow, if she wants more. Roy had done that, in the morning, in Minneapolis, holding a box of cereal.

Renny goes to a horizontal file. "Well?" he says. "The great moment of discovery is here."

All at once, she is holding what seems to be a photograph of the prow of a ship, waves lashing the sides. An old photograph, fragile, on yellowed paper, that she must hold so gently, most of her energy goes into being careful. She balances it lightly, carefully, on her fingertips. Another is placed on top: rigging, with a skeletal shred of flag hanging from a mast. Obviously, he is showing her things he admires. Things that inspired him. There are two photographs of the ship's deck and . . . coiled rope. The next photograph shows, in close-up, a hand grasping a rope. The hand is burned. Bruised? There are more photographs on paper worn and stained, with tattered edges. She holds the pile gingerly, as if someone has placed delicate flowers in her hands. In the next photograph a broken ship is nosed into a beach, slabs of wood peeling, a gash in its side. Looking at the background, she tries to guess where the battered ship is beached. The next ones are heavily damaged: torn; a stain obliterating most of the picture. Renny leans in. These seem to interest him more. As if putting down the trump card, he places the last one on top: a sea chest amid scattered coins, covered with seaweed and barnacles. There are tiny holes in the paper. Rot? Silverfish?

"Sepia-toned," he says. "They're printed on endpapers from old books. The boat's a model. I rubbed some of the prints in my armpit and put them in the sun. Not a technique you'll find in 'Hints from Heloise.' My daughter took her first steps across some of these. I started out with old postcards of seascapes and fooled around with filters. I finally realized I could create environments that were much more convincing than the backdrops I'd been using. It's called exploration art. I wish I'd gotten there first, but I'm not the only one working this territory."

She looks at him. He has to be putting her on.

"That's my hand," he says. "Why do you look so surprised? Did you think only women knew how to use makeup? You realize that a photograph like this one never would have been taken back then—right? Pictures were for documentation. They had nothing to do with *art*."

She waits to see if he's kidding.

"This one—" he says, warming to the subject. "The oars are chopsticks, roughed up and stained with dirty motor oil. The waves are a mixture of whipped cream and shaving foam. I turn on the fan over there—" He gestures across the shining floor.

She puts the photographs on the workbench and carefully flips back to his hand, manipulated to express pain. She has no idea what to say. He is correct in saying that the only human form—the anachronistic close-up—is in this one photograph. There is not even a picture of the boat in its entirety.

"Is it part of the game not to tell people you're putting them on? Do you present these as documents of a real voyage?"

"What forger would make money if it couldn't be spent?" he says.

"Renny, this is *incredible*," she says.

"A lot of work goes into it," he says. She is not sure if he makes the comment to temper her praise, or if he says it to refute her.

Pru and I took Amtrak to Philadelphia to see Janine. She and Janine didn't phone or write letters, though every now and then one would buy a funny item that reminded her of something they'd seen or done in the old days and mail it to the other without comment, Pru had told me.

Pru altered the pattern by sending Janine a note saying we wanted to take her to lunch.

We met at a restaurant near the store where Janine repaired electronic equipment. She wore a blue dress and had a tightly belted, small waist she was proud of, but her hourglass figure spread into wide hips and thick legs. It was highly doubtful that she'd ever been a ballbuster, though perhaps attractiveness was not a prerequisite. Her girlfriend was there with her. Brynn was also heavy, though her weight was more evenly distributed. Her arms had the definition of someone who worked out seriously. She made little eye contact and spoke in meaningless pleasantries. If she sensed Janine had something to say, she stopped midsentence.

The subject did not turn to Nelson until the coffee was brought. I had spaced out a little, listening to the upbeat Muzak version of "Imagine," when I heard Pru saying that when she and I met, I'd provided what she called "an interesting addendum" to the time they'd spent with Nelson: he'd told me and my cousin increasingly bizarre tales, she explained, assigning them degrading roles in his invented sex life.

"Who's Nelson?" Brynn said.

"This guy we knew at NYU a million years ago," Janine said dismissively. "Hey: we figured out he was a jerk and put him behind us, right? But"—she turned to me—"Nelson got in touch with you?"

"This was years ago. When she was a *child*," Pru said.

"In Minneapolis," I said. "I was living with my uncle. Nelson came to make a movie about our family—my cousin and my uncle and me. Actually, that sounds strange now that I say it. Why would he pick us, when he knew so many other people in town?"

"Go figure," Brynn said.

"I guess we were a little unconventional. Being raised by an

uncle." As I spoke, I was flooded with affection for Roy. I remembered the privilege of being in the garage with him, late at night,
on a winter night: the space heaters roaring, the clusters of dried
berries and ferns, the summer flowers he'd hung upside down to
dry from the ceiling beams. A cook's kitchen of delicacies, had
they been edible.

"You know what's perfectly clear to me now?" Pru said. "Nelson just didn't like women. And back then, I guess that seemed
like a challenge. Remember your old Pontiac, Janine? We were
always driving him around, telling him his ideas were so cool. So
he repaid us by using us as fodder for his fantasies."

"All you can do is move on." Brynn shrugged.

"I had sex with him exactly once," Pru said. "Midway through
a film he was making of me."

"What can you do, hon?" Brynn said. "You move on."

"I guess what I was saying was that I felt manipulated," Pru
said. "What's a worse word—*manipulated* or *humiliated*? He was
pretty much responsible for my flunking out of school. I've never
gotten things back on track with my mother. You move on, but
people's shit hurts you."

"Exploitation," I said, echoing what Renny had said in Savannah. "Like rape," I said. "Telling those things to my cousin and
me, making us the audience for his mean-spirited fantasies."

Pru looked at me. "Are you crazy?" she said. "E-mailing a bunch
of crap wasn't the same thing as somebody forcing himself on you.
You could have turned off the machine. You weren't helpless."

It was obvious what she'd said. I had the terrible feeling that
she had heard it herself, too. It was even obvious to Brynn, who
could not manage one more banal word.

Janine put her hand on Pru's arm. "It was a long time ago," she
said. "You're okay."

"Then if I'm so okay, why don't you ever get in touch with me?
How come my only friend is somebody my sister, who lives in
another country, sent around to meet me? I never went back to

school. I'm never going to get a decent job. I just have to pretend it's great to carry plates, and every now and then I get to make a brilliant suggestion, like 'Why don't we have a magazine rack?'" Her voice broke on *magazine*.

The Muzak continued, but whatever song it was was unrecognizable, it had been so denatured. Janine raised a finger, as if she could read my mind and wanted to tell me the song's title, but of course she was summoning the waiter for the bill.

That night, back in the city, worried about Pru, I spent the night on her couch. The things you discovered when you went on a fact-finding expedition, oblivious to your own self-absorption. *Your* past; *your* pain. What I'd found out about was Pru. Who had been right to take me to task when I'd made a self-serving analogy, presenting myself as more helpless than I'd been.

All those years missing Gladys—all those years of missing *us*—and not long after Roy decided to take another chance, not long after he came back from the pound with a beagle mix, he died. He threw a stick, the dog tore off after it and returned to Roy, who'd fallen to the grass. The neighbor saw it all.

Except for people from the neighborhood, and a few people from the company he'd retired from, except for Roy's dentist's assistant, whose bottom lip quivered when she offered her condolences, and Elizabeth Brown, the former boarder, who flew in from Phoenix, everyone at the funeral was male. Nelson's mother rushed over at the reception afterward to introduce herself. "My Nelson had the best time of his life getting to know the people in your household," she said. "Roy, and you, and your cousin. Oh, Roy was one in a million. When Nelson wanted to make a film about real people, *regular* people, I knew just where to send him. I said, 'Nelson, why wouldn't you make a film about people in New York City?' and he said, 'They don't make eye contact in New York City. The way that city works is that everybody steers clear of everybody else.' Well: it sounds funny, but I think maybe he was right. I've had a wonderful life in Minneapolis, supported by warm, helpful people, and I'm not so sure decent people do behave that way elsewhere. Such good friends. Such helpful people."

Someone had put one of Roy's wreaths on a stand beside the food table. Where a portrait might have sat, there was a large wreath decorated with Roy's trademark dried berries and silver-sprayed acorns. Even though I wouldn't look at her, Mrs. Crawford wouldn't let me go. "Do you know what I thought, when I heard you were coming?" she said. "I thought, you've *got* to show her that picture." She opened her handbag and removed an over-exposed picture from an envelope. I might have given the photograph only a cursory glance if not for the presence of Gladys in the foreground, costumed in a nurse's cape, head hung in shame.

"My Nelson!" she said. "He certainly did like that Polar Bear Club. And look here: that's your uncle." Indeed it was. A sailor's hat was tipped on Roy's head, and he wore the same striped bathing trunks as the others, with the logo of a polar bear's head at the hem. His hand was draped around the shoulder of the almost faceless young man next to him. Next came Nelson, no sillier than the others in his long scarf . . . no: two scarves, intertwined. It was a black-and-white photograph, but I remembered the colors as being red and pink, and that there had been a time in my life when I'd thought that one of the brashest and most wonderful things I'd ever seen. I also remembered the story of the melting snowman, which we'd been told had been attired in a scarf. . . . Nelson had e-mailed Renny that he and I should play the strip-poker snowman game, and we had both been scandalized. The final figure in the picture, of course, standing a little apart from the others, was Renny.

She rattled on: "You were your uncle's favorite. If a man has a fondness for a lady, no one else can come close. My husband, God rest his soul, he passed a year ago, he said to me, 'Nelson's my boy, but you're number one in my life.' Parents aren't supposed to say things like that, but it's true, you know."

The way the woman was compulsively talking suddenly infuriated me. Did she have any idea what she was saying—did this woman have any idea of *anything*?

It wasn't just that I'd been excluded, but that I hadn't had a clue. How many times had Renny gone swimming with the Polar Bear Club? He'd never mentioned it, ever.

"So—did Nelson ever get a movie made?" I heard myself asking, with a real edge in my voice.

"Oh, *yes*. He did a film that was shown at Sundance about migratory workers. It was a big success. It upsets me that people don't keep in touch with their friends. Why did you say your cousin wasn't at the funeral?"

"Hello!" I called to the dentist's assistant, whom I'd met before the service began. She was uncomfortable being there, awkward. She looked startled that, having only met me briefly, I was now calling out to her as if she were my dearest friend. "Excuse us," I muttered, drifting away. The girl looked at me, wide-eyed: we were rudely turning our backs on an old lady.

"This photograph is for you!" Mrs. Crawford called. "Nelson would have been here today, but he's with a film crew in Nepal."

"Nepal," the girl said, letting the word itself transport her.

"You'll never get there, or anywhere else, if we don't get away from that woman," I said, steering her toward a table where there was a punch bowl and food.

"Oh, I'm really sorry . . . this is the first funeral I've ever been to. Dr. Richardson asked me to come because he was out of town. I don't really know what I should do."

"Avoid old windbags," I said.

A man ladling punch extended a glass, pretending he hadn't heard me.

"If I'd stayed another second, I'd have told her my opinion of her son the filmmaker," I huffed.

The girl looked at me. She had no idea what the story was, but she picked up on the undercurrent. She said gently, "You're okay."

It took me whizzing back to Philadelphia. To Janine's hand on Pru's arm. To Pru, crying on the train. I went back in time to the night I'd spent on her couch, and how useless I'd felt, how guilty that what I really wanted was to drift off to sleep . . . really: What could I do for Pru, after the fact? Then, that summer, the café was sold, and after that she got involved with the soon-to-be-famous sculptor, then discovered he was still secretly seeing his ex-wife. She got a job, but quit after the first day, returning to her apartment and her CDs that had provided the café's background music; all she would do was lie in bed listening to the sad ones. She knew this was upsetting me, but she wasn't about to snap out of it because I wanted her to. After a couple of weeks I stopped going there and phoned instead, but things were never the same, and after a while I realized that things had worked out to her satisfaction. If I disappeared, she wouldn't have to deal with what I knew about her, and she wouldn't have to feel embarrassed in my presence.

"Are you feeling better?" the girl asked. She held a cup of punch. She took a sip. "I know what that's like, feeling like you're cornered," she said. "Sometimes patients talk and talk and they don't want to let you go. They tell you all this stuff because they're really nervous, sitting in the chair."

She was nice. I could imagine the report she'd make to the dentist about Roy's niece, who was jumping out of her skin, desperate to get away from some old lady.

Or maybe it wasn't all that bad for her. She might have felt proud that she'd done what was expected of her, she might go home, kick off her shoes, not think much of anything about where she'd been, how the people—not just me: the people—had been. Gay men. That was who constituted most of the people.

That night in the attic, in Savannah, Renny realized he'd caught me by surprise, but he wouldn't embarrass me further by letting on. He was adept: the same Renny who'd clicked on e-mails and left, leaving me to consider them in private.

He'd done the same gentlemanly thing in detaching himself from his own life. If it was too late and too unlikely to be one kind of explorer, he'd set off on a different kind of voyage—one that he'd record, then (how true) say that he wasn't ready for a show. His wife thought that he was photographing dried flowers. She'd mentioned to me that she'd gone upstairs and seen dried flowers from the garden on the worktable. Implied in her statement had been a question that went unanswered, though I came to find out why they were there. As Renny explained to me that night, certain parts were useful for the ship: leaves as miniature hulls; a white anemone petal the perfect sail; aperture stopped down, filter fogged with hair spray.

He'd taken a fantastic trip—no more or less than travelers do every day—but then, no different from many people who have been hurt, he ironized it. "Real" pictures of "real" trips (Nelson: the air-drawn quotation marks around the word *typical*) . . . other photographers who'd done something similar had their work in museums: Harvard had faked exploration art in its collection, he'd told me. Before we went downstairs, he'd said, "Do you know who Captain Lawrence E. G. Oates was? Okay—he's hardly a household name. He was a captain who went on an expedition to the South Pole, and he got frostbite, and he knew he was going to die, and that he'd be a burden to everyone because he wouldn't die quickly. So he took his leave from the party with what came to be a famous line. At least, a famous line if you'd ever heard the story of Captain Lawrence E. G. Oates. He said, 'I'm just going out now, and I may be some time.'"

A writer's interest would be in Oates's thoughts as the snow hit his face. A good writer could make up anything. You'd assume it would involve fear; or Oates might feel a heavy resignation, in contrast to the filmy snow. Something unexpected might happen— something that would shake him from his own resolve and make him laugh on his way to his speeded-up death. Things—whole lives; details—could get clarified, or complicated, which in this case (for once) would amount to the same thing, since there would be the same amount of time to sort things out.

The wind must have been the reality. A paradoxical wind, real and metaphoric (whether Oates wanted it to be or not), that froze his face into a self-indulgent smile, or into a more predictable frown. As long as the writer made it credible, the reader would feel the cold. The wind was in the hands of the writer. It could be the unexpected seepage of air through a skylight into an attic. The swirl of air made by a dog's tail as she thumped down for sleep. It might also be a totally benign breeze from the pages of a storybook read by a solicitous uncle that would blow the children safely on their way.

"My mother's picking me up. Would you like to stand outside with me?" the girl said.

Did I do the right thing to shake my head and let her go?

That Last
Odd Day in L.A.

KELLER went back and forth about going into Cambridge to see Lynn, his daughter, for Thanksgiving. If he went in November, he'd miss his niece and nephew, who made the trip back East only in December, for Christmas. They probably could have got away from their jobs and returned for both holidays, but they never did. The family had gathered for Thanksgiving at his daughter's ever since she moved into her own apartment, which was going on six years now; Christmas dinner was at Keller's sister's house, in Arlington. His daughter's apartment was near Porter Square. She had once lived there with Ray Ceruto, before she decided she was too good for a car mechanic. A nice man, a hard worker, a gentleman—so naturally she chose instead to live in serial monogamy with men Keller found it almost impossible to get along with. Oh, but they had white-collar jobs and white-collar aspirations: with her current boyfriend, she had recently flown to England for all of three days in order to see the white cliffs of Dover. If there had been bluebirds, they had gone unmentioned.

Years ago, Keller's wife, Sue Anne, had moved back to Roanoke, Virginia, where she now rented a "mother-in-law apartment" from a woman she had gone to school with back in the days when she and Keller were courting. Sue Anne joked that she herself had become a sort of ideal mother-in-law, gardening and taking care of the pets when her friends went away. She was happy to have returned to gardening. During the almost twenty years that she and Keller had been together, their little house in the Boston suburbs, shaded by trees, had allowed for the growth of almost nothing but springtime bulbs, and even those had to be planted in raised beds because the soil was of such poor quality. Eventually, the squirrels discovered the beds. Sue Anne's breakdown had had to do with the squirrels.

So: call his daughter, or do the more important thing and call his neighbor and travel agent, Sigrid, at Pleasure Travel, to apologize for their recent, rather uneventful dinner at the local Chinese restaurant, which had been interrupted by a thunderstorm grand enough to announce the presence of Charlton Heston, which had reminded Keller that he'd left his windows open. He probably should not have refused to have the food packed to go. But when he'd thought of having her to his house to eat the dinner—his house was a complete mess—or of going to her house and having to deal with her son's sour disdain, it had seemed easier just to bolt down his food.

A few days after the ill-fated dinner, he had bought six raffle tickets and sent them to her, in the hope that a winning number would provide a bicycle for her son, though he obviously hadn't given her a winning ticket, or she would have called. Her son's expensive bicycle had been taken at knifepoint, in a neighborhood he had promised his mother he would not ride through.

Two or three weeks before, Sigrid and Keller had driven into Boston to see a show at the MFA and afterward had gone to a coffee shop where he had clumsily, stupidly, splashed a cup of tea onto her when he was jostled by a mother with a stroller the size of an infantry vehicle. He had brought dish towels to the door of the ladies' room for Sigrid to dry herself off with, and he had even—rather gallantly, some might have said—thought to bite the end off his daily vitamin-E capsule from the little packet of multivitamins he carried in his shirt pocket and urged her to scrape the goop from the tip of his finger and spread it on the burn. She maintained that she had not been burned. Later, on the way to the car, they had got into a tiff when he said that it wasn't necessary for her to pretend that everything was fine, that he liked women who spoke honestly. "It could not have been all right that I scalded you, Sigrid," he'd told her.

"Well, I just don't see the need to criticize you over an *accident,*

Keller," she had replied. Everyone called him by his last name. He had been born Joseph Francis, but neither Joe nor Joseph nor Frank nor Francis fit.

"It was clumsy of me, and I wasn't quick enough to help," he said.

"You were fine," she said. "It would have brought you more pleasure if I'd cried, or if I'd become irrational, wouldn't it? There's some part of you that's always on guard, because the other person is sure to become *irrational*."

"You know a little something about my wife's personality," he said.

Sigrid had lived next door before, during, and after Sue Anne's departure. "So everyone's your wife?" she said. "Is that what you think?"

"No," he said. "I'm apologizing. I didn't do enough for my wife, either. Apparently I didn't act soon enough or effectively enough or—"

"You're always looking for forgiveness!" she said. "I don't forgive you or not forgive you. How about that? I don't know enough about the situation, but I doubt that you're entirely to blame for the way things turned out."

"I'm sorry," he said. "Some people say I'm too closemouthed and I don't give anyone a chance to know me, and others—such as you or my daughter—maintain that I'm self-critical as a ploy to keep their attention focused on me."

"I didn't say any such thing! Don't put words in my mouth. I said that my getting tea dumped on my back by accident and the no doubt very complicated relationship you had with your wife really don't—"

"It was certainly too complicated for me," Keller said quietly.

"Stop whispering. If we're going to have a discussion, at least let me hear what you're saying."

"I wasn't whispering," Keller said. "That was just the wheezing of an old man out of steam."

"Now it's your age! I should pity you for your advanced age! What age are you, exactly, since you refer to it so often?"

"You're too young to count that high." He smiled. "You're a young, attractive, successful woman. People are happy to see you walk into the room. When they look up and see me, they see an old man, and they avert their eyes. When I walk into the travel agency, they all but duck into the kneeholes of their desks. That's how we got acquainted, as you recall, since calling on one's neighbors is not the American Way. Only your radiant face met mine with a smile. Everybody else was pretending I wasn't there."

"Listen: Are you sure this is where we parked the car?"

"I'm not sure of anything. That's why I had you drive."

"I drove because your optometrist put drops in to dilate your pupils shortly before we left," she said.

"But I'm fine now. At least, my usual imperfect vision has returned. I can drive back," he said, pointing to her silver Avalon. "Too noble a vehicle for me, to be sure, but driving would be the least I could do, after ruining your day."

"Why are you saying that?" she said. "Because you're pleased to think that some little problem has the ability to ruin my day? You are being *impossible,* Keller. And don't whisper that that's exactly what your wife would say. Except that she's a fellow human being occupying planet Earth, I don't *care* about your wife."

She took her key ring out of her pocket and tossed the keys to him.

He was glad he caught them, because she sent them higher into the air than necessary. But he did catch them, and he did remember to step in front of her to hold open her door as he pushed the button to unlock the car. Coming around the back, he saw the PETA bumper sticker her husband had adorned the car with shortly before leaving her for a years-younger Buddhist vegan animal-rights activist.

At least he had worked his way into his craziness slowly, subscribing first to *Smithsonian* magazine and only later to newsletters with pictures of starved, manacled horses and pawless animals with startled eyes—material she was embarrassed to have delivered to the house. In the year before he left, he had worked at the animal-rescue league on weekends. When she told him he was becoming obsessed with the plight of animals at the expense of their marriage and their son, he'd rolled up one of his publications and slapped his palm with it over and over, protesting vehemently, like someone scolding a bad dog. As she recalled, he had somehow turned the conversation to the continued illegal importation of elephant tusks into Asia.

"You always want to get into a fight," she said, when she finally spoke again, as Keller wound his way out of Boston. "It makes it difficult to be with you."

"I know it's difficult. I'm sorry."

"Come over and we can watch some *Perry Mason* reruns," she said. "It's on every night at eleven."

"I don't stay up that late," he said. "I'm an old man."

Keller spoke to his daughter on the phone—the first time the phone had rung in days—and listened patiently while she set forth her conditions, living her life in the imperative. In advance of their speaking, she wanted him to know that she would hang up if he asked when she intended to break up with Addison (Addison!) Page. Also, as he well knew, she did not want to be questioned about her mother, even though, yes, they were in phone contact. She also did not want to hear any criticism of her glamorous life, based on her recently having spent three days in England with her spendthrift boyfriend, and also, yes, she had got her flu shot.

"This being November, would it be possible to ask who you're going to vote for?"

"No," she said. "Even if you were voting for the same candidate, you'd find some way to make fun of me."

"What if I said, 'Close your eyes and imagine either an elephant or a donkey'?"

"If I close my eyes, I see . . . I see a horse's ass, and it's you," she said. "May I continue?"

He snorted. She had a quick wit, his daughter. She had got that from him, not from his wife, who neither made jokes nor understood them. In the distant past, his wife had found an entirely humorless psychiatrist who had summoned Keller and urged him to speak to Sue Anne directly, not in figurative language or through allusions or—God forbid—with humor. "What should I do if I'm just chomping at the bit to tell a racist joke?" he had asked. The idea was of course ludicrous; he had never made a racist joke in his life. But of course the psychiatrist missed his tone. "You anticipate the necessity of telling racist jokes to your wife?" he had said, pausing to scribble something on his pad. "Only if one came up in a dream or something," Keller had deadpanned.

"I thought you were going to continue, Lynn," he said. "Which I mean as an observation, not as a reproach," he hurried to add.

"Keller," she said (since her teenage years, she had called him Keller), "I need to know whether you're coming to Thanksgiving."

"Because you would get a turkey weighing six or seven ounces more?"

"In fact, I thought about cooking a ham this year, because Addison prefers ham. It's just a simple request, Keller: that you let me know whether or not you plan to come. Thanksgiving is three weeks away."

"I've come up against Amy Vanderbilt's timetable for accepting a social invitation at Thanksgiving?" he said.

She sighed deeply. "I would like you to come, whether you believe that or not, but since the twins aren't coming from L.A., and since Addison's sister invited us to her house, I thought I might not cook this year, if you didn't intend to come."

"Oh, by all means don't cook for me. I'll mind my manners

and call fifty-one weeks from today and we'll set this up for next year," he said. "A turkey potpie from the grocery store is good enough for me."

"And the next night you could be your usual frugal self and eat the leftover packaging," she said.

"Horses don't eat cardboard. You're thinking of mice," he said.

"I stand corrected," she said, echoing the sentence he often said to her. "But let me ask you another thing. Addison's sister lives in Portsmouth, New Hampshire, and she issued a personal invitation for you to join us at her house for dinner. Would you like to have Thanksgiving there?"

"How could she issue a personal invitation if she's never met me?" he said.

"Stop it," his daughter said. "Just answer."

He thought about it. Not about whether he would go but about the holiday itself. The revisionist thinking on Thanksgiving was that it commemorated the subjugation of the Native Americans (formerly the Indians). Not as bad a holiday as Columbus Day, but still.

"I take it your silence means that you prefer to be far from the maddening crowd," she said.

"That title is much misquoted," he said. "Hardy's novel is *Far from the Madding Crowd*, which has an entirely different connotation, *madding* meaning 'frenzied.' There's quite a difference between *frenzied* and *annoying*. Consider, for instance, your mother's personality versus mine."

"You are *incredibly* annoying," Lynn said. "If I didn't know that you cared for me, I couldn't bring myself to pick up the phone and let myself in for your mockery, over and over."

"I thought it was because you pitied me."

He heard the click, and there was silence. He replaced the phone in its cradle, which made him think of another cradle— Lynn's—with the decal of the cow jumping over the moon on the headboard and blue and pink beads (the cradle manufacturer having hedged his bets) on the rails. He could remember spinning the beads and watching Lynn sleep. The cradle was now in the downstairs hallway, used to store papers and magazines for recycling. Over the years, some of the decal had peeled away, so that on last inspection only a torso with two legs was successfully making the jump over the brightly smiling moon.

He bought a frozen turkey potpie and, as a treat to himself (it was not true that he constantly denied himself happiness, as Lynn said—one could not deny what was rarely to be found), a new radio whose FM quality was excellent—though what did he know, with his imperfect hearing? As he ate Thanksgiving dinner (two nights before Thanksgiving, but why stand on formality?— a choice of Dinty Moore beef stew or Lean Cuisine vegetable lasagna remained for the day of thanks itself), he listened with pleasure to Respighi's "Pini di Roma." He and Sue Anne had almost gone to Rome on their honeymoon, but instead they had gone to Paris. His wife had just finished her second semester of college, in which she had declared herself an art history major. They had gone to the Louvre and to the Jeu de Paume and on the last day of the trip he had bought her a little watercolor of Venice she kept admiring, in a rather elaborate frame that probably accounted for the gouache's high price—it was a gouache, not a watercolor, as she always corrected him. They both wanted three children, preferably a son followed by either another son or a daughter, though if their second child was a son, then of course they would devoutly wish their last to be a daughter. He remembered with bemusement the way they had prattled on, strolling by the Seine, earnestly discussing those things that were most out of their control: Life's Important Matters.

Sue Anne conceived only once, and although they (she, to be honest) had vaguely considered adoption, Lynn remained their only child. Lacking brothers and sisters, she had been fortunate to grow up among relatives, because Keller's sister had given birth to twins a year or so after Lynn was born, and in those days the two families lived only half an hour apart and saw each other almost every weekend. Now Sue Anne and his sister Carolynne (now merely Carol), who lived in Arlington with her doctor husband (or who lived apart from him—he was forbidden to inquire about the status of their union), had not spoken for months, and the twins, Richard and Rita, who worked as stockbrokers and had never married—smart!—and shared a house in the Hollywood Hills, were more at ease with him than his own daughter was. For years Keller had promised to visit the twins, and the previous summer, Richard had called his bluff and sent him a ticket to Los Angeles. Richard and Rita had picked Keller up at LAX in a BMW convertible and taken him to a sushi restaurant where at periodic intervals laser images on the wall blinked on and off like sexually animated hieroglyphics dry-humping to a recording of "Walk Like an Egyptian." The next morning, the twins had taken him to a museum that had been created as a satire of museums, with descriptions of the bizarre exhibits that were so tongue-in-cheek he was sure the majority of people there thought that they were touring an actual museum. That night, they turned on the lights in their pool and provided him with bathing trunks (how would he have thought to pack such a thing?—he never thought of a visit to sprawling Los Angeles as a visit to a *beach*), and on Sunday they had eaten their lunch of fresh pineapple and prosciutto poolside, drinking prosecco instead of mineral water (the only beverages in the house, except for extraordinarily good red wine, as far as he could tell), and in the late afternoon they had been joined by a beautiful blonde woman who had apparently been, or might still be, Jack Nicholson's lover. Then he went with Rita and Richard to a screening (a shoot-'em-up none of them wanted to see, though the twins felt they must, because the cinematographer was their longtime client), and on Monday they had sent a car to the house so Keller wouldn't get lost trying to find his way around the freeways. It transported him to a lunch with the twins at a restaurant built around a beautiful terraced garden, after which he'd been dropped off to take the MGM tour and then picked up by the same driver—a dropout from Hollywood High who was working on a screenplay.

It was good they had bought him a ticket for only a brief visit, because if he'd stayed longer he might never have gone home. Though who would have cared if he hadn't? His wife didn't care where he lived, as long as she lived in the opposite direction. His daughter might be relieved that he had moved away. He lived where he lived for no apparent reason—at least, no reason apparent to him. He had no friends, unless you called Don Kim a friend—Don, with whom he played handball on Mondays and Thursdays. And his accountant, Ralph Bazzorocco. He supposed Bazzorocco was his friend, though with the exception of a couple of golf games each spring and the annual buffet dinner he and Bazzorocco's other clients were invited to every April 16—and except for Bazzorocco's calling to wish him a happy birthday, and "Famiglia Bazzorocco" (as the gift card always read) sending him an enormous box of biscotti and Baci at Christmas . . . oh, he didn't know. Probably that was what friendship was, he thought, a little ashamed of himself. He had gone to the hospital to visit Bazzorocco's son after the boy injured his pelvis and lost his spleen playing football. He'd driven Bazzorocco's weeping wife home in the rain so she could shower and change her clothes, then driven her, still weeping, back to the hospital. Okay: he had friends. But would any of them care if he lived in Los Angeles? Don Kim could easily find another partner (perhaps a younger man more worthy as a competitor); Bazzorocco could remain his accountant via the miracle of modern technology. In any case, Keller had returned to the North Shore.

Though not before that last odd day in L.A. He had said, though he hadn't planned to say it (Lynn was not correct in believing that everything that escaped his lips was premeditated), that he'd like to spend his last day lounging around the house. So they wouldn't feel too sorry for him, he even asked if he could open a bottle of Merlot—whatever they recommended, of course—and raid their refrigerator for lunch. After all, the refrigerator contained a tub of mascarpone instead of cottage cheese, and the fruit drawer was stocked with organic plums rather than puckered supermarket grapes. Richard wasn't so keen on the idea, but Rita said that of course that was fine. It was *Keller's* vacation, she stressed. They'd make a reservation at a restaurant out at the beach that night, and if he felt rested enough to eat out, fine; if not, they'd cancel the reservation and Richard would cook his famous chicken breasts marinated in Vidalia-onion sauce.

When Keller woke up, the house was empty. He made coffee (at home, he drank instant) and wandered out through the open doors to the patio as it brewed. He surveyed the hillside, admired the lantana growing from Mexican pottery urns flanking one side of the pool. Some magazine had been rained on—it must have rained during the night; he hadn't heard it, but then, he'd fallen asleep with earphones on, listening to Brahms. He walked toward the magazine—as offensive as litter along the highway, this copy of *Vogue* deteriorating on the green tiles—then drew back, startled. There was a small possum: a baby possum, all snout and pale narrow body, clawing the water, trying futilely to scramble up the edge of the pool. He looked around quickly for the pool net. The night before, it had been leaning against the sliding glass door, but it was no longer there. He went quickly to the side of the house, then ran to the opposite side, all the while acutely aware that the drowning possum was in desperate need of rescue. No pool net. He went into the kitchen, which was now suffused with the odor of coffee, and threw open door after door looking for a pot. He finally found a bucket containing cleaning supplies, quickly removed them, then ran back to the pool, where he dipped the bucket in, missing, frightening the poor creature and adding to its problems by making it go under. He recoiled in fear, then realized that the emotion he felt was not fear but self-loathing. Introspection was not his favorite mode, but no matter: he dipped again, leaning farther over this time, accepting the ludicrous prospect of his falling in, though the second time he managed to scoop up the possum—it was only a tiny thing—and lift it out of the water. The bucket was full, because he had dipped deep, and much to his dismay, when he saw the possum curled up at the bottom, he knew immediately that it was already dead. The possum had drowned. He set the bucket down and crouched on the tile beside it before he had a second, most welcome epiphany and realized almost with a laugh that it wasn't dead: it was playing possum. Though if he didn't get it out of the bucket, it really would drown. He jumped up, turned the bucket on its side, and stood back as water and possum flowed out. The water dispersed. The possum lay still. That must be because he was watching it, he decided, although he once more considered the grim possibility that it was dead.

He stood still. Then he thought to walk back into the house, far away from it. It was dead; it wasn't. Time passed. Then, finally, as he stood unmoving, the possum twitched and waddled off—the flicker of life in its body resonated in Keller's own heart—and then the event was over. He continued to stand there, cognizant of how much he had loathed himself just moments before. Then he went out to retrieve the bucket. As he grasped the handle, tears welled up in his eyes. What the hell! He cried at the sink as he rinsed the bucket.

He dried his eyes on the crook of his arm and washed the bucket thoroughly, much longer than necessary, then dried it with a towel. He put the Comet, the Windex, and the rag and the brush back inside and returned the bucket to its place under the sink and tried to remember what he had planned to do that day, and again he was overwhelmed. The image that popped into his mind was of Jack Nicholson's girlfriend, the blonde in the bikini with the denim shirt thrown over it. He thought . . . what? That he was going to get together with Jack Nicholson's girlfriend? Whose last name he didn't even know?

But that *had* been what he was thinking. No way to act on it, but yes—that was what he had been thinking, all along.

The water had run off, though the tiles still glistened. No sign, of course, of the possum. It was doubtless off assimilating its important life lesson. On a little redwood table was a waterproof radio that he turned on, finding the classical station, adjusting the volume. Then he unbuckled his belt and unzipped his fly, stepped out of his pants and underpants, and took off his shirt. Carrying the radio, he walked to the deep end of the pool, placed the radio on the rim, and dove in. He swam underwater for a while, and then, as his head broke the surface, he had the distinct feeling that he was being watched. He looked back at the house, then looked slowly around the pool area. The fence that walled it off from the neighbors was at least ten feet high. Behind the pool, the terrace was filled with bushes and fruit trees and pink and white irises— Keller was crazy: he was alone in a private compound; no one was there. He went under the water again, refreshed by its silky coolness, and breaststroked to the far end, where he came up for air, then used his feet to push off the side of the pool so he could float on his back. When he reached the end, he pulled himself out, then saw, in the corner of his eye, who was watching him. High up on the terrace, a deer was looking down. The second their eyes met, the deer was gone, but in that second it had come clear to him— on this day of endless revelations—that the deer had been casting a beneficent look, as if in thanks. He had felt that: that a deer was acknowledging and thanking him. He was flabbergasted at the odd workings of his brain. How could a grown man—a grown man without any religious beliefs, a father who, in what now seemed like a different lifetime, had accompanied his little daughter to *Bambi* and whispered, as every parent does, "It's only a movie," when *Bambi*'s mother was killed . . . how could a man with such knowledge of the world, whose most meaningful accomplishment in as long as he could remember had been to fish an animal out of a swimming pool—how could such a man feel unequivocally that a deer had appeared to bless him?

But he knew it had.

As it turned out, the blessing hadn't exactly changed his life, though why should one expect so much of blessings, just because they were blessings?

Something that *had* profoundly changed his life had been Richard's urging him, several years before, to take a chance, take a gamble, trust him, because the word he was about to speak was going to change his life. "Plastics?" he'd said, but Richard was too young: he hadn't seen the movie. No, the word had been *Microsoft*. Keller had been in a strange frame of mind that day (one month earlier, to the day, his father had killed himself). At that point, he had hated his job so much, had stopped telling half-truths and finally admitted to Sue Anne that their marriage had become a dead end, that he assumed he was indulging the self-destructiveness his wife and daughter always maintained was the core of his being when he turned over almost everything he had to his nephew to invest in a company whose very name suggested smallness and insubstantiality. But, as it turned out, Richard had blessed him, as had the deer, now. The blonde had not, but then, very few men, very few indeed, would ever be lucky enough to have such a woman give them her benediction.

"You're *fun!*" Rita laughed, dropping him off at LAX. On the way, he had taken off his white T-shirt and raised it in the air, saying, "I hereby surrender to the madness that is the City of Angels." It had long been Rita's opinion that no one in the family understood her uncle; that all of them were so defensive that they were intimidated by his erudition and willfully misunderstood his sense of humor. Richard was working late, but he had sent, by way of his sister (she ran back to the car, having almost forgotten the treat in the glove compartment), a tin of white-chocolate brownies to eat on the plane, along with a note Keller would later read that thanked him for having set an example when he and Rita were kids, for not unthinkingly going with the flow, and for his wry pronouncements in a family where, Richard said, everyone else was "afraid of his own shadow." "Come back soon," Richard had written. "We miss you."

Back home, on the telephone, his daughter had greeted him with a warning: "I don't want to hear about my cousins who are happy and successful, which are synonymous, in your mind, with being rich. Spare me details of their life and just tell me what you did. I'd like to hear about your trip without feeling diminished by my insignificance in the face of my cousins' perfection."

"I can leave them out of it entirely," he said. "I can say, quite honestly, that the most significant moment of my trip happened not in their company but in the meeting of my eyes with the eyes of a deer that looked at me with indescribable kindness and understanding."

Lynn snorted. "This was on the freeway, I suppose? It was on its way to be an extra in a remake of *The Deer Hunter*?"

He had understood, then, the urge she so often felt when speaking to him—the urge to hang up on a person who had not even tried to understand one word you had said.

"How was your Thanksgiving?" Sigrid asked. Keller was sitting across from her at the travel agency, arranging to buy Don Kim's stepdaughter a ticket to Germany so she could pay a final visit to her dying friend. The girl was dying of ALS. The details were too terrible to think about. Jennifer had known her for eleven of her seventeen years, and now the girl was dying. Don Kim barely made it from paycheck to paycheck. It had been necessary to tell Don that he had what he called "a considerable windfall from the eighties stock market" in order to persuade him that in offering to buy Jennifer a ticket, he was not making a gesture he could not afford. He had had to work hard to persuade him. He had to insist on it several times, and swear that in no way had he thought Don had been hinting (which was true). The only worry was how Jennifer would handle such a trip, but they had both agreed she was a very mature girl.

"Very nice," Keller replied. In fact, that day he had eaten canned stew and listened to Albinoni (probably some depressed DJ who hadn't wanted to work Thanksgiving night). He had made a fire in the fireplace and caught up on his reading of *The Economist*. He felt a great distance between himself and Sigrid. He said, trying not to sound too perfunctorily polite, "And yours?"

"I was actually . . ." She dropped her eyes. "You know, my ex-husband has Brad for a week at Thanksgiving and I have him for Christmas. He's such a big boy now, I don't know why he doesn't put his foot down, but he doesn't. If I knew then what I know now, I'd never have let him go, no matter what rights the court gave that lunatic. You know what he did before Thanksgiving? I guess you must not have read the paper. They recruited Brad to liberate turkeys. They got arrested. His father thinks that's fine: traumatizing Brad, letting him get hauled into custody. And the worst of it is, Brad's scared to death, but he doesn't dare *not* go along, and then he has to pretend to me that he thinks it was a great idea, that I'm an indifferent—" She searched for the word. "That I'm subhuman because I eat dead animals."

Keller had no idea what to say. Lately, things didn't seem funny enough to play off of. Everything just seemed weird and sad. Sigrid's ex-husband had taken their son to liberate turkeys. How could you extemporize about that?

"She could go Boston, London, Frankfurt on British Air," Sigrid said, as if she hadn't expected him to reply. "It would be somewhere around seven hundred and fifty." She hit the keyboard again. "Seven eighty-nine plus taxes," she said. "She'd be flying out at six p.m. Eastern Standard, she'd get there in the morning." Her fingers stopped moving on the keyboard. She looked at him.

"Can I use your phone to make sure that's a schedule that's

good for her?" he said. He knew that Sigrid wondered who Jennifer Kim was. He had spoken of her as "my friend, Jennifer Kim."

"Of course," she said. She pushed a button and handed him the phone. He had written the Kims' telephone number on a little piece of paper and slipped it in his shirt pocket. He was aware that she was staring at him as he dialed. The phone rang three times, and then he got the answering machine. "Keller here," he said. "We've got the itinerary, but I want to check it with Jennifer. I'm going to put my travel agent on," he said. "She'll give you the times, and maybe you can call her to confirm it. Okay?" He handed the phone to Sigrid. She took it, all business. "Sigrid Crane of Pleasure Travel, Ms. Kim," she said. "I have a British Airways flight that departs Logan at six zero zero p.m., arrival into Frankfurt by way of London nine five five a.m. My direct line is—"

He looked at the poster of Bali framed on the wall. A view of water. Two people entwined in a hammock. Pink flowers in the foreground.

"Well," she said, hanging up. "I'll expect to hear from her. I assume I should let you know if anything changes?"

He cocked his head. "What doesn't?" he said. "You'd be busy every second of the day if you did that."

She looked at him, expressionless. "The ticket price," she said. "Or shall I issue it regardless?"

"Regardless." (Now, there was a word he didn't use often!) "Thanks." He stood.

"Say hello to my colleagues hiding under their desks on your way out," she said.

In the doorway, he stopped. "What did they do with the turkeys?" he said.

"They took them by truck to a farm in Vermont where they thought they wouldn't be killed," she said. "You can read about it in yesterday's paper. Everybody's out on bail. Since it's a first offense, my son might be able to avoid having a record. I've hired a lawyer."

"I'm sorry," he said.

"Thank you," she said.

He nodded. Unless she had two such garments, she was wearing the same gray sweater he had spilled tea on. It occurred to him that, outside his family, she was the only woman he spoke to. The woman at the post office, women he encountered when running errands, the UPS deliveryperson, who he personally thought might be a hermaphrodite, but in terms of real female acquaintances, Sigrid was the only one. He should have said more to her about the situation with her ex-husband and son, though he could not imagine what he would have said. He also could not get a mental picture, humorous or otherwise, of liberated turkeys, walking around some frozen field in—where had she said? Vermont.

She took an incoming call. He glanced back at the poster, at Sigrid sitting there in her gray sweater, noticing for the first time that she wore a necklace dangling a silver cross. Her high cheekbones, accentuated by her head tipped forward, were her best feature; her worst feature was her eyes, a bit too close together, so that she always seemed slightly perplexed. He raised his hand to indicate good-bye, in case she might be looking, then realized from what he heard Sigrid saying that the person on the other end must be Don Kim's stepdaughter; Sigrid was reciting the Boston-to-Frankfurt schedule, tapping her pen as she spoke. He hesitated, then went back and sat down, though Sigrid had not invited him back. He sat there while Jennifer Kim told Sigrid the whole sad story—what else could the girl have been saying to her for so long? Sigrid's eyes were almost crossed when she finally glanced up at him, then put her fingers on the keyboard and began to enter information. "I might stop by tonight," he said quietly, rising. She nodded, talking into the telephone headset while typing quickly.

Exiting, he thought of a song Groucho Marx had sung in some movie which had the lyrics "Did you ever have the feeling that you wanted to go, and still you had the feeling that you wanted to stay?" He had a sudden mental image of Groucho with his cigar clamped in his teeth (or perhaps it had been Jimmy Durante who sang the song?), and then Groucho's face evaporated and only the cigar remained, like a moment in *Alice in Wonderland.* And then— although Keller had quit smoking years before, when his father died—he stopped at a convenience store and bought a pack of cigarettes and smoked one, driving home, listening to some odd space-age music. He drove through Dunkin' Donuts and got two plain doughnuts to have with coffee as he watched the evening news, remembering the many times Sue Anne had criticized him for eating food without a plate, as if dropped crumbs were proof that your life was about to go out of control.

In his driveway, he saw that his trash can had been knocked over, the plastic bag inside split open, the lid halfway across the yard. He looked out the car window at the rind of a melon, then at the bloody Kleenex he'd held to his chin when he'd nicked himself shaving he had taken to shaving before turning in, to save time in the morning, now that his beard no longer grew so heavily—as well as issues of *The Economist* that a better citizen would have bundled together for recycling. He turned off the ignition and stepped out of the car, into the wind, to deal with the mess.

As he gathered it up, he felt as if someone were watching him. He looked up at the house. Soon after Sue Anne left, he had taken down not only the curtains but the blinds as well, liking clear, empty windows that people could go ahead and stare into, if such ordinary life was what they found fascinating. A car passed by— a blue van new to this road, though in the past few weeks he'd seen it often—as he was picking up a mealy apple. Maybe a private detective stalking him, he thought. Someone his wife had hired, to see whether another woman was living in the house. He snatched up the last of the garbage and stuffed it in the can, intending to come out later to rebag it. He wanted to get out of the wind. He planned to eat one of the doughnuts before the six o'clock news.

Sigrid's son was sitting with his back against the storm door, his knees drawn in tight to his chest, smoking a cigarette. Keller was startled to see him, but did his best to appear unfazed, stopping on the walkway to extract a cigarette of his own from the pack in his pocket. "Can I trouble you for a light?" he said to the boy.

It seemed to work. Brad looked taken aback that Keller wasn't more taken aback. So much so that he held out the lighter with a trembling hand. Keller towered above him. The boy was thin and short (time would take care of one, if not the other); Keller was just over six feet, with broad shoulders and fifteen or twenty pounds more than he should have been carrying, which happened to him every winter. He said to the boy, "Is this a social call, or did I miss a business appointment?"

The boy hesitated. He missed the humor. He mumbled, "Social."

Keller hid his smile. "Allow me," he said, stepping forward. The boy scrambled up and stepped aside so Keller could open the door. Keller sensed a second's hesitation, though Brad followed him in.

It was cold inside. Keller turned the heat down to fifty-five when he left the house. The boy wrapped his arms around his shoulders. The stub of the cigarette was clasped between his second and third fingers. There was a leather bracelet on his wrist, as well as the spike of some tattoo.

"To what do I owe the pleasure?" Keller said.

"Do you . . ." The boy was preoccupied, looking around the room.

"Have an ashtray? I use cups for that," Keller said, handing him the mug from which he'd drunk his morning coffee. He had run out of milk, so he'd had it black. And damn—he had yet again forgotten to get milk. The boy stubbed out his cigarette in the mug without taking it in his hands. Keller set it back on the table, tapping off the ash from his own cigarette. He gestured to a chair, which the boy walked to and sat down.

"Do you, like, work or anything?" the boy blurted out.

"I'm the idle rich," Keller said. "In fact, I just paid a visit to your mother, to get a ticket to Germany. For a friend, not for me," he added. "That being the only thing on my agenda today, besides reading *The Wall Street Journal*"—he had not heard about the boy's arrest because he never read the local paper, but he'd hesitated to say that to Sigrid—"and once again forgetting to bring home milk."

Keller sat on the sofa.

"Would you not tell my mother I came here?" the boy said.

"Okay," Keller said. He waited.

"Were you ever friends with my dad?" the boy asked.

"No, though once we both donated blood on the same day, some years ago, and sat in adjacent chairs." It was true. For some reason, he had never told Sigrid about it. Not that there was very much to say.

The boy looked puzzled, as if he didn't understand the words Keller had spoken.

"My dad said you worked together," the boy said.

"Why would I lie?" Keller said, leaving open the question: Why would your father?

Again, the boy looked puzzled. Keller said, "I taught at the college."

"I was at my dad's over Thanksgiving, and he said you worked the same territory."

In spite of himself, Keller smiled. "That's an expression," Keller said. "Like 'I cover the waterfront.'"

"Cover what?" the boy said.

"If he said we 'worked the same territory,' he must have meant that we were up to the same thing. A notion I don't understand, though I do suppose it's what he meant."

The boy looked at his feet. "Why did you buy me the raffle tickets?" he said.

What was Keller supposed to tell him? That he'd done it as an oblique form of apology to his mother for something that hadn't happened, and that he therefore didn't really need to apologize for? The world had changed: here sat someone who'd never heard the expression "worked the same territory." But what, exactly, had been Brad's father's context? He supposed he could ask, though he knew in advance Brad would have no idea what he meant by context.

"I understand Thanksgiving was a pretty bad time for you," Keller said. He added, unnecessarily (though he had no tolerance for people who added things unnecessarily), "Your mother told me."

"Yeah," the boy said.

They sat in silence.

"Why is it you came to see me?" Keller asked.

"Because I thought you were a friend," the boy surprised him by answering.

Keller's eyes betrayed him. He felt his eyebrows rise slightly.

"Because you gave me *six* raffle tickets," the boy said.

Clearly, the boy had no concept of one's being emphatic by varying the expected numbers: one rose instead of a dozen; six chances instead of just one.

Keller got up and retrieved the bag of doughnuts from the hall table. The grease had seeped through and left a glistening smudge on the wood, which he wiped with the ball of his hand. He carried the bag to Brad and lowered it so he could see in. Close up, the boy smelled slightly sour. His hair was dirty. He was sitting with his shoulders hunched. Keller moved the bag forward an inch. The boy shook his head no. Keller folded the top, set the bag on the rug. He walked back to where he'd been sitting.

"If you'd buy me a bike, I'd work next summer and pay you back," Brad blurted out. "I need another bike to get to some places I got to go."

Keller decided against unscrambling the syntax and regarded him. The tattoo seemed to depict a spike with something bulbous at the tip. A small skull, he decided, for no good reason except that these days skulls seemed to be a popular image. There was a pimple on Brad's chin. Miraculously, even to a person who did not believe in miracles, Keller had gone through his own adolescence without ever having a pimple. His daughter had not had similar good luck. She had once refused to go to school because of her bad complexion, and he had made her cry when he'd tried to tease her out of being self-conscious. "Come on," he'd said to her. "You're not Dr. Johnson, with scrofula." His wife, as well as his daughter, had then burst into tears. The following day, Sue Anne had made an appointment for Lynn with a dermatologist.

"Would this be kept secret from your mother?"

"Yeah," the boy said. He wasn't emphatic, though; he narrowed his eyes to see if Keller would agree.

He asked, "Where will you tell her you got the bike?"

"I'll say from my dad."

Keller nodded. "That's not something she might ask him about?" he said.

The boy put his thumb to his mouth and bit the cuticle. "I don't know," he said.

"You wouldn't want to tell her it was in exchange for doing yard work for me next summer?"

"Yeah," the boy said, sitting up straighter. "Yeah, sure, I can do that. I *will*."

It occurred to Keller that Molly Bloom couldn't have pronounced the word *will* more emphatically. "We might even say that I ran into you and suggested it," Keller said.

"Say you ran into me at Scotty's," the boy said. It was an ice cream store. If that was what the boy wanted him to say, he would. He looked at the bag of doughnuts, expecting that in his newfound happiness the boy would soon reach in. He smiled. He waited for Brad to move toward the bag.

"I threw your trash can over," Brad said.

Keller's smile faded. "What?" he said.

"I was mad when I came here. I thought you were some nut-case friend of my dad's. I know you've been dating my mom."

Keller cocked his head. "So you knocked over my trash can, in preparation for asking me to give you money for a bike?"

"My dad said you were a sleazebag who was dating Mom. You and Mom went to Boston."

Keller had been called many things. Many, many things. But sleazebag had not been among them. It was unexpected, but it stopped just short of amusing him. "And if I *had been* dating Sigrid?" he said. "That would mean you should come over and dump out my trash?"

"I never thought you'd lend me money," Brad mumbled. His thumb was at his mouth again. "I didn't . . . why would I think you'd give me that kind of money, just because you bought twelve bucks' worth of raffle tickets?"

"I'm not following the logic here," Keller said. "If I'm the enemy, why, exactly, did you come to see me?"

"Because I didn't know. I don't know what my father's getting at half the time. My dad's a major nutcase, in case you don't know that. Somebody ought to round him up in one of his burlap bags and let him loose far away from here so he can go live with his precious turkeys."

"I can understand your frustration," Keller said. "I'm afraid that with all the world's problems, setting turkeys free doesn't seem an important priority to me."

"Why? Because you had a dad that was a nutcase?"

"I'm not understanding," Keller said.

"You said you understood the way I feel. Is it because you had a dad that was nuts, too?"

Keller thought about it. In retrospect, it was clear that his father's withdrawal, the year preceding his death, had been because of depression, not old age. He said. "He was quite a nice man. Hardworking. Religious. Very generous, even though he didn't have much money. He and my mother had a happy marriage." To his surprise, that sounded right: for years, in revising his father's history, he had assumed that everything had been a façade, but now that he, himself, was older, he tended to think that people's unhappiness was rarely caused by anyone else, or alleviated by anyone else.

"I came here and threw over your trash and ripped up a bush you just planted," Brad said.

The boy was full of surprises.

"I'll replant it," Brad said. He seemed, suddenly, to be on the verge of tears. "The bush by the side of the house," he said tremulously. "There was new dirt around it."

Indeed. Just the bush Keller thought. On a recent morning, after a rain, he had dug up the azalea and replanted it where it would get more sun. It was the first thing he could remember moving in years. He did almost nothing in the yard—had not worked in it, really, since Sue Anne left.

"Yes, I think you'll need to do that," he said.

"What if I don't?" the boy said shrilly. His voice had changed entirely.

Keller frowned, taken aback at the sudden turnaround.

"What if I do like I came to do?" the boy said.

Suddenly there was a gun pointed at Keller. A pistol. Pointed right at him, in his living room. And, as suddenly, he was flying through the air before his mind even named the object. It went off as he tackled the boy, wresting the gun from his hand. "You're both fucking nutcases, and you were, too, dating that bitch!" Brad screamed. In that way, because of so much screaming, Keller knew that he had not killed the boy.

The bullet had passed through Keller's forearm. A "clean wound," as the doctor in the emergency room would later say, his expression betraying no awareness of the irony inherent in such a description. With an amazing surge of strength, Keller had pinned the boy to the rug with his good arm as the other bled onto the doughnut bag, and then the struggle was over and Keller did not know what to do. It had seemed they might stay that way forever, with him pinning the boy down, one or the other of them—both of them?—screaming. He somehow used his wounded arm as well as his good arm to pull Brad up and clench him to his side as he dragged the suddenly deadweight, sobbing boy to the telephone and dialled 911. Later, he would learn that he had broken two of the boy's ribs, and that the bullet had missed hitting the bone in his own forearm by fractions of an inch, though the wound required half a dozen surprisingly painful sutures to close.

Keller awaited Sigrid's arrival in the emergency room with dread. His world had already been stood on its head long ago, and he'd developed some fancy acrobatics to stay upright, but Sigrid was just a beginner. He remembered that he had thought about going to her house that very night. It might have been the night he stayed. Everything might have been very different, but it was not. And this thought: If his wife held him accountable for misjudging the importance of their daughter's blemishes, might Sigrid think that, somehow, the violent way things had turned out had been his fault? Among the many things he had been called had been provocative. It was his daughter's favorite word for him. She no longer even tried to find original words to express his shortcomings: he was *provocative*. Even she would not buy the sleazebag epithet. No: he was *provocative*.

In the brightly lit room, they insisted he remain on a gurney. Fluid from a bag was dripping into his arm. Sigrid—there was Sigrid!—wept and wept. Her lawyer accompanied her: a young man with bright blue eyes and a brow too wrinkled for his years, who seemed too rattled to be in charge of anything. Did he hover the way he did because he was kind, or was there a little something more between him and Sigrid? Keller's not having got involved with Sigrid hadn't spared her any pain, he saw. Once again, he had been instrumental in a woman's abject misery.

Trauma was a strange thing, because you could be unaware of its presence, like diseased cells lurking in your body (a natural enough thought in a hospital) or like bulbs that would break the soil's surface only when stirred in their depths by the penetrating warmth of the sun.

Keller remembered the sun—no, the moon—of Lynn's cradle. The cradle meant to hold three babies that held only one. He had suggested that Sue Anne, depressed after the birth, return to school, get her degree in art history, teach. He had had a notion of her having colleagues. Friends. Because he was not a very good friend to have. Oh, *sometimes*, sure. It had been a nice gesture to buy a plane ticket for someone who needed to visit a dying friend. How ironic it was, his arranging for that ticket the same day he, himself, might have died.

Sigrid was wearing the gray sweater, the necklace with the cross. Her son had blown apart her world. And Keller was not going to be any help: he would not even consider trying to help her put it together again. All the king's horses, and all the king's men . . . even Robert Penn Warren couldn't put Sigrid together again.

Keller had tried that before: good intentions; good suggestions; and his wife had screamed that whatever she did, it was *never enough, never enough*, well, maybe it would be enough if she showed him what strength she possessed—what strength he hadn't depleted with his sarcasm and his comic asides and his endless equivocating—by throwing the lamp on the floor, his typewriter against the wall (the dent was still there), the TV out the window. These thoughts were explained to him later, because he had not been home when she exhibited her significant strength. The squirrels had eaten every bulb. There was not going to be one tulip that would bloom that spring. He suspected otherwise—of course the squirrels had not dug up *every* bulb—but she was in no state of mind to argue with. Besides, there were rules, and his role in the marriage was not to be moderate, it was to be *provocative*. His daughter had said so.

And there she was, his daughter, rushing to his side, accompanied by a nurse: the same person who had once been shown to him swaddled in a pink blanket, now grown almost as tall as he, her face wrinkled then, her face wrinkled now.

"Don't squint," he said. "Put your glasses on. You'll still be pretty."

He stood quickly to show her he was fine, which made the nurse and a doctor who rushed to his side very angry. He said, "I don't have health insurance. I demand to be discharged. The gun got discharged, so it's only fair that I be discharged also."

The nurse said something he couldn't hear. The effort of standing had left him light-headed. Across the room, Sigrid appeared in duplicate and went out of focus. Lynn was negating what he'd just said, informing everyone in a strident voice that of course he had health insurance. The doctor had quite firmly moved him back to his gurney, and now many hands were buckling straps over his chest and legs.

"Mr. Keller," the nurse said, "you lost quite a bit of blood before you got here, and we need you to lie down."

"As opposed to up?" he said.

The doctor, who was walking away, turned. "Keller," he said, "this isn't *E.R.*, where we'd do anything for you, and the nurse isn't your straight man."

"Clearly not," he said quickly. "She's a woman, we assume."

The doctor's expression did not change. "I knew a wiseass like you in med school," he said. "He couldn't do the work, so he developed a comedy routine and made a big joke of flunking out. In the end, I became a doctor and he's still talking to himself." He walked away.

Keller was ready with a quick retort, heard it inside his head, but his lips couldn't form the words. What his nearest and dearest had always wished for was now coming true: his terrible talent with words was for the moment suspended. Truly, he was too tired to speak.

The phrase *nearest and dearest* carried him back in time and reminded him of the deer. The deer that had disappeared in the Hollywood Hills. His own guardian angel, appropriately enough a little mangy, with hooves rooting it to the ground, instead of gossamer wings to carry it aloft. And his eyes closed.

When he opened them, Keller saw that his daughter was looking down at him, and nodding slowly, a tentative smile quivering like a parenthesis at the sides of her mouth, a parenthesis he thought might contain the information that, yes, once he had been able to reassure her easily, as she, in believing, had reassured him.

In appreciation, he attempted his best Jack Nicholson smile.

About the Author

Ann Beattie has published seven novels and seven collections of stories. She has been included in three O. Henry Award collections and John Updike's *Best American Short Stories of the Century*. She has received an award in literature from the American Academy of Arts & Letters, a Guggenheim Fellowship, and the PEN/Malamud Award for achievement in the short story form. She and her husband, the artist Lincoln Perry, live in Maine; Key West, Florida; and Charlottesville, Virginia, where she is the Edgar Allan Poe Professor at the University of Virginia.